P9-CEG-074

F
JESS   Jess-Cooke, Carolyn

            The guardian angel's
            journal

DATE DUE

JUN 2 8 2011		
AUG 1 7 2011		
OCT 1 9 2011		
NOV 0 9 2011		
JAN 0 4 2012		
FEB 2 7 2012		
MAR 1 5 2012		

MAR 1 6 2011

LEVI HEYWOOD MEMORIAL LIBRARY
55 W. LYNDE ST.
GARDNER, MA 01440-3810

DISCARDED BY THE LEVI
HEYWOOD MEMORIAL LIBRARY

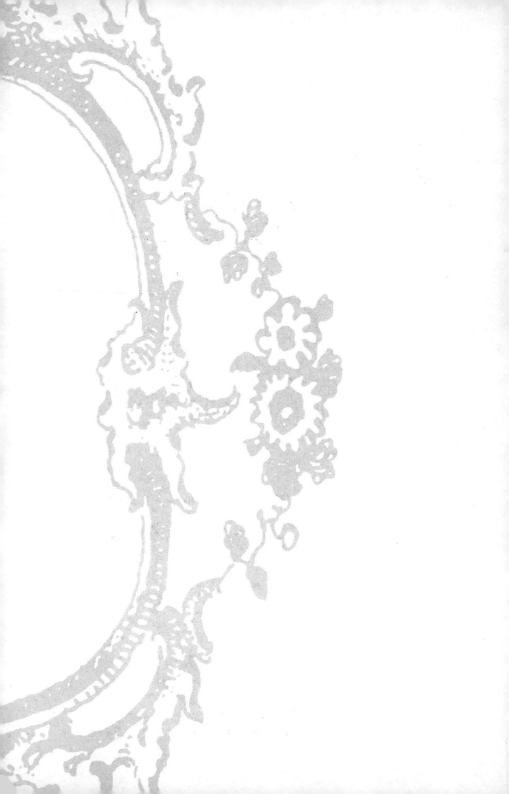

THE
*G*uardian
Angel's
Journal

CAROLYN JESS-COOKE

F JESS

Guideposts
New York, New York

The Guardian Angel's Journal

ISBN-10: 0-8249-4879-3
ISBN-13: 978-0-8249-4879-5

Published by Guideposts
16 East 34th Street
New York, New York 10016
www.guideposts.com

3 | 11   Ingram $14.99

Copyright © 2011 by Carolyn Jess-Cooke. All rights reserved.

This book, or parts thereof, may not be reproduced, stored in a retrieval system, or transmitted in any form or by any means, electronic, mechanical, photocopying, recording or otherwise, without the written permission of the publisher.

Distributed by Ideals Publications, a Guideposts company
2630 Elm Hill Pike, Suite 100
Nashville, Tennessee 37214

Guideposts and *Ideals* are registered trademarks of Guideposts.

The characters and events in this book are fictional, and any resemblance to actual persons or events is coincidental.

Library of Congress Cataloging-in-Publication Data

Jess-Cooke, Carolyn, 1978-
  The guardian angel's journal / [Carolyn Jess-Cooke].
    p. cm.
ISBN 978-0-8249-4879-5
1. Guardian angels–Fiction. 2. Self-realization in women–Fiction.
3. Future life–Fiction. I. Title.
PR6110.E78G83 2011
823'.92–dc22

                                                            2010035370

Cover design by Georgia Morrissey
Cover art/photo by Archangel Images
Interior design by Lorie Pagnozzi
Typeset by Aptara

Printed and bound in the United States of America
10 9 8 7 6 5 4 3 2 1

For Melody

*Angels are spirits, but it is not because
they are spirits that they are angels.*

They become angels when they are sent.
—Saint Augustine

Acknowledgments

THIS SECTION SHOULD REALLY BE TITLED "CHOCOLATE-DIPPED GRATITUDE," BECAUSE THAT'S EXACTLY WHAT I WISH TO CONVEY HERE TO THE FOLLOWING PEOPLE.

First and foremost, my husband, Jared Jess-Cooke. There is no other person on this earth who has encouraged, cajoled, reasoned with, loved, and championed another human being as much as you have done to me throughout the writing of this book. I can't begin to describe my gratitude at your insistent powers of positivity and faith in me; for preventing the house from falling apart while I wrote; for reading drafts and giving the most honest and trustworthy kind of feedback. At the very least, I owe you a lie-in.

I am extremely fortunate to have landed such an astute, proactive, and genuinely lovely agent as Madeleine Buston. Thank you a million times over for your passion for and belief in this book.

I am also incredibly grateful to have had Emma Beswetherick as both my editor and my pregnancy partner! Thank you, Emma, for all your comments and suggestions that undoubtedly steered this book toward its potential, and for making the editing process an utter pleasure. I am also indebted to my US editor, Beth Adams. Thank you so much for your enthusiasm for the book.

I wish to thank the team at New Writing North, particularly Claire Malcolm, for their encouragement throughout the past few years. Marching us all down to London to show off our wares was a turning point in my career, as was the afternoon I whispered my idea for this book to Claire, whose response— "How *fabulous!*"—prompted me to think that, maybe, it actually was.

As always, thanks to my mother-in-law, Evita Cooke, for providing the most dedicated and reassuring kind of childcare while I wrote; to my mother, Carol Stewart Moffett, for carefully reading an early draft, and—not least—for instilling in me a passion for stories at a young age.

I would also like to thank Lorna Byrne for her book *Angels in My Hair*. Of all the research I carried out while writing this novel, none was so inspiring as your autobiographical account of angels.

Finally, I want to thank my children, Melody, Phoenix, and Summer, for doing nothing to assist the actual writing of this book but everything to aid its inspiration. My three precious jewels, you bring me joy every day.

Celestial Pen

WHEN I DIED I BECAME A GUARDIAN ANGEL.

Nandita broke the news to me in the afterlife without any ice-breaking small talk or comfort-inducing chitchat. You know the way dentists ask what your Christmas plans are right before they yank out a tooth? Well, I can tell you there was none of that. There was simply this:

Margot is dead, child. Margot is dead.

No way, I said. I'm not dead.

She said it again. *Margot is dead.* She kept saying it. She took both my hands in hers and nodded with the reverence of a bow. I know how hard this is, she said. I left five kids behind in Pakistan with no papa. Everything will be all right.

I had to get out of there. I looked around and saw that we were in a valley surrounded by cypress trees with a small lake a couple of yards away from where we stood. Bulrushes fenced the edge of the water, their velvet heads like microphones waiting to broadcast my reply. There wouldn't be one. I spotted a scribble of gray road in the distance among the fields, and I started walking.

Wait, Nandita said. There's someone I want you to meet.

Who? I said. God? This is the summit of Absurdity, and we're hammering in the flag.

"I'd like you to meet Ruth," Nandita said, taking my hand and leading me toward the lake.

Where? I leaned forward, looking among the trees in the distance.

There, she said, pointing at my reflection.

And then she pushed me in.

Some guardian angels are sent back to watch over siblings, children, people they cared about. I returned to Margot. I returned to *myself*. I am my own guardian angel, a monastic scribe of the biography of regret, stumbling over my memories, carried away in the tornado of a history that I cannot change.

I shouldn't say "cannot change." Guardian angels, as we all know, prevent our deaths a thousand times over. It is the duty of every guardian angel to protect against every word, deed, and consequence that does not correspond to free will. We're the ones who make sure no accidents happen. But change—that's our business. We change things every second of every minute of every day.

Every day I see behind the scenes, the experiences I was meant to have, the people I was meant to have loved, and I want to take some celestial pen and change the whole thing. I want to write a script for myself. I want to write to this woman, the woman I was, and tell her everything I know. And I want to say to her:

Margot.

Tell me how you died.

1

*B*ecoming Ruth

I DON'T REMEMBER HITTING THE WATER. I don't remember dragging myself out of the other end of the lake. But what happened during that brief baptism into the spiritual world was an immersion in knowledge. I can't explain how it happened, but when I found myself in a badly lit corridor, dripping on cracked tiles, the understanding of who I was and what my purpose was poured through me as clearly as sunlight through branches. Ruth. My name is Ruth. Margot is dead.

I was back on earth. Belfast, Northern Ireland. I knew the place from my formative years, and by the sound of bands practicing at night. I was guessing it was the month of July but had no clue what year.

Footsteps from behind. I spun around. Nandita, iridescent in the darkness, the sheen of her dress untainted by the sickly glare of the streetlight opposite. She leaned toward me, her dark face filled with concern.

"There are four rules," she said, holding up four ringed fingers. "First, you are a witness to everything she does, everything she feels, everything she experiences."

"You mean, everything I experienced," I said.

Immediately she waved her hand in the air, as if my interjection was a speech bubble she was swiping away.

"This is not like watching a movie," she corrected. "The life you remember was only a little piece of the jigsaw. Now, you get to see the whole picture. And some of the pieces you get to fit. But you must be very careful. Now, let me continue with the rules."

I nodded in apology. She took a breath.

"The second rule is that you protect her. There are many forces that will attempt to interfere with the choices she makes. Protect her from these. This is vital."

"Wait right there," I said, holding up my hand. "What exactly do you mean by 'interfere'? I already made all my choices, you know? That's how I wound up right here. . . .'

"Haven't you been listening?"

"Yes, but—"

"Nothing is fixed, not even when you go back in time. You can't understand this now, but . . ."

She hesitated, unsure as to whether I was smart enough to get what she was saying. Or tough enough to deal with it.

"Go on," I said.

"Even this, right now, you and me—this has already happened. But you're not in the past the way you remember what a past felt like. Time no longer exists. But you are present here, and your view of the future is still clouded. So you will experience many, many *new* things, and you must consider the consequences very carefully."

4

My head hurt. "Okay," I said. "What's the third rule?"

Nan pointed at the liquid oozing from behind my back. My wings, you might say.

"Third rule is, you keep a record: a journal, if you like, of all that happens."

"You want me to write down everything that happens?"

"No, much easier than that. If you keep to the first two rules you don't have to do anything. Your wings do it all for you."

I was afraid to ask what the fourth rule was.

"Lastly," she said, her smile returning. "Love Margot. Love Margot."

She kissed the tips of her fingers and pressed them against my forehead, then closed her eyes and muttered a prayer in what I guessed was Hindi. I shifted my feet and bowed my head awkwardly. At last, she finished. When she opened her eyes, the darkness of her pupils was replaced by white light.

"I'll be visiting you again," she said. "Remember, you're an angel now. You have no need to fear."

The white light in her eyes spread throughout her face, in her mouth, down her neck and arms, until in a great burst of light, she was gone.

I looked around. There was a low moan at the end of the corridor to my right. Tenement flats. Bare brick interior walls, occasional graffiti. A narrow front door that lay open into the street, and beside it a grid of apartment intercoms covered in a sticky film of Guinness. A drunk curled up at the bottom of a stairwell.

I stood for a moment, considering my environs. First impulse: Walk out into the street and far away from this place. But then the urge came over me to follow that sound, the grunting at the end of the corridor. When I say an urge, I don't mean curiosity, or suspicion—I mean somewhere between the sort of intuition that prompts a mother to inspect a toddler that's been too quiet for too long and finds him on the verge of tumble-drying the family cat, and the sort of deep-seated gut instinct that tells you when you've left the door unlocked at home, when you're about to get fired, when you're pregnant.

⁂

So I found myself padding along the corridor, past the drunk, and up three steps to a landing. Along the corridor, five doors, two on either side, one at the end. All painted black. The noise—a deep, animalistic growl—was closer now. I took another step. A cry. A name. A woman's voice, whimpering. I made my way towards the door and paused.

Next thing, I was inside. A living room. No lights on, midnight dark. I could make out a sofa and the small cube shape of an old television. A window was open, the curtain flapping against the windowsill and then against the table inside, uncertain as to whether it wanted to be in or out. A long, agonizing scream. How is no one else hearing this? I thought. Why aren't the neighbors hammering the door down?

A riot had started outside. Police sirens wound up in several directions. Bottles smashed. Shouting, feet pounding pavement. I made my way through the living room toward the woman's screams.

A bedroom, lit by a flickering lamp on a bedside table. Peeling, lilac wallpaper, marks of mold and damp spotting the far wall like flicked soot. A messy bed. A young blonde woman in a long blue

T-shirt, alone, kneeling beside the bed as if in prayer, panting. Both arms thin as flagpoles and badly bruised, like she'd been in a fight. Suddenly she sat up on her knees, her eyes squeezed tight, face arched to the ceiling, jaw clenched. I saw she was heavily pregnant. Around her ankles and knees was a puddle of red water.

You have got to be kidding, I thought. What am I meant to do, deliver the baby? Raise the alarm? I'm dead. Ain't nothing I can do but watch this poor girl pound the bed with her fists.

The contraction let her out of its grip for a moment. She sagged forward and leaned her forehead against the bed, her eyes half shut and rolled back into her head. I knelt beside her and, very tentatively, put my hand on her shoulder. No response. She was panting, the next contraction building and building until she arched back and screamed for a full minute, and then the scream withered into relief, and she was back to panting again.

I placed my hand on her forearm and felt several small holes. I looked closer. Clustered around her elbow, ten purple circles, smaller than pennies. Needle marks. Another contraction. She rose up on her knees and panted deeply. The T-shirt rode up to her hips. More needle marks on her thin white thighs. I scanned the room quickly. Teaspoons and saucers on the dresser. Two syringes poking out from under the bed. Either she was a diabetic tea lover or a heroin junkie.

The pool of water around her knees was growing bigger. Her eyelids were flickering now, the moaning growing quieter instead of louder. I recognized that she was losing consciousness. Her head rolled to one side, her small wet mouth drooping open. "Hey," I said loudly. No response. "Hey!" Nothing.

I stood up and paced the room. Every so often the girl's body would jerk forward and from side to side. She just sat on her knees, her pale face turned to me, her thin arms straight by her sides, wrists rubbing the filthy, flea-ridden carpet. I'd a friend once who had a booming business as a self-employed junkie reviver. He spent long hours on our couch giving blow-by-blow accounts of celebrities he'd rescued from the brink of death, reaching into hell with the long arm of his adrenalin syringe and dragging them off Satan's lap. Of course, I couldn't quite remember what the procedure was. I doubt my friend had ever rescued junkies during childbirth. And certainly not while he was dead.

Suddenly the girl slid off and on to her side, her arms bunched together as if handcuffed. I could see blood seeping from her now. I bent down quickly and pushed her knees apart. An unmistakable crown of dark hair between her legs. For the first time, I felt the water streaming from my back, cold and sensitive as two extra limbs, alert to everything in the room—the smell of sweat and ash and blood, the palpable sadness, the sound of the girl's heartbeat growing slower and slower, the galloping heartbeat of the child . . .

I pulled her legs firmly toward me, planting her feet on the ground. I dragged a pillow off the bed, then yanked the cleanest bedsheet off the mattress and spread it under her thighs. I squatted between her legs and cupped my hands by her buttocks, trying not to think too hard about it. Any other time I would have run a mile from this kind of thing. My breathing was fast, I felt dizzy and yet incredibly focused, curiously determined to save this little life.

I could see the child's eyebrows and the bridge of the nose. I reached up and pressed against the top of the girl's womb. More water drenched the pillow under her buttocks. And then quickly, like a fish, the whole baby slithered out of her, so fast I had to catch it—the damp dark head, the scrunched face, the tiny blue body covered in chalky vernix. A girl. I wrapped her in the bedsheet and kept one hand on the thick blue cord, conscious that in a few minutes I'd have to pull again and guide out the placenta.

The baby was mewling in my arm, the small mouth puckered like a beak, open, searching. In a minute I'd put her to the mother's breast. But first I had business to attend to. The business of keeping the mother's sorry soul in that battered body.

The umbilical cord was loosening in my grip. I gave it a quick tug. I could feel the large sac at the other end. It felt like fishing. Another tug, a slight twitch. Slowly and firmly, I pulled the whole thing out, until at the entrance it plumped out in a thick bloody mass onto the pillow. It had been almost twenty years since I did this thing. What was it the midwife had done? Cut the cord close to the navel. I looked around for something sharp. I spotted a switchblade on the dresser. That'll do the trick. But wait. Something else. The midwife had inspected the placenta. I remembered her showing us that it had been delivered perfectly, that no parts of it had been left inside, at which Toby had bent into the nearest basin and repeated his lunch.

This girl's placenta was not the rich red brainlike substance I recalled. This one was small and thin, like roadkill. There was still a lot of blood seeping from her. Her breathing was shallow, her pulse faint. I would have to go and find someone.

I stood up and set the baby on the bed, but when I looked down I saw that she was blue. Blue as a vein. Her small mouth was no longer searching. Her handsome little doll's face was falling into sleep. The waterfalls flowing from my back like long wings felt like they were weeping now, as if every drop was plummeting from deep within me. They were telling me she was dying.

I picked the baby up and gathered the long folds of my dress—white, exactly like Nan's, as if heaven had only one tailor—around her small body. She was pitifully thin. Less than five pounds in weight. Her small hands, held close to her chest in tight fists, started to loosen, like petals unfurling from the stem. I leaned down and put my lips around her mouth, exhaling sharply. Once. Twice. Her little abdomen inflated like a tiny mattress. I pressed an ear against her chest and tapped lightly. Nothing. I tried again. Once. Twice. Three times. And then, the sensation of intuition. Instinct. Guidance. *Place your hand over her heart.*

I picked her up and lay her across my arm, spreading my palm across her chest. And slowly, amazingly, I could feel the small heart as if it was in my own chest, stumbling and faltering to work, rattling around like a sputtering engine, a boat flailing in chopping waves. From my hand, a small amount of light. I did a double take. There, in the dark orange haze of that disgusting room, a white light sandwiched between my hand and the child's chest.

I could feel her heart stirring, anxious to awaken. I closed my eyes tight and thought of every good thing I'd ever done in my whole life, and every bad thing I'd ever done, I forced myself to feel bad about, a kind of prayer, a quick self-qualification to be the kind of guardian angel this child needed right now, to be worthy of bringing her back to life by whatever force my body possessed.

The light grew stronger until it seemed to fill the room. The little heart stumbled over its paces like a calf running on shaky legs across a paddock. And then it pounded in my own chest, it thumped hard and forcefully, so loud in my ears I actually laughed out loud, and when I looked down, I saw the whole tiny chest heave in and out, in and out, the lips pink again, puckering as each breath moved in and out of the small mouth.

The light died down. I wrapped her in the sheet and lay her on the bed. The mother was lying in a pool of blood, her blonde hair now pink, her white cheeks streaked red. In between her loose breasts, I searched for a heartbeat. Nothing. I closed my eyes and willed the light to happen. Nothing. Her chest was cold. The baby was starting to whimper. She's hungry, I thought. I lifted the mother's T-shirt and held the child to the breast for a minute, and with her eyes still closed she leaned into the nipple and drank and drank.

After a few minutes I placed her back on the bed. Quickly I placed my palm against the mother's chest. Nothing. *Come on!* I yelled. I put my lips to hers and breathed, but the breath puffed up her cheeks and slid out of her empty mouth again, redundant.

"Leave her," a voice said.

I turned around. By the window, another woman. Another woman in white. Clearly a common thing in these parts.

"Leave her," the woman said again, softly this time. An angel. She looked similar to the woman lying dead on the floor—same thick, butter-blonde hair, same bee-stung mouth. Maybe a relative, I thought, come to take her home.

The angel scooped up the woman and headed for the door, carrying the limp body in her arms, though when I looked back at the floor, the body was still there. The angel looked at me and smiled. Then she glanced at the baby. "Her name's Margot," she said. "Look after her well."

"But," I said. Within the word was a knot of questions.

When I looked up, the angel was gone.

2

The Plan

THE FIRST THING THAT TOOK SOME GETTING USED TO WAS THAT I DIDN'T HAVE WINGS. At least, not wings with feathers.

As it turns out, it wasn't until the fourth century that artists started painting angels with wings, or rather, with long flowing constructions that emerge from shoulder and trail to toe.

These are not feathers, but water.

The many sightings of angels throughout the history of the world have filtered down the idea of a birdlike creature, capable of flying between mortality and divinity, but occasionally witnesses have differed on the notion of wings. A man in Mexico during the sixteenth century wrote of "dos ríos," or "two rivers," in his journal, which his family burned on the quiet once he'd kicked the bucket. Another man—Serbia, this time—spread the word that his angelic visitor had two waterfalls cascading from his shoulder blades. And a little girl in Nigeria drew picture after picture of a beautiful heavenly messenger, whose wings had been replaced with flowing waters trailing into the river that flows eternally before the throne of God. Her parents were very proud of her active imagination.

The little girl was well informed. What she didn't know, however, was that the two spouts of liquid flowing from the sixth vertebra of an angel's spine to the sacrum forms a link—an umbilical cord, if you will—between the angel and his or her Protected Being. Within these "water wings" is a transcription process of every thought and action, just as if the angel was writing it all down. Better, even, than CCTV or Web cam. Instead of mere words or visuals, the whole experience is saturated within the liquid, to tell the full story of any given moment—the sensation of falling in love for the first time, for instance, linked by a network of smells and memories and chemical responses to a childhood abandonment. And so on.

An angel's journal is in his or her wings. As is instinct, guidance, knowledge about every living thing. If one is prepared to listen.

The second thing that took some getting used to was the thought of re-experiencing my life as a silent witness.

Let me put it bluntly. I lived a full life. But I did not live a good life. So you can imagine how I felt about the idea of living it twice.

I figured I'd been sent back as punishment, a kind of thinly veiled purgatory. Who actually enjoys watching themselves on screen? Who doesn't cringe at the sound of their voice on a voice-mail message? Multiply that experience by a gazillion, and you've got somewhere in the range of where I'm at. Mirror, video camera, plaster cast . . . each of them have nothing on standing right beside your own self in the flesh, especially while that self is busily screwing up your whole life.

I saw other angels all the time. We'd rarely communicate, not like buddies or companions or as if we're in the same boat. For the most part, I found them sombre, aloof creatures—or should

I say boring stiffs?—all of them watching their Protected Being as intensely as if he or she were staggering along the guttering of the Empire State Building. I had that feeling again, right like I was back at school, of being the kid who wore a skirt when all the other girls were wearing pants. Or the teenager who dyed her hair pink twenty years before it became cool. Call me Sisyphus—I was right back where I'd always been, wondering where I was, *why* I was, and how I was going to get out.

Once the baby started breathing again—once *Margot* started breathing again—I rushed out of the flat and kicked awake the drunk curled up at the bottom of the stairs. When he finally came to, he turned out to be a lot younger than I'd thought. Michael Allen Dwyer. Recently turned twenty-one. Chemistry student at Queen's University (barely—his grades, I learned, were teetering on failing). Goes by the name of Mick. I got all this information just by squaring my foot into his shoulder. I have no idea why that didn't work with the dead girl minutes earlier. It might have saved her life.

I got him up and on his feet, then leaned into his ear and told him that the girl in flat 4 had died and that there was a baby in there too. He turned slowly toward the landing, then shook his head and rubbed his hands through his hair, shaking the notion off. I tried again. *Flat 4, you moron. Dead girl. Infant. Needs help. Now.* He stopped in his tracks, and I held my breath. *He can hear me?* I continued talking. *Yes, yes, that's it, keep going.* The air around him had changed, as if the words from my mouth had cleared the slim space between him and gravity, entering his blood cells, nudging at his instinct.

He put a foot on the first stair, struggling to recall what he was doing here. As he strode up the last two steps I could see neurons and glial cells buzzing around his head like small streaks of lighting, a little slower than usual because of the alcohol, though zinging with synaptic fusions.

From that point, I let curiosity take him by the hand and guide him inside. The black door was wide open (thanks to me). The infant ~~(surely not? surely she can't be me?)~~ was crying now, a pathetic little rattling wail like a kitten about to be drowned in a rain barrel. The noise of this caught Mick's ears keenly and slapped him into sobriety.

I was there when he tried to revive the mother. I tried to stop him, but he insisted on spending a good half hour rubbing her hands and shouting in her face before it occurred to him to call an ambulance. Then it dawned on me. They had been lovers. This was his child. He was my father.

An aside is necessary here. I never knew my parents. I was told that my parents died in a car crash when I was very young, and that the series of people who looked after me until my teens might have been dirt-eating criminals of various shades but, hey, they kept me alive. Barely.

So I had no idea what was about to happen at this point of my existence, and absolutely no sense of how I could contribute to a better outcome. If my father was alive and well, why did I end up where I ended up?

I sat on the bed beside the baby, watching the young man as he sobbed beside the body of the dead girl.

Let me try that again: I sat on the bed beside myself, watching my father sobbing over the body of my mother.

He got up occasionally to slam his fist into something shatterable, kicking the syringes around the room and eventually emptying the contents of the chest of drawers in a rage.

I learned later that they'd had a fight only hours before. He'd stormed out and fallen down the stairs. She'd told him it was over. But she'd said that before.

Eventually someone called the police. An older male officer took Mick by the arm and led him outside. This was Superintendent Hinds, served with divorce papers earlier that morning by his French wife, largely due to the amount of money he lost over a horse that tripped at the last jump and a nursery that remained empty. Despite his mood, Superintendent Hinds felt sorry for Mick. There was some dispute in the corridor over whether or not they should cuff him. It was clear the girl was a user, Superintendent Hinds had argued with a colleague. It was clear she'd died in childbirth. The colleague—a woman— insisted that the young man be treated by the book. That meant a good hour's questioning. It meant no gaps in the paperwork, and, therefore, no disciplinary action from HQ.

Paperwork. It was because of paperwork that my father and I got separated. It was because of paperwork that my young life took the direction it did.

Superintendent Hinds closed his eyes and pressed his fingers against his brow line. I strode up to him, itching to lean into his ear and scream who I was, that Mick was my father, that he needed to take the baby to the hospital. But my ranting got me nowhere. I could see it now, the difference between Mick and Superintendent Hinds, the reason I had been able to get through to one and not the other: the blanket of emotions and ego and memories surrounding Mick had revealed a crack, right at the moment I spoke to him, and like a wind disturbing pebbles from their footholds in the cracks of a wall, briefly allowing raindrops to seep in, for moisture to unite with the stone, so, too, did I get through to Mick. But Superintendent Hinds was a tough nut to crack, so to speak. I encountered it again and again. Some people heard me, others didn't. Most often, it was a case of luck on my part.

Margot let out a loud squeal. Superintendent Hinds cracked the whip of his ranking order.

"Right," he barked at the team of officers who'd assembled along the hallway. "You." He pointed at the first officer to his right. "Take the boy down to the station for questioning. You." He pointed at the second officer to his right. "Get an ambulance down here pronto." The female officer looked at him expectantly. He sighed. "Call the coroner."

Out of frustration I ranted at Superintendent Hinds and his team, begging them not to arrest Mick. And then I screamed about the fact that no one could hear me, about the fact that I was dead. And then I watched them cuff Mick and lead him away from Margot for the last time. Beside him, in a parallel state of time that opened up like a small tear in the fabric of the present, I watched him being released the following morning and picked up by his father, and I watched as days and weeks and months went by as Mick forced the thought of Margot further and further to the back of his head, until she was no more than an abandoned child being fed by tube at the Ulster Hospital, the white sticker on the plastic crib bearing her name: Baby X.

But that was the moment that my plan took flight. If everything Nan had said was right, if nothing was fixed, I decided that I would change everything about my life: my education, my romantic choices, the bog of poverty through which I waded until my forties. And the life sentence for murder that my son was serving at the time of my death. Oh yes, all that was about to change.

3

Extraterrestrial Goggles

I SPENT WHAT TURNED OUT TO BE ABOUT SIX MONTHS AT THE CHILDCARE UNIT OF THE ULSTER HOSPITAL — I KNOW THIS BECAUSE MARGOT WAS SITTING UP ON HER OWN BY THE TIME THEY LET HER GO. I PACED THE CORRIDOR, WATCHING THE DOCTORS AS THEY INSPECTED MARGOT, SMALL AND JAUNDICED AND STILL IN HER INCUBATION UNIT, SURROUNDED BY TUBES.

More than once, Dr. Edwards, the pediatric cardiologist in charge of Margot's recovery, asserted that she wouldn't last the night. More than once, I reached through the incubation unit and placed my hand over her heart, bringing her back to earth.

Now I'll admit, it did cross my mind that maybe I should just let her die. Knowing what I knew about Margot's childhood, there wasn't a whole heap to look forward to. But then, I thought of the good times. Mornings drinking coffee with Toby on our creaky balcony in New York. Writing bad poetry on Bondi Beach.

Finally launching my own business, signing up K. P. Lanes. And I thought, Okay, kiddo, let's do this. Let's stay alive.

I discovered several things during that time:

First Discovery: Watching, protecting, recording, and loving Margot meant barely leaving her side. Once or twice I figured I'd go sightseeing, you know—do some exploring, have a mini-vacation somewhere warm. But I could barely bring myself to leave the building. I was bound to her, and not just because she was me. I felt a sense of duty that I'd never felt anytime during my life, not even as a wife.

Second Discovery: My vision changed. At first, I reckoned I was going blind. But then everything would switch back to the way it always is: a kettle is a kettle, a piano is wooden with white and black keys, etc. More and more, I'd find myself viewing the world as if through a pair of extraterrestrial goggles. Dr. Edwards would switch from a Cary Grant look-alike to a neon mannequin, surrounded by psychedelic strands of colored light that spiraled from his heart and around his head, around his arms, around his waist like hula hoops, right down to his toes. Kind of like infrared, but a hundred times weirder. And that wasn't the only way that my vision changed: Sometimes I'd see parallel time frames (more of that in a minute), and sometimes I'd find I had X-ray vision and be able to see into the next room. I saw things as if through a massive magnifying glass.

Once, I saw Dr. Edwards's lungs—filled, I could see, with clumps of black tar, courtesy of his fondness for cigars—but the weirdest was when I saw Nurse Harrison's embryo, conceived just that morning, rolling along her fallopian tubes like a misshapen ping-pong ball, until finally it dropped into the velvety chambers of her womb, like a stone dropped into a pond. I was so mesmerized,

I followed Nurse Harrison right into the hospital parking lot until I remembered Margot and raced back to that dour room filled with infant screams.

Third, and Most Important, Discovery: I have absolutely no concept of time. No circadian rhythms to tell me it's nighttime, no ability to remember when Christmas is. It's like this: I can *see* time, but the notion of a clock no longer holds any meaning for me. Think of it this way—when you see rain, you see small silver globes of water, no? Sometimes in the form of a thick curtain streaming down the window. When *I* see rain, I see billions of hydrogen atoms grinding against their oxygen neighbors. It kind of looks like small white plates spinning among gray buttons on a countertop. The same with time. I see time as an art gallery of atoms, wormholes, and light particles. I slip through time the way you put on a shirt, or the way you punch an elevator button and find yourself on the twenty-fifth floor. I see parallel time frames open up all over the place, revealing the past and future like the actions happening on the other side of a street corner.

I don't exist in time. I visit it.

As you can imagine, this poses an ever-so-slightly major obstacle to my plan. If I can't get a grasp on time, how am I meant to change Margot's life?

I spent my whole stint at the hospital calculating the ways I would influence Margot to change. I would whisper in her ear the answers to all her school exam papers. I'd even yell at her to stay well away from complex carbs and sugar, perhaps drum up an urge deep down in her gut to take up athletics. Then I'd nudge her all the way into financial brilliance. It is this last goal that was most important. Why? Take it from me, poverty doesn't just mean hunger pains. It means all your life choices being rubbed out in front of your face.

I told myself, maybe *this* was the reason I had returned as my own guardian angel: not only to see the whole jigsaw, as Nan had put it, but to change the pieces slightly so that a different picture emerged, to put *choice* back in the main frame.

4

Strand of Fate

THE FOSTER PARENTS THAT COLLECTED MARGOT FROM THE
HOSPITAL WERE SURPRISINGLY DECENT PEOPLE. Decent in a
white-shirt and silk-dress kind of way. Decent in every other way
too.

I found out immediately that they'd tried—and failed—to have
children for fourteen years. The man, a barrister called Ben,
trudged up the hospital corridor with his hands shoved deep into
his pockets. His life had taught him to expect the worst and let the
best surprise him. I could relate to that. His wife—a very short,
very wide woman named Una—took small, quick steps by his
side. She had her arm linked through his and used her free hand
to rub a gold crucifix around her neck. Both looked extremely
worried. It was clear that Dr. Edwards had not painted a good
picture of Margot's health.

I was sitting in the crib when they arrived, my legs through
the cold green metal bars and hanging over the side. Margot
was laughing at the faces I was pulling. Already she had such a
dirty laugh. A throw-your-head-back laugh. She had a thin mess

of blonde hair, exactly the shade I'd spent my whole life chasing with a bottle of bleach, and round blue eyes that would eventually turn gray. Two small teeth had cut their way through her pink gums. Occasionally I'd catch glimpses of her parents in her face: Mick's strong jaw. Her birth mother's full lips.

Una, the foster mother, slapped a hand to her chest and gasped. "She's beautiful!" She turned to Dr. Edwards, who stood behind them with his arms folded, serious as an undertaker. "She looks so healthy!"

Una and Ben shared looks. Ben's shoulders—raked up against his ears in suspense—slumped in relief. Both of them started to laugh. I love to see this—the spine of a successful marriage. I'm mystified by it. In Una and Ben's case, it was laughter.

"Would you like to hold her?" Dr. Edwards scooped Margot off my lap. Her toothy grin vanished, and she started to fret, but I held a finger up to my lips and pulled another face. She giggled.

Una twittered such praise at Margot that eventually she turned to her and gave her a Cheshire-cat smile. More praise from Una. Ben tentatively took one of her small chubby hands in his and made clucking noises. I laughed, and so did Margot.

Dr. Edwards rubbed his face. He'd witnessed this scene too many times. A deep hatred of blame made him spill the worst to people to avoid any kind of culpability. So he said:

"She won't live to see her third birthday."

Una's face became a shattered window.

"Why?"

"Her heart isn't beating properly. It won't let the blood circulate to all her organs. Eventually, the oxygen supply to her brain will be cut off. And then she'll die." He sighed. "I would hate you to blame me for not telling you beforehand."

Ben looked down and shook his head. All his worst fears come true. He and Una had been cursed from the day of their wedding, he told himself. So many times, so many times he'd had to watch his wife cry. So many times he'd wanted to cry himself. With each disappointment he was one step closer to the truth: that life was cruel, and it ended with a coffin and worms.

Una, however, was genetically inclined to optimism.

"But . . . how can you be sure?" she spluttered. "Might there be a chance that her heart will get stronger? I've read about babies thriving through all sorts of diseases once they find a happy home."

I stood up. Courage galvanizes me. Always has. It was the thing I liked most about Toby.

"No, no, no, no," said Dr. Edwards a little coldly. "I can absolutely assure you that we're correct in this case. Ventricular tachycardia is an unfortunate disease and, as we speak, virtually untreatable."

"Ma ma ma," said Margot.

Una gasped and squealed in delight. "Did you hear that? She called me mama!"

Dr. Edwards's mouth was still open.

"Say 'mama' again," I told Margot. "Ma ma MA!" she said, and giggled. What can I say? I was a cute kid.

Una laughed and bounced Margot up and down in her arms, then turned her back completely to Dr. Edwards.

Of course, I'd already seen Margot's heart. About the size of a prune, stuttering occasionally. The light circulating from it sometimes withered and faded in intensity. I knew something was wrong. But, I figured, I had no memory of a heart problem. I suffered many a broken heart through my teens, of the unrequited love variety. Clearly the problem wasn't as big as Dr. Edwards was determined to make out.

"She'll live," I whispered into Una's ear. She stood stock-still for a moment, as if a wish from her soul had just connected with its manifestation somewhere in the corner of the universe. She closed her eyes and said a prayer.

Just then, I saw Una's guardian angel. A tall black man appeared behind her and folded his arms around her, pressing his cheek against hers. She closed her eyes and, for a moment, a white glow surrounded her. It was beautiful to see. The light of hope. In all my time at the hospital, this was the first I'd seen of it. He looked up at me and winked. Then he was gone.

After that, it was all about forms. Sign this, sign that. Dr. Edwards wrote a bunch of medical prescriptions and made several dates for Una and Ben to bring Margot back for tests. I could see Ben starting to drain—he'd had no sleep the previous night—and Una was nodding and humming and hah-ing but hearing none of it, so I made sure I paid attention. When dates were mentioned, I prodded Una. *Best write this down, love.*

⁂

Margot received her name from Nurse Harrison, after a long discussion in the breakroom between Dr. Edwards and his team of nurses. She'd spluttered the name reluctantly after Nurse Murphy suggested the name "Grainne," a name I didn't much like the sound of. It was, *mais oui*, yours truly who put the name in Nurse Harrison's head. When the others quizzed her, she attributed the choice to Margot Fonteyn, the ballerina. Her surname, Delacroix, was after her birth mother, whose name I learned was Zola.

Ben and Una's home was in one of the richest areas of Belfast, close to the University. Ben worked a lot from home. His office occupied the roof space of their three-story Victorian house, directly above Margot's nursery, which was filled with toys of every color and variety.

The time I spent there was shrouded with suspicion. Something was up. I had no memory of Ben and Una, no knowledge that they ever played such an important role in my mortality. The ornate hand-carved mahogany crib in the nursery was rarely occupied by Margot. Instead, Una kept her cradled on her right hip by day and snuggled into her left breast by night, warm as toast between her and Ben.

There was much talk of adoption, which I heartily encouraged. Anytime Ben let his fears take hold—"But what if she *dies?*"—I tickled Margot until she laughed hysterically, or reached out her arms while she tried to take her first step. Una was in love. I was in love, too, with this gorgeously maternal woman—the sort I'd never before understood—who woke every day before sunrise with a smile, who sometimes spent hours gazing and smiling down at Margot sleeping in her arms. Sometimes the golden light around her burned so brightly I had to look away.

But then another light came into view. Like a snake finding its way unnoticed through the back door, a dull gunmetal hue ribboned one afternoon around Ben and Una as they sat at the dinner table, celebrating Margot's first birthday with a pink cupcake and a single candle, and a fresh yield of gift-wrapped toys. The light—more of a shadow, really—seemed to have an intelligence to it, as if it was alive. It sensed me and whipped back when I stood in front of Margot, then slowly made its way toward Una and Ben. Una's guardian angel appeared for a moment. But instead of stopping the light, he stepped aside. Like ivy, the light coiled slowly around Ben's leg before petering into dark dust.

I paced the living room. I felt angry. I felt like I'd been given a job to do and absolutely no ability to carry it out. How was I meant to protect anybody if there were such things I wasn't being told about?

Ben and Una carried on the birthday party unawares. They carried Margot down the steps into the back garden, where she took her first steps right in front of Ben's Polaroid camera.

I was starting to think maybe Ben was right. When things were going so well, it was merely the calm before the storm.

I paced all afternoon, and then finally I cried. I knew the fate of Margot's childhood all too well, and yet seeing what could have been was a million times more crushing than the prospect of reliving all that abuse again. I decided that I had to do something. If Margot was adopted by Ben and Una, she would be raised in a home of love. She would turn out well adjusted, more than likely less inclined to self-sabotage. Screw the riches. At this point, I would have given my immortal soul for Margot to grow up feeling worthy of love.

Sometime later, Nandita came. I told her everything: the birth, the hospital, the snake of light. She nodded and pressed her palms together in contemplation.

"The light you saw is a strand of fate," she explained. "Its color suggests it is connected to an ill wish." I made her explain further. "Every strand of fate originates from a human choice. In this case, it does not sound like the choice is good."

I was frustrated that I had not yet seen Ben's guardian angel. Again, Nandita explained.

"Give it time," she said. "Soon you will see *everything*."

"But what do I do about this *strand of fate*," I said, reluctant to say it. So very twee.

"Nothing," Nan said. "Your job . . . "

" . . . is to protect Margot. Yes, I know. I'm trying. I can't do that if I don't know what this light means, can I?"

I found out what the strand was shortly before it happened.

Ben was working at home as usual while Margot slept. The smell of fresh bread curled up from the kitchen downstairs. It tempted him away from his desk, long enough for me to catch sight of the court case he was working on: a murder charge against a terrorist. Surrounding the name of the terrorist was a thin circle of shadow.

I'm not stupid. I figured it out there and then.

Just because it was a human choice—and, therefore, I was meant to let it all happen—doesn't mean I stood back with my arms folded. When the shadow snaked in again, this time making its way stealthily up Ben and Una's bodies as they embraced in the kitchen, I stamped at it wildly. It knew I was there, of course, but this time it didn't budge. It was stronger now, the color of sky a minute before rain, palpable as a hosepipe. And nothing I did made it disappear. Not when I screamed. Not when I lay my whole body on top of it and willed it to die.

It had taken months for Ben to convince Una to allow Margot out of her sight. Now that it looked like that they would finally get to adopt, he reasoned that it was only right that he take her out to celebrate. And so, Lily, the mild-mannered old woman across the road, took Margot for a couple of hours while Ben and Una ventured out to a candlelit dinner.

I saw the shadow unfurl after their car. It had no interest in Margot. She toddled happily around Lily's kitchen, wooden spoon in one hand, naked Barbie doll in the other, beaming with a pale gold light that had rubbed off on to her from Una.

When the car bomb exploded, I saw that light dim a little, but I willed it to stay. If that much of Una's love could remain, I would settle for it. I would have to.

5

The Half-Open Door

I SHOULD MENTION AT THIS POINT THAT I WAS ENJOYING BEING A MOTHER TO MARGOT FAR MORE THAN I ENJOYED RAISING MY SON, THEO. It's nothing personal against Theo. He just arrived at a moment of my life when I was more enchanted by the prospect of motherhood than its reality. Which, in my case, involved disorientation, suicidal tendencies, and insomnia, long before the term *postpartum depression* was coined or even socially acceptable.

After a few days at Lily's, and when news of the bomb brought all the residents of the village to Margot, bearing tiny gifts in sympathy at the loss of her would-be parents, I watched as a social worker arrived to take Margot to a new foster family. This was Marion Trimble, a young woman, newly qualified, but unfortunately cursed with full-blown naïveté. A sheltered upbringing with two loving parents can sometimes lead to bad things. In this case, it led Marion to send Margot to a foster couple whose warm smiles were as false as their intentions.

Padraig and Sally Teague lived near Cavehill in Belfast, close to the zoo. Their small house backed onto a derelict building smeared with graffiti. The windows in their rundown place were boarded up; broken glass and litter was scattered across the front and back gardens. Tall overgrown hedges shrouded the place from the main road opposite. There was no reason for anyone to suspect the place was anything but empty. But it was far from it.

Their decision to become foster parents was made one sunny morning after Padraig read a newspaper advertisement requesting foster parents for the tidy sum of twenty-five pounds a week. Hey, this was the sixties: You could still buy a house for under a grand. A quick series of mental calculations later, and Padraig deduced that, as foster parents, they would be able to support their growing business in the illegal-immigration industry. Immigrant transporters asked for twenty-five quid per truckload of men and women from Eastern Europe, and it sometimes took time finding work for all of them. Once they did find work, however, Padraig and Sally took a ninety percent slice of their earnings in return for "bed and breakfast" at the derelict building. But, overeager to assist their immigrant comrades in finding their feet, Padraig and Sally ended up squeezing as many as twenty of the poor souls into one room at a time, for months on end, and, eventually, in their own grotty house.

Which is how Margot got to share her nursery with three male Polacks, all electricians, all camped out on the bare floor, morning, noon, and sometimes at night. Most of the time, they smoked. Sometimes they drank vodka and cups of soup. Most of the time, Sally forgot all about Margot and left her there all day, same diaper, same clothes, same empty belly.

Nothing I did or said to Sally had any effect. She never once sensed my presence, never once heard any of the demands I made of her on Margot's behalf, never felt the slaps I aimed at her moronic face. This was because—and more of this later—just as Sally's home was stuffed to the rafters with illegal aliens, so too was Sally's body crammed to its limit with migrant demons. All that was left of her conscience was deadened by a daily dose of cannabis.

Luckily, one of the Polacks staying in the nursery, Dobrogost, took a shine to Margot, having left behind his own one-year-old daughter in Szczecin to find employment overseas. I helped Dobrogost find work at a builder's yard near the docks, convinced him to lie to Padraig and Sally about his wage, and then finally persuaded him to buy formula and food for little Margot. She was covered in sores from unchanged diapers and bad nutrition. Occasionally I'd lift her out of the crib and help her walk around the house at night. That put the wind up Padraig and Sally— finding their toddler wandering around the hallway at 3:00 AM, giggling at thin air. Sometimes I was tempted to pick her up and have them wake in the wee hours to her hovering above the bed. But, I thought, best not.

One day, Dobrogost was gone. The new residents in the nursery whispered about a discovery of a wage slip, a body in a trunk, a weighted suitcase chucked into the sea. The new residents in the nursery did not take well to Margot's crying at night for Dobrogost. Already she was beginning to ignore me, and she craved human affection. The new residents in the nursery tried to throw her out the window. First, I jammed the window shut. When they broke the glass, I stood in front of it, then loosened their hold on Margot. But I could not stop them from slapping her so hard that her beautiful blue eyes almost disappeared beneath purple, swollen skin, nor could I prevent them from throwing her against a wall, sending small fractures shooting up the back of her tiny skull. I can't begin tell you how much I cried, how much I screamed at my helplessness. What I found I could do, however, was prevent them from killing her by softening the blows. So many times I went out to seek help, but each time, I couldn't get through. No one would listen.

Margot's third birthday came and went. Her hair was still a little cottony cloud, her face cherubic and peach cheeked. But already I could spy a hardness setting in. A loss. The gold light that had surrounded her for many months after Una's death had reduced. Now, it merely surrounded her heart.

It was early one morning when the nursery residents returned from night shift. Stoned out of their minds. They thought it would be funny to get Margot wasted. From the window something caught my eye: a bright blue light moving quickly up the street. When I looked again, I saw that it was Dr. Edwards, dressed in a white jogging vest drenched with sweat, navy shorts, and sneakers. He was running so fast that he was already more than thirty yards away by the time I made the decision to get to him. I closed my eyes and—for the first time—I pleaded with God to let me get through to him. Nan had said that nothing was fixed, and I suspected that this was, quite literally, Margot's last chance. If I didn't act now, the life I had lived would be over before I could even remember, and there would be no second chance.

No sooner had I finished my "prayer" than I found myself running beside Dr. Edwards. From our past encounter I knew I'd have to get past his love of logic. He would never act on a hunch. I'd have to sell him a story, I'd have to put it in such a way as to inspire him to act.

As I ran, struggling to think of how to get this man to walk up to the door of that house and demand entry, I found myself suddenly in front of him, stationary, with him jogging toward me. Looking right at me.

"Can I help you?" he said, slowing to a stop, panting.

I looked around. *Can he see me?* I glanced at him quickly, careful not to lose his attention and at once checking that he was talking to *me*. I could see the emotions and thoughts blanketing him, and, instead of the slivers that appeared sometimes when people allowed me to penetrate their consciousness, there was a small cord that seemed to connect somehow with my aura, bringing us for that moment into the same realm.

I quickly snapped myself out of my amazement. Time was of the essence.

"There's a child in that house," I said briskly, pointing at Sally and Padraig's house. "You saved her life once. She needs you to help save her again."

Slowly, he turned and looked at the house. He took one step toward it, another. I spotted a police car turning a corner, and I bolted. Dr. Edwards was no superhero; he'd need backup. I ran toward the police car, leaned into the engine as the driver accelerated, and yanked at a wire. It worked. The thing stalled, sputtered, and conked out. Both officers were out of the vehicle in seconds.

Dr. Edwards got quite the fright when he realized that the person who'd just divulged information about a dying child was nowhere to be seen. He walked slowly toward the house and knocked on the door. No one answered. He scanned the street, stretched his hamstrings, then knocked again. I brought Dr. Edwards to the attention of Sergeant Mills, one of the police officers who was attempting to fix the engine. Sergeant Mills had heard rumors of trouble from this house, and a scantily clad man hammering on the door at the crack of dawn raised his suspicions further.

As Sergeant Mills and Sergeant Bancroft approached, the door opened. An inch. Padraig's sour breath wafting from the crack made Dr. Edwards take a step back.

"Oh, hello there," said Dr. Edwards. He scratched his head, unsure of what to say. Padraig stared and grunted. Dr. Edwards pulled himself together. "I'm informed there's a sick child here," he said. "I'm Dr. Edwards." He dug his hospital badge out of his pocket. Neither he—nor I—knew how it found its way there.

The door opened slightly wider. "A sick child?" Padraig repeated. He knew of a child. More than likely she was sick. He wasn't too inclined to let doctors inside. But there might be trouble if he said no.

The door opened further. "Upstairs. Third door on the left. Be quick."

Dr. Edwards nodded and jogged up the stairs. Immediately he found his nostrils assaulted with the sour stench of sweat and cannabis. He could hear two, three different accents whispering in the rooms that he passed. He pressed on until he came to the nursery. He could hear shuffling noises inside from several sets of heavy feet. And a child's cry.

The police officers were outside the house now. Padraig had left the door ajar. Sergeant Mills suggested they go inside.

Sergeant Bancroft was less inclined. Breakfast, he thought, sounded much more appealing. He reasoned by insisting that they report the engine failure. They started ambling away.

Dr. Edwards pushed the nursery door open. I followed after him. What he saw made him swear out loud. Beyond a cloud of smoke he could make out a small, blood-smeared child tied to the legs of a chair. Beside her, two men and a bong. Her head lolled on her shoulders like an egg on a saucer.

A man fond of golf, silence, and lazy Sunday afternoons, Dr. Edwards suddenly found himself launching at the girl, scrabbling at the chair to set her free, but not before a ringed Ukrainian fist connected with his temple.

"What was that?" Downstairs, Sergeant Mills drew his gun and headed back to the door. Sergeant Bancroft sighed. Reluctantly, he unclipped his gun. He owed Sergeant Mills five pounds. Any other time, he would have stood his ground and gone for a pasty.

"It's the police! Open up or we'll enter by force!"

A few seconds passed. Another warning from Sergeant Mills. And then, with all the encouragement I could muster, a short, piercing squeal from Margot's lips. Sergeant Bancroft raced inside first.

It was Sergeant Bancroft who discovered the rooms downstairs filled with sunken-eyed men and women in flea-ridden clothes, eating out of cardboard boxes, sleeping in rows. Suddenly his French "O" Level broke the floodgates of his memory, and he understood what the woman under the sofa was telling him: that they were immigrants, virtually held hostage by the man who'd climbed out the bathroom window just moments earlier. That they wanted to go home.

It was Sergeant Mills who assisted Dr. Edwards in his struggle upstairs, who offloaded his gun into the arm of the man who produced a blade from his pocket and cuffed the other man to the cot. It was Dr. Edwards who scooped up Margot—so light and frail it took his breath away—and carried her out of the house into the first ray of sunlight that had graced her face in months.

As he held her there in that quiet street, checking her pulse, I reached down and touched her head. A flash of memory passed through my mind. Just a glimmer. A man's face bending over me, a streak of blood across his forehead from the scrap upstairs. I remembered this moment. His hands were trembling as he inspected Margot's little body, counting her pulse. I saw my chance.

"Take her home," I whispered into his ear.

To my relief, he heard every word.

6

The Game

GIVEN THE SEVERE URGENCY POSED BY MARGOT'S CONDITION, THE POLICE HAD NO OBJECTION TO DR. EDWARDS' DESIRE TO TREAT HER AT HIS HOME.

Margot spent the next couple of weeks in a soft clean bed with a view of rolling hills and clear skies. Not that she really looked out the window—she spent much of the time sleeping. I occupied myself with a good book—Dr. Edwards had an impressive collection of Dickens, first editions at that—on a chaise longue by the window. She was put on an IV drip and a diet of fresh fruit, vegetables, and milk. Gradually, the bruises on her legs and arms faded, as did the blue shadows beneath her eyes. But the gold light around her heart did not return.

Dr. Edwards (or Kyle, as he told Margot to call him) had a wife and two daughters, one eleven years old, the other eighteen. Pictures of them lined the mantelpiece, long shelves overlooking the spiral staircase, and the Victorian desk in his office. I sensed a bit of a schism in the family unit: the older girl, Karina, posed in every photo like a glamour model, one hand piling her long dark hair up on her head, the other arm on her waist, and always a pout and a wink. But what was more telling was that the wife, Lou, appeared in every photo with her arm around Karina, though nary a smile. Wherever the younger girl appeared—this was Kate—she stood far away from her mother and older sister, her head slightly bowed so that her straight, dark hair half covered her face, her hands clasped in front of her. Even where space dictated they stand close together, I noticed that Kate turned so that no part of her body was touching either Lou or Karina.

What's more, I recognized her. A vague image unwound itself from the docks of my memory: a bone-china table lamp dropping to the floor and shattering. A game board. Strong sunlight streaming through the door of a shed, and Kate's face, contorted in either a scream or a laugh. I looked out the window to the back of the long garden. A large wooden shed. Must be the one.

Lou, Kate, and Karina were spending the month in Dublin at Lou's parents'. Kyle filled his days attempting odd jobs around the house while Margot slept, but was clearly distracted by the state of events. A half-built birdhouse, an unpainted door frame . . . I followed him around a lot of the time, making sure that there were no nails left lying around for Margot to swallow or step on.

I could see what was playing on Kyle's mind—quite literally. He had dug out Margot's medical file from among his archives and gradually recalled the infant he had treated several years before— the infant who wasn't supposed to have survived this long, especially not in a house full of drugs and violence.

Short films of worry and confusion spooled themselves in his mind during long evenings while he stretched out in front of the

TV with a gin and tonic. Even in the bath, questions bombarded him. *How is she still alive? Ventricular tachycardia is incurable. Was I wrong to advise her foster parents of her impending death? Speaking of which, where are those guys? What was Margot doing in that house?*

He couldn't sleep. I watched him, bemused, as he tiptoed downstairs to his office in the wee hours, layering his desk with medical books and journals. And I wanted to tell him— for somehow I knew, intimately and precisely—the answer to his conundrum in detail. It wasn't ventricular tachycardia. Margot had an aortic valve stenosis, which would require a transthoracic echocardiogram, or a cardiac ultrasound. In those days, a cardiac ultrasound was as common as hen's teeth. I mooched over to Kyle's desk and flicked open one of his magazines to an article by Dr. Piers Wolmar, a professor at the University of Cardiff with a specialty in ultrasonography. I fluttered the pages a little to get Kyle's attention. He eventually approached the magazine, picked it up and held it close to his face. For the eighth time today, he'd lost his glasses.

He read intently, putting the magazine down occasionally to think aloud. He began to question himself. What if it *wasn't* ventricular tachycardia after all? And what was this procedure Dr. Wolmar described? Echocardiography? Technology was moving so fast it made his head spin.

He spent the rest of the night writing a letter to Dr. Wolmar, outlining Margot's symptoms and asking for more information on how to treat it. As the sun began to rise like a gong over Ulster, he finally fell asleep facedown on his desk.

Lou, Kate, and Karina returned from Dublin. No, they didn't merely return: they exploded into the house through the kitchen door, weighed down with an impressive number of bulging suitcases and screaming for Kyle.

Margot stirred. Kyle was by her bedside, reading more of Dr. Wolmar's articles on echocardiography. She woke up to find a stethoscope on her bare chest. She looked up quickly at Kyle, then at me. I assured her that everything was okay. She set her head back on the pillow and yawned. Yells from downstairs prompted Kyle to put his stethoscope away hastily.

"Now, Margot," he said softly, "be a good girl and stay here for a moment while I speak with my wife and daughters. They don't know you're here yet."

Margot nodded and curled up on her side. She pulled a face at me, and I pulled one back, but the next time she looked at me, she couldn't see I was there. She thought I'd gone.

I followed Kyle downstairs. Karina and Lou talked over each other, giving a blow-by-blow account of their holiday. Kate sat at the kitchen table and inspected her nails. Kyle held up both hands before Karina and Lou as if surrendering. He told them to be quiet.

"What is it, Daddy?" Karina said.

Kyle pointed upward. "Upstairs, in the spare room, we have a little girl."

Lou and Karina shared bewildered looks.

"What, Daddy?"

"Kyle, explain this right now."

He dropped his hands. "I will, but not at the moment. She is sick and probably scared out of her wits at the noise you lot are making. I'd like you to quietly come upstairs and say hello."

"But . . ."

He looked down his glasses at Lou and she shut her red lips tight. I smirked. What a joy she must've been to live with for the last twenty years. Kyle deserved a medal, or possibly a padded cell. I wasn't entirely sure.

Without a word, Kate sloped behind the rest of them as they made their way to Margot's room. The colors surrounding her troubled me. Sometimes she would give out a deep pink light, throbbing from her heart, but then it would change to blood red, and instead of throbbing, it oozed from her. Even its rhythm changed: Instead of pulsing vibrantly—and that's what most auras did, they flowed and pulsed like a heartbeat—this color moved as lethargically and heavily as lava. Sometimes it stopped at her throat, where it appeared to burn. And I realized that despite her placid, wallflower presence, she was furious. Boiling with repressed rage. I just didn't know why.

And I didn't much care, at first. It was her outfit that really got my attention. Following her up the stairs, I noticed her interest in all kinds of satanic logos: a black T-shirt with a red-horned demon splashed across the back, demon stud earrings, and—something I'm sure her parents knew nothing about—a four-inch tattoo on her right shoulder blade of an upside-down cross.

Halfway up the stairs, she stopped. Lou, Kyle, and Karina continued on without her. She turned and looked right at me. Her eyes, cesspool brown. No warmth.

"Get out," she said flatly.

Is she talking to me? I thought. And then I saw it, exactly as I had seen circulating around Kyle—Kate's layer of emotions had a link connecting her to my realm. But, unusually, her link was like a dark tentacle that connected not only to my realm, but to another side. A side I hadn't yet encountered.

When I realized she really was addressing me, that she could see me, I gathered my composure. "I'm afraid you'll have to make me," I said back.

"Okay"—she shrugged—"but I don't think you'll like it."

She turned, and continued upstairs.

I shook my head and chuckled, though I was perturbed. Her discernment had completely unnerved me. Who—or what—else could see me?

Karina fawned over Margot like she was a living doll. Before she could open her mouth, Karina lifted her under the arms and carried her into her room, where she dragged out the contents of her makeup drawer and turned Margot into a miniature beauty queen. Lou folded her arms, tapped her foot, and spat a torrent of put-out complaints to Kyle. What was he thinking, bringing a stray home? And for how long, exactly? What if her drug-addict foster parents came looking for her? Et cetera, et cetera.

Kyle tried explaining that this was the little girl whom he had cared for when she arrived at the hospital the day she was born, orphaned and almost dead, and that fate had brought them together again. He thought about telling her about me—the strange woman he'd met on the road at 6:00 AM, instructing him to break into the house across the road and save Margot—but he thought better about it.

"You *always* do this, don't you, Kyle!" yelled Lou. "You always *have* to be the savior of everyone else! What about me, eh? What about Karina and Katie?"

"What about them?" He shrugged.

She flung her hands up in the air and marched out of the room. Kyle let out a long sigh and cracked his knuckles. I gave him a round of applause. The Nobel Prize for Saintly Patience goes to . . .

My wings were twitching. I went into Karina's bedroom and sat next to Margot on the bed. She was enchanted with all the pink and blue stuff that Karina was pasting on her face. I always did wonder where my love of make-up came from; my adoptive mother never wore the stuff and I'd no older sisters. Kate was in the doorway, watching. She looked at me, then at Margot.

"Who is she?"

Karina sighed dramatically. "Go away, Kate. Margot and I are having a makeup party, and you're not invited."

"Her name's Margot?"

"Margot," repeated Margot, and smiled proudly. Eventually, Kate half smiled back.

"I think you and I are going to have some fun, Margot."

She turned and walked away.

Gradually, Margot came out of herself like a crab venturing out of its shell into warm tropical sun. She quickly became a three-year-old version of Karina: She used phrases that Karina used ("that's so *awesome!*"), insisted on wearing her clothes like Karina, and danced with her to the Beatles long past bedtime. She also developed the appetite of a horse.

I had no idea I was so adorable as a child. So funny, so innocent. Once, Margot woke up scared from a nightmare, which

I'd watched anxiously. It was a memory of her time at Sally and Padraig's. Before she could wake the others with her screams, I wrapped my arms around her and rocked her on the bed. There was such pain tightening around her heart, like a vise. I squeezed my eyes tight and tried to summon up whatever power it was that had healed her before. The soft gold light that had faded to a distant glow flickered, like a candle, in the distance. I willed it harder. It grew to the size of a tennis ball, large enough to surround her heart. Her breathing steadied, but I could see her heart now, and the danger there. Although she was filled with calm and love, there was a growing problem in her heart that needed to be fixed. I only hoped Kyle would work quickly.

The next morning, Kyle received a letter from Dr. Wolmar. He said he'd be happy to pay a visit in the future and instruct Kyle on the procedure and equipment that was needed for echocardiography. He also mentioned that, by the sound of Margot's symptoms, she was possibly suffering from aortic stenosis, which was entirely treatable.

Karina was in the dining room, teaching Margot how to jive. Lou had gone shopping. A voice from the garden:

"Margot! Margot! Come and play!"

Kate. Grinning. Kyle looked up, saw her at the window, and jumped to his feet. He was excited to see Kate wearing her annual smile. He raced into the dining room.

"Margot!" he called. "Come play with Katie!"

Karina scowled. "What, with daggers? Torturing animals?"

Kyle frowned. "Don't be like that, Karina. Come on, Margot!"

He took her by the hand and led her outside. She was hesitant when she saw Kate. She looked at Kyle, then at me. I nodded. *Yes, kiddo, I'm coming too. Don't worry.*

Kate waved her hand and invited Margot to play with her in the shed.

"Don't want to," Margot said.

"Come on, silly," Kate said, smiling. "There's chocolate. And Beatles."

"Beatles?"

"Yes, Beatles."

Margot skipped happily to the shed.

Once inside, Kate bolted the door. She checked the windows to make sure her father was still in the house, then tugged the curtains to cut out the sunlight. Dust scattered across a couple of old bikes and a dissected lawn mower. I waited in a corner. She looked up at me, then back at Margot. *What is this kid up to?*

"Now, Margot," she said. "We're going to play a little game. Games are fun, aren't they?"

Margot nodded and twirled her skirt. She was waiting for the Beatles. Kate laid out the game board on the floor, and in that instant I realized two things:

1. This was the game board from my memory.
2. It wasn't a game board. It was a Ouija board.

Kate sat on the floor and crossed her legs. Margot did the same. I thought quickly: Do I go and get Kyle's attention? Or do I stay here and see what Kate is up to?

Kate pressed her fingertips against the cardboard triangle that pointed at the letters of the alphabet on the board. "This will tell us the name of your angel," she told Margot. Margot smiled back. She turned right around and looked at me, excited.

"What is the name of the angel here?" Kate's voice, hard and cold.

Slowly, a darkness seeped into the shed. Margot looked around her, shivering. "I want to go see Karina," she said softly.

"No," Kate said. "We're playing a game, remember?" She let go of the cardboard marker. Slowly, invisible hands moved the marker to an *R*. Then a *U*. Then a *T*. Then an *H*. Hello. Very unpleasant to make your acquaintance.

"Ruth," Kate said, her eyes gleaming. "Get out."

I didn't move. We eyeballed each other for a few seconds. I was aware of dark shapes shuffling at the back of the shed. For the first time in a long while, I felt afraid. I didn't know what to expect.

"Okay," Kate said. "Servants of Satan, remove Ruth."

Margot stood up. "I want to go," she said, her lip trembling. She could sense the dark things too. I had to get her out. I took a step forward, shielding her. I could see it, the large black shape headed my way. Kate was yelling dark incantations she'd picked up from whatever evil stuff she'd filled her head with. I spoke loudly.

"Kate, you have no idea what you're dealing with—"

I hadn't finished the sentence before I felt something being flung through the air at me. I held up a hand and willed a strong beam of light to illuminate the room. At the moment that the light reflected against the thrown object it also deflected its aim, bringing it crashing to the ground. But whatever had thrown it was starting to charge, its heavy footsteps making the whole shed vibrate.

I tried to shoot another beam of light, but it wouldn't come. I could feel the thing rushing toward me, the size of an elephant. Margot screamed. I stood in front of her, closed my eyes, and concentrated hard. Suddenly the light burst out of my hand with such force that it made me stagger backward. With a loud snort, the darkness that was almost upon us disintegrated into cloud.

The shed door flung open, pouring in sunlight. It had been raining before. Now the skies were blue, and blinding sun cut through the darkness like a white blade. Margot ran to the house, crying. I stood firm, watching Kate as she lay on the ground, astonished. Beside her, an old ceramic lamp in pieces.

"I recommend you find a new game," I said, before returning to Margot.

Kate didn't touch the board again.

7

A Change of Heart

ONCE MARGOT REACHED AN AGE OF REASONABLE
COMPREHENSION, I WAS BURSTING TO GIVE HER
BUCKETLOADS OF ADVICE. *When you turn sixteen, you'll
have an unprecedented compulsion to fall head over heels for a
guy called Seth. Don't. Why? Trust me, okay? You're gonna love
New York, honey. Where's New York? It's in America. I can't
wait for you to go there. Are the Beatles there? Sorta. But, more
importantly, sweet cheeks, there's a woman called Sonya whom
you meet when your dog breaks free of his leash and starts a small
flood in the deli on Fifth Avenue. You wanna stay well clear of her.
Why? She steals your husband.*

Shortly before the Christmas of her fourth year, she began to
ignore me completely. Weeks would pass and she wouldn't look
at me. It was as if the wind was settling, as though the pebbles of
her consciousness were calming into place, allowing none of my
influence to penetrate.

I got angsty. I felt marooned, lost, and humbled. I think I
started taking my job a little more seriously at that point. And I

think the truth finally sank in: I really was dead. I really was a guardian angel.

I became obsessed with my reflection (yes, I still had one— I'm an angel, not a vampire). I couldn't take my eyes off the flowing water spouting from my shoulders, finding its way seamlessly through my woefully shapeless white dress like silvery Rapunzel-esque ponytails. I looked about twentyish, though my hair was different—not a trace of peroxide. My natural caramel brown, reaching my shoulders in springs and coils. I had breasts, genitals, even my disgusting crescent-moon toes. I had leg hair. I was also slightly luminous, as if tiny LED lights circulated through my veins instead of blood.

Margot was looking more like a female version of Theo every day. I started to feel swamped by the past, so focused on what I'd lost and what I'd thrown away and how I could never, ever make it right that I almost forgot what I was supposed to be doing. I was meant to be watching over Margot, looking out for her. Kids grow so fast. By the time I woke up from my little pity trip she'd grown several inches, had a new haircut, and was totally and irrevocably Karina-fied. She was *all* attitude. But it was a good thing. She learned how to stick it to Kate and seemed to be resisting the weaknesses in her heart by virtue of sheer preadolescent sassiness.

And then, one day, she collapsed at the park. I was lying underneath the swing, tickling the undersides of her knees as she swung like the pendulum of life's clock above me, her white skirt fluttering in the breeze, and on one swing forward she was giggling, and on the swing back she was slumped on the seat, unconscious. Karina screamed. Margot fell backward off the swing and hit the ground, but not before I'd caught her head and prevented her skull from splitting on the concrete.

Kyle was doing laps around the field opposite. Karina ran for him, leaving Margot on the ground, her legs folded oddly beneath her body, her lips polar blue. I could see the ventricles of her heart, and whereas one was fat and clear, the other was a punctured bicycle tire. I leaned over her and pressed my hand against her heart, and this time the light was golden, a healing light, banishing all the blue from around her lips and eyes. For the moment.

Kyle and Karina raced back toward us. Kyle scooped Margot up under her shoulders and checked her pulse. She was breathing, barely. He carried her to the car and drove her straight to the hospital.

I cursed myself. I hadn't been paying attention. I fumbled around the hospital, figuring out what I needed to do.

And then it happened.

First, Nan appeared, smiling and calm as usual. She laid a hand on my shoulder and directed my attention to a blank wall. I was on the verge of being irritated (a *wall?*) when a vision appeared: a 3-D "film" of the heart surgery that Margot required. Nan told me to watch, remember, and repeat everything I saw and heard to the surgeon. I got it. It was a training seminar.

So I watched. It was a vision of the future as I was to conduct it. A voice appeared in my head—a female voice, American—telling me what each action meant, what it was for, why this particular technique hadn't yet been carried out on these shores, how far to draw the scalpel, etc. I listened, and I found that every word that was said, every action, sat neatly on my memory like raindrops on a waxed car. I didn't forget anything, not a single adverb or emphasis.

When the vision faded, Nan directed me to the operating room. I didn't think any time had passed: The nurse who was masking up when the vision started was still fiddling with the strings when it ended. I quickly tied a knot for her, and she said "Thanks," not looking around to see who had helped.

Inside the operating room, Margot lay motionless on the table under an overhead lamp that bleached out her features. Worse, her aura was watery, wispy. It rose weakly from her body like smoke on water. Two nurses, Kyle, and the head surgeon, Dr. Lucille Murphy, tugged on their gloves and approached Margot. As I stepped forward, a little over Margot, I looked up again and saw that the room count had doubled: there were four other guardian angels with us, one for each member of the room. I nodded to each of them. We had work to do.

Lucille's guardian angel was her mother, Dena, a short, round woman radiating such calm that I immediately started taking slower, deeper breaths. Dena leaned her head on Lucille's shoulder, then glanced at me and took a step back, allowing me to stand close to Lucille by her left. I told her not to make an eight-inch incision down the center of the sternum, as she was primed to do. I told her to make a two-inch incision between the ribs instead. Dena repeated the instructions like a translator. Lucille blinked for a couple of seconds, feeling the sensation of Dena's guidance whirling through her conscience like a vivid thread of intelligence.

"Doctor?" asked Kyle.

She looked up at him. "Just a minute." She stared at the ground, visibly torn between decades of medical practice and the arrival of a new method in her head, which, to her surprise, made complete sense. It would take courage to act so swiftly. For an instant I wondered if she'd bottle out. Eventually, she looked up.

"We're going to try something new today, people. A two-inch incision between the ribs. We're going to try to save this young girl bleeding more than she needs to."

The team nodded. Without thinking, I reached down to the small scar between my breasts. A scar whose origin I'd never known, until now.

From that point, I repeated everything I'd heard during the vision, and everything I said, Dena repeated. And then I realized the American female voice I'd heard during the vision was Dena's. Everything really was as Nan had said: this had all happened before. I had stood here before. Time as I knew it had folded over. It made me dizzy.

When the procedure was over, everyone but Kyle, Dena, Lucille, and yours truly left the room. The four of us stood by Margot as she lay on the operating table, ghostly and motionless, willing her back.

"Why the sudden change in procedure?" Kyle said at last.

Lucille shook her head. They'd been lovers once, so she was honest. "I dunno. I dunno. But"—she took off her gloves—"let's pray it works."

Margot came home from the hospital a while later, fragile, sore, but already showing signs that she was on the mend. Her first words on waking from the surgery were to ask for chocolate cake. Karina had sent her a Beatles LP, which she clutched to her chest like a prosthetic. She thought nothing of the overheard conversations among doctors and nurses that she had almost died. She thought only of jiving in Karina's bedroom in a dust cloud of pink powder and glitter.

It was early afternoon when we arrived back at the Edwardses'. The girls were gone—Karina to a party, Kate on a school trip overseas. Kyle carried Margot upstairs and put her to bed. He spent a while fussing over her temperature, making sure her pillows were plump, stuffing teddies under her arms in case she woke up in the middle of the night and was lonely. I could see it clearly. He loved her.

He headed downstairs. I stayed with Margot, hatching a plan. Surely there was no reason for me *not* to change things, to make it so that she could stay here and grow up with a family, a warm home, a *chance*? Wasn't this refitting the pieces of the jigsaw? I stood for a moment, reflecting on the episode in the operating room. *Nothing is fixed.* I was just beginning to figure out that I wasn't merely a visitor to the past, viewing the galleries of events as they had once been, but an active participant: adding paint to the future's blank canvas, to borrow one of Nan's metaphors. Maybe I could rearrange the details a little, sketch different paths for Margot to try, as long as they all led to the same destination.

When I heard shouting downstairs, I left Margot sleeping and went to investigate.

They were in the kitchen. Lou was by the sink, looking out the back window at the darkening garden. Kyle looked like he was holding himself up on the cooker. The atmosphere was like the aftermath of a forest fire. I could barely see either of them for the mists of emotion swirling about the room, thick as smoke.

Nobody spoke for a few moments. At last, Kyle:

"A divorce." Somewhere, way at the end of the statement, was a question mark. I looked to Lou.

"I never said that."

"You said you wanted to leave."

Lou turned around. Her eyelashes were globbed with tears. "Plenty of people stay married without living together. Isn't that what we've been doing for the last six years? Cohabiting? Coexisting?"

And just then, a clearing amid the swirling mists. A divide. Kyle turned and walked out of the room. She screeched after him.

"That's the spirit, Kyle; run away from the problem!"

He turned on his heel and stormed back toward her, almost knocking me over.

"It's *you* who's been running away," he spat. "Dublin to see your parents? When you hate the pair of them? Don't take me for an idiot. I *know*."

Her mouth slung open. I could see it all now: the aura of another man all over her. A visible green current in the red river of her aura. She didn't know her own husband well enough to reckon he'd sussed it out. She studied the floor.

"What about the girls?" Kyle said, quieter. "Where'll they go?"

She'd worked everything out but that. Immediately, I could see her dreams shattering with the force of reality. All Lou and her lover had talked about was the days they'd spend on a beach at Tralee, chardonnay on ice, the horizon endless. She hadn't thought about custody.

"I'll take them with me."

Kyle shook his head and folded his arms. He'd already made up his mind in the two seconds that she'd hesitated. *He* would leave. The girls would stay with their mother in the house. He thought of Margot. For a moment, his aura retreated into his core. Reluctantly, he realized there was only one thing for it. He would have to leave her too. He drew consolation by reminding himself that she'd developed a close bond with Karina. Here, they'd all be stable. Safe. Secure. Just, without him.

My heart sank. Kyle ran upstairs and hunted for a suitcase. Then, he remembered, he didn't have one. Angrily, he yanked Lou's tortoiseshell case from under the bed. I watched on, sobered into silence and sadness, as he filled it with suits and shirts, a few medical books, a clutch of precious family photographs.

He spent a long time beside Margot's bedside, his shaking palm outstretched over her heart, a deep, aching prayer writing itself on his: *If you're there, God, if you can hear me, just make her okay.*

With each word, the light around her grew.

It was decided that Kyle's sudden departure should temporarily be explained as a business trip. Kate and Karina didn't much question it—Lou's purchase of a Labrador puppy proved a great distraction—but Margot became withdrawn. She spent long afternoons in the hallway, seated on the bottom stair, waiting for Kyle. Nothing I did made her smile. Nothing I did made her look at me. At first, I thought she was waiting for Kyle. But children are smarter than that. She was waiting to be told that he wasn't coming back.

A while later, Lou drove Karina, Kate, and Margot all the way to Scotland to drop Karina off at Edinburgh University, where she was taking up a degree in geography. On the way home, they took a surprise detour through northern England to a large gray building in the middle of nowhere called St. Anthony's Home for Children, and when they drove off again they had an empty backseat—Lou and Kate were in the front, and Margot was standing in the courtyard of St. Anthony's, a teddy bear under one arm, a small bag at her feet, her little heart pounding.

"Papa," she said, watching the car drive away. Looking up at the cataract-gray building, I shuddered.

I knew this place all too well.

8 ❧

*S*heren and the Tomb

LET ME GET OUT OF MY SYSTEM WHAT I RECALL ABOUT
ST. ANTHONY'S HOME FOR CHILDREN, WHICH I ENDURED
FROM THREE AND A HALF UNTIL THE AGE OF TWELVE YEARS,
NINE MONTHS, AND SIXTEEN DAYS.

First, I should mention that I spent much of my adult life
chasing the permanent knot left deep in my stomach by that
place with a long-necked bottle of booze. It's no excuse. And now
that I see the circumstances under which I arrived there—after I
had learned what it is to be loved, after the warmth and comfort
of the Edwardses' home, having enjoyed my own bedroom that
was the size of a twelve-child dorm at St. Anthony's, having had
an older sister to dote on me instead of a group of older kids to
smash my self-esteem into pieces every day and night—I know
now why the pain lasted so long, well after I made my way out
of there. It might have been better if I'd been left at Sally and
Padraig's a while longer so that any expectation of love would've
been beaten out of me. St. Anthony's never would've been such
a shock to the system.

As a child—and in my memories—the place was enormous. It had been a hospital until the nineteenth century, after which it became a workhouse before being transformed—by name only—into an orphanage. For some reason I recalled gargoyles at every corner of the building, but there were none. The front entrance was set back behind several pillars, and two knee-creaking steps led to a black door. Two round brass knockers—one high above for adults, another quite low for children—jutted out from the door, and I remember the first time I rapped the door, the knocker was so thick that I couldn't wrap my hand all the way around. The rooms, all twenty-five of them, seemed huge, as did the old wooden school desks and the dorms. There wasn't a shred of carpet anywhere. No radiators in the bedrooms. No hot water, at least not in the communal toilets. The only pictures on the walls were of the people who had worked there—dour sepia photos of grim masters and mistresses who'd beat the living daylights out of most of the children who had the misfortune to enter there.

Reentering the place reminded me, very definitely, that I was in the past. I'd been enjoying the 1960s—Kyle's white Citroën DS 19 was an absolute dream to ride in, and I died for Lou's flares and Karina's collection of Beatles vinyl LPs—but St. Anthony's had remained in a time warp, circa 1066. There are many places on earth that do not, will not, accept the progression of time. There are also many people like that, and Hilda Marx was one of them.

Miss Marx was the woman in charge of St. Anthony's. Glaswegian, cursed with Yorkshire-pudding cheeks and an underbite that gave her the unfortunate resemblance to a toad, Hilda Marx had a personal ethos that gave the Gestapo a run for their money. The punishment for crying was four lashes. The punishment for talking back was ten lashes. Children aged two to fifteen were expected to be out of bed by six, in bed by nine. One minute after six or nine meant a day without food. The instrument used for lashes was a small stick for young children and a leather whip for children over five, though the whip and I made our acquaintance well before I reached the designated age.

Margot stood in the rain, watching Lou and Kate drive away—neither of them looked back—and for a long time after the car had vanished and the dust from the gravel driveway had settled, Margot stayed put, the teddy still under her arm, her hair spaghettilike from the rain, her whole body full of hurt and confusion. Precocious and intelligent, she'd worked out that this was for good. Take it from me—it is terrifying to see a child so young filled with such knowledge.

I scanned the horizon. Nothing but fields and a small impoverished village for miles. I wanted to see if there was any way I could prevent her from entering those doors. Was there a car I could flag down, some loving family headed this way that would spy a three-year old girl at the roadside and take her in? What about the residents of the village? Their faces flashed before me: mostly old farmers, a few battered wives. Nobody who fit the bill.

There was a larger town about thirty miles away. We could try that. I touched Margot on the shoulder and told her to follow me. I pushed her slightly, but she didn't budge. I tried running to the entrance gate and shouted her name until I went hoarse. She wasn't moving. And I couldn't go without her. Destiny? Forget it. It's all a decision. Margot had made it without realizing or understanding it.

I reluctantly returned to the spot where she was standing. I crouched down beside her, put my arm around her, and tried to explain everything. I tried to put it in a way that my three-year-old self would digest.

You know what, Margot? You're a tough kid. You're better off without those guys. Lou's as maternal as a great white. Kate's the Antichrist. I'm right here with you, kiddo. You're gonna spend a little longer than you'd like behind these doors. But you know what? I won't leave you. I've got your corner. There are some bad people here, make no mistake. There are bad people everywhere. Maybe it's better that you meet them sooner rather than later. Believe me, the earlier you learn how not to suffer fools, the better. This is good. Now don't be scared. Don't cry. Okay, cry. Get it out. And let that be it. No more tears until you leave this place. They cost too much.

She waited until I'd finished before turning toward the front door, taking hold of the rapper and knocking it as hard as she could. A few minutes passed. The rain was turning into silver ropes. Behind the front door, the sound of heavy footsteps. A handle turning. The door swung open. In the threshold, looming above Margot, was Hilda Marx. She stared down at Margot and barked:

"What's this? A drowned rat?"

Margot stared at Hilda's knees. Hilda reached down, put her fingers on Margot's chin, and yanked her face upward.

"How old are you?"

Margot merely stared.

"What. Is. Your. Name?"

"Margot Delacroix," Margot said firmly.

She raised her eyebrows. "Irish, by the sound of it. We'll soon cut that out of you. Same for the mulishness. Well, Margot Delacroix, this is your lucky day. One of our guests has just passed, so there's a spare bed. Quickly come in, come in. Heat is best kept indoors."

Once we stepped inside, my feelings of revulsion at returning to the site of my greatest childhood terror were soon put aside by an odd encounter. Hilda's guardian angel stood by the foot of the stairwell. Slim, sad, with flowing bronze hair, she looked very similar to Hilda, like a younger, prettier sister. I nodded in her direction. Up until this point, other angels tended to keep a distance. But Hilda's angel approached me.

"Ruth," I said.

"Sheren," replied the angel, smiling weakly, coming close enough until I could see the green of her eyes. "But I was once Hilda."

I stared at her. *This was Hilda?* All at once recognition made the room spin. Yes, this was Hilda—or Sheren—and the confrontation made me breathless. I began to shake all over, my veins taut with all the tangled memories created by this woman, all the rage and terror and sadness. How could I ever forgive what she did to me?

But when she looked up, her eyes glistened. There was none of Hilda's malice in this woman's face. She took my hands. Immediately I could feel the deep, bitter sting of regret twisting deep inside her, and I stopped trembling.

"I know you were Margot," she said. "Please, please forgive me. We need to work together as long as Margot stays here."

"Why?" I managed at last. Sheren was the one shaking now, the water from her back slowly turning to red. Tears dripped from her face to her neck, forming a necklace around her pale collarbone. Eventually she spoke.

"I'm working with the angels of each child who enters here to ensure that the damage inflicted by this place—by Hilda—does not result in too much damage in the world. There have been

murderers bred here, rapists, and addicts. We can't stop Hilda
from doing what she did. But we can try to heal the injury on
these little lives as much as we can."

We both looked to Margot and Hilda as they walked upstairs.
We followed.

"How can I help?"

"You remember the Tomb?"

For a moment I thought I would vomit. I had all but pushed
the Tomb to the recesses of my mind. The Tomb was the result
of Hilda's purgatorial artistry: a small, rat-infested, completely
windowless room in which a child over the age of five could not
stand. It reeked of excrement, decay, and death. The Tomb was
reserved for occasions of special punishment. Depending on the
age of the child, Hilda would champion her most treasured forms
of torture: starvation, beatings, and attacking their sensitivities by
making monstrous noises during the wee hours through a pipe
low in the ground, scaring young, naked, and starving occupants
out of their easily-duped wits until they emerged timid, jumpy and
silent as church mice for the rest of their days at St. Anthony's.
The door would be opened daily, only for a bucket of freezing
water to be poured over the naked child inside and a small bowl
of food tossed in to keep them alive. Her favorite form of torture
was to remove the occupant after a few days, take them all the
way back to the dorm, long enough for them to feel relief, then,
after a beating, they would be escorted bleeding and screaming all
the way back to the Tomb again, this time for double the length
of time that they had previously endured.

If any child entered the Tomb with so much as a grain of love in
their soul, they emerged from that awful place knowing, without
question, that love did not exist.

I looked at Sheren. She knew I remembered all right. Hilda had made sure I never forgot it. She stroked my face.

"We need to be in the Tomb with every child that Hilda puts there."

"You want me to go back in there?"

Slowly, she nodded. She knew precisely what this meant for me, how much she was asking of me. She touched my palm with her fingers, and quickly a flash of images swept across my mind—images that Sheren had witnessed of Hilda's childhood, of her abuse at the hands of five older men for many, many years, of the particularly calculated forms of torture she'd experienced at their hands.

"I'm sorry," I said at last.

"I only show you that to make you understand how Hilda came to be Hilda."

"When do we start?"

"She puts a boy in the Tomb tonight. You stay with Margot until I call you."

"Okay."

The first child that Margot made friends with was a seven-year-old boy named Tom. Small for his age, malnourished, and slow-witted, Tom was too easily lured by his rich imagination into his fantasies for the appreciation of his teacher, Mr. O'Hare. Margot was placed in the nursery with much younger children, and as a result she was bored. She wanted to jive to the Beatles as she had done with Karina. She wanted to learn songs with the older kids. It seemed that the children in the classroom opposite were having a much better time than she was, playing with moth-eaten teddy bears and wooden bricks and babies too young to walk. She went to the open window and watched as the teacher in the classroom suddenly stopped talking, walked to the back of the class, and emerged from Margot's blind spot with Tom in tow, who was then tossed into the corridor. Mr. O'Hare re-emerged a few moments later with a wooden blackboard duster, which he walloped around Tom's head a few times before marching back into the classroom.

Tom cowered on the floor. A few minutes later, he sat upright, rubbing his ear. A few minutes after that, he began to imagine that he wasn't in the corridor, but instead was on the planet Rusefog fighting warrior chimpanzees for the pirate treasure. An invisible machine gun took shape in his arms. He aimed it at the nursery window and started making firing noises as his torpedoes landed in a mass of fireworks.

Behind the window, Margot giggled.

Tom froze at the sound of her laughter, fearful of being beaten again. Margot saw that she had his attention, stood up on her tiptoes, and waved. He didn't see her. He returned to his mission. A particularly grim chimpanzee was shunting toward him, dressed head to toe in purple armor. He'd have to blast its foot off so that it wouldn't get to him. He squatted, took aim, and fired.

From where Margot was standing, the corridor was the fun place to be. She approached the nursery leader.

"I need to pee pee, please."

The nursery leader smiled and peered down at Margot through her spectacles. "The phrase is, 'May I use the lavatory please, Miss Simmonds.' Yes, you may, Margot. Off you go." Miss Simmonds opened the door, let Margot exit and locked it tight behind her.

Margot looked up and down the corridor. There was no one around except her and Tom, who was standing on the other side, a few yards to her right. Carefully she approached him. He was so engrossed in his shooting that he didn't see Margot standing there until she waved in his face.

"Oh!" For a split second, Margot was a blonde chimpanzee. He snapped out of his reverie. "Oh," he said again. Margot smiled at him.

Tom had spent the first four years of his life in a cushioned, loving home west of Newcastle upon Tyne in northeast England. When poverty and death struck a double blow to his life, he was passed around relatives until, like Margot, he found himself at the black doors of St. Anthony's, with all but his fantasies to protect him from its damage.

He hadn't forgotten his manners. He stuck out a filthy hand. "Tom," he said. "What's your name?"

"My name's Margot," she said and shook his hand reluctantly. "Can I play with you?"

He contemplated. He chewed his cheek, hand on hip, eyes darting left to right. "Here," he said eventually, handing her an invisible machine gun. "This is a laser raptor. You use it to melt the chimps' faces. Don't bother shooting at the armor. It's impenetrable."

Margot blinked for a few moments.

"Pow, pow, pow!" Tom hissed, aiming at the blank wall opposite. Margot copied him.

"Oh no!" Tom shouted, dropping his arms to his side, his eyes wide. "Your gun's out of ammo! Here, let me recharge for you." And carefully he took the heavy weapon out of her arms and reloaded it. He looked at her anxiously. "You're going to need more than that around here, you know." He reached for his calf. Gently he slid something out of its invisible strap.

"This was my father's sword," he whispered. "It's the sword of Lennon. Use it to cut out their hearts."

Margot nodded and took the invisible blade from Tom's fingers. She was too entranced to see me jumping up and down in front of her, hissing, "Margot! Margot! Get back into class! Back into class!"

For turning a corner at the end of the hall was Hilda Marx. Sheren had run ahead of her to alert me to her presence. Tom's guardian angel, a tall thin man named Leon, stood beside him and prodded him. Eventually he got Tom's attention, but not before Tom had yelled, "Take that, you mutant devils!" in Hilda's direction.

She saw the pair of them standing there, playing silly childish games. Up to no good. Deserving a fair amount of punishment.

She smiled—which was never a good sign—and approached.

"What's this, children? Silly games?"

Tom dropped all his weapons and stared at the ground. Margot copied him.

"Tom? Why are you outside?"

He didn't answer.

"Answer me, boy!"

"I . . . wasn't paying attention, Miss Marx."

She turned her glare to Margot. "And you, Margot. What brings you out of nursery?"

"I need to pee pee, Miss."

Hilda's lips curled. She raised an arm like a thick branch, pointing down the hall. "Lavatory's that way, girl. Get to it."

Margot dashed in the direction of Hilda's arm. As she reached the door to the toilets, she turned. The slap across Tom's face echoed all the way to the end of the hall.

Mr. O'Hare's report of Tom's recklessness, failing grades, and general inability to keep still in class confirmed that the Tomb was needed to bring the boy into line.

All the angels met at lights-out on the landing above the entrance hall. Sheren told us all what would happen tonight: Hilda and Mr. O'Hare would visit Tom in the dorm once the others had fallen asleep. They would strip him, beat him, and throw him in the Tomb for a total of two weeks. No child under the age of ten had ever been placed in the Tomb for longer than ten days. The punishment was particularly harsh, Sheren told us, because Tom reminded Hilda of herself. Every angel was needed to assist Tom during that terrible time, because the possible outcomes of the experience reached far into his adult life with devastating consequences: manic depression, violence, the squandering of Tom's talent as a playwright, the destruction of his marriage, and an untimely death. All before the age of thirty-five, and all because of Hilda Marx.

I returned to Margot. It was her first night at St. Anthony's, and she couldn't sleep. Two many bodies in the room. Too much creaking, whispering, snoring, and sobbing for her to feel anything but terrified. I rubbed her hands. For the first time in months, she looked right at me. I smiled. *Hey, kiddo*, I said. She smiled right back. The smile traveled all the way from her lips to her chest, removing the great rock that sat there, then all the way throughout her body, changing her aura from muddy water to a bright, golden yellow, strong as a sunrise. Slowly, she fell into a deep sleep.

Leon walked quickly toward me. He gestured for me to come. I checked that Margot was asleep, then followed him. He led me to the next dorm, where the rest of the angels were gathered.

We waited for a few moments. Most of the children were asleep. Tom, bruised and bloody from his earlier encounter with Hilda, was wide awake, constructing an escape plan out of Rusefog to confront the alien elephants on the planet Gymsock.

Tom's guardian angel, Leon, had been his twin brother. He had died minutes before Tom was born. Same nervous energy, same bird's-nest hair. He rubbed his hands anxiously.

Sheren looked to her right, and as I followed her gaze I could hear low whispering in the hallway. Two heads caught the light of the moon streaming through a window. Hilda and Mr. O'Hare. They proceeded quietly toward the dorm. We stood aside to let them enter—which made me boil at our impotence—and watched as Tom was dragged from his bed with a hand over his mouth and a thick arm around his middle, then carried into a room downstairs. There he was stripped of his clothes, beaten with a brick, then, when he fell unconscious, roused with cold water so that he would be aware that he was entering the Tomb. This last measure was a scare tactic—the sound of a child screaming at midnight filled the rest of the children with a fear that never left them their whole lives. It made them toe the line.

I checked again that Margot was sleeping, then followed the crowd of angels to the Tomb, which was located in an outbuilding next to the sewage tank. Beetles and cockroaches and rats congregated in the pipe that poured remnants of sewage into the Tomb, filling the bottom about two inches. A large rock sat up out of the slime, allowing occupants to huddle on top and stay dry. Tom was pleading, vomiting, dragging his bare feet on the gravel until they rubbed raw. We filed inside the Tomb. I was the last to enter. I stood for a moment, remembering the time I entered here as an eight-year old girl, a moment which so terrifyingly shaped my life, which was also the bass note of every nightmare, the bottom rung of my downward ladder into alcoholism.

I held my breath and climbed in. The door was closed, but we could all see the trio headed our way: Mr. O'Hare and Hilda on either side of Tom, half carrying, half dragging him. When he realized where he was, he fought with his last ounce of energy. They let him holler for a few minutes. A cold fist against his little jaw knocked him unconscious. He landed facedown in the slime. The door locked tight behind him.

To prevent Tom from drowning, Leon had to maneuver him so that he could breathe. Carefully he lifted Tom onto the rock. One of the blows had caused a blood clot in his head. Left untreated, it would travel to his brain and kill him by morning. Leon put both hands over Tom's head. Immediately, a gold light poured from his palms, and the blood clot evaporated.

When Tom woke up, his body shook violently with cold and shock. His own imagination couldn't have conjured something as awful as the Tomb. The creatures from the pipe came out, masters of this territory, and started crawling through his thick hair, inching toward his genitals, chewing his feet. Sheren sent out a blue flash and they scuffled away. They didn't bother him again. But fear and the smell from the sewage made him spew from both ends of his body until his stomach was raw. He spent the rest of the night sobbing and calling for his mother. He didn't realize that Leon was holding him, weeping.

I moved back and forth from the Tomb to Margot, making sure she was all right. On the fourth night, Tom was hallucinating with thirst and hunger. He was certain he could see his parents. Worse, he was certain they were being murdered in front of him. His screams reached the main building. Hilda sent

Mr. Kinnaird, the caretaker, with a bucket of cold water and a slice of bread to take care of the Tomb's occupant. Sheren saw to it that Mr. Kinnaird misheard Hilda, and took an entire loaf to poor Tom, who wolfed it down.

Each night, as the sun lowered and Tom's terror escalated, we formed a circle around him, palm to palm, our collective light forming a dome around him until he felt an overwhelming sense of calm and, at last, fell asleep. On the last night, as Leon finished his healing of Tom's worst injuries, he allowed a bruise on Tom's brain to remain.

"Why?" I asked.

"Forgetfulness," he replied. "He'll forget the worst of this if I let this stay."

And so it was that the naked, skeletal boy that Hilda and Mr. O'Hare eventually trailed out of the Tomb survived. Mr. Kinnaird, who also doubled as the house doctor, ordered two weeks' bed rest for Tom, and suddenly found himself inclined to top up the boy's pathetic platefuls of slop with extra meat and vegetables. Tom found his imagination brought to full activity—courtesy of Leon— which, on many a dark night, saw him creating escape routes out of dark places where previously none had existed, finding swords in hidden boxes with which to fight his imaginary foes.

About a year later, an older cousin arrived at St. Anthony's to take Tom into his home. Leon left with him and, I heard, made sure that Tom's mind transformed all the experiences— both conscious and subconscious—of St. Anthony's the way an oyster transforms grit.

Hilda's attention, however, was now turned to other devious miscreants under her care.

One of these was Margot.

9

The Song of Souls

IT FELT LIKE I WAS LIVING INSIDE A DREAM.

Memories of my life at four, five, and six years old are sodden with childish emotion, messy with interpretation and re-enactment, too entwined with my behavior and beliefs later in life to exist solely as memories.

In other words, each time Margot got flogged by Hilda, beaten by older kids, or alienated by the kids in her dorm so that she felt completely and utterly forsaken, the pain of watching her suffer conjoined with the deeper agony of my memories. Sometimes, it was unbearable.

We heard stories of angels whose Protected Beings were pedophiles, serial killers, terrorists, and all that they had to stomach on a daily basis. *Watch. Protect. Record. Love.* Angels who'd spent their mortality in the service of the church, or as Pollyanna housewives tending to children and grandchildren within the floral, apple-pie innocence of their own home now found themselves spending another lifetime following drug dealers and pimps around heroin dens, watching them abort unwanted babies, having to protect them against anything that frustrated human choice. Having to love them.

Why?

It just had to be done, was Nan's response. *God leaves no child alone.*

My own situation felt worse than the tales passed around by the angels at St. Anthony's. Nothing, absolutely nothing compared to an existence in which the terrible memories of the past flooded into the present. Nothing compared to spending every day up to my neck in full-blooded regret. I already knew the outcome. And I could do nothing about it.

It seemed a bit of lottery. I bombarded Nan with questions. How did we get paired up with our Protected Beings? How did I end up with Margot? Was it to do with the way I died?

I cornered Sheren and asked her how she'd died.

"Fifty aspirin and a bottle of sherry."

"So suicides end up as their own guardian angels? You're saying I killed myself?"

"Not necessarily."

"So, what else?"

"I met another angel once who had to go through what we go through. He said it was down to the way we lived."

"Meaning what?"

She gestured toward Hilda, who was shoving an arthritic finger in the face of a four-year-old girl for wetting the bed.

"You do know about the Song of Souls?"

"The what?"

Sheren shook her head and rolled her eyes. I felt stupid.

"It's the difference between us and other angels. When you protect your mortal self, you have an increased ability to influence and protect that person. Watch."

She walked toward Hilda. Already thoughts of the Tomb were spiraling above Hilda—clearly she planned to send the little girl there. Sheren stood next to Hilda and began to sing. The melody sounded like a traditional Scottish lullaby, though the words were in a language I didn't recognize. Slow, mysterious, beautiful. Her voice was resonant and loud, increasing in volume until the floor vibrated. As she sang, Sheren's wings lifted and began to move around Hilda, encircling them. Their auras became the same shade of purple. Hilda's thoughts gradually turned away from the Tomb. Instead, she sent the girl to bed without supper.

I approached Sheren.

"Where did you learn that?"

"The Song of Souls is whatever music harmonizes you and Margot, whatever connects you spiritually, despite the stage she's at as a human. What song do you remember as a child? What music was significant to you?"

I thought hard. All that came to mind were nursery rhymes—heaven knows I'd sung enough of them to Margot to get her to stop crying at Sally and Padraig's—but then I remembered something that Toby used to sing while he was struggling to write. It was an Irish song. "She Moved Through the Fair." And then I remembered: Una had sung it to Margot too.

"Okay," I said. "So how does it work?"

"The Song of Souls joins your will to Margot's. You're still Margot, just with a different name and form. You have the same will, the same choice."

"So I can make her choose differently?"

Sheren shook her head. "Not all the time. *She's* the one with the body. She has the upper hand. You can only influence."

My head hurt. I headed off to Margot. Song of Souls, huh? Maybe I could sing her all the way out of here.

At eight years old, Margot stood head and shoulders above the other kids in her age group. She knew her age, because every year, on July 10, a teacher would acknowledge that today she'd turned a year older, and that would be that. But she could easily pass for eleven or twelve, which meant that any eight-year-old nonsense was punished. No eight-year-old wanted to be her friend, and the twelve-year-olds didn't want her either. Wait, that isn't entirely true. Two twelve-year-old girls, Maggie and Edie, paid rapt attention to Margot. They were jealous of her long white-blonde hair. They saw to it that they dyed it red every so often from a bloody nose, or blackened her eyes so badly that she resembled a panda.

I wanted to drown the two of them. I wanted to push the huge oak bookcase that sat at the top of stairs over the banister, right on top of their heads. And I wanted to do it not only because I was the one who wrapped my arms around Margot when she sobbed in her bed at night, nor because I had to watch as Maggie sat on top of Margot while Edie booted her in the face, but because I remembered it. I wasn't completely helpless—I once made sure that a vicious blow to Margot's head didn't snap her spine—but it sure didn't feel that I was able to do a whole lot, much less take revenge.

Like an angry parent, I took issue with Maggie and Edie's angels. Both explained the reasons behind the girls' violence. Abuse this, torture that. I waved their excuses away with my hands. *I. Don't. Care. Stop them, before I do.* Clio and Priya—the names of their angels—shared looks. When Maggie spent a night in the Tomb for answering back, she suddenly found herself thinking about the punishments she'd laid on Margot with an unprecedented sense of remorse. Edie had a dream about her grandmother—for that was who Priya had been—instructing her to be a good girl. For a while, Margot found herself without cuts and bruises.

That was, until I sang the Song of Souls.

I'd sensed a family move into the village nearby who were kind, hardworking folk. I'd seen them in a vision: the husband, Will, was in his early forties, a traveling salesman. His wife, Gina, had been a piano teacher for many years until the birth of their son, Todd. They'd moved north from Exeter to take care of Gina's elderly parents. I felt they'd prove a good family for Margot, and more importantly, I felt they'd take her in.

Sheren's revelation about the Song of Souls proved to me what I'd suspected: My life as Margot wasn't carved in stone. It was merely written, as if on a page, and therefore available for some editing. If I could encourage Margot to choose differently, we might get ourselves out of St. Anthony's sooner rather than later.

And so, that night, I waited until lights-out before trying out my rusty set of pipes. I stood up and, rather self-consciously, made sure the other angels weren't looking as I inhaled and prepared to sing. I began quietly. *"My young love said to me, my mother won't mind . . . "* Margot was teetering on sleep, fidgeting on the lumpy mattress, lying on her left arm. *"And my father won't slight you for your lack of kind . . . "* I was holding the tune. I got a little louder. *"And she stepped away from me, and this she did say: It will not be long, love, 'til our wedding day."* She opened her eyes.

I felt the waterfalls in my back lift up, the way I'd seen Sheren's wings rise above her like arcs of storm. I saw Margot's aura widen and deepen in color. She was looking right at me, but she couldn't see me or hear me. She could only feel something different, deep in her gut. I sang louder, until all the angels in the room looked around at me. *"As she stepped away from me, and she moved through the fair . . . "* I could see Margot's heart now, stronger, healed. And then I saw her soul, that circle of white light, egglike, filled with one wish: a mother.

As I sang, I concentrated hard on the family I'd seen in the village. I formed an escape plan in my head, with instructions to Margot:

Spread a rumor that you're spending a night at the Tomb. Hide in the boiler room until dawn, then sneak out into the yard and, as the delivery van pulls off, jump onto the back and hide under the coal sacks. As the van slows down to cross the sheep grille at the mouth of the village, jump down and run to the house with the sky blue door. They'll take you in.

When I stopped singing, Margot was sitting upright in bed, her bony knees drawn into her chest, her mind ticking over. I could see her thoughts: she was picturing my escape plan, weighing it. Yeah, she thought. The delivery van comes at 5:00 AM every Thursday—the day after tomorrow. She'd seen it a few times. Old Hugh, the driver, was deaf in one ear. She'd use it to her advantage.

The next morning, Margot confided in Tilly, the eleven-year-old girl in the bunk above, that she was going into the Tomb that night.

"Eee, what for?"

Margot hadn't thought of that. "Um, pulling faces at Miss Marx."

"You pulled a *face* at Miss Marx? You brave lass! Wait till I tell the others about this!"

By lunchtime, every table buzzed with gossip. The story had expanded somewhat. Margot had no longer simply pulled a face. Oh no. She had called Miss Marx a *pile of dung* to her face. Then, when Miss Marx tried to drag Margot into her office for a beating, Margot had slapped her, twice, before yanking up her skirt and mooning her. Margot was now facing an eternity in the Tomb.

Margot faced a problem: she couldn't very well stage her own escort to the Tomb. Recent tradition held it that Hilda and Mr. O'Hare dragged naked offenders to the Tomb from their dorms at bedtime: The public spectacle was important now in feeding Hilda's thirst for punishment. So Margot spread another rumor: She was going to hide from them, so as to make it a bit more difficult. After all, her punishment was already pretty grim. How could they make it worse?

There was an element of truth to this: Margot *did* hide. After supper, and egged on by most of the other kids, she packed a satchel with some leftovers and ducked down the corridor toward the boiler room, where she pulled a blanket over her knees and waited.

I'd informed the other angels of the event. Sheren looked at me, concerned. "You do know what happens, don't you?" I shook my head. I had no memory of this event, just a strong hope that we pulled it off. Sheren sighed and returned to Hilda's office, with a promise that she would do what she could.

Fortunately, it was Mr. Kinnaird's turn to do lights-out. As he loped around the dorms doing bed counts, he found Margot's bed empty.

"She's in the Tomb, sir," explained Tilly.

"Oh?" He checked his notes. "Ain't got anyone down for the Tomb, not tonight anyways."

"You forgot your glasses again, have you, sir?"

He had. "Oh. Yes, I have. Well, I'll tick her off, shall I?"

Tilly nodded. Whispers circulated around the room. Mr. Kinnaird didn't notice.

Margot couldn't sleep, despite the coaxing heat in the boiler room. The whine and occasional tapping noises of the pipes made her insides twist with fear in case someone had figured out her plan and was coming to drag her out. I stayed with her all night, wrapping her in my dress when she started to shake with terror, promising her that we'd make it. The vision of the family in the village became so clear, Margot could make out their faces. She burned for them. She'd hammer on their door and plead with them to take her in. *I'll bring you breakfast in bed. I'll do every scrap of housework. Just save me from St. Anthony's. Just give me a family.*

The sound of crunching gravel cut through the five o'clock silence. It was still dark, but fingers of sun teased the horizon. The sound of the delivery van's shuddering engine. Hugh's off-tone humming. *Now*, I told Margot. She picked up her satchel, opened the door quietly, and tiptoed into the biting morning air.

From the side door she could see him at the front of the house, his heavy boots thumping slowly back and forth from the van to the front door, dumping large sacks of coal, food, and clothes donated from the villages. She was scarcely breathing now, her heart beating so wildly that she looked like she might pass out. I made a move toward the van, anxious to check whether anyone might see her, but then her knees buckled. I grabbed her just as she was about to fall. With both my arms around her shoulders, she managed to pull herself together. *Maybe I'm pushing her too much*, I thought. *Maybe she isn't ready.*

Hugh got back into the van and started the engine. *Quick!* She raced across the gravel to the back of the van, flung open the door, and jumped in on top of rancid vegetables and bags of coal and firewood. The van shuffled up the path, headed for the main road.

Margot did as planned by hiding under the coal sacks. I pressed my hands to my chest and leaped in the air. *We've done it! She's escaped!* I thought of the family in the village. I thought of how I would whisper in the mother's ear that Margot was the daughter she'd never had, the daughter she'd wished for, here to receive her love and care forever.

I watched the van trundle away, and I wept. Margot was weeping too, filled with so much hope and so much fear that she thought she might burst.

And then the engine cut out. Right at the top of the lane. The van came to a dead stop. Hugh swore, turned the key, and grinded the gears. Nothing but a hoarse mechanical cough from under the hood. I looked inside the engine: flooded with oil. Easy to fix. *But be quick!* Hugh whistled happily as he opened the hood and set about fixing the problem.

Just then, Sheren appeared beside me.

"I'm sorry, Ruth," she said. I froze.

A shuffle and a yell. The van doors flung open. Before I could do anything else, hands were laid on Margot. Hilda dragged her by the hair from the back of the van to the front door of St. Anthony's, and old Hugh was none the wiser.

And right there, right then, the vision of the family in the village withered. They were as good as dead. And so was Margot.

This time, the beating was not carried out with Hilda's hands and feet, nor with the whip. It was with the aid of a small but weighty sack of coal, which Margot had been clutching as she was dragged from the van, using it as anchorage. Sheren wept as she sang to Hilda, doing everything in her power to stop her from lifting the sack high above her head and bringing it down on Margot's little body, unmoving on the ground. Likewise, all I could do was prevent every impact from the coal from shattering her skull or rupturing her kidneys. And, later, as all the angels spent night after night tending to Margot in the Tomb, we formed the circle around her, healing what damage had already been done, preventing the poison of Hilda's punishment from spreading deep into Margot's life.

✿

The escape plan I'd placed in Margot's head did not leave. Instead, it took root and grew leaves and branches.

It came to pass in a way I did not expect.

In Margot's thirteenth year, Hilda decided to kill her. Sheren divulged this information reluctantly but out of necessity. She had not decided simply to kill Margot, but the plan she had for her would result in her death if we did not intervene. Margot's second near escape was final evidence that her wings needed to be clipped permanently. She would go into the Tomb for a month: the longest spell for any child at St. Anthony's, ever.

It would not be enough for us angels to comfort Margot every night in the Tomb. We had to prevent her from entering it at all. Sheren told me to follow her lead. I looked at her for a moment. It had been a long time since I'd acknowledged who she'd once been, *what* she'd once been to me. I'd forgotten my hate for her. I'd forgiven her.

Sheren told us to let Margot be dragged from her bed that night. Hilda and Mr. O'Hare trailed Margot into the toilets on the ground floor, stripped her, then knocked her unconscious on the old, rusty radiator. I was at the end of my tether, the end of standing back. I turned to Sheren.

"Repeat this to Margot," she said quickly. I knelt down beside Margot, holding her head. She was bleeding badly from a cut above her eye. Her breathing was shallow. She was still unconscious. Hilda told Mr. O'Hare to remove his belt.

I repeated what Sheren had said:

When Hilda was little, she loved Marnie more than anything in the whole world. And Marnie loved her. But Marnie died, and Hilda was very, very sad. Marnie watches Hilda now, and she's the one who's sad. Now, repeat after me, Margot. Say the words, "If Marnie could see you now, she'd kill herself all over again."

Margot coughed and came to.

"When you please, Mr. O'Hare," Hilda told him, as he took aim with his belt. But his angel stopped him—a brief moment's mercy had enabled Mr. O'Hare's angel to step in and hold his arm in midair. Slowly he dropped it and looked at Hilda. He couldn't hit Margot while she was lying down.

With Sheren and me on either side of her, Margot stood to her feet. Half-naked and bleeding, she turned to Hilda. She drew a deep, angry breath, and before Mr. O'Hare could talk himself out of his remorse, she said:

"If Marnie could see you now, she'd kill herself all over again."

Hilda's mouth slung open. Her eyes creased.

"What did you say?"

Sheren whispered something else, which I quickly passed on to Margot.

Margot's jaw clenched. She spoke loud and clear.

"What was it Marnie said to you before she died? Be a good girl so I can see you in heaven. And look at you now, Miss Marx. *Hilda.* Marnie's sad. You've become just like Ray and Dan and Patrick and Jim and Callum."

The names of Hilda's abusers. This time, her eyes did well up. Her aura turned red, her face ugly with hate. She lunged at Margot and slapped her across the face. I caught the sting of it. Margot turned her head and stared at Hilda and Mr. O'Hare. Neither of them budged. She picked up her clothes, turned, and walked out of the building.

Now, run.

As soon as she saw that they weren't coming after her, she pelted it out of there. Dragging on her skirt and jumper and not much else, she flung open the front doors and ran to the top of the driveway. And there, between the two stone pillars, we both stopped and looked back. Margot was panting—the adrenalin was bringing so much spit into her mouth she could hardly contain it—and I was waving. Waving at all the angels who had gathered at the front of the building, telling me good-bye. It would be the last time I would see most of them. I searched for Sheren. She lifted up both arms, as she had done when she told me about the Song of Souls, and I nodded. I knew what she meant.

Once Margot had caught her breath, we both took our journey toward the village. Freezing, half dead, and groping through the dawn, Margot found the sky blue door and hammered on it until a disheveled, worried man answered. She fell to her knees and wept at his feet.

10

*G*rogor's Proposition

THE MAN WHO ANSWERED THE DOOR WAS NOT THE MAN I'D SEEN IN THE VISION.

As it turned out, the family from the vision had sold up and moved back to Exeter, and the man who opened the door had been the current occupant for over a year.

But when I saw him, I whooped. I jumped up and down. I wrapped my arms around him and kissed his face. Then I paced, wringing my hands, talking to myself like a nutcase as Margot explained to him who she was, why she was crawling on his doorstep at five o'clock in the morning, looking like she'd been dragged from the depths of the sea.

I felt like Aeneas entering Hades and finding the ones he'd loved and lost. This was Graham Inglis, the man I called Papa for ten long, beautiful years. I never got over his death. It took me weeks to get over the fact that he was here again, red-faced, warty as an old sow, given to monstrous flatulence and belching, a man who incessantly gabbled with his mouth full of meat pie, who would cry at the drop of a hat. Ah, Papa. His heart wasn't merely on his sleeve. He slapped it into your hand at first greeting and let it bleed into your own veins.

Graham wrapped an old, filthy blanket around Margot's shoulders, took her inside, and offered her a hot drink. He told her to stay there a minute while he fetched Irina—my mamma for all of a year—and while they led Margot calmly into the living room, I stood in the hallway, hyperventilating. It was all too much. I was frozen to the spot, babbling amazement to myself and staring at Mamma as if she was about to disappear any second, soaking up all the things I had missed so much: her smooth, plump hands, always held in offering, the way she'd elbow Graham in the gut for saying something jokey or inappropriate while she stifled a giggle, her habit of running her ponytail through her finger and thumb when deep in thought. The velvet, rose-scented depth of her embrace. If they'd been around when Theo was born . . . let's just say, I think life would've been a little less rocky.

Anyway, I digress. I kind of lost the plot for a while. I headed for the back garden where Gin, the most loving black Labrador in the entire world, bounded toward me. Standing under the apple tree was Nan. I wrapped my arms around her and sobbed.

"Nan!" I cried into her thick, warm shoulder. "Do you know who I just saw?"

She nodded and gripped me by the shoulders. "Yes, yes, of course. I know, just . . . take it easy."

I swallowed my amazement. Whatever Nan was doing to my shoulders was bringing me back to earth, so to speak. She calmed me right down.

"Sorry," I said. "I was just—"

She held up a finger to my lips. "Walk with me," she said. "We need to have a chat."

Before I get into our chat, a memory.

It was the week before Mamma died. A Saturday morning. I woke up with a strange feeling. There was a stillness in the air that was too palpable, too weighted with fear to be peaceful. An unrest, a sense of limbo. My heart was sprinting for no reason. I got up and checked on Mamma. She was still in bed, her face a yellow stain amid the white sheets. I looked out the window and saw Papa heading off on his morning walk with Gin. I splashed cold water on my face. The feeling was screaming now, my gut knotted, and I began to think, *something's going to happen.*

We already knew that Mamma was sick. It wasn't her death I sensed. I wondered if there'd been a murder in the fields in the night—that sort of heavy, eerie anticipation. Was someone in the house? Even as I walked down the creaking stairs, I took each stair as slowly and as softly as I could so as not to make a sound. At the bottom, I told myself to get a grip. I lifted Papa's empty coffee mug from the windowsill and padded into the living room. And when I walked through the door I screamed, for leaning over the fire was a very tall man in a pinstripe suit, but he had no legs, just wisps of thick black smoke as if he was burning or dissolving where he stood, and when he turned and looked at me, his eyes were entirely black, no whites, and so I dropped Papa's mug and it smashed, and when I looked again, the man was gone.

I have never told anyone this memory. You can understand why.

I mention it now, because what Nan told me next brought me back to that time. She referred to the memory as if she'd been there herself, and she referred to the man with no legs not as a figment of my imagination, not as a ghost, but as Grogor. Grogor is a demon, she told me. He was already here. And I'd be making his acquaintance very soon.

Up until this point, I'd encountered demons only as shadows and brooding atmospheric influences, never as individuals. I'd seen the demons that lived in Sally. Sometimes her face would look superimposed when a demon was close to the surface, and her aura would often change like a sky in storm, from orange to midnight black. I'd seen a dark fog hovering in the entrance hall at St. Anthony's, which grew so dense—like a black bush—that all the angels had to walk around it. And sometimes, when I looked closely at Hilda, what I thought was an extension of her aura had appeared as a brooding atmospheric influence, full of her malice and contempt. Until now, however, we'd coexisted without too much fray.

But now, it seemed one of them wanted a confrontation. Happy to.

"Why does he want to meet me?" I asked Nan.

"Bear in mind that he's here on business," Nan said. "He has a proposition for you."

I stopped walking and turned to face her. "You mean he's here because I'm here."

"I'm afraid so."

"What's the proposition?"

"He wants you and Margot to leave."

"Or what?"

Nan sighed. She didn't want to break it to me.

"Or he'll give Mamma the illness."

I understood now why Nan was so hesitant. My knees weakened slightly, and I held on to her as I digested the news.

Mamma had become sick very suddenly about a month after Margot showed up on their doorstep. No one understood it. Doctors couldn't find anything wrong with her. Medicine made no difference. Right up until the minute she died, Papa was utterly, completely convinced that she would pull through. And so was I.

What Nan told me made me crouch down to my knees, press my face into my lap, and weep.

She was saying that I was the reason for Mamma's death. If I'd never turned up at their door, if they'd never taken me in, she would've lived another twenty, thirty happy years. Papa wouldn't have been so destroyed.

I had to gather my courage and face him. Nan and I headed back to the cottage. As she returned to the apple tree, she reached out and touched my face.

"Remember, you're an angel. You have all of God's power behind you. Much of it, you still can't see."

With that, she was gone.

The scene inside the cottage lifted my mood. Margot sat beside the open fire, huddled in the filthy blanket, holding a steaming mug of tea on her skinny knees. She was stuttering and shaking as she told Graham and Irina how she'd ended up on their doorstep. She told them all about St. Anthony's, how she'd ended up there, what went on there, and she told them all about the Tomb and the kids that got beaten with bricks, and how the bruises on her face were from the beating just hours before. She said it so matter-of-factly that they didn't dispute a word of it, just handed her more tea and, eventually, took notes. When Margot was finished, she let out a long cry. Graham threw his raincoat on and headed to the police station.

As Irina brushed past me, information about her that far exceeded my knowledge of her filled my head. I saw her father—a cold, stiff-lipped man—despite never having met him or seen a picture of him in my life. I saw arguments with Graham that had never been resolved, I saw her deep love for that man, rooted in her soul like an ancient tree, and then I saw her sorest regret. An abortion. Graham at her side. Both of them very young. *Mamma, I'm sorry*, I thought. *I never knew.*

Irina continued on into the kitchen, unaware of what had just happened. I walked behind her and wrapped my arms around her wide waist. Just then, she turned and stared ahead. At first, I thought she was staring at the kitchen door. Then I saw what she was looking at: she was watching Margot through the crack of the door. She smiled. Such a pretty girl, she thought. *Yes, she is*, I thought back. I think she's telling the truth, she thought. *Yes, she is. She is.*

✵

During the next couple of weeks, Nan's news of Grogor moved further and further from my mind. Graham's visit to the police station resulted in a surprise visit to St. Anthony's by the inspector—accompanied by two police officers—and what they found there made them shut the place down without further notice. Gossip spread round the village about a five-year-old child found locked in a room so small that the child could barely stand, and without food or water for almost a week. That child was now in intensive care. The rest of the children had been scattered around foster homes and other orphanages around the country. As for Hilda Marx, they found her in her office, a bottle of pills in one hand, a drained sherry bottle in the other, and no pulse.

News reports on the radio—the Inglises didn't have a TV—featured an interview with government officials who wished to comment that they were "motivated and committed" to pump more money into children's homes around the nation, and that they "sincerely promised" to raise standards of childcare. Irina looked over at Margot, who was tucking into chicken broth.

"You should be proud, darling," she said. "It's you that's done all this."

Margot smiled, then looked away. When she looked back, Irina was still standing above her. Slowly she knelt down in front of Margot—her arthritic knees always crunched when she did that—and took both of Margot's slim, cold hands in hers.

"Graham and I would like you to stay here as long as you want," she said. "Is that something you would like?"

Margot nodded very quickly. "Yes," she whispered.

Irina smiled. She smiled very much like Nan. I suppose that's why I always trusted Nan, right from the beginning. Irina's face was lined and flushed, her eyes Caribbean blue, her hair girlishly thick and blonde, her ponytail bouncing healthily. She narrowed her eyes. The smile faded abruptly. Margot wondered for a moment whether she'd done something wrong.

"Are you a ghost come to haunt me?" Irina said very seriously.

A thought lifted above Margot's head—I remember thinking it—that read: "Is she talking to me?" Confusion painted itself over her face. Irina lifted a hand and brushed loose strands of hair behind Margot's ears. By way of explanation, she said, "'It's just . . . you look very like me as a child. I just thought . . . " To Margot, it was no explanation at all. She was very confused now, worried that she was going to be thrown out onto the street. To me, Irina's explanation finally revealed itself: She thought Margot was the ghost of the child she'd aborted all those years ago. I walked over to Margot and laid a hand on her shoulder, evaporating the worry that rose up in her throat.

"Never mind," Irina said softly. "People like me get silly thoughts once we've lived too long." She stood up and left to get Margot some fresh toast.

Both Graham and Irina were writers. Graham churned out provocative, graphic crime novels under the name Lewis Sharpe. Irina was a poet with a small but devoted readership. Too shy to give readings, she penned her poetry slowly, carefully, seated beside the fire, producing a thin volume of quiet, deeply moving poems every four years. Her new collection was called *The Memory Spinner*, and she was close to finishing it.

Evenings were spent listening to the radio or, most of the time, having literary discussions. Margot found herself in the middle of a battle over whether Lady Macbeth had kids ("Of *course* she had kids! Why on earth would she talk about breastfeeding if she didn't?" "It's a metaphor, woman! It's just a ploy to get Macbeth to kill Duncan!" Et cetera.), or acting as a silent referee during a volcanic debate over whether Sylvia Plath was better than Ted Hughes ("That's an impossible thing to measure! On what grounds can he be *better*?" "No psychobabble about wasp keeping!" "You *what*?!").

Intrigued, Margot found herself spending long afternoons feasting on Plath, Hughes, Shakespeare, then Plautus, Virgil, Dickens, Updike, Parker, Fitzgerald, and Brontë. The books at St. Anthony's had been the dog-eared castoffs of charity shops and kind schools, so invariably it was potluck as to whether Margot read paperback romances or Aphra Behn. Usually, not the latter. Now, fired up with questions that begged to be answered (*Was* Heathcliff Irish?) and narrative ambiguities that demanded to be rolled flat

(Hamlet and Ophelia: siblings or lovers?), Margot read swiftly and thoroughly. She was determined to have something to say during the evenings instead of wondering whether Caliban and Aeneas were people or planets. Plus, she'd grown to love a challenge.

I should mention at this point that Nan's comment about my not being able to see *everything* in the spiritual world had played on my mind. I'd seen Irina's guardian angel a couple of times, but no sign of Graham's. I missed the community of angels at St. Anthony's. More so, I wondered why I didn't see them all the time, why I wasn't swarmed with demons and ghosts, why sometimes I felt human.

Still, I knew Grogor was there, and it bothered me that he seemed to have the upper hand with invisibility. Maybe I just had to look harder.

It happened one night while Graham, Irina, and Margot were discussing Plath's "Three Women." Graham had cracked a joke about the Polanski film *Rosemary's Baby*, and he and Irina laughed—Margot made a mental note to watch it, determined not to be caught out of the loop. Still laughing, Irina got up out of her chair and walked into the kitchen for a glass of water. Carefully she shut the door on the other two. I watched as her smile faded quickly. She leaned on the kitchen sink and looked out of the window in front of her at the night. Slowly, she hung her head and let hot, fat tears drip into the sink.

As I moved to comfort her, a man appeared at her side. He put his arm around her and leaned his head on her shoulder. For a second I assumed it was her guardian angel, until I saw the pinstripe suit, then the hideous black smoke belching where two legs should have been. He was holding her like a lover, whispering in her ear, stroking her hair.

Irina's guardian angel appeared on the other side of the window. He looked angry and baffled, pressing his hands against the glass and shouting a muffled plea to be let back inside. It was as if he was locked out, somehow. I looked from Grogor to the angel on the other side of the window. I couldn't understand it. Whatever Grogor was saying to Irina was making her more and more upset, and for some reason her guardian angel could do nothing.

I stepped in.

"*Oi!*" I said loudly.

Without moving his arms from Irina's shoulders, Grogor turned his head right around to face me. He grinned. I looked away from his disgusting black eyes, his pupils swimming in what looked like tar, his strange, melted skin that seemed to be made of wax.

"I hear you wanted to see me," I said.

Very slowly, he turned to Irina again.

"Hey," I shouted. "I'm talking to you."

Before I or Irina's guardian angel could do anything, Grogor reached into her body as easily as you might reach into a cupboard and placed something there. Irina's angel banged his fists on the window, and then he vanished. So did Grogor, but a second later he was in front of me. He looked me up and down.

"So this is how you turned out?" His accent was one I couldn't place, his tone surprisingly nasal.

"My answer's *no*, so you can get lost."

He smiled—I was disgusted to see he had no teeth, just a wet, gray hole for a mouth—and nodded. "So Nandita's been to see you, has she? I bet she didn't tell you everything."

"Oh, I'm sure she told me enough," I said.

He spat at me. He actually spat at me—black, sticky gunk from the depths of that foul mouth—then vanished.

I wiped my face and retched. Immediately, Irina straightened up. She looked as though a terrible burden had been lifted, and not a moment too soon. The kitchen door opened. It was Graham. She rubbed quickly at her eyes with her sleeve and turned to face him with a smile.

"Are you all right, love?"

She picked up her glass. "Forgot what I came in for. You know what I'm like."

He nodded, unconvinced, and waited for her to follow him back into the other room.

I slept beside Margot that night, my dress wrapped protectively across her body. I felt furious at the other two angels loping around the house. Perhaps if we acted as a team, we could kick Grogor out of here. But they refused to show themselves.

Just before sunrise, Grogor appeared above me, hovering beside the lampshade like a thundercloud with a face. I ignored him. After a few minutes, he spoke.

"It's a particularly painful disease that Irina's got. Very bad way to go, poor thing. Incurable. Of course, all you have to do is take Margot somewhere else and Irina will feel much better."

"Why Irina?" I hissed. "She has nothing to do with this. This is between you and me."

He moved right up to my face, so close I could feel his breath on my skin. I gritted my teeth.

"You and me?" he said. "And who do you think stands between you and me?"

I turned away from him and curled myself tighter around Margot. When he got angry and threw a boulder of tar at me, I lifted my hand and willed a protective shield to form around the bed. Like a dome of light, the shield absorbed the black gunk. At that, Grogor dissolved into a sooty cloud, wrapping himself around the shield until he almost blotted out its brightness. I had to concentrate hard to keep the shield intact, to keep him from getting inside.

Eventually he gave up. He returned to his vile semihuman form and pressed against the dome.

"Just remember. *She doesn't have to die.*"

※

But what could I do? Every day in Irina's presence, Margot grew brighter, happier, visibly rising out of the emotional pits of St. Anthony's. I watched, my heart breaking, as the disease grew inside Irina like a virile weed. Soon she was complaining of itchy skin. One night, in the glow of the fire, her skin appeared yellow and sickly. Margot noticed it. "Are you all right, Irina?" she asked over and over. Irina ignored the question and replied, "Call me Mamma."

Margot spent afternoons reading or leaning out of her bedroom window, watching the other kids hang out in the gardens next to Graham and Irina's house, wishing for a friend. I told her, "Spend time with Mamma, Margot. You'll regret it if you don't." And so she yanked the window shut and padded downstairs to the kitchen, where Irina was sitting in her bathrobe at the table, struggling to drink a mug of soup. Her thin arms were too weak to hold the mug, her throat too tight to manage more than a drop each time. Without a word, Margot sat opposite her. Slowly she lifted a teaspoon and used it to feed small amounts to Irina. Irina cupped her bony hand around Margot's as she lifted each spoonful to her lips. Though they never broke eye contact the whole time, neither of them spoke. By the time Margot finished, the last dregs of soup were cold, and her face was a blur of tears.

It's difficult, in a way, to explain why I sought out Grogor. It wasn't as simple as not wanting to go through the pain of losing Mamma. Margot felt like a child to me, *my* child. Many times, her experiences and pain felt separate from mine. Already we were becoming different.

I told Grogor that *I* would leave; Margot would stay. I told him that I would speak to Nan and we would arrange for someone else to become Margot's guardian angel, if that's what it took. I didn't even know if this was possible, or even sensible, but I was willing to give it a shot. The look in Graham's eyes as he watched Mamma spend more and more days in bed was killing me.

Grogor's response puzzled me. "Interesting," he said. And then he left.

Though Mamma clung on for many weeks, she died painfully and without dignity. There were mercies. Irina's guardian angel made more of a regular appearance, at least at the end, strengthening her muscles so she could sit upright in bed, giving her small glimpses of heaven in her dreams, persuading her to tell Graham and Margot the things they desperately needed to hear. That she loved them. That she would always, always be with them. And that there was absolutely no way on this earth that Hamlet and Ophelia were siblings. Graham needed his head examined for even suggesting it. She agreed with Margot on the Caliban theory, though: definitely, definitely a woman.

Her funeral took place on a misty Monday morning. A handful of mourners, angels, and a priest huddled around the graveside. As they began to lower the coffin into the ground, I started heading as far away from the crowd as I could, burying my cries in the folds of my dress. But then I turned and saw Margot, heaving her tears into her fists, and Graham, ashen and deflated, his face a quarry, and I realized, *I am here to carry them through this.* And so I took long strides toward Margot, put my arm around her waist, and told her to link arms with Graham. He was standing some distance away at her left. She hesitated. *I know this is hard for you,* I said. *Up until now, you've been closest to Mamma. But Graham needs you now. And you need him.*

She took another breath. The priest was reading from the Bible: "The angel of the Lord encampeth round about them that fear him, and delivereth them . . . " I watched as Margot carefully reached out for Graham's arm and, very slowly, linked his with hers. He snapped out of his thoughts, then, when he saw what she was doing, took a slight sidestep so that they were no longer standing apart.

"Are you okay, Papa?"

Graham blinked. After a few moments he nodded. Something in the first use of that word, that new title "Papa," gave him strength. He folded his rough hand around hers as she clasped his arm. I swear I saw him smile.

It took many years for me to understand how a demon had the ability to kill a human being. Later, Nan said he hadn't: Guilt had killed Mamma. Or, at least, her guilt at having an abortion all those years ago had provided fertile ground in which the germ that Grogor put inside her was able to take root. The explanation didn't make me feel any better. Instead, it sowed another kind of seed—revenge.

11

A Short Film on Arrogance

OKAY, SO I SHOULD WARN YOU. As a teenager, I was no angel.

Sorry, couldn't help it. But you know what I mean.

I hit thirteen, and suddenly the world shrunk to a small bag of glue. I found that this magical substance had the ability to stick posters of Donny Osmond to my bedroom wall *and* ferry me far away from the grief that stuck its muddy boots under our dining table after Mamma's death. Not long after I enrolled at the local school, they wanted to kick me out. Papa fought to keep me there. My grades in English Lit were top of the class, so they said okay, as long as I stop bunking off and encouraging the other kids to get high.

For a few years after Mamma's death, I trundled along like a lone wolf, writing agonizing poems at night to kill the silence, making friends with the wrong sort of people, watching Papa spend his days staring at the clock on the mantelpiece, which had stopped ticking long ago. Eventually, he completed a new novel. I read his drafts and gave detailed feedback. He chuckled at my precocious ability to spot plot holes and weak characters. He yanked his old typewriter off his desk and plonked it on my dressing table. "Write," he ordered. And I did.

A lot of drivel, at first. Then some decent short stories. Then love letters. For a lanky excuse named Seth Boehmer. He seemed to have problems standing up, or sitting still. He greased his black hair until it folded halfway across his face like a dead crow's wing. He rarely looked anyone in the eye, always had his hands too deep in his pockets. But I was sixteen. He was twenty, sullen, and drove very fast. How could I *not* love him?

I watched Margot dig a sinkhole for herself before jumping right in. I did a lot of eye rolling and talking to myself. Call me a cynic. I had very literally been there, done that, and now I wanted to projectile-vomit about it. Seth was a sort of milestone: I began to see just how far I'd come from Margot's nosedive into self-destruction.

Now, however, I was uncharmed. It was like watching a bad rom com— —you know exactly who's who, what happens, when it happens, and you could set a clock by the cues for the string music. It was tedious. And I was afraid. I was seeing things that I never, ever saw before. I don't mean spiritual things. I'm not talking about auras or fallopian tubes here. I mean: the consequences of my experiences at St. Anthony's. Although we had worked hard to prevent those consequences from wrecking the lives of the children who passed through St. Anthony's door, there were many consequences that happened nonetheless. Seth was one of them.

She met Seth at a sleepover at her best friend Sophie's house. Seth was Sophie's cousin. Orphaned at a young age, he'd spent

many years at Sophie's parents so that despite inheriting his parents' sprawling farm, he preferred to spend most evenings at his
aunt and uncle's cat-infested bungalow. Since Sophie had started
having friends to stay, Seth began showing up with his own pillow
and blanket.

A short film on arrogance.

Setting: kitchen. Time: twilight. Mood: a hair's breadth from
creepy. A sixteen-year-old girl sneaks downstairs. She rifles
through the cupboards for acetaminophen—she's got period
cramps and can't sleep for the pain. She doesn't see the silhouetted figure seated at the kitchen table, reading and smoking.
The silhouetted figure watches her for a few minutes. He had
noticed her earlier while Sophie and her gang of bratty friends
were dolling themselves up with makeup. Tall (about five foot
nine), slim in that sixteen-year-old kind of way (pot belly, narrow
thighs), thick Norwegian-blonde hair to her waist. Juicy pink lips,
irreverent eyes. And a very naughty laugh. He watches her raid
the cupboards before announcing his presence.

"You a burglar or somethin'?"

Margot spins round, dropping boxes of migraine pills to the
floor. The figure at the table leans forward and waves like the
queen. The moonlight reveals him as Sophie's cousin. "Hey," he
says, flatly. She giggles. "Um . . . hey," she says awkwardly. I hate
how awkward. "Why are you down here?"

He doesn't answer. Instead, he pats the spot on the table in
front of him. Obediently, she sits opposite. He takes a long drag
from his cigarette, testing to see how much time she'll give him.
How he can hook her without doing much of anything. She passes
with flying colors.

"So," he says, scratching his sideburns with his thumbnail. "I'm up. You're up. Why don't we do something better with our time other than stare at the moonlight?"

More giggles. Then, when he smiles, my own laugh in teenage form. "You mean, like bake a cake?"

He flicks the butt into the sink, flattens his hands on the table, and rests his chin on them, smiling up her like a dog. "You're a smart girl; you know what I mean."

She rolls her eyes. "Um, I don't think Sophie would like it if I slept with her cousin."

He straightens up, produces another rollie from behind his ear. A pretense of offense. "Who said anything about that?"

"I'm a smart girl; I knew what you meant."

No smile. Her eyes burning into him. He opens his, wide. She's a whole lot smarter than he'd thought.

"Smoke?"

"Sure."

"Say, Margot?"

"Uh-huh?"

I mouthed his next words as he said them. "What say you and I take a long walk in the park?"

Margot inhales smoke and does her best not to choke. "There are no parks round here."

"You're a smart girl, you know what I mean."

I lean into her and say very clearly, "Don't." I know I'm speaking in vain. There was never any telling me anything, not when I was forty, certainly not when I was sixteen. And I knew obstacles didn't work either—they made me even more determined. I thought carefully about my tactics. The only thing I could do in this situation was stand back and let Margot do what Margot did, and when it was all over, when all the terrible mistakes were made, I would do my best to make something beautiful out of the debris. Like wisdom.

Okay, so I never took psychology in college. I never got Freud. But something became remarkably clear to me during this time, casting a bright light over a life choice that I'd never quite understood, and never completely recovered from.

Margot got off on their fights.

No, seriously. She took the slaps and the kicks, the taunts and the lies, knowing that the kisses afterward tasted sweeter for it, that his promises and romantic gestures were all the more exciting if they followed a bruising.

Once, when Seth climbed the drainpipe into Margot's bedroom in the wee hours and insisted that she follow him to his car, I reluctantly tagged along as they drove to a bar in a larger town ten miles away. Beneath the blare of Johnny Cash on the radio, Seth:

"I love you, babes."

"I love you more, Seth."

Seth turns the volume down. "You're sure?"

Margot nods. "Yep."

"Would you die for me, Margot?"

"Of course I would!"

A pause.

"Would you die for me, Seth?"

He stares at her without blinking. His eyes are bullet gray, and he smiles an arsonist's smile.

"I'd kill for you, Margot."

She swoons. I shift anxiously in my seat.

***

Less than an hour later, Seth drags her out of the bar and slams her against a brick wall. He points in her face.

"I saw you!"

Margot catches her breath. "You saw me what?"

"That guy. You looked at him."

"No I didn't!"

"Don't *lie* to me!"

She cups his face. "Seth . . . it's you I love."

He slaps her. Hard. Then he kisses her. Softly.

And, bizarrely, she relishes every soap-opera second.

***

I consulted with Graham's guardian angel as Margot paced her room, wringing her hands and talking to herself, working out how to tell him. Graham's angel—Bonnie, his younger sister—nodded and vanished. Just as I was about to query her tactic—she *vanished?*—Bonnie reappeared with someone by her side.

It was Irina, about three decades younger, smooth-faced and clear-eyed in a long white dress. Only, no water pouring from her back. She looked over at me, reached out a hand and stroked my face. I cupped my hands to my mouth, my eyes filling with tears. "Mamma," I said, and she pulled me to her chest. After a long time she stood back and held my face in her hands.

"How have you been, sweetheart?" she said.

A wave of tears made it difficult to answer. There were so many things I wanted to tell her, so much I wanted to ask.

"I really miss you," was as much as I could say.

"Oh, honey," she said, "I miss you too. But you know, I'm really not that far away. I promise." She looked over at Graham. I knew she'd come to be with him. "How long can you stay?" I asked quickly. She glanced at Bonnie. "I don't have long," she said. "Spirits can only visit when there's a need. But we'll see each other soon." She wiped my tears away, then held my hands up to her mouth and kissed them.

"I love you," I whispered, and she smiled before sitting down beside Graham on the sofa as he lay, snoring and dribbling, and put her head on his chest.

I raced upstairs to Margot's room. She stood in front of the mirror, mouthing silent words.

I couldn't help myself. "Margot!" I panted. "Mamma is downstairs, quick!"

She ignored me and continued rehearsing her little speech. A speech I remembered well.

I know you're very disappointed in me, and I know Mamma would be too . . . Her eyes started to well up. *. . . but as Lady Macbeth said, what's done cannot be undone. Whether or not you choose to kick me out is up to you.*

I'd seen the baby when it was the size of a germ, watched it swirl and uncoil until it sat neatly now like a diamond on a red cushion, its poor heart shivering. A little boy. My son.

Margot finished her monologue and stared at herself a while longer in the mirror. For a moment, our reflections merged. We were twins from opposite ends of mortality. Only the look in the depths of our eyes was different. Margot's eyes had the look of someone approaching a bridge over a chasm. Mine were the eyes of one who had crossed it.

She walked slowly downstairs.

"Papa?"

He snorted, still asleep. She tried again. Irina gently nudged him, and he woke up. Margot immediately seized up with fear. She'd hoped he would keep sleeping and she'd be off the hook. He sprung upright and looked around. He saw Margot's face.

"Are you all right? What's happened?" He rolled upright and fumbled in his hair for his glasses.

Margot was quick to reassure him. "Nothing, nothing Papa." Wishful thinking.

"Come and sit down," he said groggily. Margot obliged, hiding her eyes. She was crying already. Graham felt his way into the kitchen. "You're white as a sheet," he said. "Are you feeling okay? Sit down; I'll make us both some tea. Dreadful to sleep so long . . . I was dreaming about your Mamma, you know."

"You were?" said Margot, tears spilling down her cheeks.

He shouted out from the kitchen. "She told me I had to look after you better. Fancy that, eh?"

Margot said nothing. Instead, she dug her nails into her thighs so as to not cry out. I watched as Irina moved close to her, wrapping her arms around her waist.

When Graham came back inside he saw Margot's face, set down the tray, and took her hands in his. Very gently:

"What is it, love?"

She closed her eyes and took a deep breath. I stood beside her and placed a hand on her shoulder.

"I think I'm pregnant, Papa."

I looked away. The sight of Papa's face aging in an instant, plummeting into sorrow, was too much to bear a second time. And yet, when I looked up and saw his expression, I realized it wasn't sorrow or disappointment or anger, at least not at Margot.

It was a portrait of failure.

And there were brushstrokes visible of his and Irina's child, the one they'd chosen not to keep.

"Easy now," Irina whispered to him. "She needs guidance, not judgment."

Slowly he leaned down close to Margot's face, so close she could see the sadness in his eyes.

"Whatever you choose to do, you must choose very, very carefully, without too much regard for the here and now, but with utmost regard for the future."

He flopped down next to her and took her freezing, quivering hands in his.

"Does he love you?"

"Who?"

"The father."

"Yes. No. I don't know." She was whispering now, tears falling off her lip into her lap.

"Because if he loves you, you have a chance. If he doesn't, you must think about your own future."

She wished he would yell at her and throw her out. His rationale was making her more confused. I reached down and placed a hand on her head. Her pounding heart slowed. After a few moments, she said:

"I need to find out whether he loves me or not."

Graham nodded. "Do, do." He looked up at the picture of Irina on the fireplace, right at the moment Irina smiled at me before vanishing to wherever she had come from. "Where there's love, nothing can stop you."

I remembered I had already known the answer. And I had already known the solution. What I had wanted was someone else to tell me what it was, to confirm that I wasn't an evil person for wanting to be rid of it.

You have to understand: Margot's thoughts were like lashes across my back. Mostly, the seventeen-year-old ignorance of what crossed her mind. She didn't once visualize another human being, an actual baby. She saw this pregnancy as a molehill in her life that she had to squash. *Stupid kid*, she thought, and I thought of Margot as a baby, being born, being abandoned, how the desire for her to survive grew and grew in me until it was unquenchable. *How am I meant to look after a baby? Why would I even want to?* she thought. And I thought, with no small amount of guilt, at how I'd wondered that maybe it would be better if Margot had died, if I hadn't lived at all. There were more thoughts I witnessed unscroll from Margot's dark mind that I can't even bring myself to write.

She found an abortion clinic in London that would do the deed for the tidy sum of two hundred pounds. She told Graham her plan, and he simply nodded, said he'd give her the money, and informed her that it would be very painful but that she must be brave.

It wasn't until a week later that she told Seth about the pregnancy. His jaw dropped ever so slightly, then he looked away and began pacing the room. She left him like that for a few minutes. "Seth?" she said at last. He turned to face her. His wide grin and gleaming eyes planted a seed of doubt in her heart. She hadn't expected him to be happy. Maybe this was a good thing.

Maybe they'd stay together. Maybe she would keep this child after all.

I knew what was coming next like the steps of a waltz. I hung my head and held out a hand to catch the force of his slap. It spun her off balance. She caught the back of an armchair to steady herself and turned back to face him, dazed and breathless.

"Seth!"

And then, from my wings, a voice that echoed throughout all the chambers of my soul. *Let be.* I stepped in to catch Seth's next moves, but suddenly I found myself on the other side of a wall. Inside I could hear each punch, the dull thud of his kicks, and I screamed on one side of the wall and Margot screamed on the other, and I pounded the cold brick with my fists.

I looked around quickly. I was in Seth's back garden among the weeds and the dying sun.

A moment later, I felt an arm around my back. I looked up. Solomon, Seth's guardian angel. We'd met briefly. He reached out for my hand to comfort me.

"Get off me," I snapped. "Just help me get back inside."

He shook his head. "I can't," he said. "You know that."

"Why are we out here?" I yelled.

Solomon merely stared at me. "Some things are meant to be," he whispered. "Some things are not. Where they make a choice, we have no power." Another scream from inside, then the sound of a door slamming. Silence. Solomon glanced at the wall. "You can go back in there now. Seth is gone," he said gently, and I marched forward and found myself back with Margot.

She was lying on the floor, gasping for air, her hair wild and matted with blood and tears. A flash of pain across her abdomen made her sit up sharply, squealing in pain. She struggled to get her breath. "Slow and deep, slow and deep," I told her, my voice breaking into sobs. She looked around, terrified that Seth might come back and yet aching for him to comfort her.

I leaned over her to fix what I knew was unfixable. The diamond inside her was gone. The red cushion unraveled its thick strands of velvet all over the floor.

I went for help, and managed to persuade a neighbor to call at Seth's home. When nobody answered, she decided to come in and check that young Seth was okay. When she found Margot on the floor, she called an ambulance.

As Margot struggled to come to terms with what had happened, she decided to move as far away from Seth as she possibly could. She spun Graham's desk globe, closed her eyes, and stretched out her index finger. It was me who stopped the globe spinning, me who lowered her finger on the best destination possible:

New York.

So nice they named it twice.

12

A Darkening Ocean

SOMETHING TO TAKE NOTE OF: WHEN YOU BECOME A
GUARDIAN ANGEL (AND NOT EVERYBODY DOES) THERE'S A
WHOLE NEW CATEGORY OF AIR TRAVEL. Forget business class.
First class is for wimps. Try Angel class. It involves sitting on
the nose of the plane or, when you want to stretch out a little,
the wing. You might assume this merely provides ample views
of clouds and sunsets. Don't be fooled. It's not a glorified window seat. Sitting on that plane, passing over Greenland, then
Nova Scotia, I saw more than clouds. I saw the angel of Jupiter,
so large that her wings—which were made of wind, not water—
enveloped that enormous planet, constantly batting away meteors
that headed toward earth. I looked down and saw stratospheres of
angels hovering above earth, listening to prayers, and intervening
to help guardian angels. I saw the paths of prayers and the trajec-
tories of human choices wind their way like gigantic highways. I
saw angels in cities and deserts shining like night images of earth
from the moon—the upturned pear of Africa, alight with the candles of Cape Town and Jo'Burg; the dog head of Australia, fringed

with gold flame; and the witch on her broom—Ireland—sending up new pennies from Dublin, Cork, Derry and Belfast: not city lights, but light from the angels.

Margot had left for New York on the notion that it was just for the summer. The damage that Seth had inflicted was not limited to the loss of the baby, nor the humility she had felt as the nurses at the hospital tut-tutted about *another pregnant teenager* and ignored both dignity and pain relief as they administered a D & C, nor the raw grief and betrayal that set in once she fully realized what Seth had done. No, he hadn't loved her. Every human has one truth that they never fully learn. They have to keep having the same sort of lessons, making the same sort of mistakes, until it sinks in. In Margot's case, it was her inability to discern between love and hate. New York, I figured, was the place where everything came together—and where it all fell apart.

But something weird was happening to me. On the day we left for the airport, I noticed my dress had a silvery shine to it. I reckoned it was reflecting another color. On the journey to New York, the color had changed to lilac. It started to change so quickly that I watched it travel through the spectrum of violets and sky blues, until, by the time we landed at JFK, I was staggering through the luggage hall gathering up my dress, wondering why on earth it was now turquoise.

When I looked around me, I got the shock of my life. I'd acquired another kind of sight, it seemed—the spiritual world finally revealed itself to me without shade. It was like a curtain had been pulled aside, bringing the two worlds—the human and the spiritual—side by side. Hundreds, no, *thousands* of angels. What is it the Bible says? *Throngs*, that's it. Throngs, choirs, scores, legions—they were all there in a colorful fog. Angels gathering

around families as they greeted loved ones at the gate, or helping potbellied businessmen yank heavy luggage off the carousel.
Ghosts—I kid you not—appearing occasionally in odd places,
disoriented, lost, and with them their angels, waiting patiently for
the day when they would realize that yes, they were dead and
that, yes, it was time to leave. And, lastly, demons.

Let me not paint a picture that insinuates the easy coexistence
of demons and angels. Now that I saw the spiritual realm clearly,
I saw that demons lived among us like rats in a barn: conspiring
to grab every mortal scrap they could, and, if left to their devices,
capable of a shocking amount of damage.

Like angels, the demons varied in appearance. I saw that their
form—whether an inky shadow or thick mist, a face suspended
in midair or, as Grogor had been, a fully-clothed being with a
face—had a strong link to the aura of the humans they followed.
I watched a young man in jeans and a tight white T-shirt cross
the airport terminal trailing a suitcase, chewing gum, muscular
and cheery. You wouldn't think to look at him that he should
qualify for not one but two demons, who walked with him, side by
side, purposeful as Dobermans. Then I saw his aura—the purple
black of an eggplant. And whatever this young man had done in
his life, he had no conscience: the light that most people have
around the crown of their head was gone. There wasn't even a
shadow.

Margot took her luggage—a single bag—off the carousel and
looked around her, dazed by the number of people coming and
going, unsure where she needed to go next. She had the phone
number of a friend of a friend who was prepared to put her up
while she found her feet. I remembered this clearly—the friend
of a friend owned a bookstore and happily exploited Margot's

willingness to work for free in exchange for a small room upstairs that had an odd, swaying black rug, which was actually a swarm of cockroaches—so I nudged an angel standing by the exit and asked for some assistance. To my delight, he spoke in a dyed-in-the-wool Bronx accent. He said he'd have a word with his "guy," who I took to mean his Protected Being. His "guy" was a taxi driver. I steered Margot in his direction.

The taxi driver happened to know a place where Margot could get some work *and* a place to sleep, smack-bang in the heart of the city. As a bonus, it was around the corner from the best little all American café in town. Pretty rockin' fritatas Margot got all fired up about her good luck. She was beaming like a Halloween pumpkin by the time the taxi driver rolled up at her stop. I, on the other hand, could not believe my luck. You want to guess where we ended up? Go on, have a go. It's not hard.

Babbington Books had the misfortune to resemble a pawn-shop instead of a bookstore. Bob Babbington—the lazy, tobacco-chewing, exploitative owner in question—had inherited the business from his father. His decision to continue the business had less to do with a passion for books—he read car manuals—or a desire to take up the mantle of the third-generation Babbington bookseller than a penchant for rent-free accommodation and employment that required near-constant sitting and smoking. You might say that you could tell Bob's heart wasn't in it from a ten-mile radius. Painted black with window boxes spewing dead weeds and beer cans, the shop exterior was as inviting as an open grave. Inside was worse.

Undeterred by the look of the place, Margot pushed open the door and called "Hello?" It was the way most customers entered—unsure whether or not they'd intruded. In the far corner of the shop she could make out a small bush of black hair and a handle-bar moustache, above which was a dancing kite of smoke, and, below, an enormous, floating white smile, which turned out to be Bob's gut, hanging out under his tight T-shirt. He took one look at the blonde, plaid-wearing gyspy queen in his doorway and thought of handcuffs. Uh-oh.

However. True to his word, Bob gave Margot a room upstairs in exchange for her "assistance" in the shop downstairs. And so I gritted my teeth as I followed them around, kicking at Pirate—Bob's blind, leprous cat—and sending out a small light to scatter the cockroaches and rats.

Margot crawled between the stained sheets of the sofa bed, thought of how much she already missed Graham, and cried herself to sleep. Me, I paced the creaky floor, watching my dress change color again like an ocean deepening its blue in the darkening sky. I waited for Nan—she usually showed up when something in my world changed—but she didn't show. So I tried to work it out.

I didn't have to think too hard. There were, you might say, a few clues. If the spiritual world had opened its doors to me just hours before, so now did the natural world. When I looked into the street below, I saw what initially appeared to be dust clouds hovering about seven feet above the pavement. Then I realized that these "clouds" were swarms of diseases into which unsuspecting men and women were walking. And I sat there and watched, horrified, as a man passed through the cloud and took away with him Kaposi's sarcoma, spreading to his gums and the skin around his knees, and then a woman walking quickly and taking with her a souvenir of a century-old pox. I signaled to their angels, and each time their answers spoke in my head, clear as a voice mail: *Look closer, newbie. These are lessons in each virus.*

It took me a long, long time to look *that* close.

As you can imagine, Margot's bedroom was the Hotel California for germs. My night was spent protecting her lungs from damp spores clinging to the air and a pretty robust form of flu embedded in the pillowcase she was curled around. But that was tame in comparison to my final preoccupation. Like a game of chess, I spent the rest of the night knocking down the markings of a path set up for Margot by three demons, whose faces I couldn't see.

Let me explain. Demons, I learned, don't resort to whispered suggestions and elbow nudges. They are scientists of human weakness. They will encourage soul mates to wed, at the same time as they'll locate the smallest fracture in their union and spend years stamping on it until, eventually, the divorce doesn't just rip up the soul mates, but also their children, and their grandchildren, and so on, until the fracture ripples through the lives of generations. Demons set up their targets well in advance. They are pack hunters. Three of them spent much of that night executing a plan they'd had in place for years: to persuade Margot to take her own life.

I saw the markings as soon as I set foot in the bookstore. The first marker was Bob. He saw Margot and thought of handcuffs. Another thought crossed his mind, like a small film: he'd keep her in that upstairs apartment for weeks, months, maybe even years. She could cook and clean, and he'd stock her up with all the weed that it took for her to reject any thoughts of escape. His ailing sense of humanity pushed the thought away, but it kept coming back. I and ten other angels formed a circle around Bob's bed and filled his dreams with memories of his mother. As the light around his head grew stronger, the three other forces in the building showed up. And this was the moment I learned of ranks in the angel world: four of the angels among us produced swords. Fat with blinding light, if you looked hard enough the blades appeared to be made of quartz. Whatever they were made of, they worked. The demons left, and their plan fell apart. But I was taking no chances. I spent all night planning a new course for Margot with the other angels. They left to do what needed to be done.

By morning, my dress was indigo blue, and I was disoriented, scared, and excited. For whatever reason, my dress had changed color just as I finally ripped the curtain of the spiritual world. Had I known how much more responsibility I'd have on my shoulders—how much more protection Margot would need—I figure I'd have left the curtain right where it was.

But it was too late.

13

Returning the Gun

I BEGAN THE NEXT DAY WITH RENEWED PURPOSE: TO DISCOVER HOW I DIED. More precisely, to find out who killed me.

Margot was verging on eighteen, naive as a duckling, pretty as a French pastry. And if that combination wasn't dangerous enough, her head was chock-full with dreams of a life that would never happen: a successful writing career while juggling six kids (three boys, three girls) in a picket-fence home in upstate New York and baking apple pies for a better-looking version of Graham. But watching her as she leaned out of the apartment window, overlooking streets scrubbed by dirty rain and yellow taxis, her fantasies painting the air around her as vividly as violets, I couldn't help but think with paralyzing regret: *When did it all change? Where did it all go wrong?*

Was it because of Hilda? Seth? Sally and Padraig? Lou and Kate? Zola and Mick? Was it because of things to come, like marrying Toby, having Theo, and sailing past a marriage breakup on a reservoir of vodka? This was the moment in my life that things *should* have soared into endless sky. A young blonde living in Manhattan at a time when all the best kinds of revolutions were flowing through the streets—social, political, sexual, economic—should not have wound up dead some two decades later in a hotel fewer than five miles from here. Sure, it happens. But not on my watch.

Margot shut the window, put on her clothes (homemade tartan pants, a navy woolen jumper), and brushed her long hair. She stood before a reflection of herself in a long free-standing mirror. I stood behind her, resting my chin on her shoulder. "Girl," I sighed, "you have got to get some new clothes." She made a little pout with her lips, slapped her cheeks, inspected her fuzzy eyebrows. She did a little twirl in her outfit—did I mention that her tartan pants were also high waisted and baggy at the hip?—then frowned. As did I.

Did I ever look like this? Why did no one arrest me?

On the shop floor, Bob was stacking books in no particular order and attempting to eat a cinnamon roll. He saw Margot and looked away sheepishly. His dreams of his mother had been stark and alarming. Gone were the lewd thoughts of imprisoning Margot. I started to see a different side to him. He was a mole in human form. Curious in a blind sort of way, grunting and shuffling through the narrow corridors of crammed bookcases, he reveled in the lack of human contact. His angel—his grandfather Zenov—followed him around with his arms behind his back, shaking his head in disapproval at the chaos of pages and jacket covers. And when I looked hard enough, I could see parallel worlds emerge on either side of him like a TV screen underwater, becoming clearer as I concentrated, as if the water was stilling: one of him as a young boy hiding in his wardrobe from his heavy-fisted father, another of him as a pensioner: single, senile, still stacking books. Both made me feel a wee bit sorry for him.

He offered Margot tea, which she declined, then showed her around the bookstore. Sorry, did I say bookstore? I should have said *literary treasure trove.* The guy had hundred-year-old copies of Plautus propping up his pool table, signed copies of Langston Hughes's gathering dust under the counter, a first edition Akhmatova being used as a coaster. As Bob rambled on about how bad his sales were, how he didn't really know why anyone bothered separating history into geographical categories, yadda yadda yadda, I finally drew Margot's attention to the Akhmatova. She picked it up and stared at the cover.

"Do you know who this is?"

At least a minute passed. "Who?"

"The woman on the cover of this book."

"Man, I like your accent. *Cuv-ah.* Say 'cover' one more time."

"She's Anna Akhmatova. She's one of the most revolutionary female poets of our time."

"Uh..."

"And this." She yanked a copy of Shakespeare's *Works* from another bookcase and flipped it open. "This is signed by Sir Laurence Olivier. We're on the doorstep of some of the finest university literature departments in the world."

She stared at him expectantly. I nodded. Too right. Bob shifted his feet.

"How long has this been sitting here?"

Bob held his hands up in surrender. "Uh, I dunno..."

She rifled through more shelves. Bob looked around like he was expecting the rest of the Spanish Inquisition to break down the door any second. Margot stopped rifling and thrust her hands on her hips.

"*Hmm*," she said, pacing. She had Bob's full curiosity now.

"What? What?"

She stopped and pointed at him thoughtfully. He tugged his T-shirt down to his belt. "You need newer stuff," she said.

"What, like newer clothes?"

"No! Newer *books*. You've too much classical stuff on these shelves." More pacing. "Car boot sales. Where do they happen round here?"

"Car *what* sales?"

"Sorry, *yard sales*, garage sales, places where people sell stuff they don't want anymore."

"Um . . ."

"We could pick up some castoffs on the cheap at places like that."

"We . . . ?"

"I'll go out and find where we can get our new stock."

"Uh, Margot?"

She turned at the doorway, her coat already on, and stared. "What?"

Bob scratched his tummy. "Nothin'. Just . . . good luck."

She smiled and left.

For those of you who don't remember it, weren't alive, or were stranded on a desert island, New York in the late 1970s was a vibrant, impoverished, crime-riddled, drug-infested, slum-spewing 24-7 urban disco. Returning to it now made me both wary and antsy with excitement. From where I stood, the place seemed to have ten angels for every human, different kinds of angels—some of them wearing white dresses, some of them as if they were on fire, others enormous and pulsing with light. Small wonder the city throbbed with a sense of invincibility, as if it had a set of wings that could lift it above whatever stamped on it.

For instance, the streets that Margot walked that morning had very recently been marked with blood, reporters, and rats following the Son of Sam murders. For a while the area had felt the weight of fear and suspicion, making the air hard to breathe, the sidewalks too slippery to tread. But now, such a short time after, life was in bloom again. Poppies grew defiantly from cracks on the concrete that had recently been cordoned off by the cops. And I remembered that *this* was why I had felt safe despite getting mugged four times in eighteen months, *this* was why I had loved the place: not the coffee shops that doubled as Black Panther hideouts, not the beat poets on Sixth Avenue or the revolutionaries, but the resilience that vibrated here, the feeling that I could climb over all the high walls of my past and use them to reach higher.

It had started to rain. Margot pulled her coat above her head and tried to make sense of her street map. She confused a right with a left and, before long, found herself walking on a residential street, East Side. It had been a long time since she'd seen homes bunched together so tightly, like logs stacked in the back of a barn. She stood for a few minutes, looking up at the row of three-tiered white houses with steps leading up to the front doors.

A few feet ahead, a wild-haired preppy guy and a tall black woman in a yellow maxi dress were carrying boxes back and forth from an open doorway and loading them into the back of a pickup truck. They appeared to be in the middle of a fight. The woman shook her open palms at each side of her head, her eyes wide, her lips moving fast. As soon as Margot got within earshot, Preppy Guy dropped his box and stormed inside. The woman continued shifting boxes as if nothing had happened. Margot approached.

"Hi. Are you moving?"

"No. But he is," the woman snapped, nodding at the empty doorway.

Margot looked at the box that the woman was carrying. It was full of books.

"Do you fancy selling those?"

"*I'd* give them to you. They're not mine, though. I'll have to ask *him*."

The woman snorted and set the box down, then picked out a book and used it as an umbrella as she ran back inside the house. Margot walked slowly over to the box and inspected the contents. Salinger, Orwell, Tolstoy . . . The reader had taste.

Preppy Guy appeared at the doorway. Not so preppy up close, as it turned out. Vampirishly pale, a tumbleweed of black hair and dark liquid eyes that had witnessed too much pain.

"Hey," he said to Margot. "You want my books?"

Margot smiled. "Um, yes, please, if you're interested in selling them. Or giving them, whichever you prefer." She laughed. His eyes lit up.

"Where are you from?" He took a step forward. The woman reappeared. She twitched her mouth and grunted under the weight of the box. I searched my memory for this encounter.

"England. Well, Ireland originally," Margot replied, no longer feeling the rain. "I just got here, actually. I'm working at a bookstore."

"Which part of England?"

Now I recognized him. The deep, jet-black eyes, the Dumbo ears . . .

"The northeast."

"Uh-huh?"

"Can we get a move on, please?" His girlfriend, Miss Irritated. Oh, butt out, I said. Her guardian angel glared at me.

"Oh. Right," he said, snapping back into boyfriend mode. "Sorry, I'm moving today. No time for memory lane. Just take that box, it's yours."

"You're sure?"

"Free to a fellow countryman. Or, in this case, country-woman."

I felt a tap on my shoulder. I turned around to see Leon, my fellow angel from St. Anthony's.

"Leon!" I shouted, wrapping my arms around him. "How are you?" I glanced from him to Preppy Guy. And then the penny dropped.

Preppy Guy was Tom from St. Anthony's. Tom, defender of the planet Rusefog, the first child I'd protected in the Tomb, the boy I vaguely remembered handing me an invisible gun.

"How have you been?" Leon was asking, but I was caught up in my own thoughts. Tom turned and walked back inside and a parallel world opened up right there in the heavy space be-tween them—or maybe it was a projection of my own wishes, I can't be sure—of Margot and Tom, two soul mates living out her fantasies with the zillion kids and evenings spent dis-cussing Kafka across the dining table. I yelled at her, "It's him, it's *him!* It's little Tom! Tell him who you are! Tell him about St. Anthony's!"

Maybe I got through to her, maybe I didn't: either way, Margot picked up the boxful of books and left, but not before she'd scribbled her name and address inside a copy of Philip K. Dick's *Minority Report* and left it on his doorstep.

A few days later, he walked into the bookstore and asked for Margot.

"Who's askin'?" Bob, in fine amphibian form.

"Tell her it's Tom. The Philip K. Dick fan."

"He can't write to save his life, man."

"Is she here?"

"Dunno."

Tom sighed, pulled out a notepad from his jacket pocket and wrote his number down. "Give her this, will you please?"

I made sure he did. I made sure Margot phoned him back. And I made sure that when he asked her to dinner, she said yes.

And so, Margot and I—both of us similarly nervous, similarly excited—took a taxi on a rainy Tuesday night to the Lenox Lounge in Harlem. And both of us imagined the future—mine of a long life with Tom, Margot's quite similar—and I marveled at how I was changing something at last. I was steering the ship of my destiny, headed to shores with neither footprint nor regret.

Tom was waiting outside the Lenox Lounge in a black suit and a white shirt, opened at the neck. He sat on a bollard, his legs crossed at the ankles, occasionally wiping rain out of his eyes. I saw Leon standing next to him and waved. Margot spotted Tom and shrieked "Stop!" at the taxi driver so alarmingly that he slammed on the brakes and did an emergency stop in the middle of bumper-to-bumper traffic. Margot threw quarters and apologies over the front seat and got out of the car. I followed. Someone on the other side of the road was waving at me. It was Nan. I let Margot run ahead and crossed the road to meet Nan.

She pulled me into a tight embrace. "Like the new color. Blue, eh? You must be seeing things differently now." She linked my arm and tugged me purposefully up the street.

"A *lot* differently," I said. "Is that what the change in color means? I mean, why would my dress change its own color?"

"Goodness, one question at a time," she laughed. "The change is to do with the progression of your spiritual journey. You've hit an important milestone, it seems. Blue is a good color."

"But what does it . . . "

She stopped and looked up at me very sternly.

"We need to have a talk about those two." She turned her head to Margot and Tom, who were chatting and flirting awkwardly.

"I'm listening."

"Don't listen. Just look."

And right there on Lenox Avenue, the clouds above the bulimic trash cans and leprous buildings parted to reveal a vision.

It was a young boy, about nine, with dirt on his face and dressed in clothes reminiscent of a street urchin circa 1850: tweed beret, grubby shirt, short trousers, and a ratty blazer. He held up his arms and opened his mouth, as if he was singing. A second later I saw he was onstage. Among the hundred-strong crowd was the black woman in the yellow dress that we'd encountered earlier. She was older now, her hair cut close to her head, her eyes twinkling, focused intently on the performance. And I realized: the boy onstage was her son. A curtain rustled backstage, and the boy ran off. The man whose arms he ran into was Tom. His father.

"Have you worked out yet why I'm here?" Nan raised an eyebrow.

"You want me to put a stop to any romance between Margot and Tom."

Nan shook her head. "I want you to consider the whole jigsaw before you fiddle with the pieces. You already know who Margot marries. And now, you've also seen the outcome of the choices that Tom made."

"But he hasn't made them yet! And neither has Margot." I stopped and took a deep breath. I was feeling angry. "Look, I'm my . . . Margot's guardian angel for a reason, and I think that reason is because I know all too well the things she should have done and the things she should not. And one of the things she should not have done is marry Toby."

Nan shrugged. "Why?"

I searched her face. *Why?* Where did I even begin?

"Trust me," I said. "Toby and I . . . were no good for each other. We split up, okay? What's the point in me letting Margot enter into a marriage that doesn't even work out, huh?"

Nan raised an eyebrow. "And you think things will be any different with Tom?"

I closed my eyes and leaned backward, exhaling all my frustration. It was like trying to explain neuroscience to a caveman.

"You know, I found out about the Song of Souls," I said at last.

She flicked her eyes up at me. "Oh yes? And how did that work out for you?"

I stopped walking. "There's something more than the Song of Souls, isn't there? I can actually change things."

"Ruth—"

"I can find out who killed me and stop it from happening. I can rearrange the outcome of my life . . . "

We were outside the Lenox Lounge.

Nan raised her eyes to meet mine. "There are many, many things that you can do as a guardian angel, particularly in your case. But it's not about 'I can.' 'I can' is a human concept, a mantra of the ego. You're an angel. God's will is what's important now." She started to walk away.

Now it was my turn to play the "why" game. "Tell me why that's important, Nan," I said. "I haven't even seen God yet. Why shouldn't I change things when I know exactly how good things could have been, huh?"

"Do you?"

The pity across her face disarmed me.

I continued, albeit a little less convinced. "Even if I'm dead, I can still experience Margot's life vicariously. Maybe I can even turn things around so that instead of dying in my prime and leaving my relationship with my son in tatters, I can live to a ripe old age, maybe do some good in the world."

She was disappearing now, zoning out of my protests. I bit my lip. I hated ending our talks in turmoil. "Be safe," she said, and then was gone.

I turned and looked behind me. A dark mist, and in a car window, a reflection: Grogor's face. He winked.

I stood in the rain, feeling the water from my back pulsing. I could not tell if the heart beating in my chest was my own or a memory of my own, if the choices Margot was making were mine or hers, and I did not know, for the first time in my life, what say I had in anything anymore. And it infuriated me.

It was midnight. Margot and Tom, arm in arm, leaving the Lenox Lounge. They still didn't realize that they'd known each other at St. Anthony's. They only knew that they wished to be lovers, and soon.

They embraced, then kissed for a long time.

"Same place, tomorrow night?" Tom said.

"Absolutely." Margot kissed him again. I turned away.

Tom spotted a taxi headed in their direction. "You get this one," he said. "I kinda want to walk home tonight."

The taxi slowed to a halt. Margot jumped inside. She took a long look at him and smiled. With a deadpan face, Tom pulled an invisible Magnum .44 from his inside pocket and fired it at her. For a moment a memory of St. Anthony's crossed her mind, but just as quickly it faded away. As I stood beside him, both of us lost in our memories, the taxi pulled away into a neon tide.

❈

I sat beside Margot in the backseat, watching her glance again and again out the rear window, laughing to herself as she thought of Tom. I could see the light around her heart grow larger and larger, flooding with wishes. I thought of what Nan had said. *Do you think things will be any different with Tom? Yes*, I thought. Yes, I absolutely do.

As the taxi slowed for a red traffic light, a rap on the car window. The taxi driver rolled it down and glanced out at the figure standing in the rain. A man leaned forward, shielding himself from the downpour with a leather notebook.

"Can I share your cab? I'm headed to the West Village."

I stiffened. I'd have known that voice if you'd buried it in an Egyptian tomb and set a brass band marching on top.

The taxi driver glanced in his rearview mirror at Margot.

"Sure," she said, shuffling over to make room for the new passenger.

Don't, I said, closing my eyes.

The traffic light turned green. A young man in a lime corduroy suit swept his long hair back and held out his hand to Margot. "Thanks," he said. "I'm Toby."

I screamed. A long, anguished yell. The yell of the damned.

"Margot," Margot said, and I cried.

"Pleased to make your acquaintance."

14

Three Degrees of Attraction

IS THERE A WAY THAT I CAN POSSIBLY CONVEY TO YOU THE SCENE IN THAT CAR, THE FEELING THAT SLUNG ABOVE US LIKE AN AWNING FAT WITH STORM WATER, READY TO BURST? The rain bounced off the windshield with the sound of radio garble. The windshield wipers pumped like an EKG and the taxi driver warbled "Singin' in the Rain" in Hungarian.

There were three types, or three *degrees*, of attraction in that car:

1. Margot looked at Toby and found herself curiously drawn to his fine, long hair, the color of autumn leaves, the gentleness in his eyes, the sincerity in his "thanks."

2. Toby looked sideways at Margot and thought "nice legs." Despite my frustration, it stirred something inside me. He had assumed, right off the bat, that Margot had a boyfriend, that she was a student at Columbia (it was the short, moss green tweed skirt, doing the rounds among the student

cohort that summer), and that there was no way in high heaven that she'd give someone like him the time of day. And so he smiled politely, pulled a notebook from his pocket, and continued jotting down notes for his short story.

3. As I sat between them, my own attraction to Toby was the deep, loyal, war-savaged connection to the man who fathered my child, my husband, my client, and, once, my best friend. The cable that had once ran thick as a tramline between us had finally snapped back and smacked me in the face. And now, as I sat so close to him that I could see the chain of orange freckles under his eyes, the smoothness of his cheeks where he prayed for stubble to prove that he was—finally—over twenty-one, I shivered with love and desire and hatred and hurt.

Although I had no breath to hold, I held it like a precious gift, rigid as a statue, until he got out of the car, rapped good-bye on the window, and disappeared into midnight. I unknotted my fists, and laughed until the nervous tremor in my voice was convincingly steady. I knew they'd meet again, and the part of me that still hated him roared at the part of me that wanted them to.

Amid this angelic conflict, an oversight: when I turned back and looked at Margot, she was reaching down for something that had fallen out of Toby's pocket as he'd stepped out of the car. Before I could do anything, before I had time to reinsert myself in the present, she was reading.

It was a short story, maybe an essay, scribbled in small, spidery handwriting—the handwriting of an intellectual, but with fat round vowels, suggestive of Toby's deep sense of empathy. It was written, oddly, on a page that had once belonged to a turn-of-the-century edition of Boccaccio's *Decameron*, so old that the page was custard yellow and the text was almost rinsed away by time.

Toby was what you would call the definitive starving artist. He was so thin that his corduroy suit was a sort of suit-shaped sleeping bag, and his long, thin hands were always mottled, always cold. He lived off his quarterly stipend from New York University, which meant that he depended on the scraps from an old college buddy's hotdog stand for nutrition and the loft of the all-night café on Bleecker Street for a place to lay his head. He would never, ever admit that he was poor. He gorged on words, feasted on poetry, and felt like a millionaire when bestowed with a pen filled with ink and clean sheets of paper. He was a writer; the worst thing about this for Toby was that he believed—even championed— that outright poverty was part of the package.

So if you can imagine a fragile piece of paper with faded Italian script peeking out from beneath the ink-blotted artistic scrawls of a fountain pen, you have an idea of what Margot picked up from the floor, unfolded, and read.

The Wooden Man

by Toby E. Poslusny

The wooden man was not a puppet; unlike Pinocchio, the wooden man was a real man, while everyone around him was not. In this land of puppets, the wooden man found life very difficult. Employment opportunities were nil, unless you had strings attached to your limbs and could keep your mouth completely still while talking. There were no houses or office blocks either, and there had been a recent dearth of churches; instead, the whole planet had turned into a giant stage upon which the puppets strutted and fought, and the wooden man found himself becoming increasingly lonely. You see, the wooden man was not made of wood, but his heart was; rather, his heart was a tree with many branches, but neither peach nor pear grew there, and no bird ever came to sing.

Although Margot knew nothing about the man she had sat next to for all of seventeen blocks, she felt as though she'd been given a window into his world, a page from his journal, a love letter. The naked loneliness that crouched within the words found a foothold in her sympathies. I, of course, read it as self-conscious, intertextual drivel, huffy in tone, reeking of reflexive post-McCarthyism. The young Toby Poslusny was not a literary master; it would be many years before he mastered his craft. But to a young, slightly homesick lover of literature who could recite passages of *Wuthering Heights* verbatim, Toby's palimpsest was a minefield of deliciously confessional symbolism.

And so, the man who pushed Tom out of Margot's thoughts was not Toby, but one of his characters. Tom called five more times at the bookstore. Each time Margot was out on the streets, pillaging other bookstores for the kind of material Bob ought to have had on his shelves, her mind fixed on Toby's story. She became increasingly frustrated at the dusty tomes of dead white males taking up floor space in Bob's bookstore; even though she painted the outside white, replaced the flickering light bulbs, and spent a whole weekend fixing the "Babbington Books" sign, customers who ventured inside simply didn't want Hemingway or Wells. They wanted the new, enraged voices springing up from the ghettos of Detroit, the squats of London, Manchester, Glasgow, the projects of Moscow. After JFK, Vietnam, Watergate, and a serial killer on their doorsteps, the new generation of twenty-something readers wanted literature that gave a voice to the craziness.

I eventually came to terms with the lost opportunity with Tom and encouraged Margot's next move with vigor, though of course I knew the cost: to study literature at NYU.

She called Graham.

"Hey, Papa! It's me! How are you?"

A muffled snort. "Margot. Margot? Is that you?"

She checked her watch. She'd gotten the time zones mixed up again. It was 4:00 AM back home.

"Margot?"

"Yes, Papa. I'm sorry, did I wake you?"

"No, no." A cough like shoveled gravel and the sound of spitting. "Absolutely not, no. I was just getting myself ready for the day. You sound excited, what's happened?"

And so she breathily explained what she wanted. He chuckled at her choice of words: "the chance to prevent myself from becoming like the Philistines who run our country." He asked how much it would cost. In less than a minute, her wish was granted. He'd pay the fees and wire some money to Bob for her accommodation for another twelve months. He had one request: that she read his latest novel and give feedback. Done deal.

I watched Midtown West carefully, nudging Margot occasionally to overlook its apocalyptic wastelands and consider instead its proximity to Times Square, to ignore the gang wars and cop raids in favor of its unimaginably cheap market price. When Graham's money cleared in her bank, it was enough to buy forty-five thousand square feet of land. The bank would certainly fork out the rest to let her build a modest hotel. I ran the idea past her in her dreams, added some images of airy hotel rooms with pressed linen sheets, pink peonies on the bed stand, an open fire in the lobby . . . I felt like a film director, though I needed no camera, just my own imagination and my hand pressed against Margot's forehead. When she woke up, she had sudden longings for a softer bed, a hot shower, and room service. But the hotel idea never took hold. NYU was calling. She was pretty much baptized in her own academic ardor.

So I traipsed behind her like a jaded old goat through Washington Square Park to NYU, up the stairs of the old Victorian building with the leaking roof, tentatively taking her seat in a drafty, high-ceilinged room with a blackboard sitting on the marble fireplace. The other students in the class—fifteen of them—were silent, primed, close to vomiting their opinions on poststructuralism all over the professor, who hadn't yet shown up. One girl, a skinhead Chinese heiress named Xiao Chen, kitted out in gold satin leg warmers over fifteen-hole Doc Martens boots and a leather motorcycle jacket covered in spikes, looked up at Margot and smiled. I looked at Xiao Chen and thought immediately of tequila shots and a mugger lying half dead in an alley. Ah yes, Xiao Chen. She introduced me to the art of theft.

As the trees turned red, then white, then naked as pitchforks, Margot and Xiao Chen immersed themselves in several forests' worth of pages, and I watched, tortured, as brick after brick of a new development was laid on the wasteland of Midtown West like slabs of gold bullion.

❧

Toby had worked at NYU at the same time I had studied there. He'd been hired to teach a few seminars when Professor Godivala took time off to nurse her kid. Toby's course, Freudian Shakespeare, was filled within hours of being posted to the notice board. Margot stood, pen poised, eager to sign her name. I saw the name of the course tutor—*Mr. Tobias Poslusny*—and belted out the Song of Souls, much to the shock of the other angels among the crowd of students vying for the board. Margot hesitated, then scribbled her name down. Mercifully, Xiao Chen approached and saved my neck.

"You are *not* taking that class."

"Yes I am. That's why I'm putting my name down. What, you're not?"

Xiao Chen shook her head. "The seminar's on *Monday mornings* at eight thirty. Anyways, you hate Shakespeare. Come do the modernism class with me."

Margot hesitated.

"My round at the bar if you say yes," said Xiao Chen, and she yanked the pen out of Margot's hand, crossed out her name, then shoved her in the direction of the modernism board. Margot signed her name and they hightailed it to the student union.

But as I followed behind them, noticing the seeds in the hard ground of Washington Square Park ripening like green hearts, preparing for the long journey to sunlight, I saw Toby, alone on a bench, writing. Two jocks bumped into Xiao Chen and kept her and Margot flirting and giggling while I approached Toby.

In the branches of a willow tree behind him sat an angel with long, silvery hair and a long, sober face. She was so bright that from a distance the scene resembled a waterfall in sunlight pouring through the middle of the branches. As I approached, I became aware that this was Gaia, Toby's guardian angel, and also his mother. We had never met while I was alive. Gaia looked at me and nodded, though her mouth didn't quite make it to a smile. I sat down beside Toby. He was scribbling intently, one leg crossed over the over, deep in thought.

"It's good to see you, Toby," I said.

"Good to see you too," he said absentmindedly, though he faltered at the "too" and looked up, confused.

I stood up sharply. Toby peered around him, scratched his head, then went back to his writing. As he wrote, the blanket of emotions and thought processes—which often appeared as a pulsing wall, full of colors and textures and little sparks—became pitted with crevasses as new connections were made rapidly among all the ideas that ballooned from that blanket, and I saw my opportunity.

I had to ask.

I had to know, because if he was the one who killed Margot, if my life had ended so abruptly because of this man, I needed to work out a way to get her as far away from him as possible.

"Did you kill Margot, Toby?"

He kept writing.

I spoke louder. "Did you kill Margot?"

Gaia looked up.

I strained to see images of his past and future appearing next to him as parallel worlds, anxious for clues. But all that appeared were the faces of his students, the character of the wooden man dancing all alone in the land of puppets, a poem that was still an iambic embryo.

And a flash of Margot in the taxi.

I took a step closer. He grinned as if he was indulging in a private longing, then carried on writing. Then again. Above his head, Margot's face, smiling from inside the taxi: seeds growing in winter.

I looked over at Margot and Xiao Chen, consensual prisoners of the blue-eyed jocks, and I sunk down beside Toby.

"My son's no murderer." Gaia stood in front of me, silvery as a new blade.

"Then who killed Margot?"

She shrugged. "I'm sorry, I don't know. But it wasn't Toby."

She walked away. A burst of wind shuddered through the park, blowing up a girl's skirt and creating scattered applause. It swept over Toby and me, but didn't stir his thoughts.

I allowed myself to study him, taking in the earthy palette of his aura, drawing breath when I noticed how bad a state his kidneys were in, how fragile his bones. And I looked over his calm, feminine face, the gold, penetrating eyes; I saw the white light of his soul contract and expand as he stumbled upon an idea that resonated with his deepest desires, and I saw those desires tumbling out of the center of his being like small screens bearing the projections of hope: to be loved. To write books that moved the world into a state of compassion and change. To achieve tenure at NYU. To father a child with the right woman.

The jocks were leaving, and Margot and Xiao Chen were following. It would be many months before Margot and Toby would meet properly. I bent down and kissed him, softly, on the side of his face. He looked straight at me, and what he thought was a dark cloud shattering into rain was my heart shredding itself into a thousand pieces of regret.

I was falling in love with him again.

15

A Dog and a Deli

MEANWHILE, MARGOT WAS BUSY FALLING IN LOVE WITH NYU'S ICE-HOCKEY TEAM. She tossed her love in the direction of their coach, until his wife found out, and then she spread her love around the male component of the karate club. Her love was so hungry it gobbled up half the faculty. Then, she devoured Jason. But Jason was Xiao Chen's boyfriend. After robbing a baker's dozen of Connecticut blondes of their devoted jock boyfriends, Xiao Chen had started moving her things into Jason's apartment. Xiao Chen had no right to be so surprised. Where Margot was concerned, it was simply a case of the student outwitting the master. Suffice it to say, their friendship ended with a bang.

For my part, I was starting to loathe Margot more and more each day. Margot, I'd tell her. How I hate thee. Let me count the ways:

1. I hate your fake American accent.
2. I hate your pseudocommitment to feminism and your religious devotion to whoredom.

3. I hate your lies to Papa. When he finds out that you're flunking, it will devastate him.

4. I hate your drugstore philosophies and your deep smoker's voice. I hate it because you never hear mine.

5. Most of all, Margot, I hate that I was once you.

Exam time came around. I got a group of angels together and we worked hard getting our Protected Beings to knuckle down and reach for better futures. Bob, however, had been paying attention to Margot's little escapades upstairs with every Tom, Dick, and Harry that crossed her path. He figured he might get lucky too. So, the night before Margot's first exam, he slicked back his fuzzy afro, tucked his best T-shirt into his tightest jeans, and knocked on her door.

"Margot?"

"I'm sleeping."

"No, you ain't; 'cause if you were, you wouldn't be answerin'."

"Go away, Bob."

"I got some wine. It's red. *Cha-bliss.*"

The door swung open. Margot in her nightgown and her most disingenuous smile. "Did someone say Chablis?"

Bob inspected the bottle, then looked up at Margot. "'Um. Yeah."

"Come right on in."

I succeeded in preventing Bob's wishes from coming true but at the cost of them both passing out in the kitchenette. Too much Cha-bliss make the white man sleepy, as Bob would say.

I had less success getting Margot to hear my answers to her exam. She sat in the exam room, slung over the desk, mentally clambering over the jagged wall of her hangover. I threw my hands in the air and stalked off toward the window. Seated at the exam supervisor's desk at the front of the room was Toby. I sat on the desk beside him and watched him write.

I recognized some of the sentences he was writing; they'd show up later in his first novel, *Black Ice*. A couple of times he tutted and drew several heavy, punishing lines through a word or sentence, until Gaia placed an arm over his shoulder and encouraged him to keep going. Once, I saw her reach forward as he scored his pen deep across the page, but she couldn't touch him. A few minutes later, she could. I watched closely. As his thoughts traced the landscape of ideas rising in his mind, his aura would contract suddenly, and a thick barrier—it looked like glacial ice—would enclose him for all of a moment. Once or twice it remained for ten seconds or so. Gaia called his name over and over until the barrier seemed to dissolve. And it didn't dissolve into the ether—it dissolved into Toby.

"What is that?" I asked Gaia after a while.

She flicked her eyes at me. "It's fear. Toby's afraid he's not good enough. You never encountered it with Margot"?

I shook my head. Not like this.

"I guess it takes different forms." She shrugged. "This is Toby's way. It shields him. But I'm worried. Lately it's shielding him from good things. And I can't get through."

I nodded. "Maybe we can work together on it."

She smiled. "Maybe."

She continued trying to shake him out of his mold, but the shield would go up and once he'd triggered his fears, only Toby could get it to dissolve. There was no fighting it. Had he shaken himself out of it, he might have noticed Margot packing up her stuff and leaving an hour early.

I followed her outside. She wrapped her arms around herself and looked out over the Hudson. Then she started walking, fast, until she broke into a run, and she didn't stop until we were both pelting at high speed, sweat beading on her face, her hair streaming behind her like the tail of a comet.

We ran and ran until we found ourselves on the George Washington Bridge. Margot was gasping for air, panting and leaning over her knees, her heart galloping in her chest. She looked at the traffic below, then leaned against the grid of railings and looked out at the skyline of Manhattan. The sun was still high, forcing her to hold up a hand to protect her eyes. She looked as if she was searching for someone, squinting at the Twin Towers, then Pier 45, until finally she staggered toward a public bench and sank down.

All around her, sorrow and confusion flashed like small bursts of lightning. As she sat hunched over her knees, hundreds of small pink lights darted out from her heart, circulating around her body and seeping into her aura. Her eyes were closed tight, and she was thinking of Mamma, her chin wobbling. All I could do was put a hand on her head. *There, there, kiddo. It isn't all that bad.* When I sat next to her, she dug her elbows into her thighs, her head against her palms, and wept long, bottomless sobs. Sometimes the longest distance is between despair and acceptance.

She stayed there as dozens of cyclists breezed past, as the sun drifted through its shades of gold until, finally, the city glowed bronze, and the Hudson burned.

I searched my memory for this moment, but it wasn't there. So I stopped searching, and I started talking.

"Are you thinking of jumping off this bridge, kiddo? 'Cause I'm telling ya, the suicide squad is one step ahead." I tapped the grid of railings.

She started to cry again. I softened my tone. Not that she could hear me. But, perhaps, she could feel me.

"What is it, Margot? Why are you still here? Why aren't you putting your head down, studying like you promised, making something of yourself?" And then I found myself launching into statements like "the world is your oyster," and I sighed. I changed tactics.

"All these guys you're sleeping with, do any of them make you happy? Do you love any of them?"

Slowly she shook her head. "No," she mumbled. Tears dripped down her face.

I persisted. "Then why do it? What if you get pregnant again? Or HIV?"

She looked up and wiped her face, then laughed. "Talking to myself. I really am going crazy." She leaned over her folded arms, staring beyond the skyline now, looking as far into the horizon as she could.

"We really are all alone in this world, aren't we," she said quietly.

It wasn't a question. And I remembered then, the powerful, soul-stripping urge to be rescued. I remembered that I felt on that bridge as if I was a million miles from land, stuck on a rock in the middle of space. And no one came.

Except, I was there. I wrapped my arms around her, then felt another set of arms on top of mine, then another, and when I looked up, I saw that Irina and Una were there, spirits visiting from the other side, embracing both me and Margot, telling her softly that it was okay, that they were here, that they were waiting. I cried and touched each of their hands, wanting to hold on as long as I could, and they kissed me and held me and told me that they were always there, that they missed me. I wept until I thought my heart would crack. The light around Margot's heart flickered like a candle at sea.

Eventually she got up, and her jaw was set. She walked slowly down the ramp and took a cab home, and the stars hid their secrets behind impenetrable cloud.

The bad news, of course, was that she failed all her exams. There was some success amid the failure. She had failed more than any other student in her year. You might say she failed stupendously. Bob threw her a book and booze party, and the two of them enjoyed an irritatingly raucous evening celebrating her tremendous academic catastrophe.

The good news was that she could repeat her freshman year. I managed to get through to her to encourage her to devise a plan. There was no way she could tell Graham she'd wasted hundreds of pounds on a prolonged hangover. So, she figured she'd get another couple of jobs, save up all summer, then pay her own way through round two of her freshman year.

She got a job at an Irish pub waiting tables on weeknights, and another job walking dogs for rich folk on the Upper East Side. I took one look at the barking pom-pom on the end of the leash and groaned. We were headed for Sonya, no doubt about it.

There were two reasons why I didn't do more to prevent a reunion with Sonya Hemingway.

First of all, Sonya was a scream. Tall, curvaceous, with butt-brushing, Valentine-red hair that she ironed for half an hour every morning, Sonya liked heights, hard drugs and half truths. She had absolutely no long-term goals. She was also a distant relative of Ernest Hemingway, a fact (or not) that she touted to designers, drug dealers, and anyone who would listen. It paid off. Among the benefits of her tall tales were a skyrocketing modeling career and a constant blizzard of hallucinogenic white powder.

Second, there was a question mark hanging over me. Did she or did she not have an affair with Toby? I figured that being in a position to resolve this particular existential tidbit, I might as well take advantage.

But we were headed away from her. The dog—Paris—was obediently padding alongside Margot, its leash intact. I turned and scanned the street for Sonya. She was still on the other side of Fifth Avenue. Perhaps I better intervene, I thought.

I leaned down and ruffled Paris's fluffy ears, then pressed my hand against his forehead. "Lunch time, isn't it, boy?" Paris slobbered enthusiastically. Immediately I sent images of all kinds of doggy cuisine into Paris's head. "What tickles your fancy, huh? Turkey? Bacon?" Roast turkey and bacon on a spit appeared in Paris's head. He barked. "Wait, I know," I said. "A megaton of salami!"

At that, Paris took flight. A little faster than I anticipated, and with surprising force. He yanked Margot forward, straight across the road, forcing two cabs and a Chevy to a halt, just inches in front of Margot. She screamed and let go of the leash. Paris darted onward, his little tail whirring like a propeller, bringing another car to a dead stop and sending a cyclist over his handlebars into a hotdog stand. He was not pleased.

Margot sheepishly crossed the road, waiting for the "WALK" sign by way of apology. Once she reached the other side, she bolted for the deli. I stood by the door and laughed—second time around was much more fun. Paris had made straight for the new delivery of pork at the back of the deli and, in his little poochish angst to get the biggest piece, knocked over the watercooler, spilling the contents all over the shop floor. The owner ranted and waved Paris out of the shop. Paris happily complied, his jaws wrapped around a baton of meat. Margot grabbed Paris, smacked him on the nose a few times, and dragged him back inside to apologize. She faced the owner, who was struggling to collect the scattered remnants of meat.

"I'm so sorry! I promise I'll pay for all of it! Please write down the list, and I'll get it back to you as soon as I can, somehow."

The owner glared and told her—in Italian—to stick her apologies where the sun don't shine. Margot turned her gaze to the girl with long red hair in the corner, drenched from the fallout of Paris's escapades, inspecting her wet clothes and laughing. It was Sonya.

"Hey, sorry about that," Margot said. "He's not my dog . . ."

Sonya wrung out her red hair. "You're English, huh?"

Margot shrugged. "Sort of."

"You don't sound much like the queen."

"I'm really sorry about your shirt. Is it ruined?"

Sonya walked toward her. She had this habit of demolishing the rules of personal space. She'd approach virtual strangers—like Margot, in this case—and get so close that they'd almost bump noses. She'd learned the hard way, at too young an age, that people responded to confrontation. Sometimes in a good way, sometimes bad—either way, she got the attention she wanted.

"Hey, Sorta English, you got a date tonight?"

Margot took a step back. She could see the whites of Sonya's eyes, the red lipstick on her teeth.

Sonya took another step forward. Paris licked her arm. "Your dog likes me, huh?"

Margot found her composure. "Sorry about your shirt. It's lovely."

Sonya looked down at her violet silk ruffled top, which was sticking to her chest. "No matter; I got loads more like it. Here." Out of nowhere, she produced a black business card and slipped it under Paris's collar. "You can make it up to me by coming to my party tonight."

She gave Margot a saucy wink, then walked out into Fifth Avenue, still dripping.

Dogless, clueless, Margot showed up that evening at Sonya's town house in Carnegie Hill, squinting at the address on the black business card, convinced she'd gotten the wrong place. She pressed the bell. Immediately the door swung open to reveal a beaming Sonya in a skin-tight, leopard-print dress. "Sortof!" she yelled, pulling Margot inside. I giggled. Sortof. What a cheek.

Sonya introduced Margot to her guests—she had to shout their names over Bob Marley, who hollered through two enormous speakers at the front of the house—until finally she reached the man she introduced as "Mr. Shakespeare, Who Likes to Spend My Parties Buried in a Book." I caught my breath. It was Toby.

"Hello," Margot said, extending a hand to the book-shielded figure in the chair. Hi, he said from behind the book, and when he saw her he said "Hi" once more, but with an exclamation mark at the end of it.

"Toby," said Toby, standing up.

"Margot," said Margot. "I think we've already met."

"I'm gonna leave you two to chat," said Sonya before wafting off.

Margot and Toby eyeballed each other, then awkwardly looked away. Margot sat down and picked up the book he'd been reading. Toby fiddled with the belt straps around his trouser-waist before sitting down beside her. A glance at Sonya as she flirted and laughed at the opposite end of the room confirmed my suspicion: he had always preferred her instead of me, right from the get-go.

"So," said Margot. "You're Toby."

"Yes," said Toby. "Yes, I am."

Had it *really* been this awkward? I always recalled our first meeting as much more dynamic. And so it continued.

"Is Sonya your girlfriend?"

Toby blinked for a few seconds, then opened his mouth and closed it.

"Uh, how to describe our relationship . . . She used to steal my pacifier as a baby. I think there was an episode where she took all her clothes off and climbed into my crib, but other than that our relationship has been pretty platonic."

Margot nodded and smiled. Gaia stepped forward and leaned over Toby's shoulder.

"Margot's the One, Toby."

Just like that, she said it. And what's more, Toby heard her. For a moment, he turned toward Gaia, his heart racing at the sudden flash of knowledge that had been imparted to his soul, and I watched on, struck by wonder and humility. Gaia knew

I had been Margot, and she had watched me accuse her son of murder. And yet here she was, encouraging him to be with her.

Toby turned to Margot, suddenly eager to get to know her a little better. She'd become engrossed in his book.

"You like books, I'm taking it?"

She turned a page. "Yep."

"Everyone's so anti-Shakespeare these days, but you just gotta love *Romeo and Juliet*, ya know?"

I laughed. Toby was utterly wanting when it came to small talk.

Margot, however, was inclined to bulldozing conversation. She looked up from the book, crossed her legs and looked at him very seriously.

"*Romeo and Juliet* is a chauvinist's fantasy of romance. I think Juliet should have poured a vat of burning oil over that balcony."

Toby's smile withered like a fern in flame. He looked away, searching his mind for a comeback. Margot rolled her eyes and stood up to walk away. Immediately Gaia was by his side, whispering. I watched Margot search the room for someone else to talk to, someone much more inclined to play hard to get, and I felt myself rising to Toby's defense.

None of Gaia's whisperings were getting through to Toby, so chaotic were his emotions at the sudden desire that overwhelmed him to make a connection with Margot. He felt nervous, tense, uncertain as to why he was so attracted to someone who was so not his type.

At last I stepped forward. "Toby," I said firmly. "Tell her to take a running jump."

I said it again. And again. Gaia looked at me as if I'd lost all reason. Finally Toby stood up.

"Margot," he said loudly as she walked away. "Margot!" he said again, and she stopped. A pause in the music. Several heads turned to look at them both. Toby pointed at her.

"You're wrong, Margot. That play is about soul mates overcoming all odds. It's about *love*, not chauvinism."

The music started up again: the opening bars of "I Shot the Sheriff." Sonya ousted everyone out of their seats to groove to the music. Margot looked across the crowd at Toby, meeting his stare. For a moment she wanted to hurl back some offhand remark. But something in his gaze prevented her. And so she walked away, out of the front door and back to her apartment above Babbington Books.

16

The Wave of Lost Souls

OVER THE MONTHS THAT FOLLOWED, I HAD MY FAIR SHARE OF CLASHES WITH DEMONS. Sonya's angel—her twin, Ezekiel, who had been stillborn minutes after her own screaming arrival into the world—patiently paced the hallway of her home, regularly ousted by Sonya's dependency on two demons, Luciana and Pui. Unlike Grogor, they were hard to tell apart from any one of the many beautiful humans that crossed the threshold of Sonya's house. I know they spent a lot of time with Sonya, but most often I couldn't see them.

And here's where I learned a thing or two: demons could hide themselves remarkably well. Like the millions of insects that prowl around the cubbyholes and floor gaps of your own home, so, too, do demons insert themselves in the pocket spaces of the living. I watched as Sonya took off a necklace with a heavy mother-of-pearl pendant, and as she set it on her dresser, I saw the faces of Luciana and Pui staring up from inside it. Sometimes they'd take a ride in her designer handbag; at other times, they'd curl around her forearm like an amulet. Because Sonya was, shall we say, fickle in terms of her lifestyle choices—for instance, on a Monday you might catch her doing yoga and sipping aloe vera, on a Tuesday you'd be likely to trip over her unconscious, drug-riddled body facedown in vomit—Luciana and Pui were either lolling on Sonya's enormous couch in full humanlike form or reduced to dark stains on Sonya's soul. But they never left her.

Within a couple of weeks, Sonya invited Margot to move in. She said she felt sorry for Margot, what with having to work three jobs and, worse, living in Bob's vile apartment. In truth, Sonya was lonely. Even the presence of Luciana and Pui was bound up with her loneliness. She never understood why, when she gave in to the drugs, she suddenly felt less alone. She put it down to the effects on her brain. Wrong. It was because Luciana and Pui laced themselves around her like ivy around a tree, the most devoted and nefarious of companions.

I made it clear from the outset that I would not be pacing any hallway while those two annihilated Sonya's soul. They made her a bad influence on Margot. Already, she was sampling a little grass here, a little crack there, and I saw what was coming like the headlights of a steam engine bearing down on her lying on the rail tracks. Luciana and Pui didn't take too kindly to my confrontation. They changed form, rising up like two cobra-shaped pillars of red smoke, spitting balls of fire in my direction. And just like in real life, I found myself in a situation for which I'd received no training, no forewarning. Just like in real life, I acted on instinct: I raised both hands and stopped the fire, and then I closed my eyes and imagined the light in my body growing and growing, which it did, and when I opened my eyes again, the light had become so strong that they backed down into a corner, like shadows at noon, and didn't show their faces to me for quite some time.

Ezekiel returned to Sonya's life in rude health. She found herself thinking about kicking the drugs, turning to a healthier lifestyle, maybe even settling down with a nice man. For keeps.

"What do you think about Toby?" Sonya to Margot over morning coffee.

Margot shrugged. "He seems nice. Quiet."

"I'm thinking of dating him."

Margot gave an exaggerated cough. "*Dating* him? Are you also gonna start, I dunno, baking and knitting scarves?"

Sonya —and you have to imagine this girl, hunched over her latte in a silk, black robe and a red velvet push-up bra, her unironed hair crazed and gashing down her pale face like a head wound—was affronted. She was more affronted by the fact that she wasn't, actually, affronted by the thought of baking and knitting scarves.

"I think I'm getting old."

"Do you and Toby have a past?"

Sonya shook her head. For once she was telling the truth. "We went to kindergarten together. He's like my brother. Yuck, what was I thinking. Anyway, didn't you two have a bit of a *thing* at my party a few months ago?"

"I insulted him."

"And . . . ?"

"And nothing. I haven't seen him since."

"Would you like to?"

Margot thought about it. At last, she nodded.

And so, Margot and Toby found themselves on an unofficial date.

He showed up at Bob's bookstore. Bob was in his usual position behind the counter in a chair, smoking a mixture of weed and tobacco and reading up on the new Cadillac Fleetwood Brougham. He glanced at Toby and flicked his cigarette in his direction.

"I'm here for Margot?

A cough from behind the counter. Toby glanced over the new-arrivals shelf.

"Some good books here. Never heard of this place before."

"Uh-huh."

"So. Margot around?"

"You'd have to ask her."

I always admired Toby's infinite patience. I glanced at Bob's angel, Zenov, leaning on the counter, and mimicked the action of smacking Bob upside the head. Zenov shook his head like "Whaddyagunnado?"

Toby clasped his hands behind his back and considered Bob's suggestion. Then:

"Margot?" bellowed Toby at the top of his lungs. Bob fell off his seat and smacked his rear on the ground.

"Margot Delacroix, it's Toby Poslusny, here for our unofficial date. Are you here, Margot?" He roared from his calm, nonplussed stance with the volume and command of an evangelical preacher, all while smiling and fixing his gaze on Bob.

Bob rose to his feet while Zenov laughed into his hand. "Uh . . . lemme just go check if she's here . . . "

"Thank you," Toby, still smiling, nodded at Bob.

Margot emerged from the room divider a few minutes later in a green tulle 1950s party dress two sizes too small. She was still pinning her hair in place, flushed with nerves. I watched Toby do a double take, drinking in her dress, her ballerina neck. Her legs.

"Hi," she said. "Sorry to keep you waiting."

Toby nodded at her and held out a bent arm, gesturing for her to link arms.

She did so, and they swept out of the shop.

"I'm lockin' up at eleven," coughed Bob, but the door slammed before he could finish.

They say that the first two weeks of any relationship give the full picture of the whole kit and caboodle. I say it's less than that. First dates are a map of the territory.

Toby didn't do regular. He didn't do dinner-and-a-movie dates He did a rowing-boat ride in the Hudson. Margot found the whole thing hilarious. An important relationship milestone. Then Toby lost an oar and started reciting W. B. Yeats. Margot found this fascinating. And then—well, didn't she just have to?—she produced cocaine. Which Toby found distasteful.

"Put it away, I don't do that stuff."

Margot looked at him as if he'd grown a second head. "But, you're friends with Son, aren't you?"

"Yeah, but that doesn't mean I'm a junkie . . . "

"I'm not a *junkie*, Toby. I'm interested in a bit of fun, that's all . . . "

He looked away. I looked away, embarrassed. I hated myself. I loathed this moment, one of many blights on what could have been a decent landscape of a relationship. And, as always, my bad.

Margot took umbrage. "Well, if you won't, more for me!" She snorted both lines.

Toby inspected the buildings on the other side of the river. Street lamps were starting to shimmer along the fringes of the water, sending gold and red ribbons streaking toward the boat.

He smiled. Then he set down his oar. He took off his jacket, his shoes. Then his shirt.

"What are you doing?" Margot asked.

He continued undressing, right down to his Y-fronts. Then he stood up, pushed his skinny white arms outward, leaned his bony torso to his knees in a diver's pose, and jumped into the river.

Margot dropped her coke and leaned over the side of the boat, stunned. He was under an awful long time. She waited, fidgeting with her hands. Still no sign of him. She wondered whether she should shout for help. Eventually she took off her jacket and shoes and jumped in after him. At this, he surfaced, laughing his head off.

"Toby!" she screamed, her teeth chattering. "You tricked me!"

Toby laughed and cuffed water at her. "No, my sweet Margot; it is you who are tricking yourself."

She looked at him. *How wise he is*, I thought. *How crazy he is*, thought Margot.

"Huh?"

He doggie-paddled toward her. "You really think that doing coke makes you a fun person?" he said. "Because if you do, you're a whole lot dumber than I took you for."

Water was dripping off his nose, and the cold was making his voice tremble. Margot stared at him, and just as the thought crossed her mind to kiss him, he leaned in and kissed her. It was— and I can vouch for this—the softest, most sincere kiss of her life.

※※

I spent the months after that in Toby's tiny loft space above the all-night café, studying Margot and Toby carefully as they fell deeper and deeper into a spiritual crevasse that began to feel like love. At first, I told myself that the two of them were falling in love with love itself, that it was circumstance and not love that kept them together, despite having no money, no future, and not a whole lot in common. But watching them wrapped in towels on the shaky balcony on the fifth floor overlooking the West Village, drinking coffee and reading the morning papers like an old couple, I thought, *Hold on a second. What am I missing here? What did I miss first time around?*

Watching them together was like witnessing the biochemical marriage that takes place between a lily and the sun. Slowed down and close up, the process by which light feeds the bloom like invisible nectar and, simultaneously, of the oxygen pluming up from the leaves like small balloons rising to take their place in the mosaic of the universe—witnessing the spectrum of their union was like watching a new river cut its way through the mudflats of a land so thirsty that the fusion of water and earth is nothing short of the symmetry of the sacred. It was the flowering of love, in all its spiritual, chemical, and psychological fusions and refinements.

Did I feel like a third wheel? Well, let's just say it helped that Gaia was there. I took the time to get to know her. During Toby and Margot's more intimate moments, moments I wanted to respect and cherish in terms of their privacy and sanctity, Gaia and I chatted about Toby's childhood. She'd died of cervical cancer when he was four. Until that time, Toby's guardian angel had been his aunt Sarah. Oh, I'd said in surprise. I thought guardian angels were singularly assigned to one person. "No," Gaia said. "Just as long as we're needed, when we're needed. A person can have twenty different guardian angels in his or her lifetime. And you'll probably guard more than one person too."

The thought of it made my head spin.

Toby had told me that he only had one memory of his mom. She was teaching him to ride his bike. He was scared of falling off and stayed put in the doorway of their home, gripping the handlebars. He remembered that she told him to ride only as far as the end of the garden path, and if he could make it that far, he could try to ride to the end of the street, then to the end of the next block, and so on. When he made it to the end of the path— all of four meters—she applauded with such enthusiasm that he started pedaling all the way to the other side of town, until she dragged him home. He told me that since then he'd used a similar tactic in his writing—he would write to the end of the page, then to the end of the chapter, and so on, until he'd finished an entire novel. And he always kept that image of his mother applauding at the forefront of his mind.

Gaia smiled. "You know, I remember that, the bike adventure."

"You do?"

"Yeah. But what's funny is, Toby wasn't four then. He was a year older. And I was no longer living. I was his angel at that point."

"I stared at her. You're sure?"

She nodded. "Toby's been able to see me on and off his whole life. He doesn't know I'm his mother, or his angel. Sometimes he thinks I'm someone he recognizes from school, or maybe an old neighbor, or just some crazy woman in the bookstore standing too close. It's rare, but it happens."

I looked over at Toby and Margot, lying on Toby's battered leather couch, lacing and unlacing their fingers, and I wondered and hoped: Would Toby ever see me? What if he did? Could I ever apologize to him? Could I ever, ever make up for what I did?

✺✺

The wedding took place in the Chapel of the Flowers in Las Vegas, nine blissful months after that disastrous first date. I tried—and failed—to convince Margot to hold out for a wedding back in England, a more sumptuous affair that would provide Graham with the sole opportunity to give away his only child in marriage. I'd spent my life making up stories about that wedding, beefing it up a little the way I'd have liked it in retrospect. But, the fact is, Toby showed up at the Irish pub where Margot was working one evening. He'd applied for tenure at NYU, and it looked like he was set to get it. So he bought himself a 1964 Chevy and a present for Margot—a modest diamond solitaire.

She looked at him. "You're serious?"

He winked.

"It's too big for my wedding finger, you know."

His smile dropped. "It is?"

"It fits my thumb. I'm taking it this isn't an engagement ring, then." This time she winked and took a deep breath. *Is this really it?* she thought. *Yes,* I told her. *This is it.*

She looked at Toby. "Aren't you supposed to ask me something?"

He dropped to one knee and took her hand. "Margot Delacroix . . ."

"Yes?" She fluttered her eyelids saucily. I stood beside her, watching him carefully. I wanted her to buck up, be serious, soak up this moment. I wanted to be in her place, to say yes and mean it with all of my heart.

"Margot Delacroix," Toby said again, very seriously. "Argumentative, self-indulgent"—her smile dropped—"passionate, feisty, beautiful Juliet of my heart"—her smile grew—"the woman of my dreams, please, *please*, refrain from pouring a vat of boiling oil over my head and, instead, become my wife."

She looked at him, her eyes smiling, chewing her cheek. At last, she spoke. "Toby Poslusny, Romeo of my soul, introspective slave to literature, sufferer of martyr syndrome . . ." He nodded. All true, in fairness. But, there was more. She kept him waiting. " . . . sweet, loving, patient Toby . . . "

A minute passed.

"Margot?" Toby pumped her hand. His knees were hurting.

"Didn't I say yes already?"

He shook his head.

"Yes!" She jumped in the air. He gasped in relief and struggled to his feet.

She admired her ring, then had a lightbulb moment. Or, in hindsight, a moment of insanity. Ready? Here goes . . .

"Let's get married in Vegas!"

I promise you, I tried to talk her out of it. I even sang the Song of Souls. She was having none of it.

Toby considered. He painted a picture of a white wedding the following year in a quaint English chapel, dripping in lilies and roses, Graham walking her up the aisle. I mouthed her words. "Boring," she said. "Why wait?"

Toby compromised. To his eternal credit, he did the honorable thing. He found the nearest pay phone and called Graham to ask for Margot's hand in marriage. No, Margot wasn't pregnant,

Toby assured him. He simply loved her. And she simply wouldn't wait a moment longer. Silence on the other end of the phone. At last, Graham spoke, choked up with tears. Of course, they had his blessing. He would pay for the whole ceremony and a honeymoon to England. Margot screeched "Thank you!" and "I love you, Papa!" into the receiver—she couldn't even wait long enough to have a decent chat with him, for which I wanted to kick her up the backside—before dragging Toby to the car. The receiver dangled in midair, and Graham's best wishes went unheard.

And so, they set off for Vogue. A mere three-day drive. They swung past Sonya's and acquired a bridal outfit—a borrowed leopard-print dress with red-patent stilettos—and a gold hoop earring in Margot's jewelery box that sufficed as Toby's wedding band. Food? Provisions for the long journey? Don't be silly. They were in *love*—what more did they need?

The sun was beginning to slip behind the distant hills when Nan appeared in the back of Toby's Chevy.

"Why, hello, Nan," I said. "Come to tell me I should prevent them from getting hitched after all?" I was still a little sore after our last meeting. She stared straight ahead, scowling.

"What's wrong?"

She leaned toward me without taking her eyes off the darkening landscape outside.

"Margot and Toby are driving right into the center of a Pole House."

I blinked. "What's a Pole House?"

"It's a gathering of demons. This Pole House in particular is very big. They will know that Toby and Margot are traveling to be married, and they'll seek to prevent it."

"Why?"

She glanced at me. "Marriage equals love and family. It is what every demon opposes most, aside from life itself."

I followed her gaze out the window. Nothing but the orange wink of a retreating sun, the flash of headlights passing by on the other side of the road.

"Maybe we passed it already."

Nan shook her head and continued to glance outside anxiously.

Suddenly the car rocked from side to side, fishtailing wildly across the road. I gripped the back of Toby's seat, reaching forward to protect Margot.

"Not yet," Nan said calmly, but the car keeled heavily to the left, and for an instant I thought we would either tip over entirely or crash into the oncoming traffic. I felt Nan grab my hand.

"What do we do?" I shouted.

"Now!" yelled Nan, grabbing my arm, and right then we were outside with Gaia, holding on to the hood as it thundered down the highway, yanking it back to the right-hand side. Car horns sounded ahead. Several cars swerved toward the ditch. Toby wrestled with the steering wheel and yanked the car out of the way of the flashing headlights of a truck.

The car straightened its course and Toby rolled it to a stop on the dirt path next to a sign that read "Welcome to Nevada." The engine shuddered to a stop, and I tried to gather my senses. I could hear Margot and Toby laughing in the car.

"Wow, that was scary!"

"I'll check under the hood."

Voices from the front seat. Excited. Unnerved.

Nan had started to walk toward the edge of the yellow plain, silhouetted by sun. I held a hand up to my eyes and strained to see what she was looking at.

"What do you see?"

No answer. I looked around. Beyond the contours of the purple hills, I could see figures starting to move toward me. I started to walk toward them, holding up an arm, ready to send out my brightest light. And then I saw them. At first, I thought it was hell's finest. So bright I had to look away. A hundred or more gold, flaming beings, much taller than I, their wings made of fire. I went to turn and call to Nan, but she was already beside me.

"Archangels," she said. "Just letting us know they're here."

"Yes," I said. "But why are they here?"

"Haven't you sensed it?" Nan said. "Look at your wings."

Folding around me, so that the water crisscrossed against my chest and flowed toward my feet, my wings were full and dark, like the overspill of a reservoir. And I felt it then, as intense and as frightening as reaching the precipice of hell: We were being hunted.

Toby dropped the hood shut and wiped his hands on a rag. "Fear not, young damsel, all is well," he called to Margot, who was hanging out of the passenger window, giggling. He jumped back into the car and started the engine.

I started to get back into the car, but Nan held me back.

"Look." She pointed at the car.

I watched as black smoke trickled, then bellowed, from under the hood, wondering for a moment why Toby wasn't shutting off the engine to check what was going on. Instead, the car took off smoothly, and the smoke continued curling out from the hood, up and over the roof, right down over the trunk, until it enveloped the whole car like a skin, or a barrier—almost like the one I'd seen around Toby.

And then a face amid the smoke.

Grogor.

I shot after the car and jumped on the hood, then the roof. The last ribbons of sunlight dissolved into the horizon, leaving me for that moment in shadow, unable to see the volume of smoke growing around my feet. In the distance behind me, Nan held up a ball of light high above her head. It began to travel toward me, growing brighter as it came closer. I looked down and saw the smoke parting around me in a circle, but it continued to thicken elsewhere, rising steadily like a mud bank.

"Ruth!" Nan shouted in the distance. Immediately a wall of black smoke rose above me like a tidal wave. As the ball of light reached me and hovered directly overhead, I could see it wasn't smoke—it was hundreds of coal black hands, reaching for me.

"Nan!" I yelled. My wings were pulsing. The tidal wave came crashing down on top of me with the force of an avalanche.

When I came to, I was lying on the side of the freeway, unable to move. I strained to look for Nan. I turned my head and saw, right there among cars and eighteen-wheelers in the middle of the freeway, a war. Hundreds of demons were attacking the archangels I'd seen in the desert, hurling huge balls of flaming boulders and arrows set alight, which the archangels fended off with swords. Occasionally I'd see an archangel drop to the ground and vanish. *Are they dying? How could that be?*

I could hear someone coming behind me. I tried to get up. *Nan*, I cried, but as I said it, I knew it wasn't Nan. It was Grogor.

The footsteps ended at the side of my head. I cranked my head and looked up. Above me, not two legs made of smoke, not a face with a shotgun blast for a mouth, but a very human being. A tall, knifish man in a dark suit. He gave my legs a slight kick to make sure I was immobilized. Then he crouched down beside me.

"Why don't you come join the winning team?" he said.

"Why don't you go become a priest," I said. He smirked.

"You really want to end up like that?" He glanced over at an archangel who had taken a ball of flame straight in the chest. I watched, amazed and horrified, as she fell to the ground and vanished in a burst of light.

"As if it isn't bad enough that you lot just stand around watching on as humans mess everything up," he continued, tutting. "But I think I have you all figured out, Ruth. You'd prefer to change things, make them better. And why not?"

Suddenly, I felt my wings pulsing *into* me, the current traveling inward. And on the current, a message, a voice in my head: *Get up.*

Just as I struggled to my feet, a burst of crimson light and a hard tremor pulsing the ground beneath me, as if a bomb had exploded underground. I looked up and saw the archangels circling the demons, their swords uniformly pointed toward the sky. And then, plummeting from the clouds, a huge blast of fire shattering all the demons into a thick cloud of dust. When I looked again, Grogor was gone.

Through the ball of flame Nan came running straight toward me. She grabbed my hand and pulled me to my feet. "Are you all right?" she said.

"I thought they couldn't hurt us."

She looked me over carefully. "Of course they can hurt us, Ruth. Why else do you think we have to defend ourselves?"

"I thought you said I had nothing to fear?"

She dusted down my dress. "What did Grogor say to you?"

I shook my head. I didn't want to repeat it, to admit that what he'd said was true. Nan raised an eyebrow.

"You can't afford to feel guilt, doubt, or fear, or any of the barricading emotions you felt as a human. You're an angel. You've got God behind you and heaven before you."

"So you keep telling me."

Dawn was breaking over the hills. The other angels looked to it and started to vanish into the pink sky.

"The worst is over," Nan said. "Go find Margot. I'll visit with you again very soon." She turned toward the hills.

"Wait," I said. She turned.

"I'm in love with Toby," I said. "And if I don't find a way to change things, I'll never see him again. Please help me, Nan." I was begging now. Desperate.

"I'm sorry, Ruth, but it's like I told you. You already had one life to make all your choices. This life is not about remaking them. It's about helping Margot make them."

"So that's it?" I screamed. "I only get once chance? I thought God was all about second chances!"

But she was gone, and I was alone in the middle of Route 76, looking to the skies, looking for God.

"So you love me, huh?" I yelled. "Is this how you show it?"

Nothing but the sudden, slow falling of rain, the sound of wind that sounded like *shh*.

17

A Seed

I REACHED VEGAS NOT LONG AFTER. Gaia attempted to fill me in on the details of the wedding, but—rather grumpily, I admit—I told her not to bother. I remembered it distinctly. The chapel's broken neon sign flashing a cracked heart, like a bad omen. The kitschy plastic flowers and elevator music warbling from an electric organ in the lobby, the registrar's toupee flapping in the air-conditioning like a dead bird's wing, Toby sniggering through his vows. Being hesitant when I said yes, wanting instead to ask what marriage was like, how you were supposed to know if this was the right person or not. How it felt to be truly in love instead of, as I had been so many times, up to my neck in a deep-seated need to be told I was worthless. And I remembered that this was perhaps not the best time for that sort of discussion, that perhaps I should stick to a simple yes, and we would live happily ever after. Of course.

The honeymoon took place a week later. Using all of their savings they bought two return tickets to Newcastle upon Tyne in northeast England. Margot raced through the small terminal, tugging Toby along behind her, eager to see Graham for the first time in two years.

They made it as far as the exit doors, but still no sign of Graham.

"Do you think he might have forgotten?" Toby asked. "Maybe we should just take a cab over there."

Margot shook her head and scoured the airport anxiously. "Of course he hasn't forgotten. It's not like he's got fifty daughters, you know."

Toby nodded and sat on top of the suitcase.

When I saw the shaded figure emerge at the other end of the terminal, I leaned toward Margot and said, painfully, "He's here."

She turned her head and looked right at the figure by the doorway.

"Is that him?" said Toby, following her gaze.

"No. That guy's too thin. And he's got a walking stick. Papa would be running over here by now."

The figure stood for a moment, watching her. Then, very slowly, a man emerged out of the shadows to reveal himself, with each hobbled step, as a very gaunt, very aged Graham.

For a moment Margot struggled to reconcile the image of the man walking slowly toward her with her mind's portrait of Papa. I recalled this moment with such aching clarity that I could hardly bear to look on, for what appeared before Margot was a series of startling replacements—the Santa Claus belly, wide shoulders, and fat butcher's hands had been replaced while she was gone with a version of Graham that looked like he had just stumbled across the Sahara Desert. His thick storm of hair was now a fistful of salt grass, his round, ruddy cheeks were sunken into his cheekbones and his eyes—the most shocking of all—were without wit or fight.

"Papa?" Margot whispered, still rooted to the spot.

Toby read the panic in her voice. He looked from Margot to the man shuffling toward them with his arms loosely held forward, and strode forward.

"Graham, I presume?" he said cheerfully, reaching for Graham's limp hand, managing to catch him right at the instant that he missed a step and staggered forward into Toby's arms.

Margot drew both hands up to her face. *Easy now,* I told her. *Get it together, sweetheart. The last thing Papa needs right now is for you to start the waterworks.* And yes, these were brave words, for I too was aghast at the sight of him, not because of his physical form, but because of his aura: the light around his heart was shattered into dozens of strands that drooped and pulsed weakly, like small bleeds from an unhealing wound. Above his head, the energetic fireworks of his intelligence and creativity were damp fuses, lolling slowly as if in fog.

True to character, Graham thumped Toby on the back in an approving manner before moving him out of the way to touch Margot. Tears dampening her cheeks, she pressed her face into his shoulder and held him tightly.

"Papa," she whispered, breathing in his scent.

Graham didn't reply. He was sobbing into her hair.

Back at Graham's, Margot went straight to bed to sleep off jet lag while Toby inspected the novels lining the bookshelves bearing the name Lewis Sharpe and Graham's photograph. Gaia, me, Bonnie, and the two men sat around the dancing fire. For a moment, silence. Then, Graham:

"So how'd you get her to say yes?"

Toby coughed into his fist. "Ah, the proposal. Well, I produced the ring, as leverage of course, and I asked the question of all questions . . ."

Graham smiled weakly. He leaned forward, resting his elbows on his knees. I noticed that his mouth drooped slightly to the right. "No. What I mean is, this is Margot. Easier to lasso a hummingbird than make a missus out of Margot, that's what my wife used to say. Margot always was a wild pony. What's changed?"

It took a moment or two for Toby to consider what Graham was saying. I looked at the photos of Margot and Irina along the fireplace and felt sad. I didn't know that this was how Papa saw me.

"Well, sir," Toby said, scratching his beard. "I know Margot can come across like that. You hit the nail right on the head right then. But deep down, I think she wants this more than anything in the whole world. She acts flighty and noncommittal because her life has taught her that commitment means pain."

Graham nodded. Slowly he leaned toward the whisky bottle on the coffee table in front of him and poured them both a drink.

"I need you to know something," he said quietly.

Alert to the tone in Graham's voice, Toby took a seat opposite him and nodded.

Graham drained his glass, set it noisily on the coffee table, then looked at Toby.

"I'm dying," he said.

A long pause as the gravity of those words sank in. "I'm . . . that's . . . I'm really very sorry to hear that, sir."

Graham waved his hands slightly from side to side like flags of surrender. "That's not what I need you to know. That's just the prelude." He cleared his throat. "I'm dying, which is completely fine by me. I have a wife somewhere out there. I'm looking forward to seeing her again. But you see"—he edged forward in his seat toward Toby, so close that Toby could see the firelight dancing in the old man's eyes—"I can't die until I know that you'll take care of Margot for me."

Toby leaned back and read the anxiety in Graham's face. Now, it was all very clear. He scratched his beard and smiled. For a moment, the weight of Graham's news was lifted by an overwhelming sense of gladness. He was glad, I could see, that Graham cared this much. He was glad to sense that Graham trusted him with something as precious as his only daughter.

Eventually, he gave the only answer he could guarantee.

"I'll never let go of her. I promise."

The fire was dying down. Smiling at Toby's choice of words, Graham leaned back in his chair and promptly fell asleep.

Later, as Toby lay in bed beside Margot, still on New York time, he watched her sleeping and thought of Graham's request. He rubbed his face, already constructing a way to tell her. Then he thought of what Graham had said about her. *Easier to lasso a hummingbird than make a missus out of Margot.* He chuckled to himself. Then, out of nowhere, the ice barrier formed all around him. Gaia and I shared looks. The barrier was thicker than we'd ever seen it, hard and glassy. We watched on as Toby stared at Margot, and I realized he'd taken a huge risk marrying me. Toby's greatest paralyzing fear was losing me, and not just because of the promise he'd made to Graham. I had always known that he had lost his mother at a young age, but now I saw that that loss had filled every corner of his life. It was written all over his beliefs, his view of the world. What if Margot *did* leave him? What if it all ended? What then?

My focus from that point was making it work. I'd sing the Song of Souls every minute of every day, if I had to. I'd whisper all Toby's good points into her ear, instruct her about what she needed to do to make their marriage a paradise instead of a purgatory.

But who was I kidding? How did I know how to make it work?

A week later, it was time to leave. Margot reluctantly and tearfully said her good-byes to Papa, not at the airport, but at the doorway of his home. Here he didn't seem so diminished by the hustle and noise of the outside world; at home, he seemed less broken, enlivened by the unchanged surroundings of the open fire, the photos of Mamma, the slumbering presence of Gin coiled in the corner.

When Margot and Toby arrived back in New York, however, they were met by a couple of surprises:

1. Toby's application for tenure at NYU had been denied, and his classes canceled. He was no longer required.

2. His apartment above the all-night café was being turned into an extension of the café. What had been a living room was now filled with dining tables and menus. Toby's belongings had been tossed into cardboard boxes and stored in the kitchen beside the meat freezer, so that all his books and notepads forever reeked of dead cow.

They had two options: move in with Bob or move in with Sonya. She'd offered them the top floor of her place until Toby found work. They moved all Toby's stuff into Sonya's and, for the first few nights, the place was pretty cozy. Sonya stayed out of their way. Margot carried on waiting tables at the Irish pub, secretly stowing away quarters for another trip back to England. Toby stayed up until the wee hours, smoking on the balcony, watching the people in the houses opposite, struggling with the worst of all the recent turn of events: He had writer's block.

⁂

The young guy caught Margot on her way to work. She'd recently dropped out of NYU—she was taking a "year off," she'd told everyone, including herself—and was working seven days a week to save for a deposit on an apartment. But she was lonely, homesick, and depressed. Toby was trying to finish his novel—a literary opus about a tragic hero who ironically fails to overcome his fear of failure, written in the form of a series of letters—while looking for work. He even tried the docks. The guys in dirty overalls took one look at him and told him to hit the road. They didn't need a guy who could write an essay. They needed someone who could lug forty pounds of coal from one spot to another a hundred times a day.

Which was why the arrival of the young man seemed—no, *was*—expert timing on the part of Luciana and Pui. Oh yes, they were still around, despite Sonya's recent conversion to religion and healthy living. She was now a Buddhist and a vegan. Despite her irritating compulsion to convert everyone around her ("Did you know milk actually causes cancer?"), she was healthier, happier, and a lot more pleasant to be around. She was also a much better influence on Margot. I had almost forgotten the grudge I'd held against her for many, many years. The grudge that was beginning to take root in Margot.

The seed of that grudge lay in the pocket of the young man. A sample, he said, of the stuff he used to sell to Sonya. If Margot liked it, if it worked out for her, he could come back next week and sell her some more at a discount. Margot looked him up and down. He was no more than seventeen. There was nothing particularly shifty about him—a different story from where I was standing, I can tell you—and, in fact, he was quite likable. What's it called? She asked. The *stuff*. He smiled. Lysergic acid diethylamide, he said, commonly referred to as the happy pill. With that, he waved good-bye.

I wrung my hands and struggled to recall this moment. Trouble with drugs is they tend to *frappé* the mind. Finally I said a prayer and talked to her very seriously. "Margot," I said. "That stuff is *toxic*. You don't want to be putting that into your body. It will *ruin your life*." Wisdom is defiled by its necessary clichés.

She didn't hear me. And so, when the boy showed up next week, and the week after that, and the week after that, Margot bought more and more of his seeds, and they took root, and bloomed into awful flowers.

Toby's book was almost finished. His writer's block had been cured by virtually barricading himself into the small room adjacent to his and Margot's bedroom for days and nights, pounding at Graham's old typewriter. Up until now, he hadn't noticed the change in Margot. He typed the words "The End"—a tradition of his, even though the publisher always removed them—then stood up on his chair and punched the air. He undid all the door locks and announced:

"Margot? Margot, my love! I have finished! Let's eat!"

He found her pacing the living room, pulling books out of the bookcase and dropping them to the floor, tugging cushions off the sofa, picking up shoes and banging them upside down as if something was stored inside. Surrounding her, a blizzard of white feathers from the mattress she'd sliced open.

"Margot?"

She ignored him and carried on searching.

"Margot, what's wrong? Margot!" He grabbed her by the shoulders and looked at her. "Honey, what have you lost?"

Her mind, I wanted to say, but this wasn't a time for jokes. Toby couldn't see it—he'd never done so much as a joint—but she was in the grip of an addiction that I knew, all too well, would take years to undo. And that's just what it looked like. Similar to the strand of fate I'd witnessed at Una and Ben's, Margot's addiction wound itself tightly around her heart, then outward until each one of her organs and arteries and blood cells was gloved in need.

Margot stared blankly at Toby.

"Get off me."

He let go and looked at her, puzzled and hurt.

"Look, just tell me what you've lost and we'll find it together."

"No, you can't. He's coming."

A pause.

"Who's coming?"

"I don't know his name."

"Why is who coming? Is he coming here? Margot?"

He tried grabbing her again, but she pushed him away and ran downstairs. Toby, Gaia, and I followed.

Sonya was in the kitchen, drinking miso soup and reading. Margot marched up to her, her hand outstretched.

"I need a hundred dollars." A chunk of change in the 1980s.

Sonya stared at her. The thought crossed her mind that this was some sort of joke. Then she saw Margot's eyes, the sweat pouring down her face, her trembling hand. She set down her soup and stood up.

"Margie, what have you taken, sweetheart. This ain't like you at all . . ."

Toby interjected. "I think she's sick. Isn't yellow fever going around just now?"

Sonya held up a hand to shut him up. "It ain't yellow fever, babes."

"Babes?" Margot. Paranoia was kicking in something fierce. She looked from Toby to Sonya. They were stopping her from getting what she wanted. They were acting together. They wanted her out. No, wait. They were lovers.

"Did you sleep with her?" Margot to Toby.

"We need to get her to a doctor, and fast." Sonya to Toby.

"Will someone tell me just *what* is going on here?" Toby to the air.

A knock on the door. Ah, Mr. Seventeen-Year-Old Drug Dealer. Come right on in.

Sonya marched across the living room and swung open the door. She recognized him immediately.

"Patrick?"

"Hey." He looked past Sonya at Margot.

"I told you guys I wasn't . . . are you here for *Margot*?"

Patrick thought about it. "'Um. No?"

Toby let go of Margot and approached Sonya.

"Who is this guy? What does he want with Margot?"

Patrick had something in his hand.

"Show me that!" shouted Sonya, and before he could tuck it back into his pocket Toby reached forward and yanked the object out of Patrick's hand.

A gold locket.

"Is this for Margot?" Toby said quietly. He looked behind him at Margot, his breath quickening, the ice barrier forming all around him.

"No, it's mine," said Sonya, grabbing the locket from him. "Look." She opened it to reveal two miniature photos of her parents. "Why did you have this, Patrick? Did you steal it from me?"

Patrick stuttered. "It's worth less than she said," he said, pointing at Margot. And then he bolted.

Ah yes, my finest hour. Of course, I had no memory of this at all. I was on the far side of reality. Margot was pacing an exact circle around the bearskin rug in front of the fire, flapping her hands and sobbing. Toby approached her.

"Honey? Margot?" She stopped pacing and looked at him. "I'm sorry, sweetheart. I'm the cause of this. I've been spending too long at my *stupid* book . . ." Gently he raised his hands and held her face, his eyes filling with tears. "I'll put this right. I promise."

He leaned in to kiss her. She pushed his face away roughly and walked toward Sonya.

"You can't just go around sleeping with people's husbands!" she screamed, raising her hand in the air and bringing it hard across Sonya's face.

Sonya reeled back, holding a hand to her cheek. She inspected her lip: fresh blood from where Margot's wedding band had caught her mouth.

"I want you and your stuff out of here." She looked over at Toby.

He nodded. "Let me get her to a doctor first."

And then, Luciana and Pui, emerging from the corners of the room and circling Margot like wolves. They whispered to her, soft as kittens:

"He's always preferred Sonya to you. Isn't that the only reason he married you? To get close to Sonya. Beautiful, funny Sonya. Not like you."

For a moment I considered fighting the two of them, but then, a familiar sensation in my wings, a voice carried on their current: *put your hand on her head and think of Toby.* And so, I stood right in front of Margot, and I placed my hand against her forehead and filled it with every good memory of her and Toby, of the night they rowed up the Hudson, of the car journey to Vegas, of his promise to her to always be faithful, of the feeling, deep down in her heart, that he always would be.

She sank to her knees, heaving hollow, dry sobs.

Sonya scrambled around the kitchen and returned a few moments later with a glass of water and a Xanax. "Give her this," she said to Toby.

"No!" he shouted. "No more drugs."

She thrust it into his hand. "It'll put her to sleep while you figure this out. She looks like she hasn't slept in days."

She was right. Margot hadn't. And Toby hadn't noticed.

Reluctantly, he gave Margot the pill.

Is it the happy pill, Toby? Yes, Margot, it's the happy pill. Okay, Toby. Drink the water too, Margot. Okay.

Soon after, she was curled up on the sofa, fast asleep.

Sonya emerged from the kitchen and handed Toby a mug of coffee. "I'm sorry, Tobes, but ain't no way I'm letting her take my stuff. This was my mom's." She held up the locket.

Toby sank down beside Margot and sobbed quietly as Sonya explained the effects of the drug, what he needed to do from this point, how they could help her kick this thing. And I thought, for the first time in decades: She was a true friend. The truest of all my friends.

And I didn't blame her when she stuck to her word and insisted that Toby and Margot move out once Margot had spent two weeks in bed, two weeks without drugs. She promised to remain friends. She even helped them move all their things into the new place on Tenth Avenue.

The journey back from this fall from grace was a ropeless climb up a steep cliff face. Margot refused to seek help. Instead, she did rehab old-school: in bed, with the door locked, surrounded by books, water, and pillows, into which she'd scream when the fist of addiction squeezed. Quietly, Toby set about the routine of regular coffee refills and short-and-sweet updates on the world outside. *Pat Tabler just got traded from the Yankees to the Cubs. Reagan appointed the first female Supreme Court justice today. Simon and Garfunkel just gave a free concert in Central Park. No, I didn't go. I wanted to make sure you had enough coffee.*

As she started venturing out of the bedroom and out of her addiction, Toby found work at a local high school. At Gaia's behest, he put Margot to work, editing his new book before he sent it out to publishers. She thrived on the opportunity to immerse herself in books again. As did I. Seeing the rough draft of Toby's first book—which, I can tell you, sold its print run within two months—was a real treat. I read alongside her, making suggestions, sharpening her editorial eye, making her question every scene, every character. For the first time in a long while, she listened.

And then, a morning I recognized. School kids running along the street wearing pumpkin heads and masks of ghosts. The loose change of autumn gathering in the outside stairwell. *You're pregnant*, I told Margot. *No, I'm not*, she thought. *Well, then, do a test*, I said. *You'll see. You'll see.*

18 ❧

$\mathscr{M}$essages in the Water

I GUESS IT'S JUST AS THEY SAY: MOTHERHOOD IS BETTER THE SECOND TIME AROUND.

Or maybe I was just ready for it this time. I don't know. But as I watched that small grain of light deep inside her, I willed its heart to begin its Morse code, its anxious rhythm of being. I watched, my own heart in my mouth, as dozens of times Margot's body threatened to drown the soft melody of this new life with viruses, toxins, hormonal tides. But the light clung inside, like a small figure huddled against a drowning mast rocking in red squalls.

She told Toby. Gaia whooped and jumped in the air—I'd held off telling her, just to watch this reaction—and Toby took a step back, reading the disappointment in Margot's face, struggling to contain his excitement.

"A baby? Oh man, that's heavy. That's . . . I mean, it's wonderful, huh? Isn't it?"

Margot shrugged and folded her arms. Toby took her by the shoulders and pulled her close.

"Honey, it's okay. We don't have to keep it if you don't want—"

She pushed him away. "I knew you'd never want a kid with me."

Projections of her own feelings. I stood away from the glare of the sun, wrapping myself in shadow.

"I've already tried to get rid of it," she sighed, her eyes filling with tears. Lies. She was testing him.

Toby's face caved in. A long pause. A grave stare. This is where the landslide started, I thought.

"You did?"

"Uh-huh. I . . . tried falling down the stairs. It didn't work." More lies. She wrapped her arms around herself.

Relief and anger drew themselves across Toby's face. He closed his eyes. Gaia put her arms around him and spoke to him: *She needs to know you won't abandon her.*

He let her walk away to the window, his arms dropping to his sides. "I won't leave you, Margot. This is *our* baby." And then, with less conviction, "This is our marriage."

Very tentatively, he approached her. When she didn't flinch, he put his arms around her from behind, pressing his palms against her stomach.

"This is our baby," he said softly, and she smiled and turned very slowly, receiving his embrace.

⁂

I spent much of Margot's pregnancy recalling with stinging clarity all the things I had done to try to sidestep reality, swaying between shame and excitement. Shame at the marijuana she'd smoke at Sonya's while Toby was at work, shame at the lies she'd tell ("Isn't that bad for the kid, Margie?" "Not at all. If I'm relaxed, the baby gets more vitamins."). Shame at the effects of the drugs I'd watch descending down inside her to the faltering light. Shame at the thoughts she'd have ("Maybe I *should* try falling down the stairs; maybe I'll get lucky and lose it.") And then, gradually, she grew excited, as did I. We shared excitement at the shadows of Theo's face sculpting the light in Margot's womb, excitement at Margot's surprise at a tiny foot leaning against the wall of her womb, her sudden, full realization that an actual baby was inside of her, that this was real.

Luciana and Pui had taken up residence on the windowsill of Toby and Margot's apartment. "Cats among the pigeons, huh?" I'd shout out at them, and they'd scowl and call to Margot, enticing her to go round to Sonya's, to give the baby more vitamins. And then I'd make Theo kick, and Margot decided she didn't want to visit Sonya. She decided she wanted to walk to Inwood Hill Park for fresh air and a different view. So she did, every day.

I recognized the old, maroon-colored door of the apartment opposite, long strips of ancient paint curling up from the bottom. Margot had noticed newspapers and milk bottles collecting outside. She was pretty sure someone lived there. Occasionally the living room light was on in the wee hours, but by morning it had been switched off. The curtains were always drawn. In a neighborhood like this, neighbors kept to themselves. Margot hesitated. Should she go check it out? Yes, I told her. She looked down at her pregnant belly. It's all right, kiddo, I said. Ain't nothing gonna hurt you. Go on, go on.

The front door was slightly open. Still, she took the precaution of giving a knock. No answer. "Hello?" she called. She opened the door a little wider, her fingertips meeting dust. "Anyone home?"

The smell hit her like a flung rag. Garbage, damp, and excrement. She gasped and drew her hand up to cover her nose and mouth.

I hesitated. Yes, I knew who lived here, but I was no longer so sure I should encourage this meeting. And then, messages in the water flowing from my back: *She is needed here. Send her inside.*

Before Margot could convince herself to walk away, a rasping voice: "Who's there?"

A woman's voice. A very old, very sick woman's voice. Rose Workman. I rushed inside ahead of Margot into the dark, forgotten room to the figure on the couch, eager to see Rose's face, wrinkled like a sheet of paper that had been crumpled in a bin then spread flat, the heavy rings on her long black fingers like coins balanced on her knuckles, each of which had a story. Stories that had never left me.

The figure on the couch was not Rose Workman. A fat white man, naked to the waist, threw back a blanket and growled at me. He was a demon. I jumped back, startled and confused.

"Hello? Who's there?" Rose's voice from the kitchen, the tap-tapping of her walking stick, guiding her shuffling feet through the darkness.

Margot approached very slowly.

"Hi," she said, relieved and repulsed. "I live in the apartment opposite. Just wanted to say hello."

Rose lifted her glasses and peered up at Margot. She gave a wide smile, warmer than a homecoming, her eyes becoming dark slits in the deep folds of her face. "Well, c'mon in, child. Don't get many visitors, no ma'am."

Margot followed her into the kitchen, taking in the bare, damp walls, the sheet of dust on the rotten dining table, the echo of her heels on naked floorboards. As she walked past the old man on the couch, she shuddered. She wanted to leave. And so did I.

The demon jumped up and stalked toward me. Three hundred pounds of bald white flesh with pinprick eyes and a scowl, naked to the waist. He loomed over me and growled, then shoved me backward. "You ain't got no business here," he barked.

I planted my feet firmly on the ground, keeping an eye on Margot and Rose in the kitchen, looking around for Rose's angel. He launched himself at me a second time, but I held up a hand, and from it, a cannonball of flame.

"Touch me again, and I'll turn you into burger meat," I said firmly.

He raised an eyebrow and snorted. Clearly, witty comebacks weren't his forte. He screwed up his face and pointed a finger.

"Stay out of my business," he rumbled, then flumped back down on the sofa and covered himself with the blanket. I stumbled around the room, stunned by the encounter, struggling to figure out why a demon was here, but no angel.

A while later, Margot returned from the kitchen carrying a plateful of cookies wrapped in aluminum foil. Rose had her arm around Margot's shoulder, telling her the story behind the ring on her left index finger. It involved her eldest son, killed in the war. They headed for the front door.

"Sorry I have to run," Margot said. "I told my husband I'd meet him at the park. But I'll call again."

"You betcha," said Rose and waved her off. I followed, bewildered. No angel? Didn't Nan say God left no child alone?

⚜

I began to take more notice of the messages I'd receive from my wings. Sometimes they'd feel like whispers in my head, at other times it was strong instinct, a clear set of instructions rising from every cell in my body. Gradually, amid the messages, a picture formed. A picture of Margot's future. It didn't much resemble the life I remembered, and so I ignored it.

Margot visited Rose the following day, and the day after that, and the day after that, until she was popping back and forth three times a day. Just as I'd once loved these visits, basking in the jolly reassurance of a woman who'd given birth thirteen times and, to my delight, made birth and motherhood sound so much more of a gift than the purgatory I'd believed it to be, so now did I dread the sight of that flaking door, the threats and taunts resounding from the couch, the constant attacks.

Finally, I called on Nan. She hadn't been to visit since the battle in Nevada, and I figured we'd parted ways. But I missed her. And, above all, I needed her.

A few minutes later she appeared beside me. I started off on a note of penance.

"Nan, I'm sorry," I breathed. "I'm sorry, very sorry."

She waved my apologies out of the air, always so selective about what she did and didn't wish to hear.

"It's okay," she said, pulling me into a hug. "It's your first time as an angel; you still have so much to learn."

I explained to her the situation with Rose's demon.

"Why is there no angel assigned to Rose?" I asked. "And *who* is the walrus living on Rose's couch?"

She looked surprised. Genuinely so. "But . . . didn't you . . . Margot is Rose's angel."

Come again?

She laughed, then saw the look on my face and got serious. "You know that a human being can have more than one guardian angel?"

Uh-huh.

"And you know that Rose's guardian angel was recently reassigned?"

"Nope. But continue."

She sighed. "My dear, you really must start using these." She tapped my wings. "Right now, Margot is acting as an angel to Rose."

I stared at her. There appeared to be some holes in the details. Like the fact that Margot was mortal.

Nan shrugged. "So what?" she said. "It's not only the dead who act as angels, my dear. Otherwise what would be the point of parents? Or friends, siblings, nurses, doctors . . ."

"I get it," I said, though I didn't.

"Your job right now is to protect her against Ram."

"The demon?"

"Yes. You've probably figured out that he's got quite a hold on Rose."

I considered this. I had worked out that, for whatever reason, he'd been able to take up residence in Rose's life like a husband she couldn't bring herself to leave. But, as far as I could see, he didn't do much tempting. Rose went to church. She had no addictions. She hadn't killed anyone. She couldn't even bring herself to step on the cockroaches that scuttled happily across her kitchen floor.

"Look closer," advised Nan. "You'll see his purpose, and the strength of his grip on Rose."

It happened the day that Rose told Margot the story behind the gold sovereign ring on her wedding finger.

"'This ring," she said, tapping it thoughtfully, "it came into my life one afternoon when I was a girl, no more than twelve. I was on my daddy's farm, you know, gathering apples from the orchard next to the barn. It was so hot you could roast a joint right there in the fields, yes ma'am. Even the cows were keelin' over, their barrels of water running dry as dunes before they could stumble across the field. I knew I shouldn't, but I couldn't help it. I went down to the bayou, stripped myself down to my naked self, said a prayer and slipped right into that cool, black liquid. I even let my head go under. I can still feel those slivers of water running through my hair, between my bare legs . . . I woulda stayed there all afternoon if I coulda held my breath long enough.

"As it turns out, I had to hold my breath longer than I thought. At first, I thought the tuggin' was the current, you know, pulling me downstream. And then I felt a warmth around my ankle, a warmth that turned into a burn, and a burn that made me squeal like a pig at Christmas. When I opened my eyes, the blood even looked like fire. Beyond the bubbles and blood I could see a long tail. A gator, long as a pickup truck. I remember my daddy tellin' me their eyeballs was vulnerable, so I leaned down to its snout and jammed my thumb right where its eye was. For a second it let go of me, and in that second I kicked my legs and broke the surface, long enough for some air. But then the gator went for my other leg, and this time it rolled me right under. I seemed to stay under there so long that I figured, one more second and I'm with Jesus. But right then, a man pulled me out into the heat of the day, into the heat of a new life. He was the one who gave me this ring."

Who knows if these stories were even true? But every time Rose told them, the light around her shined so brightly that Ram shunted off the couch and growled his way to the back door, like a bear with a headache.

"My first husband, he gave this to me," Rose said, smiling up at a cobwebbed photo of a handsome man hanging on the wall. "He told me, never stop tellin' your stories, tell them to the *whole worl'*. He went out and bought me a fine pen and leather notebooks and made me write them down. And I never stopped."

"These notebooks," said Margot. "Where are they?"

Rose waved a hand. "Oh no, I ain't diggin' those out. Too many!"

Margot lifted a new, hardback notebook from the floor. "Is this your latest one?"

Rose held up her twisted fingers. "Yes, but my hand hurts too bad. Can't write no more."

Margot started to read out loud. As she did, the small parallel worlds that faded in and out of Rose's aura fanned outward until they filled the whole room. I watched as a montage of images flashed before me of Rose as a child, being called upon by her parents to tell stories to the rest of their family in Louisiana, then a mother, scribbling down tales beside a crib, and then, Rose, the age she was now, but thinner, fitter, seated at a table beneath the crisscross windows at the Low Library at Columbia University, surrounded by men and women in suits and dresses, smiling as if for a photograph, and then someone handing her a certificate. As I strained to read the text, it startled me: the Pulitzer Prize for Fiction.

And then the vision cut to a closeup of the same certificate, framed and hanging on Rose's living room wall, but it wasn't the living room she was sitting in: the one in the vision was three times larger, with a marble fireplace, wall-to-wall carpets, and ivory, satin curtains framing bay windows. A maid busied herself sweeping the endless gilt-framed photographs of Rose's beloved sons and grandchildren, and—this is what made me weep—the images in the photos showed her sons' graduations, their service photos, one of them shaking hands with President Reagan. To my knowledge, none of her children had ever graduated from high school.

The vision folded, and I stood there, stunned and breathless, until I noticed that Ram had returned.

Margot was flicking through Rose's notebook. "This is incredible," she said. "Why haven't you published this?"

And then Ram, sitting beside Rose, gently took her hand:

"You ain't good enough, Rosie."

Rose repeated it, shaking her head. "I ain't good enough, child."

"Books are for rich folk, not like you."

Rose, like a robot: "Books are for rich folk, not the likes of me."

"That's rubbish," interjected Margot. Ram threw her a look. "This is beautiful. You write like a dream."

Ram got louder. "You ain't interested in money. Money makes good people turn bad."

A shadow fell across Rose's face. She repeated Ram's words.

Margot looked confused. "I'm sorry you feel that way," she said softly. Then, an idea. I had nothing to do with it. "Can I take your notebooks to show my husband? He's a writer too."

Ram stood up. He opened his foul mouth and bellowed at Margot. Rose held her ears as if she was having a fit. Margot reached for her.

"Rose, what's wrong?"

Rose whimpered. "Just go. Please."

But then she leaned forward and, with trembling hands, curled her knobbly fingers around Margot's, pressing them around the spine of her notebook on Margot's lap. Ram looked on, stamping his foot on the floor next to Rose in protest. Rose opened her mouth to speak, but she could feel the air around her sag with Ram's discontent. "Go," she whispered again.

Margot looked from Rose to the notebook in confusion, then took a step toward the door.

Ram craned his head back and glanced at the old wooden fan hanging above Margot.

"Don't you dare," I said, stepping forward. He smirked at me, then swung up and tugged on it.

"Quick!" I yelled at Margot before launching myself at Ram's gut and knocking him to the floor.

I watched as Margot closed the door of the apartment behind her, cracked plaster trailing from the ceiling fan. Rose howled. Ram picked himself up and glared at me, his nostrils flaring. He bent his knees and made to charge, but just then, without warning, the water in my back turned to flame. His jaw dropping open, Ram cowered, before hiding himself like a cockroach in the picture frame of Rose's first husband.

And then, something I didn't understand. Rose stood in front of me, serene, smiling. She was looking directly at me.

"I'm ready," she said. "Make the man bother me no more. Take me home."

She held out a hand, and I took it. I felt her walk into my body and through my wings, and then she was gone.

❧

I stayed the night in Rose's apartment, pacing the floor, looking at the photographs she'd treasured, weeping at the empty kitchen cupboards, the rats living tamely under her bed, the filthiness of the water that choked from the ancient tap. I struggled to discover why she'd chosen this place, why she'd allowed herself to cower in the fist of a demon instead of living out the life she was supposed to live. But I found no answer.

Instead, I did what was needed. When Margot came the next day and found Rose's body curled on the couch, when she gasped and sobbed on the floor, I wrapped my arms around her, whispering in her ear to be brave, calming her, reminding her of the notebooks. After she called the ambulance, she ventured upstairs to the wardrobe next to Rose's bed. Inside, no clothes, but dozens of notebooks filled with Rose's handwriting. She filled several suitcases with the books and enlisted the help of Toby in dragging them across to their apartment before the ambulance arrived.

A while later, a call from Toby's publisher. He was interested in Rose's notebooks, but they would need a fair amount of editing, and he just didn't have the time. Was Margot available the day after? She looked down at the small planet erupting from her abdomen and prayed the baby would stay in there a little longer.

"Yes," she said, "I'm available."

I should mention: This was a dream come true. It had been growing in me like a secret I'd been sworn not to share, like the baby, I guess, for a long time. I'd never had a sense of what I wanted to *be* when I grew up—I guess I'd never been sure when I *would* officially grow up—but now, having pored over the books at Graham and Irina's, having spent so many hours dissecting Toby's novels to find the truth in the fiction, the flower in the bud, I knew exactly what it was I wanted to *do*.

And ain't that the funny thing—I stumbled right into my perfect job. And I didn't even see it. At least, not at the time. I walked that morning alongside Margot with confidence and purpose. *Buttercup,* I told her, *if I could do it all over again, this would be the one thing I wouldn't change.* Finally, I thought, things were going the way they ought to be.

The publisher's office was above the famous deli on Fifth Avenue, the one Margot had so memorably desecrated years before. She hid her face as she walked past the owner, and we hiked all the way to the third floor.

Hugo Benet, managing director of Benet Books and a man with the whitest, straightest and largest teeth I'd ever laid eyes on, was a veteran of the publishing world. Despite his best efforts, he'd been unable to find a decent assistant in all the time he'd been based outside his native Toronto. The notebooks were quite a find, he told Margot. They were going to publish the first batch, after they'd been through the usual editing process. Was she interested in taking on that job?

She wasn't sure.

Of course you are, I told her.

"Of course I am," she said, feeling the slow trickle of water against her thigh, the lightening bolt of pain across her stomach, resisting the sudden urge to scream.

19

The Bus

TEN HOURS INTO HER LABOR, MARGOT DECIDED SHE DIDN'T WANT TO GIVE BIRTH ANYMORE. She had decided motherhood wasn't her cup of tea, she didn't actually want a baby, and could she go home now please.

Another contraction hit before she could finish her little plea to Nurse Mae. "No, Mrs. Poslusny," said Nurse Mae firmly. "Just another push and we're there. If you could reserve your breath for pushing instead of screaming, we might get this child out quicker. Thank you."

Margot hollered bloody murder. Toby paced the corridor outside, finding himself chanting the Shema for the first time in years.

Nurse Mae reached between Margot's legs and felt the position of the baby. Still high up in the cervix. But instead of a head, a leg. She looked up at Margot. "I'll be right back," she said, and rushed out to find a doctor.

Another contraction rolled like a steel tank across Margot's body. Boy, did I remember what that felt like. They say you forget, but you don't. And, of course, watching it all over again certainly jogs the memory. I watched the bloody jaws of the contraction bite down, hard, and I closed my eyes and laid my hands on her pelvis. And then, beside me, another angel. A young man, early twenties, with cappucino hair that brushed against his jaw and a quiet intensity about his eyes. Something about him was very familiar. I squinted at him.

"Do I know you?"

He looked at the scene on the hospital bed and winced. "James," he said quickly without taking his eyes off Margot. "I'm Theo's guardian angel."

Margot screamed again. She struggled to get off the bed.

"Hold on," I told her. "I'm trying to turn Theo."

"Theo?" she moaned. I looked up. She'd heard me. Another shocker: She was looking at me as if she could see me.

"Nurse," she pleaded, reaching out for me. "Give me drugs. Give me anything. I can't take much more of this."

My eyes, I daresay, were wide as saucers. It had been well over a decade since she'd last seen me. I wondered for a moment what I appeared like to her. Then she yelled again and I snapped out of it.

"The baby is coming out breech," I said calmly. "I'm going to try to turn him. But you need to stay as still as you can." I flashed a look at the door. I could hear voices at the end of the corridor: the nurse and doctor returning.

"How can you see it's a boy?" she panted.

I ignored her and placed my hand on top of her stomach. I glanced at James, who looked a little scared. "Get over here," I said. "You're Theo's angel, right?"

James nodded.

"Then get that little guy to turn the way he's supposed to."

James placed his hands on top of mine, closed his eyes, and immediately gold light flooded across Margot's body. I tried to absorb some of the pain as I had done so many times before. I squeezed my eyes shut and, when the next contraction hit, I grabbed it, pulled it like a metal bar, and yanked it toward me. And just like Rose had walked inside me, so did that metal bar journey all the way through me to my wings, traveling through them to some other part of the universe. Margot sighed in relief.

I could see the baby now, little Theo, frightened and confused, starting to gravitate upside down. Margot was screaming again, the contractions collapsing on top of her like toppling skyscrapers. I moved closer to her head and placed my hand on her heart.

"You need to try and be as calm as you can," I said. "Theo needs you to breathe slow, slow, *slow*."

She breathed as slowly and as deeply as she could, and just as James turned the baby into its final position, lowering him down toward the cold entrance to the world, the doctor and the nurse walked in.

"Oh my word!" the nurse said, for the baby's head was right there, and she arrived just at the moment that Margot gave that last, amazing push, feeling the whole child exhale out of her, head first.

"Mrs. Poslusny," the nurse said, gasping, "you've quite the little boy, here."

Margot struggled to lift her head. "Theo," she said. "I think his name is Theo."

Theo Graham Poslusny, all ten pounds of him, curled into Margot's breast and didn't stop nursing until nightfall.

Margot had problems with her placenta, and so they kept her in the hospital a few days, wheeling the baby into the children's unit at nights so she could sleep. I suppose I should have let James do his job while I watched over Margot, but I couldn't help it. I was smitten by the pink loaf mewling in the plastic crib, his lick of flame-red hair covered by the woolen hat that Rose had knitted several months before. He was so hungry that he spent all night searching for an invisible breast, but the nurses shushed him with a pacifier, and I stroked his beautiful face.

Eventually, James approached me. I figured he was very brave.

"Look," he said after several moments of standing silently beside me by Theo's crib. "It's my job to be watching over Theo. You're supposed to be with Margot."

I glanced past him at Margot, who I could see through the closed curtain of her hospital cubicle. She was fast asleep.

"What, you think I'm not watching her? I can see her fine. Or had you forgotten I'm an angel? We can do these things, you know."

He cocked his head and frowned

"Maybe I should explain my relationship to Theo—"

I cut him off. "All I care about is that you make sure he doesn't wind up serving a life sentence for murder."

From the corner of my eye, I saw him take a step back. Maybe I'd been a little abrupt, I thought. He was probably some distant relative of Toby's. An uncle, or something. In any case, I had no need to bite his head off. But the truth was, I wanted Theo all to myself. I had an opportunity that I thought I'd never had—and never believed I'd ever want—to experience the miracle of my firstborn child all over again. I felt like a she-wolf, snarling at predators. I wanted James to take a backseat. But, clearly, he was a little more dedicated than that.

I turned to face him. "I'm sorry, all right?" I said, holding my hand out as a gesture of sincerity.

He met my gaze and ignored my hand. For a while we stared at each other like that, me sinking deeper into the echo of my careless words, James silently refusing my apology. Finally, when Theo began to whimper, he stood up. I moved to stroke Theo's cheek, but James got there first. He placed his hand over Theo's head, and immediately he began to drift back to sleep.

"You don't have to like me," James murmured without meeting my eyes. "But I ask you to trust me."

I nodded. A second apology formed itself silently in my mouth. James turned his back to me, and I slipped quietly back to Margot.

Several days later, Margot arrived home to a sparkling clean apartment, replete with a freshly painted nursery, kitted out with every single baby item she'd oohed and aahed at in the baby store. Toby, well ahead of his time, insisted that his employer grant him a week's paternity leave. When his request was denied, he took it anyway, and promptly received the sack. But doesn't the sight of a newborn fill the world with hope? Jobless, penniless, and with the resounding screams of cop cars all around, Toby felt his little family was invincible.

The best was yet to come: He informed Margot that, with the last of their savings, he had paid for Graham to fly into JFK the next day to meet his grandson. And this is where I sang the Song of Souls for the first time in a long while.

"Call Papa," I told Margot, and at first the idea sank like a stone amid her excitement.

"Call him?" she thought. "But I don't have time . . . . I have so much to do before he gets here."

I urged her again, and finally she relented.

I listened, crying tears of joy and sadness at the phone call I never made, relieved that somehow, someone out there allowed me to rearrange the pieces just a little, just enough to say the things I had never said.

"Papa!"

The gravelly sounds of hacking and coughing. As usual, she'd messed up the time difference. But, no matter.

"Papa, Toby's just told me! How long are you staying? Are you getting the first flight tomorrow morning?"

A pause. "Yes, yes, Margot, my love. The flight leaves at seven, so a taxi is coming for me around four..." Theo started to wail. "Is that my grandson I hear?"

Toby passed Theo to Margot and she held the phone receiver close to Theo, letting him howl all the way to England. Eventually she passed him to Toby. He latched immediately onto Toby's pinky and started suckling.

"I think he's hungry," Toby whispered. She nodded.

"Papa, I have to go. But I can't wait to see you tomorrow. Travel safely, okay?"

Silence. "Papa?"

"I love you my sweet girl."

"I love you too, Papa. See you soon."

"See you soon."

�֍֎

And while Margot fidgeted and bounced all day, unable to be still with excitement, I paced the room, at once overwhelmed with relief at being able to fit the piece that was always missing and devastated at what was to come. For I knew I could only change so much. Even now, there was so much beyond my control.

The phone call came late the following morning from Mrs. Bieber, Graham's next-door neighbor, to inform Margot tenderly and tentatively that she'd received a knock on the door just an hour ago from a taxi driver who had discovered Graham sitting at his doorstep, briefcase in hand, cold and unmoving. He had passed quietly, she said, and without pain.

Margot would not be comforted. I sat beside her, locked inside the small bathroom, and wept the same tears that dripped steadily into her palms.

You know, I'd managed to convince myself that the feelings that set in soon after Theo's birth were of my own making. Now, seeing the hormones knotting themselves in Margot's head, witnessing nerve cells accelerating until they collided, I saw the physiological portrait of postpartum depression firsthand. Each time Theo screamed—which he would often do, for hours on end—a red wave would travel across her body, and her nerve cells would travel faster until her whole body trembled from the inside out. She seemed to feed him all day, every day. She was anemic—though the doctors assured her she wasn't—and a cervical infection had gone unnoticed. And she found that she suddenly hated Toby. She hated him because he had the magical gift of being able to sleep soundly while the baby howled from the crib right by his head. She hated him because he didn't have to turn himself into all-milking, all-bleeding baby machine. She hated him because she was exhausted, confused, and scared out of her wits by the thought of another day enduring the chaos.

I watched as Toby struggled to please her. And then, a pleasant surprise. Toby's book, *Black Ice*, hit the national best-seller list.

Now, this I did know. But I didn't know it until months after the fact. Toby took the phone call and thanked his publisher, watching Margot as she struggled to feed Theo for the seventh time in an hour, her face red with tears. I could see now what I didn't understand at the time—Theo wasn't getting any milk. The swallowing noises he was making were gulps of air. And while his little tummy ached with hunger, Margot's breasts were ablaze with excess milk.

"Do something!" I hissed at James.

He flicked his eyes at me. "I'm trying."

Gaia stepped in. "Let *me* try." She whispered something to Toby.

He put down the phone and approached Margot.

"Honey?"

She ignored him. He put an arm on her shoulder.

"Margot?"

"What is it, Toby?"

"Why don't you go out for a few hours. I can watch the baby."

She looked up at him. "You don't have breasts, Toby. He'll need feeding again in another ten minutes."

Toby smiled. "No, but I can feed him powdered milk. Go on, take yourself to a hair salon, or something. Treat yourself."

"You're serious?"

"Absolutely."

"We don't have any money."

He looked away. He was a bad liar, even when it was doing some good. "Let's just say, I saved a little for moments like this."

"Really?"

"Really."

"How much?"

"Stop asking! Just take the checkbook and go! Get a facial, a pedicure, whatever it is you girls do to your nails, just go on, get out of here.'

She was out of there faster than you can say "Swedish massage."

I followed her down the steps, along the street toward the bus stop. My wings were pulsing with messages: *Encourage her to walk. Don't let her take the bus.*

Why? I thought. I looked at the bus approaching. *Why?* I asked again, but no response. *Fine,* I thought. *You ain't telling me, I ain't listening.*

We took our seats at the back. Margot pressed a handkerchief against her head, the pain across her chest easing in the cool breeze rushing in from the open window. The bus stopped at Eleventh Avenue. Another handful of passengers came onboard. One of them made her way toward us and sat in the seat opposite, facing Margot. And my stomach turned.

The woman was the double of Hilda Marx. The bright orange hair threaded with silver and piled up on her head, the forever-red nose startling her face, the bulldog underbite. I watched Margot draw her breath sharply, staring as the woman shook off her coat—a black trench coat, so similar to the one Hilda had worn outdoors—and chomped her jaw, exactly the way Hilda had done. After a moment or too, it was clear that the woman wasn't Hilda. Someone further down the bus recognized her as Karen, and when she smiled and chatted, her face took on a different appearance. Her voice registered her as born and bred in New Jersey.

And of course, I should have remembered this. I looked on helplessly as Margot's thoughts turned to St. Anthony's. Her skin crawled with memories of the Tomb, the fear and humiliation and hopelessness that infused her memories of the place dredged to the forefront of her mind like a wreck rising to the surface, all its bloated, dead bodies showing their vile faces to the sun. She stared at her feet and panted. I pressed my hands on her shoulders and soothed her: *You're right here, right now. All that is behind you. You are safe.* She took slow, deep breaths and struggled to ignore the images that flooded her vision: Hilda beating her with the coal sack. Hilda dragging her out of the Tomb, only to drag her back in again. Hilda telling her she was nothing.

She got off the bus at the next stop and walked quickly, though she wasn't quite sure where she was or where she was going. The idea of a massage had long disappeared. In its place was an overwhelming desire to get wasted. She wished for a moment that she could call Xiao Chen and head to the bar at NYU. Within a second, it was decided that she would go by herself.

Okay, I said out loud. To God, I think. *I'm listening now. Send me messages, some clue of what I'm supposed to do here. You see, I know what happens. I know she spends fifty dollars on rows of shots, and I know she makes out with some guy whose name escapes me, and I know she rolls out of there at midnight, having all but forgotten that she's got a husband and a home. Oh, and a kid.*

And you know what? Nada. Not a whisper. No messages in my wings, no instinct. Of course, I talked to Margot, I yelled at the top of my lungs, I sang the Song of Souls . . . But she tuned me out. The worst of it was, when we reached the bar, there was Grogor, waiting at the entrance. As Margot walked inside, he put his arm around her waist and escorted her in. And I could do nothing.

The reason that Toby didn't tell Margot about his success with *Black Ice* is because, for weeks afterward, they didn't speak. An old NYU colleague called him from the bar when he spotted Margot necking cocktails and snogging a student. The call went like this:

The phone rings in Toby and Margot's kitchen at eleven at night. Toby's out of powdered milk, and all the stores are shut. Theo is screeching.

"Hello?" He immediately holds the phone away from his ear. There's loud music on the other end.

"Hey, buddy. Jed here. Say, Tobes, didn't you have a kid recently?"

A beat. "Uh-huh."

"And ... didn't you get married to a blonde chick called Margot?"

"Uh-huh."

"And where might she be right about now?"

Toby looks around. He fell asleep a while ago. He checks the bedroom.

"Not sure. Why?"

"Buddy, I don't know how to tell you this. I think she's here."

"Where?"

❈

And so, Toby picks up the baby, wraps him up, and both of them drive all the way to where Margot is holding hands with another guy while puking her lungs up beneath a lamppost.

I watched, helpless and penitent—more penitent than you can ever imagine—as Toby pulled up alongside Margot, checking on Theo before jumping out of the car. Gaia and James stayed in the car. I looked away. Toby approached Margot, and she knew he was there but refused to answer, until at last he said, "Theo needs you," and something of that responsibility, that love, sank in, and she staggered to the car, almost falling on top of Theo on the front seat.

※○※

There are no words.

There are no words to describe what happened to me that night.

All I know is:

I wanted to change everything. I wanted to rip away the curtain that divided me and Margot and I wanted to leap back inside her flesh and beg forgiveness from Toby. I wanted to pick Theo up and I wanted to run away with him, I wanted to take him far, far away from this terrible, broken woman, and at the same time I wanted to heal all her wounds, I wanted to turn back time and I wanted to meet God and rant at him for all that had happened to make her this way.

From that night, a marriage that had been fatally stabbed before it even began lay bleeding in the silence between Toby and Margot, and Toby spent his days writing, and Margot edited Rose's notebooks, and Theo looked from one sad face to the other, and then at me. I told him I loved him, that I loved his father. That I was sorry.

And I prayed that someone, somewhere, would hear me.

20

The Chance to Change

WHEN THE SHEER AWFULNESS OF THAT NIGHT HAD REDUCED TO THE SIZE OF A BAD MEMORY, WHEN TOBY FINALLY, FINALLY LISTENED TO GAIA'S SUGGESTION THAT HE FORGIVE MARGOT, THEY DECIDED TO TRY AGAIN.

It was the happiest day of my life, both before and after my death.

Margot had seen a poster for Toby's book on a bus stop. She came home, stooped over with a sack of groceries, and was met with his back.

It was a familiar greeting. But this time, she was angry. And she was hurt.

"How come you never told me about your book?"

A beat. "Huh?" He didn't turn around.

She dumped the groceries on the floor. "Your book," she said again. "Your 'international best-selling' book. Why am I the last to know? Everyone at Port Authority knows about it. I'm your *wife*."

At last, he turned. She suddenly realized it had been over a week since she'd looked into his eyes.

"My wife," he whispered, trying out the word like a foreign language. "My wife."

Her face softened. Suddenly, without knowing why, she burst into tears.

"My wife," Toby said again, rising from his seat, slowly making his way toward her.

"I'm sorry," she said through tears.

"I'm sorry too," Toby said, wrapping his arms around her. She didn't pull away.

I can tell you, every time one of those messages came via my wings, I listened, and I acted as instructed. I didn't question who, what, where, or why again. It simply didn't matter if it was God or another angel or my own conscience sending those messages. The fact was, had I listened, had I encouraged Margot *not* to get on that bus, the iceberg that almost sunk their marriage may well have been avoided.

And I saw that it wasn't just their marriage that had been wounded. Toby was a different person. His eyes were filled with a sadness that hadn't been there before. He took to adding whisky to his coffee. First a splash, then a shot. He looked at other women and thought: *What if? What if I married the wrong woman?*

It was unbearable. The memories of our breakup came fast and thick, with all the animosity and betrayal that accompanied it. And I thought, I caused it. I caused him to cheat.

But still, a question mark continued to hang above that issue like the sword of Damocles. I'd never actually caught him in the act. In fact, much of the reason why I believed he'd cheated had faded into the ether. Actual evidence aside, it had always been pretty unquestionable. He had slept with Sonya. And I had despised him for it.

✿

Shortly after Theo's first birthday, when Margot and Toby's joy at witnessing Theo's first efforts to walk were soured by the realization that their chubby little boy could now negotiate the living-room window, which swung open above concrete some four stories below, they relocated to a place in the West Village, close to Toby's old loft apartment, though five times the size of that place. A healthy royalty check for Toby's book afforded the kind of home interiors that realized Margot's ideals of comfort and security: a cast-iron bed, too many couches, their first TV, and eventually, a telephone. It was as if a giant net had suddenly appeared under Margot's world. At last, she felt safe. And she was happy.

And so the rest of the household was happy. James and I even managed to put our little power struggle well behind us. James, Gaia, and I, forming our own little family of angels, watched over the other trio, Theo, Toby, and Margot, who slowly but surely moved away from the junkyard of their past to a more promising, less destructive future. Toby spent evenings writing his new book while Margot critiqued and copyedited his drafts, and during the days they took Theo to the park, teaching him all the names of the animals in the zoo, holding him tightly between them when he cried at the sound of sirens, gunshots, or arguments from next door.

Eventually, Toby managed to persuade Margot to strike up her drowning friendship with Sonya.

THE GUARDIAN ANGEL'S JOURNAL •

"No way," she argued. "Are you crazy? After she kicked us out of her apartment with nowhere to go?"

Toby considered bringing up Sonya's stolen locket, but bit his tongue.

"Fine," he said. "I just . . . I hate seeing you alone, you know? Moms need a support network." He'd been watching Oprah again. He sighed. "I just think it would be healthy for you to have female company. And you and Son used to be like . . . "

"Like what?"

"Sisters, man. You were like *that*." He crossed his middle finger over his index. "Tight, you know?"

Yes, I thought. We were. Once upon a time.

Margot insisted that Toby make the call. Satisfied that Sonya wasn't going to reject her, she took the receiver from him. Eventually, with Toby mouthing the words from the other side of the room, she managed to say, "Why don't you pop over for dinner?" though she said it as a statement, not a question. She hated having to beg.

I wasn't completely sold on the idea either. My suspicions were not diminished, not in the slightest. But I did nothing. I watched as the three of them spent a perfectly pleasant evening sprawled out on the new leather couches, toasting Toby's success while Theo, now four years old, slept like a log. And I waited.

Sonya had been living in Paris for the last couple of years. Thinner, towering in her six-inch platform shoes, she peppered her conversation with French words and the names of celebrities and famous photographers. Margot fidgeted in her armchair. She looked down at her tatty yard-sale sweater with holes under the armpits, the jeans that were starting to rub holes at the knees.

Then she looked over at Sonya, dripping in Parisian couture, her long swimsuit legs. *She's so beautiful*, Margot thought. Forget it, I told her. She's bulimic and lonely. *Why couldn't I have been like her? Maybe Toby would've been better off with her instead of me.* And for the first time, I saw it: like an anorexic who finally looks at the photos of their skeletal self and says, Yes, I really *wasn't* fat, I thought, Yes. I get it now. It wasn't Toby who didn't love me. It was *me* who didn't love me.

So I persisted with the rant. Toby loves you, I told her. But as she watched Sonya direct her tedious account of the artistic community of Montmartre to Toby, reaching over every so often to flick an invisible speck of dust from his trouser leg, Margot descended into the gloom of her self-defeat. Eventually Sonya grabbed Toby's hand and pumped it up and down. "Promise you'll come visit me in Paris, Tobes, please!"

Gaia struggled to bring Margot's expression to Toby's attention. It had been a while since he'd had four gin and tonics on the trot. As a result, he was leaning closer and closer to Sonya, agreeing to go to Paris and then, to add injury to ignorance, cracking jokes about a past that Margot had had no part of. Finally, Gaia broke the membrane surrounding Toby's lucidity and prodded his conscience. He glanced over at Margot and withdrew his hand from Sonya's.

"Are you okay, honey?" he said softly.

She looked away, disgusted. Just then, a yell from Theo's bedroom.

"I'll get it," Margot said, and walked out of the room.

Toby wasn't so drunk as to remain oblivious to Margot's mood. He turned to Sonya and made a big deal of checking out his wristwatch, holding it close to his nose.

"Hey, Son, it was great to see you, but it's getting kinda late . . . "

Sonya threw a look at him before draining the contents of her glass. She inched forward, holding his gaze.

"Did you tell Margot about our conversation at the diner?"

Margot, in the hallway outside, heard her name being mentioned in hushed tones. She froze at the door, all ears.

Slowly Sonya swung her long legs off the couch and moved closer.

"No," said Toby. "Why?"

Sonya shrugged and smiled. "Hey, you're a married man, I'm not telling you what to do. It's just . . . " She glanced at the door.

"What?"

A wider smile. "I was wondering whose idea it was to have me over for dinner. Yours or hers?"

I remembered this statement as if it had been hardwired into my neuroses. Margot, listening outside, let the questions wrapped around those words carve themselves on her suspicion.

Toby blinked at Sonya, unsure as to what she was getting at. "Mine, I guess."

Sonya nodded. "And what other ideas do you have, may I ask?"

I watched as she slid a hand up Toby's leg, stopping just below the crotch, then giggled. Toby put his hand on top of hers and squeezed.

"Son," he said. "What are you doing?"

At the doorway, Margot could hear the flirtation in Sonya's voice. She placed a hand on the door handle.

Sonya leaned back. "What do you think I'm doing, Toby? Isn't this what you want?"

I was breathing so hard I felt faint. Gaia stood next to me and said *Watch, watch,* and I told her I couldn't. In the doorway,

Margot felt the same. Half of her wanted to burst in, and the other half wanted to run away.

So I watched. Toby, always such a quick draw with words, stuttered incoherently.

"Was that a yes?" Sonya, putting words into his mouth. She pulled his hand toward her thigh. He pulled it away.

Suddenly he sobered right up. "Son, don't be like that." He sat upright, shaking his head. Gaia looked at me, very seriously. He didn't sleep with her? I thought. Didn't?

Sonya lay casually against the back of the sofa, crossing her long legs and playing with the ruffles on her dress. "Just tell me one thing," she said, very serious. Toby looked up at her. "That time you said you loved me—did you mean it?"

I saw Margot in the hallway raise a hand to her mouth. I watched carefully.

"That was so many years ago . . . " Toby mumbled to his feet.

"Did you mean it?" Sonya, insistent. Desperate, even. Ezekiel emerged from his space in the corner and placed a hand on her shoulder. There was a vulnerability, an ache, to her question, rooted in something far beyond Toby.

Toby looked up at her. "Yes."

She darted forward, sweeping her right leg across him, straddling him, then leaned down to kiss him.

And yes, this was the moment Margot came back into the room.

This was the moment all hell broke loose.

This was the moment my marriage ended.

Margot made him pack his bags the next morning. Her emotions slammed down a fortress against all my pleadings, against all Toby's excuses. So he took a change of clothes and camped out at a friend's house. After a month, he took over the rent when his friend moved upstate. Margot was numb. I was devastated. After six months, Margot filed for a legal separation. On the morning that he received the letter, Toby pulled a mirror off the wall and smashed it on the floor, a mosaic of frustration. In every sliver my face appeared, just for an instant, before being smeared into oblivion by his tears.

My heartbreak at their separation soon turned into all-out desperation as I reflected on what I recalled about my life immediately before I died. The circumstances of my death were still unresolved: One day I was alive; the next I was looking down at my dead body and, in a flash, chatting with Nan in the afterlife. But the period before that was clear in my memory as glacier water: Theo had been sent to prison. For life. And something in my gut was starting to turn the finger of blame in my direction.

Shortly after, Grogor appeared. He decided to make his appearance in Theo's bedroom—an implicit threat, I thought—which made Theo yell out in his sleep. It distracted Margot long enough for him to have a chat with me.

I don't know why, and I don't wish to know how, but Grogor was no longer the foul-faced, burning monster I'd first encountered. He was exceedingly human. Tall, square jawed, with inky black hair slicked over his ears—the type of man I'd have found myself attracted to once upon a time. He even had a five o'clock shadow and a chipped front tooth. So human that it took me off guard.

"I come in peace," he said, holding up his hands and smiling.

"Get out, Grogor," I said, holding up a hand full of light. I hadn't forgotten our last tango.

"Please, don't," he said, pressing his hands together in penitence. "I've come to apologize. Sincerely."

I shot a beam of light at him, forceful as a car slam, and knocked him across the room. He landed against the chest of drawers and coughed on his hands and knees.

"If you don't get out, I'll kill you,' I said.

"Kill me?" He chuckled, struggling to his feet. "Now that I'd like to see."

"Fine," I said, shrugging. "I'm comfy with just blasting you to pieces." I held up another smaller ball of light and aimed it at his legs.

"Don't!" he said, crouching slightly. I cocked my head. He held up a hand. "I think I have a very generous offer to make. Hear me out."

"You have ten seconds."

He stood upright and tugged at his jacket, gathering his composure. "I know you want to change things. I know Margot is busy screwing up an otherwise wonderful life, a life you would at least like to have some good memories of, a life that you would've like to have paved a better future for Theo . . . "

I turned and faced him. My wings were sending messages, fast and furious. *Get him out now. He is wrapping lies in truth. Get him out.*

"Get out, Grogor, before I show you my nasty side."

He smiled. "Understood." He walked toward the window, then turned. "Should you change your mind, I promise you there's a way. You can prevent Theo's fate."

And with that, he was gone.

Immediately, Theo was calm. Margot stroked his face and he drifted back to sleep, his face still as morning mist. Margot sat beside him and pushed thoughts of Toby to the back of her mind. I looked at her and thought, I can still change things. I can still make it right.

21

The Usual Suspects

"What would happen if I changed the outcome of Margot's life?"

We were on the roof of Margot's apartment, looking down over the squares of orange light pulsing from the windows of homes all over the city, silhouetted figures occasionally blotting the light—embracing, arguing, solitary—like insects in amber.

She didn't answer for a long time. And then, a scolding. "You know very well that we are not here to reorchestrate the symphony. We are here to make sure the symphony gets played the way the composer scored it."

I always did struggle with Nan's metaphors. "But you've told me before that I can rearrange the pieces of the jigsaw a little, yes? What if I changed the whole picture. What if I made it better?"

"Who has been to see you?" Always such a sage.

"Grogor," I confessed.

She winced. "The demon who killed your mamma?"

"You said guilt killed Mamma."

"Did Grogor mention the cost of changing the picture, *hmm?*"

"No."

She threw her hands up. "There is always, always a cost. That's why we don't change things beyond what we are instructed: The navigator guides the plane, not the people inside it. But you already know that. Don't you?"

I nodded hastily. "Of course, of course. I was just asking."

"We are here for four purposes. Watch, protect, record —"

"Love." I finished the sentence for her. Yes, I knew all that.

"Just out of curiosity," I said after a respectable pause. "What is the cost?"

She narrowed her eyes. "Why do you want to know?"

I explained—as best I could to someone not actually in the maddening position of being their own guardian angel, of having to suffer the most soul-crushing regret on a constant basis—that there were simply some things about my past that I would have liked to have done a little better. And that I wanted so much more for Theo. So much more than a prison sentence for murder.

"The cost is this," she said, holding out an empty palm. "Right now, you have the chance to go to heaven right in the palm of your hand. Angels are not just servants, you know. We are given work to prove that we are worthy to get into heaven, because most of us didn't do enough of that sort of work in life. The cost is this." She splatted her other hand on top of her open palm. "When you finish being an angel, you don't see heaven."

I started to cry. I told her I was in love with Toby, that Margot was busy filing for divorce. Which placed a reunion with Toby on the wrong side of possibility.

She sighed. "I was once where you are now. Asking questions, feeling regret, feeling loss. You will see God. You will see heaven. And in heaven, there is only joy. Remember that."

But every time I watched the looks of longing and pain in Toby's face as he collected Theo, every time I watched Margot's dreams of her life with Toby, watched her cry and deepen the hatred at Toby's betrayal, Grogor's words rang in my ears, until the lies peeking out from behind them shrank into insignificance.

Do we ever identify the cookie-cutter moments, the moments that pressed into the dough of our lives and made an eternal shape? Could we *ever* spot such moments, even if we could go back and relive our lives, even if we could line up all the offending moments of our lives like the usual suspects, could we point them out? *Yes, officer, it's the suspect with the cutting remark. Yes, sir, he's the one—the one who resembles my father. Why yes, I recognize that one—the one that tipped my life into the gutter.*

I had all but given up on recognizing my own defining moments. Margot was who Margot was, and all I could do was what I had originally been assigned to do. I was struggling with the last, but most important, part of my job: loving her. She certainly made it tough. Consider this moment:

Margot is getting ready for work. She is also itching for a drink. She finds the bottle behind the fireplace and hurls it at a wall. It's empty. The glass shatters everywhere. Theo wakes. He is already late for school. He is seven. He has his father's calm eyes and red hair. He has Margot's temperament: fast as a whippet to anger, though just as fast to love. He adores his father. He tries to write stories like his dad, but he struggles with dyslexia. His backward letters and weird spelling make him mad.

Margot is yelling at Theo to get out of bed. She's the one who neglected to wake him, but she forgets this, and he scrambles out of his bedsheets and makes for the bathroom. He tries to pee, but while he's at it, Margot knocks him out of the way as she searches behind the tank. He shouts. She shouts back. She has a raging headache and he's making it worse. He makes everything worse, she tells him. He always has. What do you mean? he yells. You're the one who's drunk all the time. She responds to his question. What do I mean? I mean, my life would have been better without you in it. *My life would have been better if you'd never been born.* Fine, he says. I'll go live with dad. And he gets dressed for school and slams the door, and then when he comes home no one talks.

Theo's defining moment was not the moment Margot announced that she wished he'd never been born. He'd been hearing *that* kind of stuff for a while. No. Theo's defining moment was a little further down the line, but at the beginning of that line was the sight of Margot searching frantically for vodka. Despite having reached the conclusion that his ma was a wino, that she was stir crazy, and what was his dad even thinking when he married her—despite all this, a question: *What's so good about it that she's searching for it like the elixir of eternal youth?*

And on the back of this question, an answer, when presented with an open bottle of Jack Daniel's at the age of ten:

Sure.

And on the heels of that answer, a consequence. Blinding drunkenness. And amid the drunkenness, a fight with a younger kid. A younger kid carrying a knife. A knife that made its way into Theo's hand. A knife that ended up in the younger kid's gut.

And so, the New York City Department of Juvenile Justice decided that Theo needed to spend a month in a detention center with other juvenile offenders. Juvenile offenders who had a history of rape and grievous bodily harm, which they continued to carry out upon their inmates. Theo was one of them.

I learned this from James. He returned with Theo a month later, his face like petrified wood, his wings pouring blood. And when I saw Theo, I wept with James. Around Theo's bronze, shimmering aura was a jagged armor of pain, so dense and leaden that he seemed to stoop under its weight. When I looked closer, I could see strange tentacles straggling inward from the armor, cutting through his aura and traveling all the way to his heart. It was like a stiff, unyielding parachute wrapped around him, strapped to his soul. This was the worst kind of emotional fortress that any of us had ever seen—Theo was making himself a prisoner inside his own pain.

He didn't speak to Toby for days. He set his bags in his room, then dug the steak knives from the back of the kitchen drawer and stashed them under his bed. When the counselor called, Theo threatened to jump out of the window if he tried to talk to him.

That night I watched Theo's nightmares fill his bedroom. Fresh memories of his attackers in the detention center. Two boys punching him in the gut with a knuckle-duster smuggled in by a visitor. Another older boy holding his head underwater until he lost consciousness. The same boy holding a pillow over his face at night. The same boy raping him.

And if that wasn't enough, parallel worlds spiraled among the clustering nightmares, flashing images of Theo as an older man, his body smattered with tattoos, both wrists showing signs of repeated suicide attempts. At first, I was relieved to see that he was no longer in prison. But I watched as he tucked a gun into his pants, opened the trunk of his car, and helped another man drag a heavy body bag out of it. When the body bag twitched, Theo drew his gun and let off four rounds.

Another world showed him on parole. Another world showed him slapping a woman—a lover—across the face. The armor he'd grown was no longer a second skin: It had changed him into a living weapon.

What would you have done? Would it have mattered what it cost?

I walked out into the night air, made my way to the top of the apartment block, and called out for Grogor.

Instantly, a set of feet appeared in the shadows. He stepped forward, his face solemn, both eyes as penetrating as blades.

"Tell me why."

"Why what?"

"Why you've changed your mind?"

I stared at him. "Just tell me your price."

"My *price*? Am I a salesman?"

"You know what I mean."

He moved closer, so close I could see the veins in his neck, the feathery lines fanning outward from his cheekbones. So like a man.

"I think the word you're searching for is *opportunity*. To become mortal long enough to do what needs to be done, you will need to put a plug in both of these." He pointed at my wings.

"And how is that done?"

He pressed a hand against his chest and bowed. "I would be *deeply* honored. They need to be sealed up, or to put it another way, they have to be damned from the river of eternity that flows before the throne of God, so that God can no longer see what you're up to. And this is how you get the opportunity to change what must be changed. Understand?"

"Come on, Grogor. What else?"

He feigned puzzlement. I stared. He broke off my gaze and shrugged.

"Depending on your stance, there is a risk."

"And what is that?"

He paused. "What do you think God would think of one of his angels going against the rules?"

"I may never see heaven."

He applauded very slowly. "You may never see heaven."

But neither would Theo.

Do you think I even hesitated?

22

AND SO, JUST AS CINDERELLA STEPPED OUT OF HER RAGS AND
INTO THE BALL GOWN, SO DID I STEP OUT OF MY BLUE DRESS
AND INTO TIME.

I allowed Grogor to apply hot fistfuls of tar from the bowels
of hell to my wings, and then, when the water stopped, when I
began to *feel*, I screamed as the sensation of pain hit my skin from
the tar, I shivered as the wet cold from the bathroom tiles spread
beneath my bare feet, and then I staggered, overwhelmed by the
weight of my own body, as if an elephant had been dumped on
me from a great height.

Not as graceful as Cinderella. But I did leave behind a glass
slipper.

Or at least, as soon as I undressed, my blue dress shrank to
a small, blue jewel. I hid it in Margot's chest of drawers. I was
already a spy in the human world. I had to hide every trace of what
I'd done until I'd accomplished what I'd set out to accomplish.

I'd chosen my timing carefully. I had watched as Margot's
divorce lawyer advised her to spend four weeks in rehab to prove

to the judge that she was fit as a mother. To prove that she deserved full custody or, worst case, partial custody. No problem, she'd said, though she wasn't sure she really wanted either. She only knew she wanted to win something, anything, to prove she hadn't lost absolutely everything.

So, as Margot checked into Riverstone, an up-market addiction-recovery clinic close to the Hamptons, I found myself alone in her apartment, peeling through her clothes in the wardrobe, drinking her milk, occupying her space in the world. Theo was staying at Toby's place around the corner. I spent that first day, mesmerized by the feeling of skin and hair, the sensation of warmth and cold, of the sound of my hand as I slapped it on the table, of eating pizza. As I hacked that fourteen-inch, cheese-crusted deep-pan double pepperoni with extra mozzarella, I caught the tip of my thumb with the bread knife. For a moment, I stared at it dumbly, and then the blood globed from the white slice, spilling suddenly down my arm like red ink, and I almost forgot what to do about it until I glanced at the vase of sunflowers on the dining table and plunged my whole arm in, and my whole hand throbbed and burned.

Everything was so solid. When I looked at a table, I didn't see through it to the next room, I didn't see the traces of the people who had sat there or the whorls in the wood beneath the varnish. I didn't see time dancing like a dust storm of waves and particles. Anyone watching me that night would've called in the white coats, for sure. I spent a lot of time inching along the walls, cheek to plaster, amazed by the sudden, familiar materiality of this world, knocking on brick, remembering the illusion of limits that pervade mortality, the deep, unremitting acceptance that comes with a body full of blood.

Perhaps the greatest of my crimes was abandoning Margot, leaving her unprotected at a time when she was most in need. Reluctantly, I called on Nan, knowing what I was in for.

Eventually, a voice that sounded very far away, as though the speaker were at the end of the long corridor.

"Do you understand what you have done?"

I looked around. "Where are you?"

"By the table."

I looked. "Why can't I see you?"

"Because you did a deal with a demon. A deal that may cost you everything and gain you nothing."

Her voice quavered, ripped through with emotion. I made for the table. At last, I saw her. She was standing behind the vase of sunflowers, appearing as a shaft of moonlight.

"I knew you wouldn't understand, Nan," I sighed. "This isn't permanent. I've got seven days to find a way to undo what's been done."

"You may not have seven hours," she replied.

"What?"

The light around her shook as she gave a long sigh. "You are as vulnerable as a paper boat in a tsunami. Do you know what a target you are to demons right now? You don't have an angel's ability to fight them, or a human's God-given defense against them, because right now you are neither. Instead, you are Grogor's puppet. He won't wait to find out whether or not God will send you to hell. He'll try and take you there himself."

I absorbed the impact of her words. The truth of them made my knees weaken.

"Help me," I whispered.

She reached and took my hand in hers. Her skin, always dark and grooved, glittered around mine in a fine mist.

"I'll do everything I can."

And she left me alone again, leaving me to look out helplessly across the city, aching for the presence of archangels.

⚶

I slept late, rolled out of bed onto the wood floor, then burned myself in the shower when I forgot that red meant hot and blue meant cold. I tugged on Margot's jeans and black shirt and fumbled around for scraps of makeup. I glanced in the mirror: I looked younger than Margot was right now, a little slimmer, a little healthier. My hair was longer, darker, my eyebrows fairer and regrettably thicker than hers. I found some lipstick, tweezers, and blush, then poured a bottle of bleach on my head and hoped for the best. Next, scissors. By the time I had finished, I had forgotten all about the threat of demons, determined to stay on course with my plan.

⚶

I strode out into the cool Manhattan morning, deciding to take the bus to Theo's school, but then I found myself enjoying the feel of the wind on my face so much that I walked the whole thirty blocks. A woman walking by said "Good morning," and I said, "It is, isn't it?", and then a homeless guy wanted change, and I stopped to tell him how lucky he was to be alive, and he gaped at me as I walked away, laughing, reveling in how I could talk to people and they would listen and talk back.

I slowed my pace as I approached the gates to Theo's school. I had to consider my next moves very carefully. This wasn't a dream anymore, not a letter I could rewrite, not a performance I could restage. It felt like every word, every action was now being carved into stone. No, it felt stronger than that, more consequential. It felt like I was cutting into the stone that had already been carved. And if I wasn't careful, that stone might just split in two.

I figured that I would wait for the school bell, meet Theo at the front gates, invite him to take a walk. But what if Toby was there? What if Theo saw me and bolted? I decided to go into the school, take him out of class. If the teachers told him he had to go with me, he probably would. Albeit, with a groan.

I presented myself at reception. I recognized Cassie, the heavy-lidded school receptionist, and cracked a smile. She didn't return it; I remembered we'd crossed paths several times before. She looked me up and down, pursed her lips and said:

"May I help you?"

I couldn't help but giggle. I was still wowed by the fact that people were talking to me all over the place. She probably thought I was high.

"Hey, how are you? Um. Yeah. I'm Ruth . . . no, sorry. That's not right. I'm Margot. Margot Delacroix."

She stared at me, eyes wide. Yep, I'd made a pig's ear of that. *I'm Margot, Margot, Margot,* I told myself. And then I realized I'd said it out loud, which made Cassie's mouth drop open.

"I'm Theo Poslusny's mom," I continued, very slowly, as if English was my second language. "I have to take him out of class for a little bit. Got a family emergency."

I jammed my lips together. Too dangerous to talk, I thought. Cassie lifted the phone and dialed. It was fifty-fifty whether she was calling the psych unit or Theo's teacher.

"Yuh-huh, this is the front desk. We got Theo Poslusny's mom up here. She wants to talk to him. Yuh-huh. Whatever."

She put down the phone, blinked at me, then said:

"He's on his way."

I saluted and clicked my heels. I swear, it was like I had Tourette's. I looked around, spotted a chair and ran to it, crossing my ankles and folding my arms.

And then, Theo. Theo with his backpack slung over his shoulder, his blue shirt half hanging out over his pants, his red hair spiked with pomade and curling at the nape of his neck like petals. Theo, with his father's blotchy freckles, his nose still cute and mushroomy, his sneakers muddy and falling apart, his face crumpled in confusion and suspicion and hardness.

And yes, I burst into tears. And I resisted the urge to fall to my knees and beg forgiveness for everything, even stuff he hadn't experienced yet. I forced back the wave of guilt that I wanted to spew by his feet, and I struggled just to say, "Hey, Theo," as if the words couldn't fit into my mouth, as if they were too big with longing and years of waiting and the sudden, blinding ache in my heart to hold him.

He just stared. Cassie to the rescue.

"Theo," she said, smiling. "Your mom says there's been a family emergency. You just take the time you need to get things together, okay? No pressure. You know I got your back, hey buddy?" She winked. I was grateful for the interlude. I pulled myself together and gulped back tears. Theo, still bewildered, allowed me to put a hand on his shoulder and walked with me out into the sunlight.

It was at least a couple of blocks before he spoke.

"Is Dad dead?"

I forgot all about my "family emergency" fib. I stopped.

"No, no, Toby's fine. I just wanted to . . . spend some time with you, ya know? Have some fun."

Theo shook his head and started to walk away. I ran after him.

"Theo? What's wrong?"

"You *always* do this."

I did?

"What?" I said. "Do what?"

"Leave me alone," he said, and walked faster. "I knew you were lying. What is it you want this time, huh? You gonna kidnap me just to mess with Dad? You wanna poison me against him, is that it? Well, it's *not* happening."

He kept walking. Every word was like a kick in the chest. I stood and watched him for a moment, then came to my senses and bolted up the street after him.

"Theo, hear me out."

He stopped and breathed deeply, refusing to look me in the face.

"What if I said we could do anything in the world, huh? What would be a dream come true for you? What would you like to do more than anything in the whole world?"

He looked up to check I was serious, then considered

"I'd like a hundred dollars."

I thought about it. "Done. What else?"

"A Nintendo. With ten games."

"Okay. What else?"

"I want a Luke Skywalker costume, with the cape, and the boots, and the sword and everything!"

"Good choice. Anything else?"

He thought about it. I tried to steer him in the right direction.

"Anything you'd like to *do*, me and you? Like a trip to the zoo, maybe? Dinner and a movie? C'mon, my treat."

He shrugged. "Nada." And he started walking. Once again, I watched after him. Then I realized James was probably with him.

"James," I whispered. "Help me out here."

A voice. "He wants to play cards with you and Toby."

Cards? Was that all? And then a memory of the three of us flashed in my mind. A time when we trying to work things out. Theo couldn't have been more than five. Toby had started using a deck of cards to teach Theo his two times tables, and before long, we were sitting on the living-room floor, teaching Theo the basic rules of poker, laughing as he wiped the floor with both of us in less than an hour.

It was just one night, just once. And yet, suddenly that boy wanted a game of cards more than a trip to Disneyland or SeaWorld. Go figure.

"How about a game of cards?" I shouted after him. He stopped. I walked toward him quickly. "You know, you, me, and Dad. Like old times."

"You and Dad?" he said, eyeballing me. "But you hate him."

I stood back. If only you knew, I thought. "I don't hate him," was the best I could come up with. "I love your dad."

He saw the truth of it in my eyes. "No way, you don't."

I said it again, and he believed me. I think it shook him up a little, threw possibilities around his head like marbles, lit a candle deep inside.

"I don't want that other stuff," he said. "I just want to play cards."

Phew, I thought. I had no clue how I was going to come up with a hundred dollars.

We went home and I called Toby. I saw Nan there when I hung up my coat—again, she appeared as a shining mist, standing by the stairs—and I breathed a long sigh of relief. She had my back. Still, I had other things to be nervous about. I hadn't planned on dealing with Toby on this trip. It had been all about what I could do for Theo, how I could change him, how I could say and do the things that would heal the wounds I'd inflicted on his young life.

But, of all people, I should have known. Sometimes the stone breaks centuries after the strike.

I called Toby at his apartment. I knew he'd be working at home, wrapping up the edits on his new book. He heard the tone in my voice and said immediately:

"What's wrong?" His voice stiff and suspicious.

"Uh... nothing, absolutely nothing. Theo and I were wondering if you would care to join us this evening for a game of poker."

A pause. "Is this some kind of joke?"

I blinked. Theo was smiling, which was encouraging, making eating gestures at me as I held the receiver against my ear. "And... I think Theo wants us to get takeout." Theo did a kung-fu chop. "Of the Chinese variety."

"Margot." Toby's voice, stern and impatient. "I thought we agreed that you were going into rehab for a month, huh? Or have you broken that promise too?"

The anger in his voice unnerved me. I hesitated. *Gaia*, I thought. *Please let him give me a chance. Just once. Just this time.*

"Toby," I said softly. "I'm sorry. I'm sorry."

I watched Theo's face drop, no, *melt* with stunned joy. And as I listened to Toby's breathing on the other end, slowing, I imagined his mind journeying through conclusions—*Is she high?*

pregnant? terminal?—before arriving at the possibility that I was sincere.

"Look, Margot—" he said, and before he continued I jumped in.

"I'm booked into rehab next week. You have my word, Toby. I promise you. Next week, I'm off to get clean." I laughed. "Now get over here before Theo and I cut the deck without you."

And so, for the first time in over forty years, I sat with my son and my husband and played poker, a game I hadn't played in so long that both of them spent most of the time teaching me the rules all over again, explaining the point of it to me as if I were a two-year-old, finding endless hilarity in how dumb I'd become. And I ate Chinese food—with a fork instead of chopsticks, which provided more hilarity—and then I did anything and everything that made Theo laugh, anything that raised his voice like a feather, carefree into the moonlight, and I started conversations that I knew would set him off on one, the veins in his head bursting with excitement at the new Spielberg movie, at how he was going to be an actor too, and Toby looked back and forth at the two of us, holding his cards up like a peacock's tail, smiling and thinking.

When ten o'clock came, and Theo's little body was about to pop like a whole bag of corn from excitement, Toby took him to bed. A few minutes later, he came downstairs. He took his coat off the armchair, slung it across his thin shoulders, and said:

"Well, good night."

"Wait," I said. He turned the door handle and paused.

"You really have to go so fast?" I forced a laugh. It sounded forced.

He turned. "What do you want, Margot?"

I clasped my hands. "I want you to know that I'm sorry."

He clenched his jaw.

"For what? For getting wasted in front of our kid, all day, every day, for... for weeks? For sleeping with his teacher and making him the laughingstock of the whole school? For sending him out in dirty clothes, for not taking him to a doctor when he had appendicitis, what?"

I opened my mouth. No words would come. He continued.

"Or is it for the way you've treated me, Margot? Boy, we could spend all night compiling *that* list of sins, couldn't we? Tell you what. *I'm* sorry. How's that?"

"Sorry for what?"

"I'm sorry that I can't accept your apology. I don't believe it. I can't."

Without looking at me, he walked out of the room and shut the door behind him.

⚜

I took Theo to school the next day. I had woken up in a wet patch, and I realized: *my wings are coming back. I haven't got long.*

As he walked—no, bounced—alongside me, chatting about when Dad and I were going to have round two of our poker match, how cool it was that he got three aces and a jack and I only got some threes and nines, how maybe we could all go to the zoo for his birthday, I thought of Margot. There needed to be longevity to this plan. I would need to confront her, somehow, see to it that she didn't undo whatever I managed to accomplish during my short visit. I was terrified, no, out of my wits with unthinkable horror at the possibility that, after all I had done, after all I had sacrificed, Margot might ruin it all by an act as simple as asking who had taken Theo out of school that day. What if everything I did placed Theo and Toby's expectations at a greater height from which Margot would send them crashing, irreparably, to the ground?

I found the place—Riverstone—a sprawling, UFO-shaped, white building with plastic, life-size storks on the lawn and bronze Buddhas sitting placidly among the white pillars. A duck pond glimmered beyond the bushes surrounding the circular building. I followed the signs to reception.

Now, my memory of Riverstone was vague, to say the least. I remembered only splashes of short, sharp scenes: a patronizing therapist in a room that smelled like a swimming pool; looking down at my hands one morning and realizing I had grown two extra fingers on each hand—the effects of tranquilizers, no doubt, for the extra fingers soon fell off—and a woman that smiled and took my hand and told me about kangaroos.

I found the receptionist seated in a space-agey cubicle, shrouded by a dome of glass. I introduced myself as Ruth, relieved that at last I could use my own name.

"You're Ms. Delacroix's . . . sister?" The receptionist. I'd taken pains to reverse the physical similarity. Glasses. A beret. Heavy makeup. Clearly, it hadn't worked so well.

"Cousin," I said.

"I could tell." She smiled and wrinkled her nose. "Well, we don't normally allow guests—"

"It's an emergency," I said. It was true. It was. "A family member is dying, and I'd rather she hear it now, and not a month after the fact."

The receptionist's face dropped. "Oh. Um... okay. I'll call her therapist. But I'm not promising anything."

I was taken to the communal area, where Margot and the other "guests" were apparently having "quiet time." It looked enormously boring. Margot was probably going crazy. I know I would have been. The walls were covered in large, gold-framed pictures with words like *Acceptance* and capped-toothed statements like "Attitude is Altitude" at the bottom. I rolled my eyes and visualized replacing the words with *Cynicism* and statements like "Failure is inevitable." Nothing like a sharp sense of reality to aid recovery. As it was, whoever designed the place clearly equated recovery with lots of white velour couches and glass coffee tables everywhere strewn with tea lights and tulips. Classical music trickled delicately from an invisible speaker. I looked at the large Big Ben–style clock above the doorway and felt my heart quicken. If they told me to come back tomorrow, I was done for.

At the white doors to the communal room, the therapist—a short, bony Canadian with heavy black bangs named Dr. Gale—took my arm and peered down her glasses into my eyes.

"I'm afraid I can't let you see Margot," she said. "It's against company policy. But I can pass on any message you'd like to send her."

I thought quickly.

"I have to see her," I said. "Don't you understand? She'll never recover if she finds out... *Nan* died while she was inside this place. In fact, it'll probably tip her straight off the wagon..."

"I'm sorry," Dr. Gale said emphatically. "Margot's already signed a list of terms and conditions that include family tragedy. It's important for her recovery. I hope you understand."

A smile, brief as a wink. Then she turned on her heel and walked away.

I closed my eyes and breathed. I didn't expect this setback. I thought hard: how to get around this without setting the place on fire? Okay, I thought. *Here goes.* And I prayed. *Let this woman's angel give her a nudge in the right direction.*

"Dr. Gale?" I half shouted across the room after her. A few wobbly heads turned on the sofas and looked at me.

Dr. Gale stopped. "Please lower your voice," she snapped.

"I *really* need to see Margot," I said. "I promise I won't interfere with her treatment. She just needs to know something. It's me who won't be around by the time she gets out. I need to see her this last time."

Dr. Gale glanced around her. A few of her colleagues were staring. Her right foot turned to the door, but then she started heading slowly toward me.

She stood in front of me again and looked me over. "Okay," she said. "You've got ten minutes with her." She paused, then said in a low voice, "Margot has had to be sedated a number of times since her admission, so you may find that she's a little sleepy. It's normal. Just try not to speak too loud or too fast."

I nodded and followed Dr. Gale down a long corridor toward a small room at the end of it. She pushed open the door and called for Margot. No answer. A figure looked up from a chair by the window.

"Margot," said Dr. Gale calmly. "Your cousin is here. I'm afraid she has some bad news."

"My . . . cousin?" Margot muttered. Not all there, right now. She blinked very slowly and looked at me.

Dr. Gale nodded. "I'll give you ten minutes."

As soon as the door closed, I sat slowly in the chair opposite Margot, then leaned forward and reached for her hand. She pulled away and stared at her lap. Seeing her in the flesh took my breath away. The sense of my own physicality, of hers, made me want to weep. She seemed so frail, so deadened by drugs and despair. And I too felt the shame of not protecting her more. Of not making her whole.

Eventually, she let me take her hand. It lay loose and limp as a leaf in my palm.

"Margot, I need you to pay attention," I said firmly. She lifted her head to look at me. I took a deep breath and continued. "I have something very, very important to tell you, and I need you to really listen right now. Okay?"

She squinted, her head unsteady. "Do I know you?"

"Sort of."

A beat. She sniggered. I'd just reminded her of her first encounter with Sonya.

"You've a funny accent. Where're you from?"

I realized that my voice still dipped occasionally into an Australian twang from my years of living there. Years that Margot still had not experienced.

"Sydney," I said.

"In Australia?"

"Uh-huh."

A long pause. "They got 'roos, huh?"

"Ruse?"

She slid her hand out of mine and held both hands up to her face like paws.

"Oh!" I said. "Kangaroos."

She nodded.

"Yeah, they got kangaroos there."

I thought carefully about what I should say. It had crossed my mind to tell her that I was her, visiting from the future. I quickly came to my senses. I definitely, definitely couldn't ask her to trust me. I had never trusted anyone my entire adult life. Not even my own husband. Not even myself.

So I went with what had worked with me.

I told her about what happened to Theo in the detention center. I didn't hold back. I told her, in vivid, graphic detail, to the point that I cried, and Margot stared, looking farther and farther into the distance from the window, nodding every so often when I asked a question, touching her face when I spelled out what Theo had suffered, what he needed from her to make everything okay.

At last, I got to the point. The real reason I was here.

"I need you to forgive Toby," I said.

She turned her gaze to me, her head unsteady. Whatever they'd given her had drugged her into outer space. "He cheated on me. With my best friend."

"No, he didn't, Margot. I promise you, he didn't."

She stared. I wanted to shake her. She remained very still. I searched my mind for something to say to her that might break through the drugs, something that might just reach all the way past years of suspicion and disbelief, right past the layers of self-protection and hurt.

And before I could speak, she said:

"You know, I used to see angels when I was a kid. A long time ago. Do you believe in angels?"

After a few moments, I nodded, stupefied.

She didn't say anything for a long time, just stared out of the window, lost in a memory.

I leaned forward and took her hand.

"Toby's still in love with you. You have one chance—*just one*—to claim that love. But if you miss it, it's gone forever."

I picked up Theo at school, running most of the way when I missed the bus, feeling the wetness of my wings against the back of my shirt. Every second now was precious, and so I put special care into our time together. We had dinner at IHOP and went to see *Hook* at the cinema theater on Union Square. I bought him a whole new wardrobe of clothes—all of it on Margot's credit card—and we stayed up until the wee hours changing his bedroom around, putting some *Batman* posters on the walls, cleaning the rug, changing his bed linen and fixing the loose panels of his wardrobe so that the thing didn't look like it was going to collapse on top of him during the night. Finally, I fixed his blinds and folded all his clothes. I told him to get into bed and I'd bring him a glass of water, but by the time I got back, he was passed out.

I headed for Margot's bedroom. At the far end of the hall, a light. Nan, I thought. I walked toward it. Just then, Nan's voice, coming from the room to my left.

Ruth!

A second later, I hit the ground, my face bleeding and burning from whatever had whacked me, my lungs so crushed I could hardly breathe. I gasped and staggered to my feet. Right in front of me were Ram, Luciana, and Pui. They huddled together, appearing at first as three pillars of shadow. Ram was holding a spiked flail on the end of a chain.

There was only one thing for it. Run.

Ram backed up, ready to take another shot at me with the flail. I bolted for the living room, and as he reached me I raised my hands to my temple, ready for the explosion against my head. I saw Nan out of the corner of my eye, reaching out and deflecting the blow. As she did, I felt two arms wrap underneath my armpits, pinning me in midair: Luciana holding me, while Pui thrust her hand right into my chest. It felt as if she'd cut me open, and I screamed. I heard Theo call out from his bedroom. James appeared beside me and headed for Theo's room. But Luciana and Pui had seen him. "Don't you dare!" I yelled, and Pui smiled in my face, leaned forward, and dived inside me as easily as you'd lean into your closet.

In that moment, I think I saw hell. Pui was taking me there, dragging me out of my flesh and down a dark chute into a world so terrifying that I felt its cruelty in my bones.

And then, darkness.

I heard thuds, roars, and screams. But far away, as if I was being dragged to another place, another time.

※

When I woke up, I was sprawled on the floor of a white room, naked. Terrified. Was this it? Was I in hell?

I tucked my knees into my chest and shivered. "Nan?" I called. Then, "Theo? Toby"? Footsteps behind me.

I turned. It took me a moment or two to realize that the shining figure in front of me was Nan. Her face glowed like noon, her wings stretched out at either side of her shoulders, wide bands of red light. Her dress was not white as before, and it wasn't material;

it was as if she had lifted the surface of a still lake reflecting a sunset and slipped it over her head.

"Just tell me," I said, trembling so hard, the words seemed to rattle out of my mouth. "Am I going to hell now?"

"I hardly think so," Nan said calmly. "I just saved you from becoming its newest resident."

"But I am going to hell, right? In the future?"

"Only God will decide what the consequences of your choices will be."

It was little reassurance. I knew she wasn't going to lie to me. But I had to face up to it. Nan hadn't saved me from hell, not indefinitely. She'd only delayed my arrival.

I got to my feet. I reached out and touched her dress. "Why have you changed?"

"We all change," she said after a long time. "Just as you changed from a baby to an adult when you were mortal. When I saved you, I became an archangel."

"Why?"

"Each type of angel has a specific role in the service of God. Some of us will become Powers; others, Virtues. Few of us will become Cherubim, who protect and help humans come to know God. Even fewer of us will become Seraphim."

"Even fewer of us wind up in hell, huh?"

A fleeting smile. "Here," she said, and I raised my hand to protect my eyes as I looked up at her outstretched palm. She was holding out a white dress.

"What about the blue one?"

"It can't be worn again. This is all that's left." And she handed me a small blue jewel on the end of a gold chain. I slipped on the white dress, then fastened the jewel around my neck.

"What's next?" I asked. "Did I change Theo's life?"

She held out her hand again. Within it, a parallel world appeared, the size of a snow globe, then expanded until it was the size of a melon. I stood closer and peered into it. Inside, like reflections in a pool of water, an image of Theo in his late teens. Brutish, scowling. At first I thought he was sitting behind the wooden desk of an office, but then I realized he was sitting in court, dressed in standard orange inmate attire, hanging his head as the verdict was announced. A woman's voice called "Guilty!" Theo was yanked to his feet and dragged away.

"That's it?" I cried. "After all that, Theo gets a life sentence, and I go to hell?" I looked at Nan for an answer. She didn't offer one.

I dropped to my knees.

For a long time I sobbed on all fours, letting my tears rain on the white ground. It had all been for nothing. I can't even begin to tell you how that felt.

Eventually I wiped my face and stood up to face Nan.

"What do I do now?" I said. "Did I change anything?"

"Yes," Nan said. "And not all of it will please you. You might witness Margot make choices that frustrate all your plans."

"I don't have plans anymore, Nan. I'm going to hell, remember?"

"It's like I told you at the beginning," she said very seriously. "Nothing is certain."

I dried my eyes. She was giving me hope. But, for once, it felt like an act of cruelty.

"What do I do now?" I said.

For the first time in a long while, Nan smiled. "You have a job to do. Go do it."

23

The Hardest Word

I WAS THERE WHEN MARGOT RETURNED HOME FROM RIVERSTONE, STRIPPED OF HER ADDICTIONS BUT, IN TURN, STRIPPED OF HER SENSE OF WHO SHE WAS, WHERE SHE HAD COME FROM, WHY SHE WAS HERE. She set down her bags, brushed her hair out of her face, and sighed. To her surprise, Toby and Theo were waiting in the dining room. But she looked past them to the withered sunflowers in the vase

"Margot?"

She looked at Toby. "Yeah?"

"Uh," he looked at Theo. "Say, buddy, could you give your mom and I just a minute?"

Theo nodded and headed for his room. I looked over at Gaia, who was standing in the doorway. She walked toward me and put her arm on mine.

"Are you okay?" she said.

I nodded, though I was far from okay.

I watched Toby produce a bunch of papers from his oversized fishing jacket and set them on the dining table. I knew what they were. He cleared his throat and squared his shoulders, using one hand to search the pockets of his jacket for something. His certainty, I think. For a minute or two he kept his hand on top of the papers, as if letting go of them entirely was an irrevocable act, something he could never, ever change.

"Tell him you love him, Margot," I said loudly, but she continued staring at the sunflowers.

"These are . . . divorce papers," Toby said, drawing his breath. "All you have to do is sign beneath where I've signed, and we can both . . . get on with things."

Margot yanked the dry stems out of the vase and stalked into the kitchen without making eye contact. Toby followed. "Margot?"

"What?"

"Did you hear me?"

She held up the dry stems. "These died while I was gone."

"Yeah?"

"You didn't replace the water?"

"No, I didn't. I don't live here, remember? Remember, you kicked me out . . . Anyway, let's not get into all that."

I could see Theo in the doorway of his room down the hall, listening intently, the wish of his heart glowing like a coal. *Please, please . . .*

Margot looked down at the sunflowers in her hand. "You know, even if I drown these things in a bathtub, even if I drench them for days on end, they're dead. And that's it." She looked up at Toby. "You know?"

He nodded very slowly and dug his hands deep in his pockets. Then he shook his head. "No, in fact I don't know. What are you talking about, Margot? First you tell me you're sorry, and then . . . and then we're all playing cards like we're one big happy family again . . ."

She looked up quickly and said, "Cards?" as if she couldn't remember, which maddened him.

He raised his voice. "I have waited six *years* for you to forgive me, for you to open up to the possibility that maybe, just *maybe*, I *didn't* cheat on you, that maybe what you saw wasn't the whole picture, that maybe I do *love* you . . . "

She looked up at him. "You do?"

"Did," he said, looking down. "I meant, did."

He tossed the papers on the table. "You know what? Those flowers are dead. I need to get on with my life."

He left. The silence hung in the room like a suicide.

***

The next morning, a letter from Hugo Benet, thanking Margot for her editorial services and praising her for her work on Rose Workman's notebooks, for which a long-overdue royalty check was enclosed.

The check was for twenty-five thousand dollars.

I watched her fidget around the apartment, and I remembered the hollowness that had set in once I'd cut the alcohol out of my life, like a giant stone removed from the mouth of a cave. She looked at her hair in the mirror. I need a haircut, she thought. Then she touched her face. Nothing but lines and sadness.

She walked slowly down the hall to Theo's room, like a tightrope artist placing her feet carefully in line, careful not to fall. They'd applauded her when she completed her stay at rehab, thrust an elaborate bouquet of lilies and orchids in her arms, and like an anointment, pronounced her as one who was, finally, clean. They even took a Polaroid of her and the other inmates at the Riverstone entrance, the one with all the Buddhas and storks, and she'd set the picture against the clock on the fireplace as a prompt: *You're clean now. Don't forget.* But that's the thing with rehab: They scrub you so clean it feels too unnatural, too difficult to ever, ever stay that way, to stay so white, so bleached of humanity. At least, that was how I'd felt. I had wanted someone to show me how to live a normal life. How to live without pillars of empty bottles of booze propping me up.

Theo was curled up in bed, pretending to be asleep. All the stuff he'd heard Toby say played on his mind, and he did his best to work it out. James sat on the edge of the bed, trying to distract him by prodding his imagination. But it wasn't working. Theo saw Margot standing in his doorway and slowly sat upright.

"How do you feel about moving someplace new?"

She said it as lightly as possible, as if she'd fully thought it through, as if she knew exactly what she was doing.

"Like where?"

She shrugged.

"Like New Jersey?"

She laughed.

"Where, then? Las Vegas?"

She walked over to the map of the world on the wall above his desk. "You know, your dad and I got married there."

"Let's move there, then."

She inspected the map, her arms still folded. "How about Australia?"

Theo considered. "Isn't that, like, a billion miles away?"

"About ten thousand."

"No way."

"Why not? They got kangaroos."

Theo sighed and dangled his feet off the edge of the bed. "Do you *really* want to move to Australia? Or is this another way of getting back at Dad?"

"Would you move with me?"

Theo looked down at his feet and wrinkled his brow. Again, he was feeling torn in two. I looked at James. "Tell him it's okay to say no," I said. "Tell him he can stay with Toby." James nodded and repeated what I'd said.

After a long time, Theo looked up. "Mom," he said. "Can I visit you in Australia?"

It was his answer. Margot stared and smiled. "Sure."

"Like, every summer?"

"Yeah, though summertime is wintertime there."

"Can I have a kangaroo as a pet?"

"Maybe. But you can definitely come and stay as long as you like."

❈❈❈

Of course, I'd anticipated the move for a long time. Regardless of how much I credited the warm shores of Sydney for my long-overdue sense of well-being, I hated myself for abandoning Theo. It was unfair to put him in the position of choosing between Toby and me. I had been cruel, and wantonly selfish, by moving not to another part of town, not to another state, but to another continent.

And yet, after all I'd been through, after the series of events that had almost torn me apart, it was my safety net.

Margot began her self-transformation with a severe haircut—a jaw-brushing, chocolate bob that swan-necked at the ends—and a bronze spray tan. She banked Hugo's check, bought a rack of new clothes from Saks, and booked an appointment with a plastic surgeon. Blepharoplasty, or removal of the sadness around her eyes. Remove the bags all you like, I told her. The sadness is soul deep.

She decided to keep the apartment for another month or two, just in case things didn't work out. I'd told her there was no need, but since she'd returned from Riverstone, she hadn't responded to a single word I'd said. When I sang the Song of Souls—just once, to see if there was any connection left between us—she didn't bat an eyelid, didn't sit up and look around, didn't shiver with the sense of my presence. If I didn't know better, I'd have guessed she was a different person entirely.

Nan came the night before Margot flew out to Sydney. I sat, cross-legged on the roof of the apartment, under an unusually glittery sky, feeling disconnected from everything and everyone—God, my family, my own self. I took a step, right off the edge of the roof. Call me a drama queen. It was hardly a suicide bid. I wanted to see if I really had cut myself off, if my deal with Grogor had changed the rules. I dropped for about half a second and then . . . nothing. I was suspended in mid-air. For once, it reassured me.

Nan listened to my woes with her usual stoic patience. When I finished, she told me to look around me. What was moonlit blackness just a moment before was now a landscape of glowing rooftops, upon which sat endless rows of archangels, each of them like ten-foot-tall rubies shot through with light, their firm, human faces wearing expressions of determination and purpose. Strands of flame of various thickness and force orbited around their bodies, bright as comets. Some of them were armed with swords, shields, some with bows and arrows. All of them were watching me. Reminding me of their solidarity. That they were looking out for me.

Nan had said nothing the whole time that I had vented about Theo, Toby, and Margot. When I asked my usual question— "What am I supposed to do?"—she stood up and looked at a cloud that was drifting across the sequined sky like a black sheep. "What is it?" I said anxiously. "Look harder," she said.

I stared. The cloud drifted slowly toward the moon until it shielded the white thumbnail in the sky. And then, a vision.

Imagine a movie trailer: The vision was bits of an event, like scenes cobbled together awkwardly by a drunken film editor. The timing was all out of sync: Margot driving her car, singing along to the radio. Then a flash-forward to shards of metal flying through the air in slow motion. Margot's head flinging forward on impact. Another car spinning round and round on the road like a spin top. A close-up of a twisted hubcap wheeling to the sidewalk. The glass of a windshield shattering. A black Lincoln swerving and heading straight for a woman pushing a baby in a stroller along the sidewalk. Margot plunging through the windshield, her face swelling and bleeding in slow motion, hitting pavement in the hot morning sun, her arm folding up her back, shattering, her whole body flipping over, landing on her left hip, crushing her pelvis, then skidding—no longer in slow motion—all the way to the buckled tire of another car, bleeding smoke from its hood.

"What is this?" I glanced at Nan.

"It's something you have to prevent from happening," she said. "One of the effects of the changes you made is what you see before you. Unless you stop it."

My heart pounded. "What if I fail?"

"You won't fail."

"But, what if . . . ?"

"You really want to know?"

It was my turn to throw Nan a look.

She held my gaze. "Margot will be paralyzed from the neck down, confined to a wheelchair and twenty-four-hour care for the rest of her life. But, she'll be lucky. Four people will die in the accident, including a baby, a man who is about to be married, and a woman who is instrumental in preventing a major terrorist attack in the future."

I leaned over my knees and breathed deeply.

"How do I stop it?"

"Pay attention," Nan said, very stern. "This is both your training and a matter of urgency. That's as much as I've been told."

"Pay attention?" I half yelled at her. "*That's* my instruction?"

She took a step closer as the vision folded. "Look around you," she said calmly. "Do you *really* think you have anything to fear? Even now, as an angel, knowing that God exists, seeing what you see—why is fear still a part of your being?"

I shut my mouth. I didn't know the answer.

"You've been instructed to *do* something, not to fear it. So do it." She stepped toward the edge of the roof.

I turned. "What do you mean, my *training*?"

But she'd already gone.

***

Walking on eggshells? Jumping at every sound, every movement? Paranoia didn't even begin to describe my state of mind the next morning. I watched the sun rise, and I groaned. I prayed: *Please, let the messages start again. I'm listening, really. I'm sorry for screwing up. Just, please, tell me what to do.*

But my wings dribbled listlessly, impotent as drain water.

Margot had been dreaming about Sonya. She'd turned up at Sonya's house and confronted her about the affair with Toby. She took off all her clothes—the leopard-print dress and red shoes she'd borrowed the night she and Toby got married—and threw them at Sonya's feet. And then, Sonya apologized. Margot felt wretched, because she realized that all this time Sonya had been sorry. She realized that, all this time, she'd been wrong.

When she woke up she felt hollow. For the first time, I saw the trace of a dream lingering on her aura like spilled coffee: At first, its images splashed across the soft pink light rising up from her skin like morning mist, until eventually, as the hard edges of the day began to press into her sense of reality, the dream was no more than a few drips, each of which played out the image of Sonya's face, penitent, sincere.

The remaining tasks before Margot packed and headed for Sydney included storing the bigger items of her furniture and collecting her visa from the passport office downtown. She dragged on the same jeans and black shirt I'd been wearing a few weeks earlier, wondering for a moment why they were folded on the wooden trunk at the foot of the bed, then picked up her car keys and padded downstairs.

What I thought at first was an oil leak turned out to be a small stain of shadow, hovering directly under the car. I stood outside the vehicle, taking a good look around the parking lot for demons—I half wanted, half expected to bump into Ram, Luciana, Pui, or Grogor, to repay them in kind for their recent hospitality—then turned my attention to Margot's old silver Buick. She reversed, almost backing into a trashcan, and I saw the shadow wobble as if gravity was attaching it to the underside. And then, as she began to drive off down the street, I saw it for what it was: a black stem, like the darkened arch of a rainbow, leading all the way from the shadow, past the trash cans, and up, over the brow of the hill.

I thought back to the vision. I hadn't spotted anyone else, at least not for more than a few seconds. There'd been a woman on the sidewalk, pushing a stroller. I didn't see her face. Was it the choice of someone who'd decided to sleep in that morning and was about to cause a crash because they were rushing to work? Or someone who'd chosen to knock back a bottle of Jack Daniel's while driving down Lexington Avenue? Was there something wrong with the car?

And then, a detail from the vision. Right before Margot hurtled forward, launching through the windshield, she'd turned and mouthed something. I guess I thought she'd been mouthing it at me. But then I worked it out. Whoever she was talking to was sitting right next to her. Right in the passenger seat.

I got into the backseat of the car and leaned forward, close to her ear.

"Margot!" I yelled. "Do not stop. Do not pick anyone up, do you hear me? Not anyone, not if the world is ending. Do you hear me, Margot?"

She didn't. My wings were pulsing. I sobbed with relief. Yes, I thought. Give me instruction. Give me instinct. Give me anything that tells me what is going on. But then the pulsing stopped. I looked around frantically.

Right there, right next to me, was Grogor.

"Enjoy your trip?" he said. He was younger now. Late thirties. He resembled a handsome young lawyer or businessman. Clean shaven, swarthy skin. A new black suit. Keeping up with the times. I turned to face him, ready for a fight.

"Get out," I said.

He tut-tutted. "Now, now," he said. "I only dropped by to check on you. I hear you had a bit of a run-in with Ram and Co." He frowned. "This did not please me. I can assure you, punishment has been meted out."

Immediately, messages in my wings: *He is a distraction.*

I ignored him and peered out the window, taking everything in, frantically trying to match what I'd seen in the vision with what I was seeing in the here and now.

"I have another offer," he continued. "I think you ought to hear me out on this one."

I turned away, scanning the street outside. I spotted a woman pushing a baby in a stroller and jumped. But then the lights changed and we took off. Was it possible that Nan's vision was a mistake?

"You know you're going to hell," Gregor said mournfully, "And you know, there won't just be three demons there who don't like you. There will be millions."

He reached out and dipped his fingertip in my wing, just for a second. And for that long, awful moment, a flash of hell in my mind. No fire, no brimstone. Just excruciating, palpable bitterness. A dark room without carpet or doors or windows, just an interior without lights.

Then, like a searchlight, a flicker of red bringing objects into view: a young man being ripped apart by a crowd of shadowy figures. I saw them calmly stitch him together again as if he were a rag doll, ignoring his cries. I saw other rooms where people walked through the three-dimensional projections of their own lives, and extensions of those lives, screaming as they watched themselves plunge in the blade that could not be withdrawn, men trying to catch all the pieces of the bomb blast that ripped across the room like glass shattering in slow motion. I knew, somehow, that the virtual projections were on replay for the rest of time.

I saw things I can't begin to describe. I seemed to lift out of that place without exits, and I saw enormous, black buildings filled with rooms like the ones I'd seen before, filled with screams. And I saw myself, arriving at the entrance of that building. Just as I had done at St. Anthony's, I rapped on the door. Every head turned. They were coming.

"Get off me," I hissed at him. He sucked his finger. It was burned raw from my wings. He flashed me a look.

"That was just a glimpse", he said. "You imagine an eternity of that, Ruth. But, lucky you, there's an alternative."

I hesitated. "Which is?"

He looked puzzled. "Ruth . . . don't you know who I am?"

I stared at him blankly. He shook his head in disbelief. "Look," he said, "if you come with me now, I will make sure you don't get so much as a frosty stare from the millions of demons waiting for you. Immunity, if you like."

I thought about it, much longer than I should have. And I confess, part of me wanted to say yes. Much of what he said was absolutely right. I'd done the deed that meant I was slowly sliding into hell. When a cop finds himself in jail, he also finds himself rubbing noses with a lot of criminals who want his blood. I was facing a similar predicament. Only, these criminals didn't want my blood. They wanted my soul.

And then, Nan's words: *Do you really think you have anything to fear?*

I shifted in my seat and forced a smile. He smiled back and leaned forward. There was, if I'm not mistaken, a certain amount of lust in his eyes. "Well?" he said.

"You must think I'm a wimp, Grogor. So let me spell it out: I would rather take on all of hell's residents than spend another second in your company."

He didn't miss a beat. "You don't mean a word of that," he said, smiling, but in the dark reflection of his eyes, I could see someone at the window behind me.

Just then, the car door slowed at another light, and Grogor vanished. Someone climbed into the passenger seat and slammed the door. "What the . . . ?" Margot yelled at the woman sitting next to her.

"Drive." It was Sonya. A much heavier, madeup Sonya, her breasts spilling over a tight Gothic bustier, her hair orange-red and dreadlocked. The years had not been kind.

Margot met her eyes. Quickly she knocked the car into first gear and took off.

"Where are we going?"

"Shut up and drive."

"Nice to see you too, Son."

A pause. *So this is how it happens,* I thought. *Sonya makes her crash the car.* But then, I thought back to the vision. There was no sign of Sonya anywhere in the car when it crashed. Was there?

Ezekiel, Sonya's guardian angel, was outside on the hood, trapped by the glass. I thought hard and I prayed harder. *Tell me what to do . . .*

"What's this about, Son? I'm kinda busy right now . . . " Margot took a sharp corner, slamming Sonya against the passenger window.

Sonya recovered herself. She turned to Margot. "Hey, I thought, it's been a while, we should really get together and, I don't know, compare notes on how badly our lives turned out. Maybe we could have a contest."

"You picked a great time for that, Son. You always were such a planner."

Sonya scowled. "You know, I used to think I was the one who owed *you* an apology? But recently I've been thinking it's the other way around."

Margot hit the brakes at a red light, forcing Sonya into the dashboard. "As I recall it, you got a gold in the Olympics of marital destruction."

Sonya pressed her hands against the glass and pushed herself back into her seat. "You see, that's the type of stuff I'm talking about. I did *not* destroy your marriage." Her voice wobbled. "Do you know what it's been like living with that ever since?"

Margot cut her off. "Oh, was there a Pity Party I missed?" She threw the car into first gear and slammed the accelerator.

Sonya lifted her head slowly and looked at Margot. Heavy, black tears seeped from her eyes and ran down her face. "You're still not getting it, Margie," she said. "I have apologized to you many, many times. I have tried and *tried* to make amends for that night. I've spent a hundred hours in therapy. But you won't accept it. It's not enough. So now . . ." From her pocket, a small gun. She jammed it into her mouth.

"No!" Margot swerved the car, narrowly missing a cab in front. Horns sounded all around. She struggled to keep the car straight while reaching out for the gun, carefully pulling it out of Sonya's mouth. There was a moment when she wasn't sure if Sonya was going to pull the trigger. I leaned out of the car and pushed off the door of the cab alongside us, keeping us running on course.

At last, the gun lowered.

"I'm going to pull over," Margot said, her voice shaking.

"Keep driving," said Sonya, turning the gun and pressing it against Margot's temple. Margot visibly drew a sharp breath, and I froze in terror. *What do I do? What do I do?*

Sonya gritted her teeth. "Now you listen, sweetheart. I have put up with all your self-righteous accusations, slamming the phone down, bouncing my e-mails, and now all this with Toby. It is *you* that's sabotaged your marriage, not me . . ."

"You've waited years to point *that* out?"

Sonya pushed the gun against Margot's head until it tilted to one side. "You married the nicest guy I have ever met. And yeah, I wanted him. I figured, you treated him so badly that you didn't deserve him. But you know what? When I tried to take him, even when you pushed him so far out of that marriage he was ripe for the taking, he said no. He said *no*, Margot. And still you left him. Now I am telling you that I'm sorry. And I'm telling you that Toby did nothing, absolutely nothing. But I want to hear you say it. Say it, Margot. Say you believe me. Say you forgive me."

Her fingers curled around the gun.

"I believe you," Margot said in a low voice. "I forgive you."

"You mean it?"

Slowly Margot turned, allowed the barrel to brush across her forehead. She locked eyes with Sonya.

"I mean it."

A long, terrifying pause. Sonya sighed an enormous breath of relief, until her shoulders slumped forward and she lowered the gun to her lap. I watched as her aura seemed to be scraped of its color, its jaundiced yellow changing into vibrant turquoise.

And then, the whole car jerked to the left.

"What's that?" shouted Sonya. Margot struggled to keep the car on a straight course, narrowly missing another vehicle.

I jumped to attention. I saw the woman with the baby in the stroller to my right, and I darted outside. All at once, a message from my wings, loud and clear:

Trust.

And then, about ten feet away, a man in a black Lincoln pulling out of a side road. *If I just reach out,* I thought, *I can stop this.*

Trust.

The black car was so close that I could see my reflection in the windshield. "What do you mean 'trust'?" I yelled. "What am I supposed to do, just stand back and do nothing?"

It was as if the noise of car engines, chatter pouring out of the café on the sidewalk, road rage, cop sirens, subway trains, gutters running—all of it stopped dead. And only one sound piercing the air, like a whisper . . .

Trust.

So I closed my eyes, and in that moment I trusted that everything would be as it should be: the car would roll to a halt, right past the woman pushing the stroller, right past the black car with the man who was about to be married. I stood in the middle of the traffic and closed my eyes.

Right at that moment, a flash of light, shooting straight out of me and surrounding everything. It was as if I'd become a cut diamond reflecting an intense ray of sunlight, for suddenly every color imaginable poured out of me and into every corner of the street. And riding on those shafts of light, the archangels, darting in front of the woman, guiding the black Lincoln on its course, holding the tire in place as Margot pulled over, right in front of the intersection that I recognized from Nan's vision.

I stood by the car, watching as the archangels comforted the mother and her screaming baby, as they whispered to the man in the black car to continue to his destination, as they guided passersby on their way, consulting with their angels. And then they disappeared just as fast as they'd appeared, retreating into spokes of sunlight and bright discs of leftover rain.

Gradually the light around me subsided. I touched my arms and face and realized I was dripping in sweat.

I walked to Margot's car and got into the backseat again, wondering what had just happened to me. I desperately needed Nan to appear to explain it to me, but she didn't show.

Margot looked over at Sonya.

"You know, next time, you don't need to bring a gun."

Sonya looked back at her. "It worked, didn't it?" A pause. "I'm sorry, you know?"

"Yeah. I'm sorry too."

"My card," Sonya said, tossing a black business card onto the dashboard. "Keep in touch, Margie."

She got out, tucking her gun back into her purse. She paused at the window and leaned in. "Do me a favor," she said. "Get back with Tobes."

And with that, she walked away.

24

Reshuffling the Cards

THE NEXT AFTERNOON I TOOK MY SEAT IN ANGEL CLASS ON THE QANTAS FLIGHT FROM NEW YORK TO SYDNEY, LOOKING DOWN AT THE LIGHTS OVER THE EARTH, AT THE ANGELS GUARDING THE STARS AND PLANETS ABOVE ME. I thought of what Nan had said—"This is your training"—and burned a few brain cells trying to work out what she'd meant by that. Why would I be getting training *now*? A little late for that, wasn't it? Or was it training for something else?

And I thought about the message I'd felt in my wings at that crucial moment. *Trust.* I felt both relieved that I'd opted to listen and confused as to why I'd been instructed to simply trust. Hadn't I been sent in that car to *do* something, to prevent the accident? All I had done was force myself to believe that, somehow, everything would be all right. I had no clue how it worked. But something had happened when I did it, something vital. I had changed for a brief moment of time into something else, *someone* else. I was determined to give it another shot.

And I practiced the fine art of hope.

Vain hope, perhaps, but hope nonetheless. Hope that maybe I'd earn some brownie points with God, enough to push my treachery far out of his mind. Hope, despite the vision that Nan had showed me of Theo being locked up for life, that maybe there was still some way that I could do enough to help him sidestep that fate. Hope that I would find a way back to Toby. I would die trying. Even if I had to die a second time.

As Nan predicted, there were signs that things had improved, that things had changed. I recalled that when I moved to Sydney it had taken weeks to find a place to live, so I'd ended up spending a lot of time at a hostel in Coogee, a suburb in East Sydney, where I shared a dorm with some Thai students and a woman from Moscow who stayed indoors all day and night, smoking large, fat cigars and drinking vodka. My relapse had been virtually inevitable; soon, I had joined her, and my quest to find a home and a job and a life disappeared down bottle after glass bottle engraved with Russian characters.

Margot touched down at Sydney Airport in the early hours on a Monday morning in September. I thought I'd spare her the disgusting dorm room at Coogee and suggested she head straight to Manly and rent an apartment overlooking the beach. There was a strong chance that I was being a little premature in suggesting the apartment—I had rented it from the beginning of the December of that year—but the Manly idea took hold and she asked for directions. A bus and a ferry later, she was dragging her suitcase up the promenade, gasping at the row of Norfolk Island pine trees that suddenly came into view like gigantic Christmas trees, the ivory scarf of sand, the indigo quiff of ocean tumbling amateur surfers off their boards.

I gave her directions to the apartment, a message from my wings. Stronger than I had ever experienced. Not just a message but a current circulating through my body, and along that current, an image of Margot, her hair long and blonde again, walking through fields, past a lake, toward a road in the hillside. I looked around for some such place, then searched my memories. There was nowhere that resembled the place I'd just seen, not in any part of Sydney that I remembered. And then I realized: The woman in the image was not Margot. It was me.

Watch. Protect. Record. Love. It had taken me thirty-odd years to recognize the absence of the word "change" in this set of directives, as well as the omission of the words "influence" and "control." So as Margot wandered the streets of Manly, jet-lagged and overwhelmed by the beauty of the place, the newness of every shop front and street corner, I chanted those four words like a mantra. I resisted the urge to shove her in the direction of that gorgeous apartment—the open-plan living room with a balcony that jutted out over the beach, the four-poster bed, the copper bath, the coffee table with tropical fish swimming around inside it—and stood back as she fumbled around this place, around *time*, as if it had never happened before. As if it was all really happening right now.

And I guess I realized that I had spent much of the past years treating her like a parent who had completely forgotten what it is to dream about Christmas, how it feels to walk into a toy store when you're five, six, or seven years old, or why places like Disneyland require absolute mania at a thousand decibels. The privilege of living in the present was the endless opportunities for enthusiasm and surprise. Not so, in my case. As a result, I had treated Margot with the exact lack of understanding as she'd inflicted on Theo. I had treated her with an utter lack of forgiveness.

So I tried a new system: I'd let her stumble, I'd let her fall, and if she fell too far, I'd pick her up and steer her where she needed to be. Like when she switched from feeling excited and euphoric that first night in Australia to feeling lost and alone. She'd checked into a hotel on the promenade and spent twenty minutes eyeballing the minibar. *Don't,* I warned her. She hesitated, then swung both legs off the bed and yanked the door open. *Better not,* I said. *You're an addict, sweetheart. Your liver can't take it.* And so she lined up three bottles of Baileys and half a gin and tonic before she looked down at her shaking hands and thought, all by herself, *Maybe I should stop.*

Just as I remembered, she decided to create a plan. I guess you would call it a set of goals. I was never terribly good at devising lists. Much better with visuals. So she sat with a bunch of newspapers and magazines spread across the floor of the hotel room, cutting out pictures that captured what it was that she wanted out of life, and as she snipped images of a picket-fence home, kittens, a range cooker, a dove, Harrison Ford, the images that flooded my mind of my own goals were almost identical. I watched, bemused, as she reduced the image of Harrison Ford right down to a set of eyes, then cut out the jaw and nose of Ralph Fiennes, then scalped a red-headed male model. She pieced the images together, creating a collage of Toby.

Then she cut around a newspaper image that had no reference point: a photo cover of a book that bore the image of Ayers Rock morphed with a whale on the front. The title was *Jonah's Jail,* and the author was K. P. Lanes. You might want to read that book, I told her.

A phone call to the front desk.

"G'day, Miss Delacroix. What can I do ya for?"

"Is there a library open anywhere nearby?"

"Uh, nah, sorry, ma'am; it's ten thirty at night. The libraries don't open until tomorra."

"Oh."

"Anything else I can help you with?"

"Yeah. Have you heard of an author called K. P. Lanes?"

"Well, yeah, I have actually. He's my uncle."

"You're kidding? I've just seen a photo of his book in the *Sydney Morning Herald*."

"Yeah, it's a beauty. Have you read it?"

"No, I just arrived this morning. . . . "

"Would you like to read it?"

"Well, yes, actually. . . . "

"All righty. I'll send up my copy in two ticks."

"Oh. That would be wonderful!"

"No worries."

She read the book cover to cover, before passing out and sleeping for twelve hours straight.

Again, this was not how I'd experienced Sydney. It was like the hand of cards I'd been dealt during my life had been reshuffled. Whereas I'd met K. P. Lanes in the lobby of one of the many publishers that I begged for a job, Margot met him a few days later in the lobby of the hotel.

It was to be the first of many differences to my own life. I started to wonder about the reliability of memory. And then I figured: *We really are two separate people. What she does, what I do— they're not the same thing anymore.* Like Toby's fondness for writing over old, faded manuscripts, his kind of perverse intrigue at spying the pale ghosts of words peeking behind his own writing, I decided, right there in the lobby as Margot shook Kit's huge, aboriginal hand, *Let be. Let be.*

The version of events in my memory wasn't entirely different, however. Kit—or K. P. Lanes, as he was known in the literary world—was a retired detective who had been writing in various forms all his life. Tall, gentle, and very shy, it had taken him ten years to write *Jonah's Jail* and twenty years to publish it. Because he'd revealed some indigenous traditions that were deemed sacred by his clan, most of his family and friends had cut him off. As he'd once explained to me, and now explained to a tearful, awe-struck Margot, he'd only revealed the secrets of his people precisely because his people were dying out. He wanted those traditions to live on.

Jonah's Jail had been published by an independent publisher, and only one hundred copies had been printed. There had been no launch. Kit's dreams of telling the world about the beliefs and values of his people were in tatters. But he wasn't bitter. He was confident that his ancestors would help him. Margot was confident of only two things:

1. His book was amazing on a number of levels.
2. Only she could help him.

And so, the remainder of the royalty check that Hugo Benet had kindly written paid for another two thousand copies of the book to be printed, for a modest promotional campaign, and for the launch of Kit's book at the Surry Hills Library. And here's where I came in useful: At the launch, I recognized the journalist Jimmy Farrell, who had been instrumental in picking up the story of Kit's journey to tell this story, the cultural sacrifices he had made, and the glaring fact that, less than six months after the Australian High Court had overturned *terra nullius*, a controversy surrounding the right to reclaim native land, here was an indigenous Australian writing about issues of territory and identity.

Go talk to him, I told Margot, nudging her in Jimmy's direction.

By December, Kit's book had sold over ten thousand copies, and he and Margot had begun an affair. Kit left to tour the islands for four months with his book while Margot rented a small, cramped office on Pitt Street, with a half-decent view—if you stood on a stack of books and craned your neck, you could see the white dorsal fins of the Opera House—and registered her business: the Margot Delacroix Literary Agency.

And then, a phone call.

"Hi, Margot? It's me, Toby."

It was 6:00 AM. Completely deviating from form, she was already up, padding the warm floor of her kitchen in her robe, drinking her new poison: hot water with lemon and honey.

"Hi, Toby. How's Theo?"

"Well, funny you should mention our son; he's the reason I'm calling."

She remembered she hadn't spoken to Theo in over a week. She stubbed her toe against the fridge. Penance.

"Sorry, Tobes, it's been crazy over here. . . . "

"There's been some trouble." He sighed. A long pause. She realized he was crying.

"Toby? Is Theo okay?"

"Yeah. Well. Yeah, I mean, he's not injured or anything like that. But he is in the hospital. He stayed over at Harry's last night. The two of them thought it would be real cool to have a drinking contest, so now Theo's in hospital with alcohol poisoning."

She held the phone against her chest and closed her eyes. *I have done this,* she thought.

"Margot? Are you there?"

"Yeah. I'm here."

"Look, I'm not asking you . . . I'm just calling to tell you, is all."

"You want me to come home?"

"No, I . . . Why, are you coming home? How are things working out over there?"

She hesitated. She was itching to tell him all about Kit, about the book. But then she thought about her relationship with Kit. Toby hadn't had a relationship since he moved out. She'd had a handful of flings. It had been seven years. Seven years that had swept by like leaves on the breeze.

"Things are good, things are good. Say, Toby, why don't I come over for Christmas? Maybe we can play cards together."

"I bet Theo would just love that."

"Yeah?" She was smiling now. "And how about you?"

"Yes. I would like that too."

※

She flew back a week later with a suitcase full of shorts and open-toed sandals to a freezing New York–style Christmas. Already the pace of the city seemed to outrun her, as if she'd joined a sprint at walking pace. Already she felt her place in New York had been filled. The city required certain skills, and hers had been blunted by Sydney's sunny, carefree lifestyle. It took her half an hour to hail a cab. I bounced on the spot, elated at the thought of seeing Gaia and James again.

"Hey, Mom," said the rail-thin skinhead in the doorway.

Margot blinked. "Theo?"

He scowled a mouthful of silver braces, then bent forward for a reluctant embrace.

"Good to see you, son," she said quietly.

He turned and sloped back inside, yawning. Margot followed, dragging her luggage behind her.

"Dad, Mom's here."

The figure seated by the window rose. "I was waiting for you to call for a ride," he said anxiously. "Tell me you didn't cab it all the way from JFK?"

Margot ignored him and stared at Theo.

"You donate your hair to charity, kiddo?"

"I got cancer. Thanks for being sensitive about it."

Toby smiled apologetically and dug his hands into his pockets. "I see we have a tie in the Sarcasm Championships." He leaned forward and gave Margot an awkward peck on the cheek. "Really good to see you, Margot," he said.

She smiled and looked back at Theo. It struck her that his precocious wit and physical maturity were the product of a need to grow up too soon. Had *she* caused that need, she wondered?

Theo was still standing there, visibly itching for something. Toby glanced at him.

"Now listen here, young man, no later than eight, ya hear?" He threw a look at Margot that said, "I'm cutting him a little slack."

Theo saluted. "Gotcha. Later, Dad." A beat. "Mom."

He loped to the front door.

"Love you, son," Toby called after him.

"Love you too."

The door slammed.

❧

Once Theo had left, the awkwardness between Margot and Toby in the living room contrasted dramatically with the reunion between James, Gaia, and me in the dining room. While Margot and Toby sat stiffly on opposite sides of the room, tiptoeing carefully over safe topics of conversation, James, Gaia, and I stumbled over each other's news. After a long time of talking over each other we finally stopped, and burst out laughing. They had become my family, and I missed them every single day. I even cursed myself for encouraging Margot to move so far away, though I could see that the distance between her and Toby had been good for them. Suddenly, old war wounds seemed no more than tiny nicks in their relationship. They were polite to each other, glad of the company of someone familiar, someone they had once loved.

It was James I wanted to question most. Gaia filled me in on Toby's activities: mostly, due to my persistent questioning like a jealous ex-wife, of the romantic sort, which I was glad to hear were zilch. Finally, I turned to James.

"Be honest with me," I said. "Has anything I did changed things around for Theo? He looks worse than when Margot left."

James studied the floor. "I guess we have to think long term when it comes to stuff like that."

I turned to Gaia.

"Toby's a good father," she said, a little too consolatory. "He's keeping that kid in check. And James is the best angel a kid could ask for." She slapped James's leg. "Theo does occasionally respond to James's presence, which is a good thing. Sometimes, when James talks to him in his sleep, Theo replies."

I looked at James, amazed. "That's fantastic! "I said. "What does he say?"

James gave a shrug. "*Megadeth* lyrics, his twelve times tables, the occasional line from an episode of *Batman* . . . "

Gaia and James started to laugh again. I laughed too, but inside I was deflated. There was no still no evidence that anything I had done had benefited anybody, and I was still facing the price.

Things didn't improve. Theo came home after midnight, slept late on Christmas morning, then made an excuse about leaving his Sega game at Harry's and slipped out for the rest of the afternoon. Six days later, when it was time for Margot to head back to Sydney, she had managed all of four conversations with Theo that went pretty much as follows:

Margot: "Hey, Theo, I hear the Knicks have a game the night after next. You want to go?"

Theo: "Uh."

Margot: "Son, is that a transfer or a real tattoo?"

Theo: "Muh."

Margot: "Theo, it's one in the morning. Your dad said eight. What's the deal, here?"

Theo: "Nuh."

Margot: "Bye, Theo. I'll send you a ticket and, um, we'll talk, okay?"

Silence.

❧

Gaia and James assured me that they would do everything they could to protect Theo from the fate I'd seen. But when Margot returned the following summer, Theo had visited the hospital another five times for substance abuse. He had also been arrested. He was only thirteen years old.

I told her the story of the detention center over and over again.

"Remember, Margot," I'd say. "Remember what I told you at Riverstone?" And then I'd recount the terrible things Theo had suffered, and so often I would cry, and James would come forward and put his arms around me. Once he told me he'd had a message in his wings telling him that everything Theo had experienced would ultimately make him the man he was meant to be, that it would all work out for his good.

I couldn't tell him that I'd seen exactly what Theo would become. Grogor had been sure to give me the full, harrowing picture of Theo as an adult.

And then, a breakthrough.

I was repeating myself for the fiftieth time when suddenly Margot cut me off midsentence. She and Theo were at the kitchen table, cracking eggs open and buttering toast.

"You know, Theo," she said thoughtfully. "Did I ever tell you that I spent eight years of my life in an orphanage?"

He furrowed his brow. "No?"

"Oh." She bit into her toast.

He stared at her. "Why were you in an orphanage?"

She chewed and thought. "I'm not really sure. I think my parents were killed in a bombing."

"A bombing?"

"Yeah. I think so. I don't really remember. I was very young. I was only about your age when I finally ran away from the orphanage."

Theo's interest was piqued. He stared at the table and spoke fast. "Why did you run away? Didn't they catch you?"

And she told him, without holding back, of how her first attempt at running away had resulted in a beating that almost killed her, how she'd been thrown into the Tomb—and here he made her recount the dimensions and terror of that place in intricate detail—how she'd escaped, been caught, then faced Hilda and Mr. O'Hare.

Theo watched his mom, eyes open wide.

Ask him about the detention center, I told her.

She turned to him. "You know, that wasn't the first time I was beaten, Theo. It wasn't the last." A memory of Seth pushed itself to the front of her mind and her eyes welled up. She thought of the baby she had lost. James approached Theo and put his arms around his shoulders.

"Now," she said, very serious, moving her face closer to Theo's. "I know bad things happened to you in that detention center. And I need you to tell me what, because, by God, my son, I will find out who did it and I will take them down, mark my words."

His face flushed crimson. He stared at his hands, flat on the table, one on top of the other. Very slowly, he slid them off its surface and under his legs.

And then he got up and left the room. The things that had happened to him were of a nature that made him feel that there was something very wrong with him. Being punched in the face or kicked in the gut was explainable, it had a name. But the other stuff? He had no words.

Another year passed. Theo spent less time in hospital and more time in his best friend's basement drinking whisky, then sniffing glue, then smoking weed. Margot paced the floor of her Sydney apartment, unsure of what to do. It had seemed only yesterday that he was a baby, when the dimensions of his needs were as simple as feeding and sleeping. But now, in so short a time, Theo's needs were a knot she could neither untangle nor tie.

Kit approached her as she sat on the balcony, pouring her first G&T in a long time. I nodded at Adoni, Kit's guardian angel and a distant ancestor, who kept pretty much to himself.

I watched Kit carefully. He'd been in the picture far longer than I'd expected. Yes, I'd managed to change things, but was I happy with everything I'd changed? Not entirely. In my version, Kit and I had been lovers for a few months, found we preferred a working relationship, and got on with our separate lives. That version would have facilitated a reunion between Margot and Toby much more easily. But now, watching Margot pour out her complaints to Kit, watching him simply listen, nodding at the right places, I started to doubt. Maybe she should stay with Kit. Maybe he was good for her.

"What can *I* do?" he said at last, sandwiching one of her small pale hands between his.

She slid her hand out of his grasp. "I just don't know how to tackle this," she said. "Theo's doing exactly what I did. I'm a hypocrite to tell him not to."

"No, you're not," Kit said. "You're his mum. The fact that you did all of this gives you even more of a right to kick his backside for it."

She chewed a nail. "Maybe I should go over there . . . "

Kit sat back in his chair. He thought for a few moments, then said:

"Bring him here. Let me meet him, at last."

A minute passed. She considered. Was she ready for this?

Shortly after, Theo was met at Sydney Airport by a tall Aborigine with silver-flecked cornrows and scars on his face who introduced himself as Kit.

Having never met an Aborigine before—well, you can imagine Theo's reaction.

Kit took Theo to his battered jeep in the parking lot and told him to jump in.

"Where're we goin'?" Theo yawned, dumping his backpack in the seat next to him.

Kit yelled over the roar of the engine. "Put ya head down, little fella; have a rest. We'll be there in a jiffy."

They drove for hours. Theo fell asleep on the seat, curled around his backpack. When he woke up, he was in the middle of the outback, under a sky that shimmered with constellations, surrounded by the roar of crickets. Kit's jeep was parked under a tree. He looked around, forgetting for a moment that he was in Australia, wondering where his mom was.

Kit appeared at the passenger door. Except, he was no longer dressed in a polo shirt and chinos. He was stripped naked to the waist with a red cloth around his middle, his face and broad torso painted with thick, white circles. In his right hand, a long pole.

Theo just about jumped out of his skin.

Kit held out a hand. "Come on now," he said. "Jump out. By the time I'm done with ya, you'll be a true native."

Theo leaned back, away from the outstretched hand in front of him. "How long will it take?"

Kit shrugged. "How long's a piece of string?"

Three weeks later, Theo flew home. With the exception of the time he stayed at Margot's, his nights had been spent under a wide sky, waking occasionally to find a snake brushing near his pillow, then being instructed by a low voice from the shadows on how to spear and skin that snake. His days were spent lighting fires from two bits of dry wood, or making a paste from stone and water, which he then applied to his own bare skin, or to the back of a large black leaf.

"What's your Dreaming?" Kit would ask, over and over. Theo would shake his head and say something like "I want to join the

Knicks?" or "I'd like a motorbike for Christmas," and Kit would shake his head and draw a picture of a shark or pelican. "What's your Dreaming?" he'd say, until one day Theo took the stick and paste off him and drew a crocodile.

"*That's* my Dreaming," he said.

Kit nodded and pointed at the picture. "The crocodile kills its prey by dragging it underwater and holding it until it drowns. It takes away the creature's basic unit of survival." He pointed his stick at Theo. "Don't give up your own survival so easily.

"Now," he said, walking away, "we're done."

Theo looked down at his painting, at the white marks on his sunburned skin, at the red earth stubbornly rooted beneath his fingernails. He thought of the crocodile. Indestructible. Pure weapon. It was the way he wished to become.

❧

And he did, to a degree. When he returned to New York three weeks later, he numbed out the tremors of his past with any substance he could lay his hands on, any fight he could take part in. And when Margot came home each Christmas, she would tell Theo a little more about the orphanage, and every year she would ask him to tell her about the detention center, and every time she asked he would walk away.

But then a difference in Margot's life that I whooped about: She called Toby and asked him to become one of her clients. He said yes. *Fabulous idea!* I yelled. *Why didn't I come up with that one? It makes perfect sense!* And I started dreaming about the two of them getting back together, how the second time round would be so much better, so much more about *love* and less about their frail egos, how happy Theo would be, how happy we *all* would be, maybe, in heaven . . .

And then, just as Margot set the phone receiver in its cradle, the sound of footsteps in the hall.

A figure in the doorway.

"Kit?"

He stepped forward, smiling his wide, white smile, his hands deep in his pockets.

"Aren't you supposed to be in Malaysia?"

He shrugged. "I hate giving interviews."

She linked her arms around his neck, kissing his face. He scooped her up and carried her, screaming and laughing, to the balcony and said:

"Margot, my love. Marry me."

I watched, my heart pounding, as Margot looked away from him toward the ocean below. The waves flung their faces in the open palms of beach.

And then I saw it.

She looked up at Kit and smiled, but her aura was the same shade of gold as Toby's, and right then it flowed like a full river, rich and full of currents that dragged her heart all the way across the Pacific to Toby.

But she started to nod.

No! No! I yelled, ignoring the voice in my head that reminded me of the promise I'd made to stick to the four directives—*Watch. Protect. Record. Love.* How I shouldn't interfere. And I told that voice to go to hell, and I told her, *Don't marry him, Margot!* and she looked back at him and she said, with the smallest of frowns:

"Kit, I'm all yours."

25

The Unsigned Line

THERE WAS A SLIGHT PROBLEM WITH THIS PLAN, MUCH TO
MY DELIGHT.

Margot had never signed the divorce papers. In fact, neither
she nor Toby had any clue where the papers were. It had been
so long since they separated that they'd settled into the comfort
of a relationship that had never borne the awful sting of the label
"divorce" but which, at the same time, resembled a marriage as
much as a mouse resembled a mango.

She flew to New York to discuss it. The timing coincided with
Theo's eighteenth birthday, so she told Theo and Toby that that
was the reason for her impromptu visit. But Toby knew better. He
knew his soon-to-be ex-wife like the streets of Manhattan. And
of course, Margot didn't do subtle. The rock on her ring finger
was big as a horse chestnut.

"Nice ring." Toby's opening words at JFK.

"The flight was fine, thanks. I got an upgrade."

They walked in silence to the parking lot. Toby unlocked the
door to his old Chevy. They got in. After four attempts, the engine
rumbled into life.

"Cheese and rice, Tobes, you'd think you'd replace this old thing after . . . how many years old is it?"

"I'll never replace this car. I'm getting buried in it, didn't you know?"

"We drove to Vegas in this car, didn't we?"

"To get married."

"Yes. To get married."

Back at the apartment, Toby busied himself with the urgency of coffee. It was suddenly imperative that everybody in the room should have a cup of something hot in their hand, and that the cup should be cleaned, thoroughly, and he occupied himself like this so as to distract both him and Margot from the enormity of the issue that lay between them. Divorce.

Margot knew what he was doing. It saddened her. She'd hoped he could've been braver. But I can tell you, right here, right now, that if he'd given her the "so what?" treatment, she'd have blubbed like a baby. The fact was, they'd been reacting to each other for years. Now it was time for everyone to stay calm and be neutral. It was going to take a lot of work.

"I'm getting married," she said at last.

"I can see that," Toby said into his coffee. "When?"

"Once you and I have . . . you know."

"What?"

"Done the thing that begins with a capital *D*."

"Didn't you sign the papers?"

"No."

"Oh? Why not?"

"Toby . . ."

"No, I'm actually very curious to know."

"I don't know. Okay?"

Silence. "Who is he?"

"Who?"

Toby laughed. Again, into his coffee. "The guy. Mr. Delacroix."

"Kit. Otherwise known as K. P. Lanes."

"Ah. The client. Isn't that illegal?"

"No, Toby. Otherwise, technically you and I would be going to jail."

"Oh yes. Because we're still married."

"Yes. We're still married."

۞

It had been eight months since she'd seen Theo. But, of course, eight months during teenhood is comparable to the leaps of development that occur during toddlerhood, because Theo had burst out of his short, wiry frame and turned into a looming, T-shouldered soccer player. Toby's resemblance to his son suddenly appeared so unlikely that a paternity suit wouldn't have been unreasonable. Picture them, if you will, side by side: Toby, fine boned and soft jawed, his hair wispy and flecked with silver, his hands slim and feminine, his square metal glasses perched on his narrow Roman nose. Then there was Theo, stooping to avoid door frames, his nose thick and bulbous across his face. His voice was double-bass deep—courtesy of his avid fondness for weed, of course—and his chin tilted at right angles from his jawbone, coming to another angle where a dimple formed just below his mouth. His hair was long and raised off his head in a lazy, rooster-red mohican. His clothes all of them, black—sagged and trailed and slopped around him. Even his shoes.

"Hey, Mom," he'd said when Margot knocked on his bedroom door and found him, at three in the afternoon, asleep in bed. She took a minute or two to take in the difference in him—how he'd shot up all of a sudden, how his half-naked form was suddenly a landscape of biceps and triceps. She spotted a weight bench in the corner. He rolled upright and produced a bottle of vodka from under the mattress, then paused before swigging to hold a finger to his lips. "*Shh*," he said. "Don't tell Dad."

I watched her as she went to scold him, and then she stopped. What was there to say?

And so she said, "Hey, Theo," and nothing else.

It took Toby's lawyer a week to redraft the divorce papers. I watched Toby from the window of the apartment, carrying the envelope under his arm, his aura low and gray, his ever-fragile bones getting weaker and weaker. From this distance, he looked considerably older than his forty-three years. But up close, his eyes stayed the same.

He pulled up a chair opposite Margot and read over the papers. Margot twirled her engagement ring.

"Now, let me see," said Toby, figuring out where to sign, despite the enormous X that the lawyer had placed next to the line where Toby's signature was required. "Ah, here we go."

Margot watched him. She said nothing, afraid of making this harder on him than it needed to be. A large part of her put Toby's hesitance down to his inability to let go of the past. The Chevy, his old shoes, even the kind of books he wrote. . . . they all anchored him in the happiest years of his life. As she was mulling this over, I reminded her: *Margot, sweetheart, you're exactly the same. You haven't managed to outrun the past either. Not yet.*

Toby pressed his pen against the line. He clicked his teeth with his tongue.

"Do you want to do this at another time?" Margot asked.

He stared at the wall. "I just need to be very clear on just one thing," he said. And then a long pause. We all knew that he was talking about Sonya, but even bringing it up now was worth less than the vindication he craved.

Eventually Margot helped him out.

"I know you didn't sleep with Son."

The pen dropped to the table. "What?"

"She came to see me," Margot explained gently.

"Then, why . . . ?"

"I don't know, Toby. So don't ask."

He stood up, shoved his hands in his pockets, and paced the room. Eventually he whispered the obvious. "We should've done this years ago, shouldn't we?"

"Yes. We should have."

He looked back at the papers. "You sign first. Then I'll sign and take them to the lawyer. And then it's done."

"Okay." Now it was Margot's turn. She picked up the pen and stared at the line, waiting for her signature. *What, did you think it would be easy?* I said.

She set down the pen. "This can wait," she said. "Let's get some lunch."

They went to their usual place in the East Village and took a seat outside beside a table full of loud tourists. A good distraction. An opportunity to talk about how hot it was, how the seasons were all messed up, and didn't she see that documentary about global warming, how the world will be underwater by the twenty-second century? Back and forth across the table, the get-out-of-regret-free card of small talk. They talked about Toby's next book. About her root canal. Common ground.

The divorce papers were forgotten.

James came to get me. It was dark. I'd already heard cop cars screaming past. James was panting, his eyes bulbous. "What's wrong?" I said, and he started to cry.

Theo had killed someone.

The kid had been stabbed in the back of the neck, then beaten so hard he'd drowned in his own blood. Somewhere in the course of the beating, Theo had put two bullets in his leg.

"Why did he do this?" I yelled. Before James could answer, Theo burst through the front door. The noise made Toby and Margot run out of their bedrooms. When they saw Theo, both of them immediately thought the blood dripping from his hands, hair, and clothes was his own. Some of it was. He had a broken nose and a deep knife wound in his hip. The rest was the blood of a dead boy.

Margot ran to get towels and bandages for his wounds. "Call an ambulance!"

Toby fumbled to find the cordless phone receiver, until finally he pulled out his cell phone and called 911.

And then, just as Toby reached an operator and gave his address, a voice from behind the front door:

"Police! Open up!"

Toby swung the door open and quickly found himself pressed against the wall, handcuffs clicking around his wrists, as did Theo and Margot, all while Theo screamed:

"He was raping her! He was raping her!"

26

Blind Trust

IN MY VERSION, I HAD BEEN IN SYDNEY AT THE TIME. I'd dutifully acknowledged Theo's eighteenth birthday with a phone call and a bank transfer, and then I'd spent the day reading Kit's new manuscript. I'd been in the middle of a meeting with a client when Toby had called with the news of Theo's arrest. For some reason, I downplayed it in my mind. When I'd arrived in New York a few days later, I was stunned to find reports of the killing, with Theo's mugshot splashed underneath. And, as always, I believed it was entirely Toby's fault.

Gaia and I urged James to tell us what had happened. Instead of telling us, he raised his wings above his head until a small gong of water was suspended in the air, and in that gong, a reflection:

Theo, heading home after his birthday celebrations at a bar downtown, stoned and drunk. He's wearing dirty jeans, a blood-stained T-shirt, and a pretty healthy shiner from a bust-up at the bar over a girl. He stops outside an alley to light a cigarette. There are voices. An argument. A girl, crying. A guy, hissing and swearing. Then a smack. A scream. Another smack, another threat. Theo straightens up, visibly sobering. He turns into the alley. He sees, very clearly, a jock leaning over a girl, his pants around his knees, ramming his hips into hers. For a split second, Theo visibly thinks about walking away. He doesn't want to get involved in other people's business. And then, a cry. When Theo looks again, he sees the guy lifting his fist and punching the girl in the face. "Hey!" Theo yells. The guy looks up. He takes a step back. The girl falls to the ground and whimpers, pulling her legs to her chest.

"What you doing, man?" Theo yells, striding toward the guy.

The guy—blond, slightly older than Theo, in stonewashed jeans and a white jacket—zips up his pants and waits until Theo is a couple of feet away before producing a gun from his pocket. Theo holds up his hands and takes a step back.

"Woah, woah, what you doin', man?"

The guy points the gun in Theo's face. "Back off or I'll put a hole in your face."

Theo looks at the girl on the ground. Her face is puffed up and bleeding. A small pool of blood is forming at her feet.

"Why'd you do that to your girl, huh?"

"None of your business," the guy says. "Now turn around like a good boy or I'll shoot you between the eyes."

Theo claws his cheeks and stares at the girl. "Naw, man. Sorry."

"What you mean, sorry?"

Theo looks at him. In his head, images of his time at the detention center. Memories of rape.

"That ain't right," he says softly. He looks at the girl, bleeding and shaking. "That ain't right," he says again. Before the guy knows what is happening, Theo swings his arm out and wrenches the gun from his hands. He aims it at him.

"Against the wall!" he yells. "Turn around and put your nose to the bricks, or I'll kill you."

The guy simply grins.

"Against the wall!"

The guy leans forward, his face ugly with threat. He draws a knife out of his back pocket and lunges at Theo.

Theo lowers the gun and shoots two rounds in the guy's thigh. The guy screams and drops to his knees. Theo looks at the girl. "Go on, get out of here," he says. She gets up and runs.

Theo drops the gun to the ground. He is trembling. He leans over the guy, who is moaning at his feet. "Hey, I'm sorry, man, but you gave me no choice . . ."

Before he can say anything else, the guy jams his knife into Theo's hip. He screams, and out of instinct yanks the knife out of his flesh, but not before the guy smacks him in the face. Theo recoils and sticks the knife into the guy's neck. Then he punches him. And he doesn't stop until someone calls the cops.

Theo told all of this to the police. They ran a urine test. Marijuana, alcohol, cocaine. The other guy had been clean. What girl? Nobody had seen no girl. The dead guy was a straight-A student at Columbia. Theo had a criminal record fatter than the Bible.

How did I feel during all this? The rage that had fueled me when I learned what Theo had gone through at the detention center was no longer there. Instead, I felt like I had fallen through the floor of hope's basement. I missed James. I missed Theo. I watched Margot wail and weep and pace the apartment all night long, and I watched Toby struggle to comfort her and answer her questions: *Did we do this? Is it our fault?*

Toby said, "Just wait. Just wait for the trial. He'll get justice. You'll see. You'll see."

Kit arrived a few weeks later. There was some awkwardness between him and Toby. Silently, it was decided that it was better for everyone if Margot and Kit stayed at a hotel. They checked into the Ritz-Carlton, then met Toby for dinner to discuss their plans.

Toby, knowing full well that Kit was vegetarian, booked a table for three at the Gourmet Burger joint in NoHo.

"I'm sorry," Margot whispered to Kit behind the menu. He gave a slight movement with his hand that said, "It's nothing."

It made me jittery as a field mouse crossing a freeway to watch the three of them. This was the result of the changes I'd set in motion, and I felt completely and utterly helpless, like watching a train carriage freewheel down a mountainside, containing all the people I cared about.

Margot too was jumpy. She kept quiet as a chapel during Mass, unable to eat for nerves. Kit sensed her nervousness and kept an even keel at their side of the table by smiling over his plateful of burgerless bun and lettuce and being overly, ridiculously nice to Toby. He even complimented him on his novel, which made Margot squirm. She didn't realize that Kit pitied Toby. A father in Toby's position had nothing but Kit's deepest sympathies.

"Okay, Kit, let me get to the point," said Toby, once the wine had chilled his jealousy. He reached down to the briefcase between his feet and yanked out a bunch of papers.

Kit laced his fingers and looked thoughtfully at Toby.

"Margot tells me you were a detective." He set the papers on the table and drummed his fingers on them. "I don't believe my . . . *our* son killed this kid in cold blood. I believe that a rape took place, and that somewhere out there is a girl who could save my son from the guillotine."

Kit nodded and smiled but said nothing. Toby's eyes bulged slightly. Theo's dilemma had overtaken every thought passing through Toby's brain. He hadn't slept in days. Margot stepped in.

"I think what Toby's trying to say, Kit, is that your services are needed here. The NYPD aren't on our side. We need to do some inquiries of our own to help Theo."

Kit silently topped up his wine glass. Without looking at anyone in particular he said:

"I want you both to go home, get some shut-eye, and leave me to look over these files. Okay?" He leaned forward and attempted to slide the papers from under Toby's hands. But for some reason, Toby held on to them and eyeballed Kit.

"Toby?" Margot, pleading with him in both tone and under-the-table footwork to not let his anger at Theo's predicament spill over into her relationship with Kit.

Kit, sensitive to the atmosphere, smiled and held up his hands. "Later, perhaps?"

More finger drumming. Toby seemed to seethe. Finally, he looked up at Kit. "I want you to know," he said, pointing at him. "A long time ago, I promised that I wouldn't let go. And now you're forcing my hand. I want you to know that. He drained his glass, slammed it down, and shoved the pile of papers across the table.

I leaned over and put my arms around him. He thought the sensation of being held was a projection of his deepest desire, and he audibly sobbed. I let go.

As if nothing had happened, Kit pulled out his reading glasses from his inside pocket and looked over the papers intently. After a moment or so he looked up, surprised.

"What, you two still here?"

Both of them stood up and went to leave. After a second, Margot returned and kissed Kit on the head, before walking out of the diner and into the wide night.

A six-foot five, tribal-scarred Aborigine knocking on the doors of the apartments above the alley prompted many otherwise reticent residents to cough up some details.

"I have a name," he informed Margot and Toby several nights later. He slapped his notebook on the dining table and sat down. Margot and Toby hurriedly pulled up chairs. Gaia, Adoni, and I huddled round.

"What's the name?" asked Margot quickly.

"Valita. That's all I have. No family or living relatives that we know of. Teenager. Illegal immigrant. Prostitute. Someone saw her in the area during the early hours of the morning that the killing happened."

"Do we have an address? A surname?" Toby, shaking with adrenaline.

Kit shook his head. "Not yet, but I'm working on it."

Adoni looked up at Gaia and me, his perpetual scowl etched into his face. "The girl isn't ready to come forward yet," he said. "I've seen her angel."

"You have?" I almost lunged at him across the table. At exactly the same time, Margot stood up and began to pace the room.

"How do we get that address? I mean, isn't there some sort of database we can search through? Shouldn't we take this name to the cops?"

Kit shook his head.

"Why not?" I asked Adoni, and my voice chimed with Margot's as she asked Kit the same thing.

Kit spoke first. "This stays with us until we've got more details. If they know we're doing our own sniffing about, they'll keep so many tabs on us that it'll make any kind of private investigation very difficult. Trust me."

At last, Toby spoke. "I agree with Margot," he said. "I'd rather run this by the police."

Kit looked at Margot. She folded her arms and scowled.

"He's right," Adoni told James, Gaia, and I. "There's a very powerful demon working closely with the team involved in Theo's case. We need to keep this close for the time being."

I approached Margot. With great hesitation, I told her to trust Kit. When I got through to her, she melted into tears. Toby jerked beside her, about to put his arms around her on instinct, then stopped himself. Kit stood up, gave Toby a look, and walked toward Margot. He pressed her head against his shoulder and rubbed her back. She glanced over at Toby. He shoved his hands in his pockets and looked outside at the setting sun.

And then, *deus ex machina*.

Toby, Kit, and Margot were sitting at an outside coffee-shop table close to Washington Square Park. Suddenly, Adoni raced across the street to another angel in a red dress, then quickly waved back at Gaia and me to join him. The angel—an older Ecuadorian woman—was agitated, though relieved to see us.

"This is Tygren," Adoni said.

Tygren turned to us. "I was there when all of this happened. Believe me, I am working very hard to persuade Valita to go to the police, but it may be some time before I achieve this. I don't know if it'll be too late."

"Where is she?" I asked.

"Look over there," she said, pointing at a small hooded figure seated on a park bench beyond a small hedge. "That's Valita," she said. I squinted to see the girl. She was smoking. Her hand trembled with every drag.

"Why hasn't she gone to the cops?" Gaia said quickly.

"Can't you persuade her?" I said, cutting Gaia off. "We don't have much time."

Tygren held up both hands. "I'm trying," she said, "but there's a history between her and the boy who was killed that she needs to work through first. Her family's on the verge of being deported. And she's pregnant."

I glanced over at Valita again. When I looked harder, I could see shadows orbiting around her, sometimes colliding, occasionally penetrating her. And then, deep in her womb, the small light of the child. She finished her cigarette and squashed the butt under her shoe, then folded her arms around herself, withdrawing deeper inside her jacket. She looked like she wanted to simply vanish.

Adoni took both Tygren's hands in his and said something in Quechua. Tygren smiled and nodded.

Valita stood up suddenly and started walking in the opposite direction.

"I have to go!" Tygren said. "I'll meet you again, I promise."

"How will we find you?" I shouted.

A second later, she was gone.

From that point on, as Toby, Kit, and Margot spent day after day pursuing dead ends, Gaia, Adoni, and I were on the lookout for Tygren.

Christmas came and went without celebration. Eventually, and despite our persuasions, Margot and Toby finally convinced Kit to pass on Valita's name to the investigator in charge of the case. As Kit predicted, the investigator wasn't interested. No evidence, no witness statements. The pretrial hearings made much of Theo's mumbled statement, in which he'd claimed that he didn't know who the knife belonged to. It might have been his. The prosecution jumped on it. They found similar knives under his bed. The investigators threw out the possibility of a girl when the forensics reported only two kinds of blood on the scene—discounting the fact that it had rained later that night—thanks to Grogor, the accusations made during the hearings served only to enrage Theo, to the point that he came across much less an innocent victim than an aggressive lout.

Gaia, Adoni and I kept watch for Tygren, but no sign. We figured that Valita must have moved out of state or left the country altogether. Part of me didn't blame her. The other part of me yearned to see Theo and James, even if only one more time, if only to tell them I loved them both.

One night, I went all the way to Rikers Island, making my way through a sea of demons to find Theo huddled in a cramped, filthy room, suddenly so small and shrunken by the gravity of his surroundings. An inmate several cells down was yelling a woman's name and threatening to slash his wrists. I saw the crimes carried out by the men all around the block appearing inside their cells like parallel worlds, spiritual badges of their sins, and I saw their demons, all of which looked exactly like

Grogor when I first encountered him: monstrous, bestial, bent on destroying me.

But there were angels there too. Most of them men, some of them soft, motherly women, standing over the men whose crimes made me retch. Despite the horror of their crimes, their angels were still loving. Still tender.

I was suddenly aware that I had no idea who or what James had been in his mortality, but when I found him with Theo, I was certain of one thing: This boy, the one I'd been so quick to dismiss when we first met, was made of tough stuff. Theo had four demons in his cell, all of them reminiscent of Tongan soccer players, hulking over James's slim form. But they cowered in the corner, daring only to throw out the occasional taunt to Theo. It appeared that James had the upper hand.

"What are you doing here?" James said when I appeared. Immediately Theo's demons stood up to abuse me. He threw them a look.

I hugged him tight and looked over at Theo, who peered around him. "Is someone there?"

I looked at James. "He can sense me?"

James nodded. "Most likely," he said. "I won't lie to you, he's had it rough in here. But so far I think I've spared him the worst of it. The good thing is that he's appreciating how good he had it before. He thought he was a tough kid until they locked those doors. Now, he's drawing a long list of plans for when he gets out."

"So he hasn't given up hope?"

James shook his head. "He can't allow himself to. Seeing the other guys in here . . . well, it's made him determined to get free, I'll tell you that."

And so I left them, holding it together in one of the darkest places on earth, two candles in a storm, and I dared to trust that, somehow, they'd make it out of there.

Not long after, Kit left at Margot's insistence. He needed to pick up his book tour, and money was running out. Talk of their wedding plans had, I was pleased to see, all but ceased. He was watching Margot reinsert herself in New York, into a life where Kit didn't belong. In their suite at the Ritz-Carlton he'd started sleeping on the couch. Stubbornly, Margot pretended not to notice.

He was waiting for her when she returned one night from Toby's apartment. I knew they'd been discussing nothing more than what would happen to Theo if he pleaded guilty, that the evening was no more romantic than dinner in a morgue, but Kit imagined otherwise. He was jealous. It withered his dignity.

"You seem to be getting pretty cozy with Toby." Kit's voice from the corner when she entered the room. She gave a small jump.

"Give it a rest, Kit," she said. "Toby's Theo's father. What am I supposed to do? Stonewall him while our son goes down for murder?"

Kit shrugged. "Or maybe you should just sleep with him."

She threw him a look and seethed.

Kit took her silence as an admission of guilt. I sighed. "Tell him nothing happened," I told Adoni. He nodded and whispered in Kit's ear.

Kit stood up and walked slowly toward her.

"Don't you love me anymore?" he said. The pain in his voice made me wince.

"Look," she said after a pause. "This is a really bad time for everyone. Go back to Sydney, do your tour, and I'll follow you in a couple of weeks."

He was standing close to her now, his arms by his sides. "Don't you love me anymore?" he repeated.

I watched as questions and answers circulated around her head. *Do I? No. Yes. I don't know anymore. I want Toby. No, I don't. Yes I do. I don't want to be alone. I'm so afraid.*

She burst into tears. Huge, overdue tears that exploded into the palm of her hand, then into Kit's chest as he pulled her into an embrace.

Eventually, she took a step back and wiped her eyes.

"Promise me you'll come home," Kit said softly.

She looked up at him. "I promise I'll come home," she said. He bent down and kissed her forehead. Within minutes he was gone.

I should have been happy. But instead, as I watched Margot raid the drinks cabinet, spending a sleepless night soaked in tears and wine, I doubted everything. I did not know anymore what was best for her. So I prayed.

* * *

Soon after, I followed behind her as she made her way to Toby's apartment, keeping watch for any sign of Tygren. She knocked on Toby's door, but it was already open. He was expecting her.

She found him standing by the window looking down at the street, ready to swoop on any young woman that resembled Theo's description of Valita. So many days he'd spent like this, huddled in his old Aran sweater, forgetting to eat or drink, staring, his eyes slowly retreating into themselves. And as she watched him, a memory of that night in the Hudson, of those few seconds as she'd sat alone in the boat, waiting for Toby to surface. She was doing that now. And she felt just as anxious and, to her alarm, just as in love.

"I'm going back to Sydney," she said.

He turned around and looked at her, his eyes hurting from lack of sleep. He fumbled mentally through an assortment of bewildered responses. Eventually he reached the word "Why?"

She sighed. "I need to move on with things, Toby. I'll be back soon. But I need to . . . there's nothing here for me, you know?"

He nodded.

She smiled weakly and turned to leave.

"Aren't you going to sign the papers?"

She stopped in her tracks. "I forgot. I'll do it now."

She headed for the table and sat down. Toby produced the papers from a drawer in the kitchen and set them in front of her.

"Have you got a pen?"

He handed her one.

"Thanks."

She stared at the page.

Slowly, very slowly, Toby set his hand on top of hers. She looked up at him. "Toby?"

He didn't let go. Instead, he pulled her gently to her feet and put his arm around her waist. She looked into his eyes, those wintering leaves. It had been a long, long time since they'd been this close. And then he leaned in and kissed her. The softest, most sincere kiss of her life.

She pushed him away. He leaned in again.

This time, she didn't.

27

The Blue Jewel

NOW, I SHOULD MENTION AT THIS POINT THAT MY GRAND SCHEME TO GET MARGOT BACK WITH TOBY HAD ALL BUT DISINTEGRATED AMID THE CONFUSION AND GUILT I'D FELT WHEN I SAW HER RELATIONSHIP WITH KIT SHINE WITH SUCH PROMISE, ONLY TO FALL APART. I swear, I didn't do it. I didn't pull it down. In fact, I vowed to step away and let her make her own mind up.

Right now, at the crunch point, it took enormous effort for me not to step back in and sway the game in my favor.

She put her hands against Toby's chest and pulled away.

"What are you doing, Toby?"

He looked at her closely and smiled. "I'm saying good-bye." He stepped back, picked up the pen on the table and handed it to her. "You were just about to sign."

She looked at the pen. She flicked her eyes back at Toby. And when she looked again, she didn't see the Toby who had passed through the crucible of their marriage and their son's imminent conviction. She saw the Toby who had surfaced in the Hudson twenty years ago. The Toby she'd thought had drowned, the Toby she never, ever wanted to lose.

"I need to think," she said before putting down the pen.

"Don't do this, Margot," he called behind her. "Don't leave me hanging with this while you waltz off to the other side of the planet."

She turned in the hallway. "My flight's tomorrow. I'm going back to my hotel."

"So, that's it?" Toby said angrily. "You won't even sign the divorce papers?"

A pause. Then she walked toward him, took the papers and pen from his hand, and scribbled her name on the line.

She handed the papers back to him without a word.

⚘

Back at the hotel, she took a long bath. She replayed the kiss in her mind, and at first it appeared above her head like a horror film, then a comedy, until eventually she sank deeper into the water and let it replay like it happened. How it had *felt*. Home. Peace.

A phone call from the front desk made her jump out of the bath. She had a visitor, the concierge said. A Mr. Toby Poslusny. Could he come up? She hesitated. *Yes*, I told her, my heart racing. "Okay," she said.

It was like being in the deleted scenes of a movie. I thought back to this point in my life, when I'd stayed at the hotel alone during the pretrial hearings, occasionally enduring bitter meetings with Toby to discuss visiting times to go see Theo, or the date of the next hearing. Everything was so new now, and I had no idea what was going to happen.

And then I thought of my death. It had always been hazy in my memory, such a sudden event. Put a gun to my head, ask me what death was like, and I'd have to tell you to pull the trigger. I had no idea. I'd been ripped from this world faster than a pocket thief in Manhattan. One minute I was in a hotel room, the next I was standing over my body and, a split-second later, I was in the afterlife meeting Nan.

Margot wrapped herself in a white bathrobe and answered the door. Toby stood there for a moment, frowning, until she invited him in.

"Why are you here, Toby?"

"Because you forgot something."

"I did?"

"Uh-huh."

She stared at him, then threw a hand in the air, exasperated. "What did I forget?"

He stared her out. "You forgot that you have a husband. And a home. Oh, and a son."

"Toby . . ." She flopped down on the bed.

He knelt in front of her and cupped her face. "If you ask me to stop, I'll stop. I promise."

He kissed her. She didn't ask him to stop.

※❀※

It wasn't the fact that he said "I love you" that made me leap for joy, nor her own "I love you too," nor their lovemaking. It was the fact that, after many hours of pillow talk about the past and then about the future, they decided, over the noise from the park, against the glowing lights of the celebrations for Chinese New Year, to try again.

And as the music and gunshots littered the air across the city, and as Margot's aura burned golden and the light around her heart throbbed, Gaia and I hugged each other, and I wept and begged her to tell me I wasn't dreaming. That this was all really happening.

For a long time, they held each other in bed, silently lacing and unlacing their fingers as they had done all those years ago in Theo's crummy loft apartment in the West Village.

"What time is it?" Toby leaned across Margot to glance at his watch.

"Eleven. Why?"

He jumped up and threw on his shirt.

"Where're you going?" she said, rolling upright. "Tell me you're not going home?"

"I'm going home." He darted forward and planted a kiss on her forehead. "But I'll be right back."

"Why are you going home?"

"My cell phone," he said. "What if one of the investigators calls about Theo? They've no way of contacting me here."

Toby looked at her in the bed, curled around a pillow. He smiled. "I won't be long." Then he hesitated and watched her, very seriously. And I saw, for the first time in many, many years, the ice forming all around him. His fear.

"You'll wait for me, won't you?"

Margot laughed. "Tobes, where am I gonna go?" He stared. "Yes," she said, "I'll wait."

With that, he left.

I thought, this is why I had no memory of the way that I died. Because somewhere toward the end of my life, the road had forked. Whereas I had chosen one path, Margot now chose another. Somehow, these two paths had a relationship that I couldn't see. They entwined in some way to bring me to the end. And now that I could see where that path could lead, to a new life with Toby, a marriage that might actually work this time, I didn't want the path to end.

And so, when messages came to me through my wings to *let be, let be,* I couldn't.

A knock at the door. I jumped. "Room service, ma'am," said a voice. When Margot opened the door, I was poised. The young man standing in front of her holding the tray of food looked her over, then placed the tray on the bed and walked out without expecting a tip.

I watched as Margot jumped in the shower, then I checked out the hotel corridor for demons. Grogor was lurking somewhere. I could sense it.

❧

Toby returned to his apartment to find a note slipped beneath the door. He almost missed it. After digging out his cell phone and charger from the kitchen drawer, then splashing some aftershave around his cheeks and checking out his teeth, he grabbed some clean clothes and was about to head back to Margot. But then he saw it.

A white, crumpled page with childish writing. It said:

Sir—

I am writing to say I'm sorry for you son. I am the girl he talking about to the newspapers. For reasons I cant explain here I do not

*want to be identified. I will call you again and we can talk this
over, I don't want to send an innocent man to the prison.*

What your son is saying is true.

V

Toby raced out into the corridor. Old Mrs. O'Connor from the
apartment opposite was returning from her nightly stroll. Toby
grabbed her like a man possessed.

"'Mrs. O'Connor, did you see anyone come to my door this
evening?"

She stared at him. "Uh, no sweetheart, I don't think so . . ."

He lunged at another door and hammered. After a few minutes
it opened. Music blasting inside. A drunk Chinese kid in the
doorway. "Happy New Year, man!"

No point in asking. Toby ran back inside his apartment. He
grabbed the letter, his hands shaking, and read it several times.
Then he dialed 911 and prayed Margot would keep her word.
That she would wait.

Which she did. She ate the apricot glazed duck on ginger rice and
drank half the house special. She thought of what she was going
to do next. She thought of what she *wanted* to happen next. And
she returned to that dream of so many years ago: the picket-fence
house. Toby, writing. Theo, a free man.

Maybe it was within reach.

But I was at my wits' end, because I was watching her dream
and fall in love again; I was watching her body light up with the
glow of hope, the light around her heart that had been dormant all
these years now pulsing and expanding around her like a white,

blinding eclipse, and the messages that came to me said, *Let be. Let be,* and I was frantic, because I remembered what I'd seen immediately after I died: my own body, lying on this bed, on these sheets, facedown in my own blood.

Don't let anyone in, I told her. Did Toby kill me, I thought? Was it Toby? Was it Kit? Valita? Sonya? I sang the Song of Souls. *Get out! Get out!* I told her. Whoever was about to come in that door was going to kill her, I was sure of it. Finally, I told her, go look out the window at the celebrations. It's Chinese New Year. Year of the Serpent. Look, they've even got serpent-shaped floats. And fireworks. In fact, go downstairs and look. Check it out.

She picked up the last of the wine and walked over to the window, looking down at the park. Directly below was a crowd of people. A parade wound its way through the park. Fireworks rustled in the sky, masking the occasional crack of celebratory gunshots. She yanked open the window and looked back at the clock beside the bed. Almost midnight. *Oh, Toby,* she thought, *why couldn't you have been here for this?* And I told her, lock the door. But she laughed and brushed the thought clean out of her head.

And then, midnight.

The sound of a clock echoes through a set of speakers below. *One* . . . Margot presses her palms against the windowsill, looking down. *Two* . . . Toby has given up waiting for a cab and is jogging his way to the hotel. *Three* . . . I look down at the blue stone around my neck. What was it they said I'd been wearing when they found my body? A Kashmir sapphire? *Four* . . . Margot picks up Toby's jacket and wraps it around her shoulders, protecting herself against the cold. *Five* . . . In the park below, someone cheers and fires a gun high into the sky. *Six* . . . I see it. I see the bullet as it strays through the dark air. I see it as you might see a coin being tossed toward you, or a ball being hit by a racket. I see where it is headed, right for the window. And I know, I know in that instant: *I can reach it. I can stop it.* And then, the message in my wings: *Let be. Seven* . . . *Why?* I ask aloud. Eight . . . *Let be. Nine* . . . Toby reaches the hotel lobby. He thumps the escalator button. *Ten* . . . I close my eyes. *Eleven* . . . The bullet hits its destination, close to Margot's heart. *Twelve* . . . She falls backward, gasping for a moment, looking me right in the eyes as I lean over her, holding her, weeping and telling her it's okay, it's okay, it's over now. It's over. And then she looks at me, and reaches forward. I clasp her hand.

We are one.

28

The Road Among the Hills

THERE IS AN INTIMACY IN THE ROLE OF ANGELS THAT IS SINGULAR TO THE SACRED. When I was human I wouldn't have seen beyond the requirements of my angelic responsibilities without feeling weirded out about how voyeuristic it all seemed, about perversions of privacy. Only as an angel could I comprehend how compassionate this kind of protection really was, how tender this companionship. Only as an angel could I comprehend death for what it really is.

I stood up and looked down over Margot's body, re-experiencing everything I'd felt first time around, immediately after my death. The shock of seeing myself before me without a pulse. The horror at what this meant. Only, this time, I accepted it. I didn't reach forward to touch her cheek because she was me; I reached to confirm the thought that seized me: that I had come to the end of the road of mortality. I was leaving Margot behind.

Nan came just before Toby arrived. Merciful, I guess. I couldn't have coped with seeing him as he stumbled into the hotel room, his face flushed, his heart pounding, only to find the body. It was bad enough imagining it. Nan told me to follow her, and quickly.

In a blur of tears, I leaned into Toby's jacket and inhaled his smell. I had a strong urge to leave something behind, a note, maybe, some indication that, even though it was unlikely that I would ever see him again, I would always love him. But I could do nothing except follow slowly behind Nan into the night.

I found myself back in the dark, damp silence of Theo's prison cell, right next to him as he sat cross-legged on the floor, drawing. He was humming softly to himself, a song that sounded very like the Song of Souls. James stood by the window, reflected in the moonlight. He strode toward me and flung his arms around me.

"I have news," he said, squeezing my hands. "Tygren came to see me. She's confident that she can persuade Valita to speak out now."

I closed my eyes and sighed in relief. "That's wonderful," I said. And then I started to cry.

"What's wrong?" James said.

I looked at Theo. I didn't know when I would see him again, or *if* I would see him again. I tried to explain this to James, but it all came out in a series of high-pitched squeals, until he turned to Nan for an explanation. She simply shook her head as if to say, it's not my place to explain. I crouched down, reached out to Theo and put my arms around him. He looked up for a second, aware that the air around him felt different. Then he went back to drawing. He was covering the slate floor in chalk crocodiles.

"We have to go," Nan prompted me. James looked from Nan to me.

"Where are you going?"

"Margot is dead," I said, wiping my eyes and taking deep breaths. "I came to say good-bye to you and Theo." I wanted to say so much more. "I want you to know, there is absolutely nobody on this earth that I would trust to look after him as much as you." I smiled and turned to leave.

"Wait." James stepped forward, his expression serious. "Just . . . wait up, Ruth." He glanced at Nan. "This is important. It'll only take a second." He took both my hands in his and stared at me intently. "You know, you've never asked me who I was before; why I'm Theo's angel."

I blinked. "Who were you?"

"I was the diamond you couldn't save," he said. "I'm your son."

I took a step back and looked from him to Theo. And then, I saw the similarities between them pressing themselves against me like revealed truths: the defiant jaw, the square, robust palms. And I thought of watching the baby inside Margot, Seth's baby, the feeling of losing it, the confusion, the not-knowing what I had lost. Wondering on each of its would-be birthdays what my life would have been like had that child lived.

And now I was meeting him.

"We haven't got much time," Nan warned from behind me.

Through blinding tears, I walked back toward James and hugged him tight. "Why didn't you tell me sooner?"

"Would it have changed anything, really? We're family anyway." He turned to Theo. "One day, we'll meet as brothers."

I looked at them both, the man and his angel. My sons.

I kissed James's face, and before I could say anything, he was gone.

Nan and I arrived in the valley with the lake, the one where we'd first met. I felt a strange sense of symmetry. I half expected her to push me into the lake again, sending me back to earth a third time. I closed my eyes and felt the long grass brushing against my fingers, the wet earth under my toes. I braced myself for what was coming. Ahead, I could see the road again, curling through the green hills, and my heart sank. I reckoned that I knew now where it led.

"Am I going to hell now?" I asked, my voice shaking.

She stopped and stared at me.

A few moments passed. "Nan?"

Finally, Nan spoke, "You have to give your journal over to God now, Ruth."

She took my hand and led me toward the lake. "*No,*" I said when we reached the water's edge. "I'm not going back in again. No, sir."

She ignored me. "Put your journal on the water. Give it over to God. It's his now."

"How do I do that?"

"Well, I know you won't like the sound of it, but you do actually have to go into the water. I promise, you won't drown."

I stepped into the water, holding on to her hands, tight. Immediately the water flowing from my back unraveled like two ribbons, loosening from my skin, seeping into the green ripples. And within those ripples, images of Margot, images of Toby and Theo, images of everything I'd seen and heard and touched and felt. Everything I'd feared and loved, everything I'd trusted. All of it, carried within the water. A book, of sorts, traveling all the way to the throne of God.

"So, what now?" I asked. "Is hell at the end of that road up there?"

We were still in the lake. "Do you remember what happened the day you prevented the car crash?"

"I stopped it from happening."

"And how did you do that?"

"I think it had something to do with trust."

"And then what happened?"

"My body changed."

She stood closer, her dress fanning in the water. "You became a *Seraph*. The highest of the angels, the army of light, standing between heaven and hell, like a sword in the hand of God."

"A what?"

"A sword in the hand of God," she said very slowly. "A living sword. Dividing light from dark. And that is why you went through the most harrowing of experiences. You can only become a Seraph by passing through the Refiner's fire. By suffering. When you returned as your own guardian angel, time and space folded over like a rose bending in the wind. You always were your own guardian angel. And this was always the plan, you just didn't know it yet. Everything you went through, it was for this."

"But what about Grogor?" I said quietly. "And the deal I made? I thought I was going to hell."

"That might have been the case if your reasons had been selfish. But you chose to sacrifice your own happiness in order to achieve Theo's. God knew then that you were to be one of his finest angels. But you needed to learn to trust, first."

I held on to her, and I keeled over just as I had done so many years before, gasping for breath. This time out of relief, not shock. I glanced at the road among the hills.

"So . . . that's not the road to hell, then?"

"Quite the opposite."

When I got it together again I looked her in the eyes, and I thought of the question that had burned in my head all these years, the question that had underlined every one of my experiences, every dimension of my regret.

"Why did I have to go through all this?" I said quietly. "Why didn't I go back as some kindly old widow's guardian angel, or a celebrity, or someone who led a nice quiet life . . . Why did I come back as Margot's angel? Was it a mistake?"

"Absolutely not," Nan said carefully. "You were chosen as your own guardian angel because it was the only way to complete your spiritual journey. It was the only way that you could become who you are now." She leaned back and smiled. "A sword isn't made in water, Ruth. It is made in fire."

I looked at the road ahead, at the landscape around me. I thought of Toby. Would I ever see him again? Nan squeezed my shoulders.

"Trust," she said. "Trust."

I nodded.

"Okay," I said. "Let's do this."

And she led me there, right to the road, right to the end.

A sword in the hand of God.

# A Celestial Sword

IT HAS BEEN MANY YEARS SINCE I FIRST SET MY JOURNAL ON THE WATER AND LET IT DRIFT OFF TO . . . WHEREVER. I hope it was a good read. I hope it was of some use.

Since then, I have been kept mighty busy. My activities have been much more international, shall we say, than my first outing as an angel. I have prevented dozens of world wars. I have been among those Seraphim who stood in the sapphire, goose-pimpling depths of the Antarctic and held back meltwater, turning it instead into cloud, carrying it far into the stratosphere, even cracking open the earth and letting the oceans pour down, down toward its red heart. I have stepped inside the silence of tornados—yep, just like Dorothy—and driven them past houses full of children, I have lifted cattle who have drifted inside its vacuum and held them safely until it stopped, and set them on their way. I have pushed back tsunamis, like toppling walls, from land dotted with hotels, homes, small figures building sand castles on the beach, unawares.

Occasionally, I am told to let go. I am told to watch the tornado take this house, and that life, I am told to let the earthquake happen and merely pick up the pieces, I am told to let go of the tsunami. I have no idea why.

But I let go.

I still see Toby. I have watched him potter about his apartment in a threadbare cardigan and shoes that are holey as swiss cheese, I have watched him replace his glasses with thicker lenses and his teeth with more and more bits of porcelain. I have watched him as he spoke of me at Theo's wedding, hoping he didn't slip out the parts about drugs, and I watched him hold our twin granddaughters and insist that one of them receive the name Margot.

I talk to him. I tell him what things are like here. I tell him to go to a doctor, and soon, to see about that hand, that cough. Or that ache in his gut. I glance over his manuscripts and tell him where he's missing a comma, where he could improve things. I tell him I love him.

And I tell him that I'm here, always.

That I am waiting.

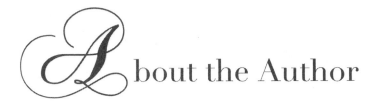

About the Author

CAROLYN JESS-COOKE IS THE AUTHOR OF THE CELEBRATED POETRY COLLECTION INROADS (SEREN, 2010), WHICH WON AN ERIC GREGORY AWARD, THE NORTHERN PROMISE AWARD FOR POETRY, AND THE TYRONE GUTHRIE PRIZE FOR POETRY, AND WHICH WAS SUPPORTED BY A GRANT FROM THE ARTS COUNCIL OF ENGLAND. Previously a film academic, she has also written and coedited four nonfiction books in the field of Film Studies and Shakespeare.

Carolyn was born in 1978 in Belfast, Northern Ireland, and now lives in England with her husband and three children. Her Web site is www.carolynjesscooke.co.uk.

SEVEN SEAS ENTERTAINMENT PRESENTS

Akashic Records
of Bastard Magic Instructor VOLUME 2

story by AOSA TSUNEMI   art by TARO HITSUJI   original character designs by KURONE MISHIMA

P9-DFV-

TRANSLATION
Ryan Peterson

ADAPTATION
Dambi Eloriaga-Amago

LETTERING
Brandon Bovia

COVER DESIGN
Nicky Lim

PROOFREADER
Danielle King
Janet Houck

ASSISTANT EDITOR
Jenn Grunigen

PRODUCTION ASSISTANT
CK Russell

PRODUCTION MANAGER
Lissa Pattillo

EDITOR-IN-CHIEF
Adam Arnold

PUBLISHER
Jason DeAngelis

ROKUDENASHI MAJUTSU KOSHI TO AKASHIC RECORD VOL. 2
©Taro HITSUJI 2015, ©Aosa TSUNEMI 2015, ©Kurone MISHIMA 2015
First published in Japan in 2015 by KADOKAWA CORPORATION, Tokyo.
English translation rights reserved by Seven Seas Entertainment, LLC.
under the license from KADOKAWA CORPORATION, Tokyo.

No portion of this book may be reproduced or transmitted in any form without
written permission from the copyright holders. This is a work of fiction. Names,
characters, places, and incidents are the products of the author's imagination
or are used fictitiously. Any resemblance to actual events, locales, or persons,
living or dead, is entirely coincidental.

Seven Seas books may be purchased in bulk for promotional, educational, or
business use. Please contact your local bookseller or the Macmillan Corporate
and Premium Sales Department at 1-800-221-7945, extension 5442, or by
e-mail at MacmillanSpecialMarkets@macmillan.com.

Seven Seas and the Seven Seas logo are trademarks of
Seven Seas Entertainment, LLC. All rights reserved.

ISBN: 978-1-626926-65-3

Printed in Canada

First Printing: December 2017

10 9 8 7 6 5 4 3 2 1

FOLLOW US ONLINE: *www.gomanga.com*

READING DIRECTIONS

This book reads from *right to left*, Japanese style.
If this is your first time reading manga, you start
reading from the top right panel on each page and
take it from there. If you get lost, just follow the
numbered diagram here. It may seem backwards at
first, but you'll get the hang of it! Have fun!!

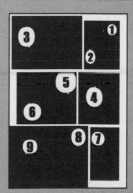

AKASHIC RECORDS OF BASTARD
MAGIC INSTRUCTOR

The author by Taro Hitsuji

Comic by Aosa Tsunemi

Character design by Kurone Mishima

Hello there! I'm Aosa Tsunemi. Thank you so much for purchasing Volume 2 of *Akashic Records of Bastard Magical Instructor*.

2015.11

I was able to safely make it through Volume 2 thanks to the support of many people. The story has moved along a fair amount and there's a lot of new characters compared to Volume 1, but strangely enough, after reading the original light novels, there were some characters that didn't leave a particularly strong impression on me. But when I started drawing them for the manga, I came to really like them or see some interesting qualities in them I hadn't noticed before and in so doing, discovered a new layer of entertainment in drawing the manga.

This is a behind-the-scenes discussion, but I talked with Hitsuji-sensei and Mishima-sensei (since they made the original light novels) about how Gene and Carell (the two characters pictured in this afterword) look, but other than a few key points they gave me for the characters, they were nice enough to give me the freedom to leave the rest of their design to my imagination. So presumptuous as it may be, I used the light novels as a reference and made up the rest. These two characters were never shown in any of the insert images in the light novels, but I'm sure those of you who have read the original light novels have envisioned them in your own way, so I hope that my illustrations align with what you imagined, if even just a little, and that they're to your liking! Of course, I hope you readers who haven't read the original light novels also enjoy them!

Staff   Thanks

Ruyoru Asahi   Taro Hitsuji
Piko   Mishima-sensei
Yuuki HB   Kishida-san
        Yoshimaru

羊太郎
Taro Hitsugi

I love seeing the expressions on the faces of the characters in this comic version of *Akashic Records of Bastard Magical Instructor*. They're all so lively and change so often that it's really a blast to read!

三嶋くろね
Kurone Mishima

Congratulations on Volume 2 going on sale! Releasing two volumes in two months in Japan must've been really rough! Good work! The magic incantation scenes are really cool to read in manga form. It's so much fun to be able to see all the different expressions from Glenn, Sisty, and Rumia in each panel!

WHAT?! FOR REAL?!

SHOCK

T-TEACH...

THE SCHOOL HAS A COMMON BATH, BUT IT'S SCHEDULED SO THE TWO SEXES AREN'T BATHING AT THE SAME TIME. IT'S *WAY PAST* THE ALLOTTED TIME FOR BOYS.

SHAKE

P...

SHAKE

H-HOLD ON THERE, WHITE CAT! THIS WAS AN OVER-SIGHT!

STOP! C'MON, I'M LITERALLY TOTALLY EXPOSED...!

IT SEEMS LIKE IT'S GONNA TAKE A LITTLE WHILE BEFORE THE TWO OF THEM ARE ON *FRIENDLY* TERMS.

BRZZT

Purple flash of the spirit of lightning!!

GYAAAAAA!!

BRZZZT

End
Special Lecture

BRZT

BRZT

IF WE LET OURSELVES GET HUNG UP ON PETTY THINGS LIKE THAT, DO YOU REALLY THINK WE'LL *EVER* BE ABLE TO GET BEHIND THE TRUTH ABOUT MAGIC, WHICH KEEPS EVOLVING EVERY DAY?

HE MAY NOT BE ABLE TO PERFORM ONE-CLAUSE INCANTATIONS, BUT THAT DOESN'T CHANGE THE FACT THAT HE UNVEILED A WHOLE NEW WORLD TO US.

......

YEAH. *PLUS* RECENTLY HE'S STARTED TO ANSWER MY QUESTIONS.

CHATTER

SHOULDN'T TEACHERS NORMALLY DO THAT?

CHATTER

HA HA! THE HECK? SO YOU DO LIKE HIM!

W-WELL, I ACKNOWLEDGE THAT WE HAVE A LOT TO LEARN FROM HIM.

E R R R ....

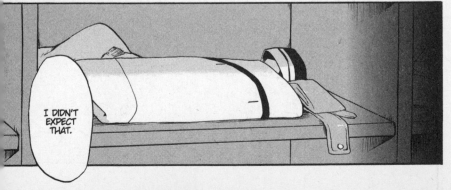

I DIDN'T EXPECT THAT.

BUT HE STILL DOESN'T REALLY OPEN UP TO OTHERS. I SENSE SOMETHING OF A *RIFT* BETWEEN US...

GIBUL'S GOT THE NEXT HIGHEST GRADES IN OUR CLASS AFTER SISTY.

I'M PREPARING FOR OUR NEXT LESSON, SO COULD YOU KEEP IT DOWN?

IT'S NOT A TOPIC I'M INTERESTED IN.

I ADMIT THAT HE KNOWS SOME FACETS OF MAGIC THAT WE'RE UNAWARE OF.

HE'S NOT WORTH MAKING A FUSS OVER.

FOR REAL? YOU DON'T CARE AT ALL ABOUT OUR NEW INSTRUCTOR?

DON'T YOU THINK THAT'S GOING A BIT TOO FAR?

GUESS YOU GOTTA POINT...

HE DOESN'T DESERVE TO BE INCLUDED IN THE SAME RANK AS OUR SCHOOL'S OTHER FAMED INSTRUCTORS.

BUT AT THE END OF THE DAY, IT'S JUST THEORIES ON HOW TO PERFORM SOME PARLOR TRICKS DEVISED BY A MAGE THAT CAN'T EVEN PERFORM A ONE-CLAUSE INCANTATION.

WELL, IT TAKES ONE UNCOUTH BOOR TO KNOW ANOTHER ONE.

I THINK PROFESSOR GLENN'S A PRETTY SWELL GUY.

OH, KASSHU.

LYNN AND WENDY, TOO.

WENDY'S A LITTLE LIKE SISTY. MAYBE IT'S BECAUSE THEY WERE BOTH BORN INTO NOBILITY.

CAN'T YOU EVEN TELL THAT I'M INSULTING YOU?

THAT'S LYNN IN THE BACK. SHE STILL SEEMS A LITTLE HESITANT AROUND THE PROFESSOR.

NOW, NOW...

KASSHU IS CHEERFUL AND CANDID.

BOARS? WHAT'S WILDLIFE GOT TO DO WITH ANYTHING?

HE'S PROBABLY THE ONE WHO TALKS WITH PROF GLENN THE MOST AMONG ALL THE BOY STUDENTS.

WHAT DO *YOU* THINK, GIBUL?

BLAH BLAH

THE THREE OF THEM HAVE TOTALLY DIFFERENT PERSONALITIES, BUT THEY'RE ALL DEAR FRIENDS TO ME.

IT'S BEEN A LONG TIME SINCE WE'VE ALL HAD SOMETHING IN COMMON TO TALK ABOUT.

THIS IS SISTY.

MY BEST FRIEND, WHO'S MORE LIKE A SISTER TO ME. SHE'S THE DAUGHTER OF THE FIBEL FAMILY, THE FOLKS WHO WERE KIND ENOUGH TO RAISE ME LIKE ONE OF THEIR OWN.

AND HERE I THOUGHT HIS CLASSES HAD FINALLY STARTED TO IMPROVE.

HON-ESTLY!

S-SURE...

ISN'T THERE ANYTHING THAT CAN CHANGE THAT BAD ATTITUDE OF HIS?!

DON'T YOU AGREE, RUMIA?!

OH? OUR CLASS'S STAR PUPIL SEEMS TO BE FUMING.

IT SEEMS LIKE SISTY DOESN'T GET ALONG WITH OUR NEW TEACHER, PROFESSOR GLENN.

YAWN! BORED.

I REALLY WOULD LOVE IT IF THEY COULD JUST GET ALONG.

HMM....

JUST LOOK, PROFESSOR!

WHAT GIVES WITH THIS "ALCHEMY TO TRANSFORM STONES INTO SOMETHING THAT LOOKS A LOT LIKE GOLD" CRAP?!

DON'T YOU EVER GET TIRED OF BUTTING IN?

....

...AND IT'S BEGUN...

I'M RUMIA TINGEL.

SHE CAN'T GO A DAY WITHOUT DOING THIS.

THIS IS THE LAST STRAW! I'M PUTTING MY FOOT DOWN TODAY!

A STUDENT AT THE ALZANO IMPERIAL MAGIC ACADEMY.

HERE WE GO AGAIN.

Akashic Records

o f *Bastard* Magic *Instructor*

Akashic Records
o f *Bastard* Magic *Instructor*

WHAT DO YOU WANT, ANYWAY?

THEY'RE *NOT.* YOU TOLD ME I *SHOULDN'T* KILL PEOPLE.

THEY BETTER NOT BE DEAD.

GOOD GRIEF. DIDN'T I TELL YOU *NOT* TO MAKE A SCENE?

YOU KNOW THE MAGIC ACADEMY IN FEJITE, RIGHT?

MISSION? WHAT KIND?

IT SEEMS WE'VE BEEN ASSIGNED A NEW MISSION.

WE'LL BE CARRYING OUT OUR MISSION ON THE SAME DAY AS THE SCHOOL'S MAGIC COMPETITION, WHICH HER IMPERIAL HIGHNESS WILL BE ATTENDING.

THERE ARE TWO TARGETS: A STUDENT, RUMIA TINGEL, AND...

SNUB

IF THAT'S ALL, I'M GOING HOME.

NO, I DON'T. I'M NOT GOING.

WAIT. JUST HEAR ME OUT.

TWITCH!!

GLENN RADARS.

HOW GRUESOME! SOMEONE CALL THE CONSTABLES!

BUZZ

CHATTER

BUZZ

CHATTER

HEY! WHAT HAPPENED HERE?

CHATTER

RE=L.

CHATTER

CHATTER

I'VE BEEN *LOOKING* FOR YOU. WHAT HAVE YOU BEEN DOING?

ALBERT.

ISN'T IT OBVIOUS?

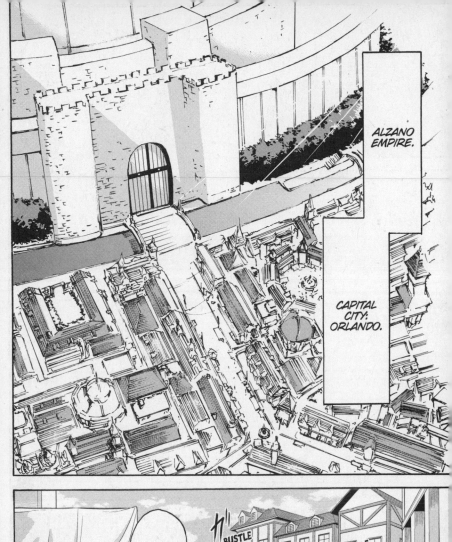

ALZANO
EMPIRE.

CAPITAL
CITY:
ORLANDO.

WHOA,
NOW.

YOU
WANNA
TRY
SAYING
THAT ONE
MORE TIME,
GIRLIE?

BUSTLE

BUSTLE

BUSTLE

IMPERIAL PRINCESS ERUMIANA.

GLENN RADARS.

WE *CAN'T* IGNORE EITHER OF THEM.

I'VE ALREADY TAKEN THE LIBERTY OF SENDING OUT "THE CHARIOT" AND "THE STAR."

SIR!

SHALL WE MAKE OUR MOVE?

WHO CAN WE DEPLOY IMMEDI-ATELY?

YES, SIR. I BELIEVE THEY'RE A GOOD FIT FOR THIS MISSION.

CERTAINLY FROM AN *ABILITY* STANDPOINT, THEY SHOULD BE *MORE* THAN ENOUGH.

THOSE TWO, EH?

SEEMS LIKE YOU'RE GONNA BE ALL RIGHT NOW...

GLENN.

LISTEN UP! NOW THAT YOU'VE BECOME AN OFFICIAL INSTRUCTOR AT THIS ACADEMY...

YOU HAVE TO STRIVE HARDER TO BEHAVE IN A MANNER BEFITTING OF THE ACADEMY! FOR STARTERS, YOU'RE WAY TOO--

CUT THAT OUT, RUMIA!!

SISTY'S TRYING TO LEARN TO COOK, SO SHE CAN MAKE YOU SOMETHING TO THANK YOU.

HEE HEE! GUESS WHAT, TEACH...

PLUS, NOW...

SHEESH, WHAT DID YOU TWO COME HERE FOR IN THE FIRST PLACE?

HONESTLY...

WHY DID YOU HAVE TO TELL HIM OF ALL PEOPLE?!

IT DIDN'T SEEM LIKE YOU WERE EVER GOING TO TELL HIM, SO I FIGURED I WOULD.

IN FACT, I WAS THINKING THE *OPPOSITE:* THAT ALL THE HUBBUB WOULD MAKE YOU WASH YOUR HANDS OF MAGIC ONCE AND FOR ALL.

NEVER IN MY *WILDEST* DREAMS WOULD I HAVE THOUGHT YOU'D ASK TO BE A **FULL-TIME INSTRUCTOR.**

YOU LOOK *HOT* IN YOUR INSTRUCTOR ROBE, BY THE WAY.

THOUGH, I *HAVE* STOPPED BLAMING MAGIC FOR ALL THE MISFORTUNE IN MY LIFE.

I FIGURED I COULD START BEING A LITTLE MORE POSITIVE.

I COULDN'T TAKE MY MIND OFF OF THAT HUEY-GUY'S DILEMMA.

AH, PRO-FES-SOR!

PLUS, NOW--

GLAD TO HEAR IT.

THEIR HANDS ARE TIED. ONLY A HANDFUL OF PEOPLE IN THE ACADEMY KNOW ABOUT RUMIA.

UGH! AND SINCE ME AND WHITE CAT INADVERTENTLY FOUND OUT THE TRUTH, THE EMPIRE'S ON OUR BACKS ABOUT KEEPING MUM.

AS IF I DON'T ALREADY HAVE ENOUGH ON MY PLATE.

THE SUPERSTITIOUS, HOWEVER, BRAND THEM AS THE "REINCARNATIONS OF THE DEVIL." SO THEY SUFFER PERSECUTION.

I'M SURE IT'S INCONVENIENT FOR THE ROYAL FAMILY THAT THEIR IMPERIAL PRINCESS WOUND UP BEING A "GIFTED." POOR THING.

ONE OF THE VERY FEW PEOPLE BORN WITH A MIRACULOUS POWER *TOTALLY INDEPENDENT* OF MAGIC.

SHE'S ONE OF THE "GIFTED."

WHAT'S IT MATTER? RUMIA'S RUMIA.

THIS DOESN'T CHANGE ANYTHING.

YOU'VE CHANGED THOUGH.

YOU HONESTLY SURPRISED ME.

ONE MONTH AFTER THE INCIDENT.

PEACE HAD RETURNED TO THE ACADEMY.

CONCERNED ABOUT CAUSING ANXIETY AMONG THE PUBLIC, THE EMPIRE EXERCISED ITS THOROUGH CONTROL OF INFORMATION.

NOT EVERYONE, EVEN THOSE WHO WITNESSED THE INCIDENT, WERE PRIVY TO THE TRUTH.

ON RUMIA BEING IMPERIAL PRINCESS ERUMIANA. ESPECIALLY SINCE SHE WAS SUPPOSED TO HAVE SUCCUMBED TO ILLNESS THREE YEARS AGO. GUESS I WOULD'VE LOST THAT BET.

Y'KNOW, I WOULD NOT HAVE PUT MONEY DOWN...

CHATTER

CHATTER

Lecture IX

Akashic Records
o f *Bastard* Magic *Instructor*

PRO-
FESSOR...

THANK
YOU!

End
Lecture VIII

PERHAPS IT DIDN'T TURN OUT HOW YOU'D ENVISIONED...

BUT THAT DOESN'T CHANGE THE FACT THAT YOU SAVED MANY LIVES.

I AM BUT ONE OF THOSE MANY LIVES THAT YOU RESCUED.

I'VE ABSOLUTELY WORSHIPPED YOU.

EVEN IF YOU NEVER REMEMBER WHO I AM. EVER SINCE THE DAY YOU SAVED ME THREE YEARS AGO...

DAY...

WHAT A...

THU

STAGGER...

NK

YOUR DREAM WAS ANYTHING BUT MEANING-LESS.

PROFESSOR!!!

TH-THIS CAN'T BE HAPPENING.

SHAKE

SHAKE

DRIP

DRIP

GACK ....!

THUMP.

WHAT KIND OF SICK JOKE IS THIS?

I REALLY THOUGHT I WOULDN'T RUN OUT OF TIME.

· · · · · · · · ·

I CAN'T MOVE AN INCH...

AND I WAS SO CLOSE, TOO.

JUST LIKE HER!

RIDICU-LOUS, ISN'T IT?! I WASTED YEARS OF MY LIFE...

OVER A STUPID *FAIRY TALE*!!

*Sc*R
IBBLE

WHAT WOULD THE POINT OF MY LIFE BE IF I RAN AWAY NOW?!

WHAT KIND OF RIGHTEOUS MAGIC-USER WOULD I BE IF I DIDN'T SAVE EVERYONE HERE?!

ALL THAT TIME AND EFFORT CAN'T BE FOR *NOTHING!*

SO QUIT YOUR YAPPING! I AIN'T DOING THIS FOR NO ONE BUT *MYSELF!*

YOU GOT A *PROBLEM* WITH THAT, GODDAM-MIT?!

GWUUUM

PWOO..
ホウ..

KRIIISH

UMRAM!!

A PICTURE BOOK I READ AS A KID...

HUFF!

HUFF!

HUFF!

THAT'S ...

THE MAGICIAN OF MELGALIUS.

IT WAS A STORY SET IN A CASTLE FLOATING IN THE SKY, WHERE A RIGHTEOUS MAGIC-USER DEFEATS THE EVIL DEMON...

— Magician of Melgaliu

AND SAVES THE PRINCESS.

THIS WHOLE TIME, THE REASON I WAS INTO MAGIC...

WAS BECAUSE I WANTED TO BE LIKE THAT RIGHTEOUS MAGIC-USER.

WIPE...

YOU MADE QUICK WORK OF THE FIRST LAYER.

WHILE I WAS TALKING, YOU WERE WORKING OUT HOW TO DISPEL THE CIRCLE?

I SEE.

NGH ...!!

ALL RIGHT, NEXT--

PLEASE, TEACH! JUST RUN!

SELFISH, STUPID BRAT!!

I CAN TELL HOW INTRICATE THIS MAGIC CIRCLE IS!

GWUUUM

THE DEEPER IN YOU GO, THE MORE WORK YOU HAVE TO DISPEL...!!

NO HESITATION, WHATSO-EVER.

YOU'RE EVERY BIT THE MAN THE RUMORS SAY.

PRO-FESSOR ?!

QUIET, YOU! I CAN'T CONCEN-TRATE!

WOBBLE

WOBBLE

WOBBLE

PRO-FESSOR! YOU HAVE TO RUN!!

Black magic ritual... Erase!!

Basis of silence, the laws of the universe should be released from its yoke here!!

DRIBBLE

End, O celestial chain!

KER-FLASH

UNLESS YOU'D RATHER STAY HERE AND ENJOY THE FIREWORKS?

YOU'LL BE ABLE TO MAKE IT OUT IN TIME IF YOU ESCAPE BY YOURSELF.

UNDERNEATH THE SCHOOL IS A LABYRINTH THAT WE USED TO BREAK IN HERE.

PRO-FESSOR!

SHEEN

RROOOO

FUU...

THE FOOL

HE'S INSANE!

MS. RUMIA, HOWEVER, IS *SPECIAL*. SO THE PLAN WAS ALTERED A BIT, AS SHE NEEDS TO BE TAKEN ALIVE.

JUST ON *THAT* REMOTE POSSIBILITY, HE'S BEEN LYING IN WAIT HERE FOR OVER TEN YEARS?!

THE HELL ...?!

ON SECOND THOUGHT, I'M NOT THAT INTERESTED.

YOU'RE *YOU* AND THAT'S THAT.

TEACHER, I....!

SO YOU'RE SAYING RUMIA IS SOME SORT OF BIG-WIG, HUH?

OH, RIGHT... I FORGOT HOW *STUPID* YOU GUYS AT THE HEAVENLY WISDOM SOCIETY ARE.

594

GLOW...

IF YOU HADN'T USED THAT SPELL, YOU'D HAVE HAD *PLENTY* OF TIME TO SAVE MS. RUMIA.

TEN MINUTES UNTIL THE MAGIC CIRCLE ACTIVATES. IF YOU WAIT FOR "THE FOOL'S WORLD" TO DISSIPATE, YOU WON'T HAVE ENOUGH TIME.

DAMMIT!

THE DARKNESS PREVENTED ME FROM SEEING THE MAGIC CIRCLE HE'S LAID OUT!!

KWOOOO

THE WHITE MAGIC RITUAL "SACRIFICE"?!

YOU'RE GOING TO PERFORM THE RITE OF *SOUL EXCHANGE*?!

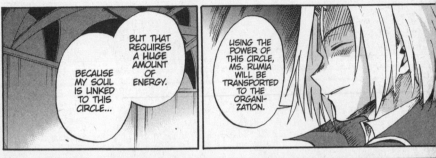

BECAUSE MY SOUL IS LINKED TO THIS CIRCLE...

BUT THAT REQUIRES A HUGE AMOUNT OF ENERGY.

USING THE POWER OF THIS CIRCLE, MS. RUMIA WILL BE TRANSPORTED TO THE ORGANIZATION.

AFTER MS. RUMIA'S JOURNEY, THE CIRCLE WILL BEGIN TO CONSUME MY SOUL TO COMPENSATE FOR THE MASSIVE MAGICAL ENERGY THAT WAS USED.

IT WILL ALSO BLOW UP THIS SCHOOL AND MYSELF ALONG WITH IT.

I'M AFRAID I AM THAT KIND OF PERSON.

YOU'RE NOT A BAD PERSON!

PROFESSOR, WHY?!

MS. RUMIA...

THIS FIGHT'S DONE.

HMPH.

IF THE ORGANIZATION HAD NEVER SET ITS SIGHTS ON YOU...

I'D STILL BE HAPPILY TEACHING RIGHT NOW.

DOESN'T MATTER WHAT SPELLS YOU HAVE. THEY'LL FIZZLE UPON ACTIVATION.

I'VE INVOKED "THE FOOL'S WORLD."

THE

HUEY...?

Lecture VIII

THE INSTRUCTOR THAT WENT MISSING?

THE ONE I REPLACED?

Akashic Records

o f **Bastard** Magic **Instructor**

I DON'T HAVE ANY IDEA WHAT'S GOING ON, BUT THE FACT HE'S A *PRETTY BOY* MEANS HE'S GOT AN APPOINTMENT WITH MY FISTS.

End
Lecture VII

!!

SO YOU'RE HERE ALREADY, HUH?

STOP DOING ALL OF THIS!!

WHAT ...?!

PLEASE!

YOU'RE THE MASTER-MIND BEHIND ALL THIS, I PRESUME?

YOU'VE GONE AND PUSHED THE KIND-HEARTED PROFESSOR GLENN UNTIL HE SNAPPED. I'D SAY MY PRAYERS IF I WERE YOU.

HA HA HA! I DON'T APPROVE OF THREATS.

ESPECIALLY NOT FROM A FELLOW TEACHER.

OH. LOOKS LIKE THEY CAN'T COME IN.

HUMANS, ON THE OTHER HAND, CAN DO ANYTHING IF THEY PUT THEIR MINDS TO IT.

UGH! I'M GONNA MAKE DAMN SURE THE SCHOOL GIVES ME WORKER'S COMP FOR THIS.

MY WOUND'S COMPLETELY OPEN NOW, THOUGH.

IN FACT, I HAVE MORE WOUNDS THAN I DID BEFORE.

AW, MAN...

SLIDE

THIS IS *EXACTLY* WHY I LOATHED WORKING.

HEE-EE-YAA-AH!!

KA-WHAM

ONCE THIS IS ALL OVER, I'M GOING BACK TO BEING A SHUT-IN.

CALM DOWN AND THINK!

I CAN'T USE "EXTINCTION RAY" AGAIN--AND "LIGHTNING PIERCE" WON'T HAVE ANY EFFECT ON THESE BIG LUGS!

ZSSH

ZSSH

ZSSH

JUST THINK AND COME UP WITH SOME SPELL THAT'LL--

THERE'S GOTTA BE SOMETHING!

KRK...

KRK...

WHOOOAAA?!

RRMBLL

ENOUGH WITH THE MAGIC CRAP!!

THAT'S IT!!

THAT ONLY TOOK DOWN **ONE** OF 'EM?!

RUUUMBLE

BUT I DON'T HAVE ENOUGH MAGIC TO "BLAZE BURST" THEM ONE AT A TIME!

I CAN BEAT THEM WITH DIRECT ATTACKS...

WHOA!!

ZA-TRUUM

PANG...

GREAT, MY WOUND REOPENED, TOO!!!

TELEPORTER TOWER: LOCATION OF THE TELEPORTER CIRCLE.

THEN HE ALTERED THE TRANSPORTER CIRCLE AND HAD THOSE TWO CARRY IN ALL THE TOOLS HE NEEDED.

THE REASON WHY, HE DIDN'T FINISH ME OFF WHILE I WAS ASLEEP IS BECAUSE HE HAS HIS HANDS FULL ALREADY!!

HAAH!

CLOP

I THINK I'VE GOT THEIR PLAN FIGURED OUT.

CLOP

HAAH!

THE LEADER SNUCK INTO THE SCHOOL SOMETIME YESTERDAY, AND MESSED WITH THE BARRIER ALL NIGHT.

CLOP

CLOP

WAS I RIGHT TO RUSH HERE TO THE TELEPORTER TOWER ALONE?!

SUCH A CON- VOLUTED PLOT JUST TO KIDNAP RUMIA ...?!

······!!

IF SOMEONE HAD LEARNED ALL THE RELEVANT SPELLS AND HAD EVERY TOOL HE'D NEED...

IT WOULD **STILL TAKE** FIVE TO SIX HOURS, I'D SAY.

PULLING OFF SOMETHING LIKE THAT IS WAY BEYOND THE SKILLS OF--

SHUT UP AND LISTEN! LET'S ASSUME THAT THERE'S SOME SPATIAL MAGIC GENIUS **OTHER** THAN YOU!!

CELICA, IS IT POSSIBLE TO CHANGE THE DESTINATION OF THE TRANSPORTER CIRCLE?

CRAP!

YANK

WHAT'S WRO--

CLICK

THWF

THANKS, SISTINE.

I WOULDN'T HAVE SURVIVED IT/IF IT WEREN'T FOR YOU.

SERI-OUSLY?

THE IDENTITY OF EACH INSTRUCTOR ATTENDING THE CONFERENCE HAS BEEN VERIFIED.

I LOOKED INTO IT, BUT NOBODY'S MADE ANY SUSPICIOUS EXITS.

SPEAKING OF MYSTERIES... THERE'S ANOTHER THING THAT'S STRANGE.

DAMMIT! WHAT'S THE DEAL HERE?!

SO THEIR MOTIVES ARE STILL A MYSTERY.

NOT THAT THIS ELIMINATES THE POSS-IBILITY OF A TRAITOR...

THE HELL ?!

THEN HOW WERE THEY PLANNING ON GETTING OUT OF HERE ONCE THEY ACCOMPLISHED THEIR MISSION?!

IT APPEARS THE BARRIER AROUND THE SCHOOL CAN NEITHER BE ENTERED INTO NOR EXITED FROM.

THIS IS GETTING MORE CON-FUSING BY THE MINUTE.

WHAT COULD THEY BE THINK--

SORRY. I RAN INTO SOME TROUBLE. I'M STILL ALIVE, THOUGH.

THANK GOODNESS! I'VE CALLED A HUNDRED TIMES, BUT YOU WEREN'T PICKING UP! I WAS WORRIED SICK!

GLENN?!

CELICA?

WHAT TROUBLE?!

CLICK

RIIIN RIIIN

ANY UPDATES ON YOUR SIDE?

THERE'S ONE GUY LEFT, PROBABLY THE BRAINS OF THE OPERATION.

I SEE.

I GOT INTO A FIGHT WITH ONE OF THE ENEMY MAGES AND... KILLED HIM.

CRAP. IF YOU WERE HERE, THIS MESS WOULDN'T HAVE EVEN HAPPENED.

ANY LEADS ON THE TRAITOR'S IDENTITY?

THE MAGE CORPS IS ON THE MOVE, BUT THEY'RE HAVING A HARD TIME LIFTING THE SCHOOL'S BARRIER.

WHATEVER THE CASE, I WON'T BE REACHING YOU ANY TIME SOON.

THE SCHOOL'S TRANSPORTER CIRCLE IS INDEED BROKEN.

AFTER MY FIRST KILL...

I WAS FILLED WITH PRIDE.

I FELT SOMETHING WAS *WRONG.*

BUT AFTER THE SECOND...

"THAT'S WHAT'S WRONG.

"I'M NOT CUT OUT FOR THIS."

AFTER THE THIRD, I REALIZED...

ACTING SO RECKLESS-- YOU REALLY ARE A FOOL!

YES.

WHITE CAT...

THIS THE SCHOOL INFIRMARY?

THANK GOD! I WAS LOSING HOPE!

WAIT, HAVE YOU BEEN CASTING HEALING MAGIC THIS WHOLE TIME?

YOU USED A TON OF MAGIC CASTING "DISPEL FORCE." IF YOU'RE NOT CAREFUL, YOU COULD DIE!

AH?!

WHAT'RE YOU DOING?! YOU CAN'T GET UP YET!

ALL RIGHT... NGH!

AT THIS RATE, YOU'RE THE ONE WHO'S GOING TO DIE FIRST!

I'M BEGGING YOU, JUST LIE DOWN!

I'M COUNTING ON YOU AND YOUR HEALING MAGIC.

OKAY, THEN.

UHN...

WHERE AM I...?

!

YOU'RE CONSCIOUS!

KI ı ı ı ı ı ı

GLENN, TOO, WAS EXTREMELY PROUD THAT HIS POWERS COULD NOW HELP OTHERS.

CELICA WAS ECSTATIC FOR GLENN, TEARS OF JOY STREAMING DOWN HER FACE.

SHORTLY AFTER, HOWEVER...

GLENN WENT THROUGH HELL.

BEFORE HE COULD GRADUATE, THEY PULLED HIM OUT OF SCHOOL.

BUT ONE ORGANIZATION DID FIND USE FOR GLENN'S SPELL.

THE EMPIRE'S MOST POWERFUL MAGES, WHO SERVED AS HER IMPERIAL HIGHNESS'S MOST TRUSTED AIDES.

THIS ORGANIZATION WAS NONE OTHER THAN THE PRESTIGIOUS IMPERIAL COURT MAGE CORPS.

THE ELDER MAGES MERELY LAUGHED OFF HIS FINDINGS.

IN PARTICULAR, THE MAGES WHOSE MAGIC INVOLVED CHANGE THOUGHT THAT HIS ABILITY WAS UTTERLY USELESS.

HIS THESIS WAS REJECTED AND ANY MENTION OF HIM CREATING SUCH A SPELL WAS EXPUNGED FROM RECORDS.

AROUND THIS TIME, IT WAS DISCOVERED THAT GLENN POSSESSED A CERTAIN ABILITY.

HE WASN'T THE BRIGHTEST, BUT GLENN WAS VERY PASSIONATE ABOUT HIS STUDIES.

EVENTUALLY, HE WAS ACCEPTED INTO THE ALZANO IMPERIAL MAGIC ACADEMY.

HE TOOK ADVANTAGE OF THESE MAGICAL CHARACTERISTICS TO CREATE AN ORIGINAL SPELL THAT ONLY HE COULD USE.

AND THUS "THE FOOL'S WORLD" WAS BORN.

THE FOOL

FATE HAD GIVEN GLENN A PREDILECTION FOR SPELLS THAT CAUSE CHANGE TO SLOW OR STOP.

SO...

BUT HE WAS NOTHING MORE THAN AVERAGE, WITH NO ACHIEVEMENTS TO HIS NAME.

HE APPLIED HIMSELF PASSIONATELY, DESCRIBING ALL HIS RESEARCH AND THOUGHT PROCESSES IN HIS SENIOR THESIS.

A LITTLE OVER TEN YEARS AGO, AFTER LOSING HIS FAMILY IN A CERTAIN INCIDENT...

GLENN WAS TAKEN IN BY CELICA, WHO CAME ACROSS HIM WHILE SHE WAS ON A MISSION FOR THE EMPIRE.

CELICA ACTED ON A WHIM, BUT OVER TIME, CAME TO LOVE HIM LIKE HER OWN.

AND HE BECAME ENTRANCED BY IT, SHOWING A LOT OF INTEREST IN HER LESSONS.

SHE TAUGHT GLENN MAGIC...

PRO-FESSOR!

PLEASE! STAY WITH ME!!

Lecture VII

Akashic Records
o f *Bastard* Magic *Instructor*

End
Lecture VI

PRO-
FESSOR!

DREDGING UP OLD STORIES I'D RATHER NOT REMEMBER.

DAMN.

GOOD JOB!

THANKS TO YOU, WE WERE ABLE TO BEAT...

HEY, WHITE CAT.

DAZE...

HUH...?

STAGGER...

PER-HAPS...

NOT.

THERE A *POINT* TO THIS STORY...?

TH-WHUD...

THE RUMORS ABOUT AN EXTREMELY SKILLED MAGE-KILLER AMONG THE RANKS OF THE IMPERIAL COURT MAGE CORPS.

AT LEAST TWENTY-FOUR PUBLICLY KNOWN, COLD-BLOODED EXECUTIONS OF MAGIC-USERS.

THERE WASN'T A MAGE IN THE UNDERWORLD WHO DIDN'T FEAR HIS CODENAME:

EACH MAGE WHO FELL WAS MORE POWERFUL THAN THE LAST. THEY SAY THE MAGES WERE KILLED USING SOME MYSTERIOUS ABILITY THAT NEGATED MAGIC.

HMPH...

"THE FOOL"...

EXCELLENT.

AH... NOW I REMEMBER...

IF THAT SPELL WORKED, IT MEANS HE WOULD'VE TEMPORARILY CHANGED MY SWORDS INTO NORMAL SWORDS.

BUT...

WHAT?! "DISPEL FORCE"?!

HE ONLY WEAKENED THEM SLIGHTLY.

SIIIZZZZ

HE DOESN'T HAVE ENOUGH MAGIC LEFT!

ENOUGH! DIE!!

I'M EMBARRASSED WATCHING YOUR FUTILE ATTEMPTS AT RESISTANCE!

TO BE TOTALLY HONEST, HE'S GOT MAD SKILLS!

I'VE ONLY BEEN ABLE TO KEEP UP WITH HIM BECAUSE HE WAS SO CAUTIOUS ABOUT MY "THE FOOL'S WORLD" ABILITY!

BUT NOW THAT HE'S FIGURED OUT WHAT I'M CAPABLE OF, THERE'S NO WAY I CAN WIN AGAINST HIM IN A STRAIGHT-UP FIGHT.

LOOKS LIKE I'D BETTER START SAYING MY PRAYERS.

DRIP...

CELICA'S ABOUT THE ONLY ONE WHO COULD BEAT SOMEONE LIKE HIM.

THIS IS THE FIRST FIGHT I'VE HAD HAD TO USE THIS MUCH OF MY STRENGTH.

SHF...

ALLOW ME TO TIP MY HAT TO YOU.

YOUR ABILITY TO PREVENT MAGIC FROM ACTIVATING IS QUITE TROUBLESOME.

BUT IT'S NOT GOING TO WORK A SECOND TIME.

GLEAM...

WHILE I AM CURIOUS ABOUT YOUR IDENTITY, I'M AFRAID YOU'RE TOO DANGEROUS TO KEEP ALIVE.

MAN, AM I IN A PICKLE...

I BLEW MY BIG CHANCE WITH THAT LAST ATTACK.

SHUDDER...

DAMN...

SO HE HAD FIGURED IT OUT, AFTER ALL.

HE'S PRETTY MUCH SEEN ALL THE CARDS I HAVE IN MY HAND. AND HE'S NOT SO DUMB AS TO LET HIS GUARD DOWN AGAIN.

PLUS, I HAVE NO IDEA WHAT ELSE HE'S GOT UP HIS SLEEVE.

WITHOUT IT, I'LL LOSE MY ONLY MEANS OF DEFENDING MYSELF AGAINST HIS SWORDS!

THE "WEAPON ENCHANT" SPELL THAT WHITE CAT CAST ON ME IS STARTING TO WEAR OFF, TOO.

GLENN RADARS...

WHO IN THE HELL *ARE* YOU?!

OH, JUST A LOWLY MAGIC INSTRUCTOR.

AND A MERE *SUBSTITUTE* AT THAT.

I THINK YOU *MIGHT* BE OVER-ESTIMATING ME.

HMPH...

YOU *COULD* KILL ME IN NO TIME IF YOU USED BOTH YOUR MAGIC AND SWORDPLAY AGAINST ME AT THE SAME TIME, YOU KNOW? AREN'T YOU GONNA DO IT?

YOU'RE QUITE THE JOKER.

NOT ONLY THAT, MY MANA WOULD HAVE BEEN IN CHAOS AND I TEMPORARILY WOULDN'T HAVE BEEN ABLE TO MOVE MY SWORDS.

IF I'D CONTINUED TO USE "BLAZE BURST," I'M SURE HE WOULD HAVE PREVENTED IT WITH HIS NEGATING MAGIC.

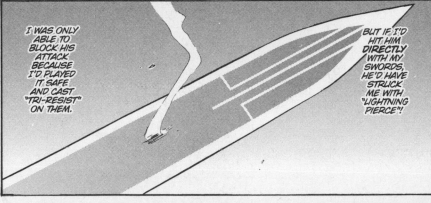

I WAS ONLY ABLE TO BLOCK HIS ATTACK BECAUSE I'D PLAYED IT SAFE AND CAST "TRI-RESIST" ON THEM.

BUT IF I'D HIT HIM DIRECTLY WITH MY SWORDS, HE'D HAVE STRUCK ME WITH "LIGHTNING PIERCE"!

CLEARLY, THIS MAN IS NO THIRD-RATE MAGIC INSTRUCTOR!

HE'S QUICK-WITTED ENOUGH TO JUST NOW COME UP WITH A PLAN THAT MUCKED UP MINE... AND HAS THE GUTS TO PULL IT OFF, EVEN THOUGH THE SLIGHTEST MISCALCULATION COULD'VE KILLED HIM...

MANA BIO-RHYTHM.

YOU JUST USED--!!

YOU SMUG BASTARD!

DANG! AND HERE I THOUGHT I'D BE ABLE TO DESTROY AT LEAST *ONE* OF YOUR SWORDS.

GRIT...!!

TO MOVE THEIR NEUTRAL MANA BIORHYTHM INTO THE LAW STATE.

IN ORDER TO CAST SPELLS, MAGES MUST FOCUS THEIR MINDS AND EMPLOY PROPER BREATHING TECHNIQUES...

ATTACK!

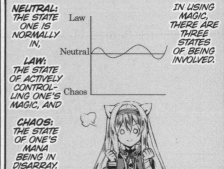

NEUTRAL: THE STATE ONE IS NORMALLY IN,

LAW: THE STATE OF ACTIVELY CONTROLLING ONE'S MAGIC, AND

CHAOS: THE STATE OF ONE'S MANA BEING IN DISARRAY.

IN USING MAGIC, THERE ARE THREE STATES OF BEING INVOLVED.

Law

Neutral

Chaos

ONCE IN THE CHAOS STATE, EVEN THE MOST POWERFUL MAGES ARE UNABLE TO USE MAGIC. THIS IS ONE OF MAGIC'S UNBREAKABLE LAWS.

AFTER EXECUTING THE SPELL, A MAGE'S BIORHYTHM PLUMMETS INTO THE CHAOS STATE. (THE DEGREE TO WHICH IT FALLS DEPENDS ON THE MAGNITUDE OF THE SPELL CAST.)

MRGH...!!

THCK THCK THCK

FROO...

Flame lion...

?!

YOU CAN'T PERFORM THE ONE-CLAUSE INCANTATION OF "BLAZE BURST"? WELL, LET ME SHOW YOU HOW IT'S DONE.

"LIGHTNING PIERCE"?! AND HE'S INCANTING ALL THREE VERSES AGAIN....

WHAT A FOOL! THERE'S NO WAY HE'LL FINISH IN TIME... UNLESS...!

With the flash of your aurora spear...

Powerful emperor of thunder...

HYOOOO

WOULDN'T BE EFFECTIVE IF I WERE UP AGAINST A TRUE SWORD MASTER.

AND AT THE END OF THE DAY, I'M A MAGE--NOT A SWORDSMAN. MANUALLY CONTROLLING THE SWORDS...

I CAN'T MAKE THE MOST OUT OF SWORDPLAY JUST BY SIMPLY IMITATING A SKILLED SWORDS-MAN.

BINGO.

THREE AUTOMATED SWORDS AND TWO MANUAL SWORDS.

IT IS THE OPTIMAL SOLUTION I CAME TO AFTER FIGHTING IN COUNTLESS BATTLES.

STUCK-UP LITTLE ....!!

SLAASH

GAH ?!

ZRSSH NGH ....!

BOTH WERE RIGHT?!

HUFF!

LET ME GUESS. THOSE SWORDS MOVE AT THE WILL OF THEIR CASTER.

OR DID YOU LEARN A SWORDSMAN TECHNIQUE THAT ALLOWS THEM TO MOVE ON THEIR OWN?

NO WAY...

HUFF!

HUFF!

!!

KRIISH

MAYBE I SHOULD DO WHAT TEACHER TOLD ME AND JUST...

WHEN ALL IS SAID AND DONE, I'M NOTHING BUT A BURDEN.

KIN

KRRK

HAS ALREADY STARTED!

THE FIGHT-ING...

KANG

WHAT...

TEACHER TOLD ME?!

RUSTLE

GAH!

I'M SURE HE DID IT TO PROTECT ME.

I SHOULDN'T BE ANGRY.

I WOULDN'T HAVE STOOD A CHANCE AGAINST THAT GUY.

HAAH... HAAH... OW...! WHAT THE HECK WAS HE THINK-ING?!

I MANAGED TO REDUCE THE IMPACT BY USING "GALE BLOW"-- BUT STILL...!

KYAAAAA!!

HMPH... HOW NOBLE.

IT WAS THAT OBVIOUS, HUH?

CRAP...

THAT MUST MEAN YOU'RE ONLY ABLE TO PREVENT A SPELL FROM ACTIVATING.

YET YOU DIDN'T USE THAT ABILITY ON THE BONE GOLEMS...

THEN YOU MUST HAVE THE ABILITY TO SUPPRESS YOUR OPPONENT'S MAGIC.

I TAKE IT GENE WASN'T EVEN ABLE TO LAY A SCRATCH ON YOU?

ZHWUU...

HERE I COME.

JUST AS WITH THESE MAGIC-POWERED SWORDS.

IN THAT CASE, I SHOULD BE FINE AS LONG AS THE MAGIC IS ALREADY ACTIVE...

WHEN A DOG CAN'T EVEN FOLLOW *SIMPLE* COMMANDS, YOU DON'T SHOW MERCY-- YOU PUT HIM DOWN.

HE VIOLATED ORDERS AND ACTED UNNECESSARILY. I SIMPLY GAVE HIM HIS *DUE*.

THINK YOU CAN MUSTER ANOTHER "DISPEL FORCE" TO NEUTRALIZE HIS SWORDS?

PSST! WHITE CAT... HOW MUCH MAGIC YOU GOT LEFT?

EVEN IF I USED ALL OF MY REMAINING MAGIC, I THINK I'D COME UP SHORT.

HIS SWORDS... THERE'S A *SUBSTANTIAL* AMOUNT OF MAGICAL ENERGY STORED WITHIN THEM.

GULP...

THAT SO?

BESIDES, I DON'T THINK HE'D EVEN GIVE ME AN OPPOR-TUNITY TO CAST THE SPELL.

GLeeeAM

I'VE GOT A BAD FEELING ABOUT THOSE FLOATING SWORDS...

LET ME *GUESS*. THOSE SWORDS MOVE AT THE WILL OF THEIR CASTER.

OR DID YOU LEARN A SWORDSMAN TECHNIQUE THAT ALLOWS THEM TO MOVE ON THEIR OWN?

AM I ON THE MONEY?

YOU KILLED ONE OF THEM *YOURSELF*.

HEY! DON'T HEAP ALL OF THAT ON ME.

JUST GONNA IGNORE MY QUESTION, EH?

IT SEEMS I *UNDER-ESTIMATED* YOU.

I DIDN'T EXPECT TO LOSE TWO MEN IN THIS OPERATION.

Lecture VI

Akashic Records
of **Bastard** Magic **Instructor**

GLENN
RADARS.

End
Lecture V

I HOPE YOU DON'T MIND ME BEING SO BOLD AS TO *ELIMINATE* YOU...

CLACK !!

Extinction Ray.

A GOD-KILLING SPELL DEVISED BY THE *GREAT CELICA ARFONIA* SOME *TWO HUNDRED YEARS* AGO DURING THE MAGIC WAR.

I'D HEARD YOU WERE *JUST A LOWLY SEVENTH STEP MAGE.*

?!

BUT IT SEEMS YOU ARE THE *GREATEST* OBSTACLE TO OUR PLANS.

EXTINCTION RAY !!!

IT'S AN ASSAULT SPELL THAT BREAKS ITS TARGET DOWN TO ITS VERY COMPONENTS, LEAVING IT NO MEANS TO RETALIATE!

THIS SPELL IS TOUTED AS THE MOST POTENT OF SPELLS A SINGLE PERSON CAN INCANT... THAT HE'S ABLE TO CAST THIS IS... ASTOUNDING!

All creation will verily break asunder here...

VWOOON

To the ends of the distant void!!

GET LOST, YOU BRAIN- LESS DOLTS!!

SHEEEEEN

THE NAME OF THIS SPELL IS...

WHILE KEEPING *THOSE GUYS* AT BAY.

YOU SEE, I COULDN'T INCANT THE SPELL I'M ABOUT TO USE...

I can both slay and take captive the Gods...

GROOOOAR

I know both the alpha and the omega...

THAT SPELL IS...!

NO WAY!

TH...

Those composed of the five elements return to the five elements; let loose the ties woven between form and the laws of the universe.

Return to the cycle of nature...

I NEED TO LOWER THE CAST TIME AND DECREASE THE ENERGY LEVEL BY 45.

MUTTER

FWOOOO

Blocking wind... Binding wind...?

MUTTER

MUTTER

Wind... Quiet... NO, THAT'S NO GOOD...

MUTTER

MUTTER

WHSSSH

DON'T LET ME DOWN, WHITE CAT!

BUT I CAN'T FEND OFF THIS MANY FOR TOO LONG.

THESE BONEHEADS HAVE ONLY BEEN GIVEN SIMPLE ORDERS TO ATTACK NEARBY ENEMIES.

RUMIA ...!

PROFESSOR ...!!

SKITTD

YOU CAN BE SO INFURI-ATING, YOU KNOW?

DASH

UGH!

SLIP...

NOW, THEN...

HEH.

I'M COUNTING ON YOU, KID.

COME AT ME, YOU BAG O' BONES!!

YOU CAN'T BE SERIOUS?!

WHILE YOU GO UP TO THE DEAD END AND INCANT A MODIFIED VERSION OF "GALE BLOW"!

HERE'S THE PLAN-- I'LL HOLD 'EM OFF HERE!

KLANK

I-I'M NOT SURE I CAN DO SUCH AN ADVANCED TECHNIQUE...

B-BUT...

THAT WAY IT'S WEAKER, BUT IT'LL LAST LONGER AND THE AREA IT'LL AFFECT WILL BE WIDER.

IF YOU CAN, I *NEED* YOU TO MAKE IT THREE CLAUSES OR SHORTER.

KA-CRACK

WHAT?!

AND IF YOU DON'T DO IT, I'LL GIVE YOU A *FAILING GRADE*!!

IF YOU'VE UNDERSTOOD ALL THE THINGS I'VE BEEN TEACHING YOU...

PULLING THIS OFF SHOULD BE EASY AS PIE FOR YOU!!

YOU CAN!!

MEANING ONCE A SPELL IS ACTIVATED, MY MAGIC'S TOTALLY *USELESS!*

THE FOOL

NO CAN DO!

"THE FOOL'S WORLD" CAN ONLY PREVENT MAGIC FROM *ACTIVATING!*

WHAT?!

I KNOW HOW TO CAST THAT SPELL!!

YOU MEAN "DISPEL FORCE"?!

THE ONLY THING THAT'LL WORK ON THESE GUYS IS A SPELL THAT WILL CANCEL OUT THEIR MAGIC...

BUT...

UP AHEAD'S A DEAD END!

"DISPEL FORCE" IS A PRETTY HIGH-LEVEL SPELL!

NO, *DON'T!*

THERE'S TOO MANY OF THEM! YOU'LL *RUN OUT* OF MAGIC BEFORE YOU CAN GET THEM ALL!!

I'M AMAZED SHE KNOWS IT AT HER AGE... I GUESS PEOPLE DON'T CALL HER A "STAR PUPIL" FOR *NOTHING!*

AH... WELL THEN...!

THERE'S NOWHERE TO RUN!

KRRRK

Y-YES,
SIR!

NOW
"GALE
BLOW,"
WHITE
CAT!

KLATTTTA

HYOOU

Great
wind!!

WE'D KILLED MORE PEOPLE THAN I CAN KEEP TRACK OF... AND *HE* SOUNDS JUST AS UNDERHANDED AS THE WORST OF US.

THAT BASTARD'S UP TO NO GOOD.

I'D WATCH MY BACK IF *I* WERE YOU, LITTLE MISS PRISSY PANTS.

DON'T YOU *DARE* LUMP HIM INTO THE SAME GROUP AS YOU! HE'S NOTHING LIKE YOU *MURDERERS!*

Y-YOU'RE AWAKE!

DO YOU *REALLY* THINK SOME THIRD-RATE INSTRUCTOR IS CAPABLE OF HOG-TYING ME LIKE THIS?

YOU KNOW NOTHING ABOUT HIM.

OH, BUT HE IS.

I'LL DO SOMETHING ABOUT THIS.

I'LL FIND THE REMAINING ENEMIES AND...

SHIVER...

KILL THEM WHERE THEY STAND!

!

TALKING SO VICIOUSLY WITHOUT BATTING AN EYE...

YOU REALLY ARE ONE OF US!

HEH HEH... AH HA HA HA HA!

DON'T PUSH YOURSELF TOO HARD. AND DON'T GO DYING ON ME EITHER.

HEARING YOU SO AGITATED OVER SOMEONE ELSE'S WELL-BEING...

YOU REALLY HAVEN'T CHANGED AT ALL.

SAY, GLENN...

LOOK, I'LL HURRY AND COME UP WITH SOMETHING ON MY END.

ARE THEY NOT COMING TO HELP?

PROFES-SOR...

CRAP.

WHAT THE HECK...?

YOU WERE RIGHT...

NOTHING GOOD COMES OUT OF MAGIC!

IT'S ALL MY FAULT THAT THIS HAPPENED TO RUMIA...

I CAN'T STAND IT... IF ONLY I HADN'T...

IF IT WEREN'T FOR MAGIC, RUMIA WOULD NEVER HAVE BEEN ...!!

NO CLUE, I'M AFRAID.

ANY IDEA WHO?

I'M SURE THEY'VE GOT SOMEONE ON THE INSIDE. WE HAVE A *TRAITOR* HERE.

THOSE GUYS MAY BE POWERFUL, BUT THEY SHOULDN'T HAVE BROKEN THROUGH THE SCHOOL'S SECURITY *THIS* EASILY.

WHA--?!

THAT WOULD PROVE RATHER DIFFICULT.

THEN PUT OUT AN ALERT AND BRING IN THE IMPERIAL COURT MAGE CORPS.

THEN EXPLAIN THE SITUATION TO THE OTHER INSTRUCTORS AND SEE WHAT THEY SAY *RIGHT NOW*.

OF ALL THE--A STUDENT'S *LIFE* IS AT STAKE!

JUST COME BACK HERE YOUR-SELF!!

FOR HIGHER-UPS TO MOBILIZE THE ORGANIZATIONS THEY RUN, YOU NEED TO CUT THROUGH A *LOT* OF BUREAUCRATIC RUNAROUNDS FIRST. BESIDES, I'M NO LONGER IN A POSITION WHERE I CAN JUST APPEAL DIRECTLY TO THE TOP.

DAMM-IT!

I'M SURE THE TRANS-PORTER'S THE FIRST THING THEY DESTROYED.

CALM DOWN AND *THINK*! THEY'RE NOT SO STUPID THEY'D OVERLOOK SUCH A DETAIL.

WE'VE GOT A TRANS-PORTER CIRCLE HERE AT SCHOOL! JUST USE THAT TO--

I NEUTRALIZED TWO OF THE CULPRITS, BUT ONE OF THE STUDENTS HAS BEEN HAULED OFF.

AND IT GETS WORSE. I THINK THESE GUYS ARE FROM...

LISTEN UP! THE ACADEMY'S UNDER ATTACK BY SOME TRESPASSERS.

WHAT ?!

THE HEAVENLY WISDOM SOCIETY!!!

I SEE.

WHAT COULD'VE BROUGHT THOSE MONSTERS TO OUR DOORSTEP?

THE HEAVENLY WISDOM SOCIETY.

AN ORGANIZATION OF MERCILESS MAGES WHO HAVE NO QUALMS ABOUT PERFORMING CRUEL--AND DOWNRIGHT INHUMANE-- EXPERIMENTS SIMPLY TO FURTHER THEIR STUDY OF MAGIC.

I KNEW IT! SO THESE GUYS REALLY ARE--

THAT EMBLEM... A SNAKE COILED AROUND A DAGGER...

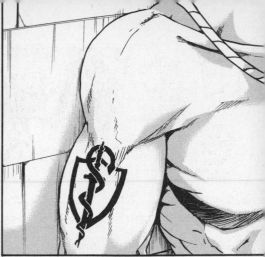

!

RIIIIN

RIIIIN

CHATTER

CHATTER

AS IF?! WHAT TOOK YOU SO LONG TO GET BACK, CELICA?!

SORRY-- I COULDN'T STEP AWAY MID-LECTURE. SO, WHAT'S UP?

GOT A BUNCH OF MISSED CALLS FROM YOU. DON'T TELL ME YOU'RE ALREADY MISSING ME?

GLENN, DARLING!

GRAB

Akashic Records
of Bastard Magic Instructor

Lecture V

I-I'M FINE. THANK YOU, PROFESSOR!

YOU OKAY THERE, WHITE CAT?

ARE YOU HURT?

BUT NOW ISN'T THE TIME TO ASK. WE'VE GOT TO--

I'M SURE YOU'VE GOT QUESTIONS.

PROFESSOR GLENN, I...

AH?!

SIR! YOUR PANTS ARE DOWN.